HOW to KISS A MOVIE STAR

Romantic Comedy by Jenny Proctor

How to Kiss a Hawthorne Brother Series
How to Kiss Your Best Friend
How to Kiss Your Grumpy Boss
How to Kiss Your Enemy
How to Kiss a Movie Star

Oakley Island Romcoms
Eloise and the Grump Next Door
Merritt and Her Childhood Crush

Some Kind of Love Series
Love Redesigned
Love Unexpected
Love Off-Limits
Love in Bloom

HOW to KISS A MOVIE STAR

JENNY PROCTOR

Jenny Proctor Creative

This one is for you, readers.
Thanks for sticking with me.

Chapter One

Flint

I'M IN A GARDEN supply store in one of the smallest towns in North Carolina, staring at a basket full of individually wrapped sugar cookies decorated to look like my face.

When I dreamed of being a famous actor, this is *not* where my brain went.

I pick up one of the cookies, noting the price tag stuck to the top of the cellophane. One cookie for more than six bucks? Ann's cookies are good, but is *any* cookie six-dollars-good?

I drop it onto the counter with a sigh. I was counting on most of Silver Creek ignoring the fact that I'm home. Everyone around here has known me since I was an idiot kid anyway.

It goes without saying that if you ever sat through one of the variety shows I put on in middle school—and by variety show, I mean a collection of badly prepared monologues and off-key Jonas Brother songs—you get a pass on being impressed with my career.

Was Flint just nominated for an Oscar? *Who cares?*

Was that him in all those *Agent Twelve* movies? *Maybe, but remember that time he skinny-dipped in the pond out by the Wilsons' pasture?*

If it were up to me, nobody in this whole town would mention my career at all.

I need normal.

I *crave* normal.

Which is why a basket of Flint Hawthorne sugar cookies is so disheartening.

I push my sunglasses onto my head and take in Ann's hopeful expression.

Ann Arney has been running the Silver Creek Feed 'n Seed for as long as I can remember. It's been years since I've seen her, but she mostly looks the same. Her hair's a little grayer, her face a little more worn. But her eyes still have the same sparkle.

"Do you like them?" she asks. "I've already sold four this morning."

Believe it or not, selling cookies right next to the bird seed and a display of gardening gloves isn't all that unusual. Ann's sugar cookies are famous in Silver Creek, and she usually has some for sale, decorated to match whatever holiday or season is coming up next. At least she did when I was a kid. Pretty sure this is the first time I've ever seen her put a *person* on a cookie, though, unless we're counting Santa Claus.

I should be flattered. I guess a part of me is. But a bigger part just wants to blend in for a while.

I take in Ann's sincere expression and sense how much she wants me to be impressed. "They look great, Ann. It's a perfect likeness."

"I used that photo they put on the cover of *People* magazine," she says. She clears her throat and leans forward across the counter. "The one that named you...sexiest man alive." She whispers the *sexiest man alive* part like she's nervous to say the words out loud.

Behind me, an older man in denim overalls, who looks like he's definitely *not* one of *People* magazine's regular readers, clears his throat.

"Tell you what," I say to Ann, pulling out my wallet. "I'm going to buy the rest of those cookies."

Her eyebrows go up. "All of them? I've got three dozen more in the back. And I'm selling them for six-fifty a piece."

I try not to wince as I do the math, but I'd rather buy them myself than have my sugar-cookie likeness reminding every single person who drops by to purchase a new shovel that I've finally moved home.

"Whatever you're charging is just fine, Ann. I'll take them all. Plus this bird seed and twenty bags of the black mulch you've got outside."

She scans the bird seed and drops it into a bag, then darts into the back room, emerging with a paper grocery sack I assume is full of pre-wrapped cookies. "I suppose you're looking to keep a low profile," she says as she slides both bags across the counter, some measure of remorse in her voice.

I offer her an easy smile as I hand her my credit card, holding her gaze long enough for a faint blush to creep into her cheeks. "Or maybe I just know who makes the best sugar cookies this side of the Mississippi."

Her cheeks flush. "Oh, you hush, Flint Hawthorne. Don't you start with me." She bats at my arm before she takes my card, the twinkle back in her eyes. "Wait. One more thing." She steps out from behind the counter and moves to the drink cooler sitting by the front door. She opens it and pulls out a Cheerwine in a tall, glass bottle. "For old time's sake."

When I was nine, Ann caught me trying to steal a Cheerwine out of this very same cooler and laid into me for over an hour, talking about representing the Hawthorne name and remembering who I am and working for the things I want instead of taking them. I had to sit in the back room until my dad drove over to pick me up, then I had to sweep the entire store to apologize for my attitude and entitlement.

The next time I was in the store, Ann offered to let me sweep whenever I wanted a soda. That way, I wouldn't need to steal one.

I take the icy cold drink and twist off the top. "I haven't had one of these in years."

"Don't they sell Cheerwine in California?"

"They sure don't."

"Shoo, then it's a good thing you moved home," she says, her words a little more Southern than they were before.

For so many reasons, I think to myself.

I take a long sip of Cheerwine. It tastes like my childhood. Like hot summers and cold creeks and hunting for lightning bugs. I lift the drink in farewell, and Ann smiles wide. "Take care, all right?"

Outside, the late summer sun beats down on the parking lot, and I'm suddenly grateful I have something cool to drink. I don't think about the scolding I'd get from my personal trainer if he could see what I'm drinking. Not to mention the forty-plus cookies I will almost certainly eat by myself.

Not that the scolding would do much.

There is a time to live like my paycheck depends on the contours of my abdominal muscles. I just spent six months shooting on location in Costa Rica, playing a lifeguard who is shirtless at least fifty percent of the time. There were actual clauses in my contract about muscle definition and the efforts I made to maintain it.

But now is not that time.

Now? It's time to eat cookies.

I head toward the far end of the building, where bags of mulch and soil and different kinds of fertilizer are stacked on pallets at the edge of the parking lot. My truck is already parked next to the mulch—something I did on purpose—so it won't take long to load up what I need.

As I round the corner, I almost collide with a massive tomato plant hustling toward the front of the store. "Hey, whoa, watch out," I say, jumping to the side.

The plant stops and lowers to the ground, revealing the woman carrying it. She looks close to my age, mid-twenties, probably, and I brace myself for the inevitable recognition. I'm not trying to be presumptuous. I'm just going off experience. Most women in their twenties and thirties recognize my face.

But *this* woman doesn't react at all.

She only stares, her eyebrows raised like she's daring me to say something else.

I lift a placating hand. "Sorry. Didn't mean to stop you. But you almost ran me over."

The woman's eyes flash, and for a moment, I can't look away. They are the most startling pale blue, clear and arresting—a contrast to the rest of her, which is clad in forest browns and greens. Her dark brown hair is pulled back into a simple pony-tail, and she's wearing utility pants, an oversized T-shirt cinched into a knot at her waist, and practical work boots. The whole look gives off a strong "don't mess with me" vibe.

The vibe only gets stronger when the woman's lips purse. "Definitely. There's so little space in the parking lot, I can see why it was so difficult for you to avoid me."

She looks around pointedly in a way that makes me grin.

Partly because she's talking to me like I'm just some random dude.

Mostly because her eyes have completely hooked me. There's a fire flashing in their bright blue depths that won't let me go.

"Fair enough," I say. "I'll keep a better eye out."

We stand there and stare at each other for a long moment before I take a step toward her. I don't know why I don't just let her leave. She's nothing like the women I normally pursue, but the impulse to keep her talking is strong.

I motion to the tomato plant beside her. It's twice as big around as she is, though she didn't seem to be struggling to carry it before. "Can I carry that for you?" I ask. She's going to say no, but maybe she'll say something else, too.

She raises her eyebrows before bending her knees and hoisting the plant into her arms like it weighs nothing at all. She turns to the side and looks straight at me, her look saying I did *not* just ask to carry her plant. "I've got it," she says.

Something sparks deep in my gut. Before I became famous, I used to love the challenge of pulling a smile out of a woman, of using my charm to crack even the stoniest expressions. It's a game I haven't played in years, but I can't keep myself from trying now.

"I can see that," I say with a grin. "Maybe I should be asking for *your* help."

She chuckles, but I don't miss the faint question flashing behind her eyes. I've made her curious, at least, if not interested. "You don't need my help," she says, but the conviction in her voice from moments before has waned the slightest bit.

I take another step forward. "What makes you so sure? I've got twenty bags of mulch to load up all by myself."

She puts down her plant, her hands going to her hips as she pointedly eyes me from top to bottom. "And you look perfectly capable."

I resist the urge to flex my biceps, but I can't keep myself from saying, "Thanks for noticing."

She rolls her eyes and huffs out a laugh. "Okay. We're done here." She crouches toward her plant, but I call out to stop her.

"Wait. Don't leave."

She leaves the plant on the ground and slowly turns to face me one more time.

When I was barely twenty years old, I auditioned for the lead role in a low-budget romantic comedy. I'd had a few minor parts here and there, but nothing big. Never the lead. I got the part, and when the casting director called to let me know, she mentioned my smile specifically and told me it would make me a star.

The movie was released to streaming platforms without even hitting the box office, but it was a surprise hit. *I* was a surprise hit. Since then, a dozen different directors have asked for that same smile, making it such a trademark, my first agent made me practice it in the mirror for hours so I wouldn't forget exactly how to replicate it.

I slip it on now, trusting it will impact this woman like it does...well, most everyone else. "What if I don't *need* your help, but I want it anyway?"

The woman doesn't move. She just stares, her gaze focused, like she's trying to puzzle me out.

My jaw tightens under the scrutiny, but I hold my ground. I've never had to work this hard, but I'm not about to give up now. This time, the effort feels different—less like the games I used to play in high school when the prize was the ego boost of knowing my charm had no bounds. I want this woman to smile for real—because I've said something to make her want to.

"I don't know what's happening here," she finally says, taking a step backward. "But you shouldn't waste your smiles on me."

I shift the bottle of Cheerwine I'm still holding from one hand to the other and run my fingers through my hair. The cool condensation from the bottle coats my fingertips and chills my scalp at the contact. "If you smile back, it won't be a waste at all."

Her eyes lift and I see a smile playing around her lips, but she never quite gets there. Which only makes me wish to see it more. "I gotta go," she says, her tone laced with humor.

I watch as she picks up her plant and heads toward the front of the Feed 'n Seed. "It was nice talking to you!" I call after her, but she doesn't look back.

I'm still standing there when my brother, Brody, eases his truck to a stop in front of me, a bright red kayak strapped into the bed. He's shirtless, which makes me think he was probably just on the river, and my eye catches on the faint scar stretching across his left pectoral muscle.

We were nine and eleven years old when I convinced Brody that reenacting the sword fight from *The Princess Bride* required actual swords. And by swords, I meant knives tied onto the ends of sticks.

Brody wound up with twelve stitches, but I wound up absolutely positive I was destined to be an actor.

I was also grounded for three weeks, but the punishment was well worth the self-discovery.

"What did you say to *her*?" Brody says as he lifts his sunglasses into his sandy brown hair.

I look across the parking lot just in time to catch the woman disappearing into the store. "I didn't say anything."

Brody lifts an eyebrow, and I grin.

"I mean, I said *something*. But I promise I was nice."

"My level of nice? Or your level of nice? And by that, I mean flirty and self-indulgent."

"Trust me, I wasn't indulging in anything. She didn't even recognize me."

Brody feigns a gasp. "The horror," he says dryly.

I pull a cookie out of the bag Ann gave me and toss it through his window and into his lap. "Shut up and eat a cookie." I turn and cross the last few yards to my truck. I finish my Cheerwine, then drop the empty bottle, the bag of cookies, and the birdseed into the front seat before moving to the back and opening the tailgate.

Brody follows slowly behind me, stopping again once his truck is perpendicular to mine. "Ann made your nose too big," he says, studying the cookie for a brief moment before taking an enormous bite of my frosted face.

He's not wrong about my nose. But I wasn't about to be *that guy* and complain. "What are you doing here? Want to make yourself useful and help me load up this mulch?"

"Just need to pick up some new carabiners. Wait, this is *your* truck?" Brody asks, like he's noticing it for the first time. He lets out a low whistle. "I thought you weren't getting it until next week."

"The dealership delivered it this morning," I say as I reach for the first bag of mulch. I lift it onto my shoulder, then toss it toward the back of the truck bed.

"They *delivered* it?"

I grab a second bag, then grin. "For a small fee."

He rolls his eyes, but he doesn't give me any more trouble than that. It's not that I'm not *willing* to go buy a car like a normal person. But Asheville's a decently sized city. Even half a dozen bystanders in a car dealership can interfere with me getting things done.

Funny the things I've started to miss over the years. Grocery shopping. Hanging out in a coffee shop and reading a book. Talking to a woman who doesn't already know my name.

I'm not saying fame isn't worth it.

I am saying it has a lot to do with why I moved back to North Carolina in the first place. I can't live completely under the radar in Silver Creek—the bag of face cookies in my truck clearly indicates as much—but I can come close. At least closer than I could in California.

I heft another bag onto my shoulder and toss a look at my brother, who has made no move to get out of his truck. "Are you seriously going to watch me instead of helping?"

He grins. "It's fun to watch you do all the work."

"At least come over to the house and help me plant," I say. "I'm finally filling in the beds behind the pool." In reality, I don't care if he actually helps. I like landscaping. The immediate payoff of working, digging in the dirt, then seeing the fruits of your labors. I've done it everywhere I've lived, even after I started making enough to pay entire crews of people to do it for me.

But helping or not, I'd happily take Brody's company. My house was finished almost a year ago, but work kept me traveling for months, and I've only been in North Carolina full-time for a couple of weeks. I was looking forward to some family time, but I've seen less of my siblings than I hoped I would.

"Wish I could," Brody says. "Kate's heading out of town, which means I've got to hurry home to get River."

A strange feeling pulses through my chest. It's weird enough that all my siblings are married now. I'm still getting used to the fact that they're also *parents*. Brody and Kate's daughter, River, is only three months old. A real, tiny human who depends on them for everything. Food. Shelter. Sleep. And Brody is acting like it's no big deal.

Most days, I feel like I can hardly take care of myself.

"You could probably call Perry," Brody says, mentioning our oldest brother. "I don't think he has anything going on today."

"Nope. Jack has a soccer game."

"Lennox?" Brody asks.

I glance at my watch. "Already at the restaurant."

"Sorry, man," Brody says. "If not for River, I really would come."

I wave away his concern. "Don't worry about it. Nate will help if I really need it."

It's not like I blame my siblings for having busy lives. It's just annoying when I've got six weeks of time to kill before the press cycle starts up for *Turning Tides*, the movie I was filming down in Costa Rica. Not long after, I'll be back in Los Angeles to film the third *Agent Twelve* movie, which is making me eager to spend as much time as possible with them *now*.

Brody nods, but his expression doesn't shift, his brow furrowed in that worried big-brother way. He hesitates another moment, then climbs out of his truck, leaving it idling in the parking lot, and helps me load the last few bags of mulch.

I close the tailgate and dust off my hands. "Thanks."

"What about Dad?" Brody says as he moves toward his truck. "I bet he'd keep you company while you plant."

I roll my eyes. "Dude. Just go home." I pull on my sunglasses. "I'm a grown man. I can put plants in the ground by myself."

"Fine. But we'll all get together next week."

"Brody. Stop it."

"Stop what?"

"Stop acting like I need special treatment. I'm fine."

"But you're—" His words cut off, and he runs a hand through his already tousled hair.

I'm alone.

I don't need to hear him say it to know that's where he was headed.

When I talked to Mom about moving home, she brought it up as a reason for concern. In a town as small as Silver Creek, it's unlikely I'll ever meet any eligible dating prospects.

I see the logic in her argument. But I can't be worse off than I was in LA. Six years in a city with millions of women, and all I have to show for it is a string of casual relationships and a fame-hungry actress ex who's still giving me trouble.

My eyes drift across the parking lot to the woman I almost ran into earlier. She's loading her tomato plant into the back of a beat-up Toyota, securing it into the bed with a length of rope she ties with enough ease, it's clear she's done this sort of thing before. She pulls a camouflage baseball cap out of her pocket and puts it on her head, pulling her ponytail through the back before she climbs into the truck.

She cranks the engine and pulls away without giving me a second glance.

Not that I care. I don't care. *Do I?*

Three hours later, my flower bed looks freaking amazing. It's a little wild—not as cultivated as the garden space outside my previous house in Malibu—but I like that it blends into the surrounding wilderness.

Seventy-five acres of wilderness, to be exact.

It used to be a research forest that belonged to Carolina Southern University. Now, it's home.

I lift my shirt and use it to wipe the sweat from my forehead. The heavy Southern humidity is bad today, and I'm half-tempted to strip down and dive into the pool to cool off.

Except, why shouldn't I dive in?

When I left California, I brought very few people with me—my private security agent, Nate, and my manager, Joni. That's it.

I *didn't* bring my chef, my trainer, my stylist, the rest of my security detail, or my housekeeper.

My agent and publicist are back in California, and they call me frequently enough to make it seem like they live with me, but for the first time in I don't know how long, I'm well and truly *alone.* Even Joni and Nate (who happen to be married to each other, thanks to my excellent matchmaking skills) have their own house at the edge of my property. They're around, but they don't hover. I don't have any neighbors, and this far into the mountains, I don't need to worry about paparazzi.

A few traveled out and sniffed around Silver Creek when word first got out that I'd sold my Malibu house, but I haven't seen any since I got back from Costa Rica. It's inevitable that word will eventually get out, but even if some desperate photographer sets out to find me, they won't get through the front gate, and that gate is the only way to access the house without hiking through miles of rugged terrain.

Point being, if I want to jump into my pool totally naked, I can jump into my pool totally naked.

I tug my shirt over my head and toss it onto a lounge chair, then unbutton my pants. I have them halfway to my knees when I see Nate walking across the deck, his frown so pronounced, I can see it all the way from here.

He's holding his iPad, and he's clearly looking for me. "Might want to keep your pants on, man."

"I'm not swimming with my pants on. It's hot. Whatever you need to talk to me about, you can talk to me about it while I'm in the pool."

He shrugs. "Fine by me. But don't say I didn't warn you when pictures of your bare butt show up all over the internet."

Pictures of my bare butt are already all over the internet, thanks to a particularly gripping scene I filmed in which I played a criminal getting strip-searched during prison intake. But I take Nate's meaning. I pull my pants back up with a sigh. "What's wrong? What's happening?"

He finally reaches me and lifts his iPad, holding it up so I can watch as he taps on the screen. "Just picked this up on the security camera over on the east edge of the property."

He pulls up a video clip and zooms in. The image is too small for me to make out actual facial features, but there's clearly a person dressed in heavy camouflage crawling through the underbrush, camera in hand.

I swear under my breath. "Did the cameras out front pick up anyone?"

Nate shakes his head. "Nobody has passed by on the main road since you got home."

"Which means what? They hiked in from the university service road? That road isn't even on the map."

"That's what makes me think it's someone local. An amateur," Nate says, "hoping they can sneak a few images and sell them for quick cash."

"A local? That's better, at least." I don't like the idea of someone sneaking around my property with a camera, but I'd rather it be someone from around here than someone who followed me here from LA. Paparazzi tend to move in packs. If you see one, you'll eventually see more.

"See the way he's dressed?" Nate says, pointing at the screen. "That's pro-level camouflage. And the way he's moving through the forest—it's someone who knows the terrain."

I sigh. "Either way, it's still trespassing. If we don't do something now, he may try again. And let other people know how to do the same thing."

Nate nods. "I'll call the cops, but I'll have to bring whoever this is up to the house. I doubt the cops will want to hike in after him."

"Just make sure you take his camera before you do."

Nate stalks off, and I turn around to retrieve my shirt.

I managed to escape a lot of things when I moved out of California.

A lot of unnecessary pressure and expectations. A toxic relationship. The constant hounding of the press.

But apparently, no matter how far into the wilderness I go, I'll never escape the kind of people who will don camo and traipse through the woods just to capture a few pictures.

I'll never escape my *fame*.

Chapter Two

Audrey

THREE WEEKS. THREE WEEKS I've been searching, and I finally found him.

I'd heard rumors about various sightings.

But I wasn't going to believe it until I saw for myself.

The implications are huge, after all. Here? In Silver Creek? I suspected it might eventually come to this—all my PhD research indicated it might—but to see actual, physical proof?

My heart squeezes. It's almost too much.

I inch forward across the loamy forest floor and lift my camera. I'm up on a bit of a ledge, a deep ravine cutting through the mountainside directly in front of me, but the height of my current position makes it easy to see, even at a distance. "Gotcha," I say as I focus my camera, zooming in to get a clearer picture.

"I'm going to need that camera," a deep voice says behind me. I jolt, and my finger slams down on the button, sounding the shutter before the camera slips from my hands, landing on the dirt in front of me.

When I look up, the white squirrel just on the other side of the ravine is nowhere to be seen.

I jump to my feet, glaring at the stranger behind me with the heat of a thousand suns.

Figurative suns, my rational, science-minded brain asserts. Because a thousand real suns would char me into nonexistence before I could glare at *anyone.*

It's a ridiculous thought, considering the giant, stern-faced stranger standing not ten feet away, but I've been with my brain for twenty-nine years now. I've learned that sometimes, there's no reasoning with it.

A flash of white appears in the distance, then vanishes behind a tree, and my jaw tightens. I was so close.

"Was that *truly* necessary?" I say as I scramble to my feet and reach for my camera. I use the hem of my shirt to wipe off the screen on the back.

The man holds out his hand, totally unfazed by my fury. "The camera," he repeats.

Does he not realize what he just disrupted? Does he have any clue how long I've been attempting to verify the presence of white squirrels in this area?

I take a step backward. "You can't have my camera."

The man is wearing some sort of utility vest over a black T-shirt, and he makes a show of sliding the vest back and propping his hands on hips, an obvious move to show off the handgun strapped to his waist.

Okay. So I probably ought to take this man seriously. Still, he doesn't look like he necessarily wants to *use* his gun. And he isn't trying to strongarm me, something he could absolutely do, though he does look poised to grab me if I try to run.

My eyes dart up to his face. There's a slim earpiece looped over the top of his left ear.

Stern expression. Armed. Wearing an earpiece. He has to be some sort of security guard.

It occurs to me that I actually have no idea who purchased the land I've been trespassing on for the past eighteen months. Trespassing with zero issues, I might add. I've never seen a soul out here, and no one has ever seen me.

"Look, we can do this the easy way or the hard way," the man says, his tone gentle, like he's trying to pacify me.

My initial frustration over losing the squirrel is fading, replaced by a sickening sense of dread. I worried I'd eventually get caught trespassing. Just not enough to actually stop.

I shrug with as much innocence as I can muster. "Do what? I'm taking pictures in the woods. I'm not breaking the law." I spare a cautious glance over my shoulder, down the deer trail that brought me to the ravine. When I look back, the Incredible Hulk—honestly, the resemblance is uncanny—folds his arms across his chest, his meaty forearms flexing.

I'd like to think I could outrun him. How fast can you truly be when you have to haul around that much muscle? But I haven't been in tiptop running shape since college.

The man takes a step closer. "You *are* breaking the law. You're on private property, for which I'm responsible. The cops are already on their way, and I'm sure they'd appreciate you coming in easily. Wouldn't want to add resisting arrest or evading a police officer to your rap sheet."

"My rap sheet? I'm just taking pictures. This really doesn't need to be a big deal."

The man frowns. "You're taking pictures *on private property*."

I barely keep myself from rolling my eyes.

I mean, *yes*. Technically, I *am* on private property. And *yes*, when Carolina Southern University sold the seventy-five acres of research forest they owned in Polk County, I was supposed to shut down the multiple experiments I had going on and relocate to the public forest land on the other side of town. But I was here first. One doesn't just *shut down* three years of research on oak ecosystem restoration, forest stand dynamics, and wildlife response to human forest management. Not to mention the water samples we've been collecting from the Broad River. I can't relocate our collection site without scrapping all our data and starting over. There are too many factors at play.

I look to my left at the house now sitting in the middle of my research forest. It's hard to miss at this distance—a monstrosity of glass and brick and poured concrete that makes my chest ache for all the trees that were sacrificed to build it. Most of the time, I'm not anywhere near it. I stay intentionally close to the river, on the back thirty acres where most of my research takes place. I'm only here now because of the squirrels.

"Ma'am, the property line is well marked. Let's not make this more complicated than it needs to be." The man shifts again, one hand moving closer to the firearm strapped to his waist. I resist the urge to ask him the diameter of his bicep because I'm pretty sure it's bigger than my entire left thigh.

My shoulders drop. "What if I just go quietly?" I motion down the deer trail, in the opposite direction of the house. "We can pretend like I was never here."

He lifts a single eyebrow—a feat only thirty to forty percent of humans can do. (I'm convinced the ability is inherited, though some argue it's simply a matter of muscle dexterity. I'd need to do my own research to fully rule out the genetic component.)

"You give me your memory card, and I'll think about it," the man says, reminding me that there is more at stake here than eyebrows.

I press my camera against my chest. There's way too much research on my memory card—at least two months of documentation, not to mention potential photos of a rare and possibly monumental white squirrel. I'll go to jail before I give it up.

"No way," I finally say. "You can't have my memory card."

He nods as though he expected my response. "Then you're coming with me," he says. *"Now."* He moves forward and reaches for my elbow.

I jerk it out of his reach. "Fine. But I'll walk by myself, thank you very much."

He gestures for me to go ahead of him, pointing through the trees. "That way," he grunts.

I push through the undergrowth for fifty yards or so, then follow Bruce Banner's lead as he cuts around a thick stand of rhododendron and lands us on a rough trail that looks like it's only recently been cut in. It isn't quite wide enough for a car, but the utility vehicle sitting a few feet away clearly fits just fine.

My feet slow, this whole situation suddenly feeling very real.

Am I really going to let this enormous man drive me somewhere? What if he isn't actually a security guard? What if he's just some random dude with a hidey-hole on the other side of the mountain where he plans to fatten me up like Hansel and Gretel before feeding me to the coyotes?

He motions toward the passenger seat. "This will be faster than walking."

I take a step backward, then lower my camera into the bag secured across my shoulder and around my hips. "I don't—" The words catch in my throat, and I swallow against the knot there. With the adrenaline firing in my brain right now, I probably *could* outrun this guy. But then I see a flash of blue through the trees—a police car making its way down the drive leading to the house. It's only visible for a moment before it disappears again. Weirdly, this brings me comfort. If I'm not getting away from this guy, I'd at least choose real jail over a hidey-hole.

"Ma'am?" the guy says.

I breathe out a resigned sigh and climb into the utility vehicle beside him.

"Who lives here anyway?" I say as we make our way up the trail. "You could have just asked me to leave, and I would have. This seems like a lot of fuss over a few pictures."

He eyes me warily. "Very funny," he says, no trace of actual humor in his voice.

Very funny?

Fear tightens my gut, but I do my best to will it away. All I've been accused of is trespassing, something that, even with official charges, only carries a fine. *Annnnd* possibly thirty days in jail. But probably—hopefully?—it will just be a fine. It's not like I have an actual criminal record. I'm a model citizen! A distracted scientist who ignored private property signs because she was so focused on finding the ever-elusive white squirrel.

A surge of satisfaction pulses through me.

I actually found him.

I resist the urge to look through my pictures to see if I captured a clear image before the Incredible Hulk scared me half to death. I'm desperate to know, but I don't want to get into any more trouble than I already am.

The ground levels out before us, then turns to pavement, and Brucey Hulk eases us to a stop directly in front of a Polk County Sheriff's car, lights still flashing blue in the fading afternoon light.

The house looms in the distance, though *looms* isn't really the right word. It *is* big, as big as I thought it was when I was seeing it across the ravine and through the trees, but from this angle, it's surprisingly pretty, its muted browns and greens and grays blending into the surrounding mountainside like it somehow belongs here.

I'm still bitter I lost access to seventy-five acres of forest land so someone can live here, but even I have to admit—the house is really lovely.

The doors on either side of the cruiser open, and two deputies climb out.

Okay.

I'm also bitter that I'm about to get arrested.

This is really happening.

I'm going to have a mugshot and ink smears on my fingertips. I'm going to be given one phone call on a sketchy payphone while a heavily tattooed man waits behind me, telling me I'd better hurry up or else.

Will I have to wear an orange jumpsuit? Or stripes? Do they still make prisoners wear stripes?

Apparently, *words* have been exchanged during my existential crisis, and now one of the deputies is moving toward me, his mouth set in a grim line.

Next thing I know, my camera bag has been lifted over my shoulders and is in the hands of giant Mark Ruffalo.

And I'm in handcuffs. Real. Actual. Handcuffs.

"Do you understand your rights?" one of the deputies says from behind me.

"My rights," I repeat. I *know* I should be listening, but Hulky Banner has pulled out my camera and is scrolling through my pictures. If he would just turn to the side a tiny bit, I'd be able to see the digital display on the back. Even just a flash of white would make me happy—

"Ma'am, are you listening?" the deputy repeats.

"Yes, but—I'm sorry, can you just tell me if I managed to get a picture of the squirrel?"

Mark Bulky Man looks up. "The squirrel?"

I nod. "White? With a little pink nose? Dark brown eyes?"

He looks through a few more pictures. "You were taking pictures of a squirrel?"

I scoff. "Trying to," I say, unable to curb the snottiness of my tone, despite my best effort. "Before you scared him away."

The man levels me with a long look. "Why?"

Something like hope flickers in my chest as all the pieces click into place.

This isn't *just* about trespassing. This is about my pictures. And this guy thinks I was taking pictures of an actual person—a person *he* is supposed to protect.

I square my shoulders. "Because I just finished my PhD research on the migratory patterns of Sciuridae as a response to climate change and the environmental impacts of urbanization and suburban sprawl."

All three men—Incredible Bruce and the two sheriff's deputies—blink in unison. Finally, Security Hulk clears his throat. "What?"

"Squirrels. Marmots. Small rodents. I've been hunting for white squirrels in these woods for weeks. And I finally spotted one."

The man's expression clears. "You're a..." He hesitates. "Scientist?"

"A wildlife biologist." I look toward the fancy house in the distance. "Look, I don't even know who lives here. I promise I wasn't trying to trespass, and I wasn't trying to take photos of anything but the squirrels."

His expression shifts, and he lifts an eyebrow. "You really don't know who lives here?"

I shrug. "Should I?"

He exchanges a quick glance with the deputies, like they're all part of some special club and I'm the dumb one who doesn't know the secret word for admittance. "Give me just a second," he says. He sets my camera down on the hood of the sheriff's car, then walks toward the house, his phone lifted to his ear. A minute or so later, another man leaves the house and meets him, then they walk back to the rest of us together.

The closer the new guy gets to me, the more my stomach fills with dread.

I know this guy. Or, I *sort of* know this guy. He's the man who almost ran into me at the Feed 'n Seed this morning when I was rescuing a nearly dead tomato plant from the back of Ann's garden center.

He stops a few feet away from me, his arms crossed over his chest, recognition flashing in his eyes. "We meet again," he says easily.

"Do we?" I say, feigning innocence. "I'm not very good with faces."

My sisters tell me I shouldn't use this as an excuse since my inability to recognize faces is *willful*. I *could* do better. I just *choose* not to. But is it truly my fault that I like science more than people? I came this way—hardwired to be hopelessly nerdy and unsociable. I can't help it that I remember the coat patterns of American marsupials more easily than I remember a man's face.

The trouble is, I *do* remember this man's face.

I also remember the thrill of emotion that shot through me (it was really just adrenaline and a spike of dopamine—it doesn't have to mean anything) when he smiled at me.

I may not be particularly adept at reading social cues—a surprise to absolutely no one—but I'm not so helpless to have missed that this guy was flirting with me.

I did not flirt back for three very specific reasons.

One—I cannot flirt. Flirting requires nuance, something I've never been able to achieve.

Two—he is much too pretty to be interested in someone like me, which means he had to be messing with me. Sadly, this isn't the first time this has happened. Experience has taught me it is much easier to keep my walls up before any real damage can happen.

And three—even if he *wasn't* messing with me, I know what kind of men I've been compatible with in the past. And they are much more the bookish, lab-coat-wearing type than the muscled, sunglasses-wearing type. As soon as this man got to know me enough to actually *know* me, he'd be out of town faster than the mayfly's life cycle.

My sisters argue I'm selling myself short and will never be happy if I can't stop *sciencing* my love life. (Their word because I only use real words, and *sciencing* isn't one.) But it's who I am.

This isn't hypothetical. It's a fact: men with faces this perfect do not fall for women like me.

He lifts a hand and rubs it across his jaw, then props both hands on his hips. The motion stretches his T-shirt across his sternum and pectoralis muscles, which—*yes,* I notice. Unfortunately, his face is not the only part of him that's perfect, and while I am undoubtedly a scientist with very specific opinions, I'm also *a woman.* I'd have to be dead not to notice.

"You really don't have any idea who I am?" he asks.

By itself, the question might sound arrogant. But there's a hope in this man's voice that negates his presumption. It's almost as though he doesn't *want* me to know who he is.

I wrack my brain, trying to think of somewhere I might have met him. Or *seen* him, since, going by the enormous house and the security guard, this guy is probably someone famous. A singer? An actor, maybe? Either way, I'm out of luck. I haven't listened to anything but classical music in years, and I haven't watched a movie since before my PhD program.

According to my sisters, *not liking movies* is one of the things that contributes to my hopeless misanthropy and should not be admitted out loud in any social situation. It's number three on the list, actually, right under my dissertation for my PhD program and the number of small rodent skeletons I have stored in my attic.

(FOR SCIENCE. I promise I don't hang out with them or anything.)

My obvious social ineptitude aside (it's shameful how much I actually need my sisters' help), I'm positive I have no idea who this man is.

"I really don't," I finally say.

He nods and looks toward the cops standing on either side of me. "You can let her go. This was obviously a misunderstanding."

Relief surges through my chest, and I take a deep breath, maybe the first one I've taken since this whole shenanigan began. As soon as my hands are free, I step forward to get my camera from the hood of the sheriff's car.

The man clearly in charge of this situation, the one with the impressive pectoralis muscles and the bright blue eyes, beats me to it. He picks it up and scrolls through several photos. "You were photographing squirrels, you say?"

I nod, resisting the urge to yank the camera from his hands. "White ones. Or, *one* white one. Though I'm hopeful there are more."

He stops on what must be the last photo I took before my...abduction? This is not the right word, I know. But my brain is full of norepinephrine from all the stress, and I'm not thinking clearly enough to land on the correct one.

"Huh. Look at that," he says. "I've never seen a white squirrel before."

I smile wide, elation filling my chest.

I got it. I got the picture. It would have been better had I been able to track the squirrel for a while, figure out where he's nesting, but a photograph is a good start.

The man looks up and startles the slightest bit, his eyes dropping to my smile, which I quickly shift into something less enthusiastic. I might as well wear a T-shirt that says, *Please ignore me. I'm too weird for regular human interaction.*

He's still looking at me, though. *Staring* at me, even. My system must still be dealing with some sort of adrenaline flood because it almost feels like there's a weird kind of energy sparking between us.

I brush the impression aside—I am stronger than the chemicals inside my brain—and clear my throat. "White squirrels don't typically live around here," I say, sounding more professorial than I would like, but it's my default mode, and in the present circumstance, it's all I'm capable of. "That's why I was tracking him. I did my PhD research on the migratory patterns of—" My sisters' threats echo in my brain, and my words trail off. What do they always say I should do? Dumb things down for regular people? "What I mean is, white squirrels aren't typically native to Polk County. The fact that they're here is new. And a big deal."

He lifts an eyebrow like I've said something to amuse him. "Is it?" he says through an easy grin.

I shrug. "A big deal to *me*."

He hands me the camera, our hands brushing in a way that makes my skin tingle. I rub at the back of my hand like I can wipe away the sensation, and the man eyes me curiously before taking a giant step back and pushing his own hands into his pockets.

He looks at his security guard, a question in his eyes. It's clear they're having some kind of wordless conversation, because eventually, the security guard shakes his head, and the other man nods, his expression resigned.

"Just the same, this *is* private property," he says. "I can't have you wandering around my woods." He looks to the sheriff's deputies. "Could you give her a ride back to...wherever she came from?"

The younger deputy nods. "Absolutely, Flint. Consider it done."

The deputy sounds like an overeager puppy, hoping to please, corroborating my belief that this man is someone famous. Also, his name is *Flint*. If that doesn't sound like the name of a star in one of my sister Lucy's romantic comedies, I don't know what does.

"Wait," I say, stepping forward. I reach for Flint's arm, which immediately has the security guy stepping toward us both like he's prepared to toss me over his shoulder like a ragdoll if that's what it takes to protect his boss. Not that *Flint* looks like he needs protecting, based on his own obvious (and very impressive) upper body strength.

I hold both my hands up, taking a step away. "Sorry. I just—if I'm only looking for squirrels," I say. "Taking pictures of *only* squirrels. Can I come back? I swear, I won't take pictures of anything else. And I'll stay in the woods, far away from the house."

Flint studies me, his arms folded over his chest. He takes a step forward, his eyes trained on me, and suddenly it feels like we're the only two people on the planet. His security guard is hovering beside us, but he is nothing but a blurry blob in the background of whatever this moment is. "What's your name?" Flint says softly.

I swallow and clear my throat. "Audrey," I croak out.

"Nice to meet you, Audrey," he says smoothly. "I'm Flint." He holds out his hand, and I slip my palm into his. I cringe when I notice the dirt staining my fingers, lining the beds of my nails, but his hands are just as dirty as mine—like he's been digging in the dirt all afternoon. Something about this makes me like him—notable because I don't generally like people at all. But if he *is* big and famous and important—and I'm beginning to sense that he must be—I like that he's not above doing his own yard work. "This is Nate," he says, gesturing to the giant behind us. "He's head of my security team."

"I gathered," I say simply.

"I believe you're a scientist, Audrey," Flint says, before letting out a light chuckle. "You look like a scientist."

I'm not sure if I should take this as an insult. I *am* a scientist, so I suppose I ought to look like one, but something tells me my sisters would not take the remark as a compliment. Regardless, I'm pretty sure Flint is about to cave and let me come back. He can insult me all he wants if it means I get to find my squirrels.

"Flint, it's not a good idea," Nate says, and my jaw tightens.

It IS a good idea, Flint. It really, really is.

"I promise I'm harmless," I say, my eyes pleading.

He holds my gaze for a long moment, then slowly shakes his head. "I wish I could make an exception, but I take my privacy very seriously. My property is off-limits."

"But the squirrels—" I start to argue. My words cut off when Nate steps in front of me, blocking my view of Flint. Blocking my view of *everything. Geez,* I didn't know humans could even BE this big.

"It was nice to meet you, Audrey," Flint says from behind the brick wall of a man now blocking my view. "Good luck with your research."

I almost ask him about the loneliness he mentioned earlier, about the implication that he'd like to spend some time with me. If I were a different woman, one well-versed in playing the games that men and women play, I might. Instead, I yell out, "There won't *be* any research if I have to stay off your property."

Flint doesn't even turn around.

"Time to go, ma'am," the younger deputy says. "I assume you've got a car parked out here somewhere?"

I sigh. "A couple miles down the road."

He nods and opens the back door of the cruiser, holding it for me while I climb in.

Seconds later, we're driving past the main house—it doesn't look so gorgeous anymore—and passing Flint, who is standing on the stone walkway that leads up to the front door. His thumbs are hooked on the front pockets of his pants, and he looks casual and comfortable and stupidly delicious.

We make eye contact through the window, and I give him my most serious glare.

His eyebrows lift the slightest bit, but otherwise, his expression remains neutral.

I hope he understands exactly what I'm trying to say.

He may have won this battle, but he isn't going to win the war.

For the squirrels.

Chapter Three

Audrey

It's nearly dark by the time I pull into my driveway. The lights inside my house are blazing, which can only mean my twin sisters, Lucy and Summer, who rent the basement apartment of my cozy mountain bungalow, have decided they'd rather hang out at *my house* instead of their own.

I shouldn't be surprised. I have a better kitchen than they do, and Lucy loves to cook. I've learned not to argue. They always make enough to share, and since I *don't* like to cook, it's a situation that works out for all of us.

I'll even begrudgingly admit that since my little sisters graduated from college a couple of years ago and turned into actual adults, we've had a much easier time getting along.

I push through my front door and take a deep breath. *Mmm.* Something Italian. "Please tell me you made homemade pasta again," I say as I drop my bag in the entryway and pull off my boots.

Summer pops her head around the corner. "She totally made homemade pasta. And a pesto that's going to blow your mind."

"Yes, please. Is there bread? I really need bread." I follow Summer into the kitchen.

"Brown butter garlic bread," Lucy says from the stove, and I try not to moan in anticipation.

"How was your squirrel hunt?" she asks as she ladles sauce over the three plates lining the counter.

I settle into a chair at my small kitchen table. "Successful until the Incredible Hulk put me in handcuffs for trespassing."

My sisters both stop in their tracks and turn to face me. "Umm, what?" Lucy asks.

I grab a piece of bread out of the basket in the center of the table. "So I guess I was *technically* trespassing on some famous person's property, and I got caught. But it was totally stupid because they thought I was trying to take pictures of the guy who actually lives there. Which—why would I ever do that?" I take a bite of bread which is delicious enough to make me cry real, happy tears. "Anyway, the security guy told me I could go if I gave him my memory card, but there was no way I was giving it up after I got a picture of a white squirrel *fifty miles away from its native home.*" I shrug and cram the rest of my bread into my mouth, suddenly feeling famished. It occurs to me that I haven't eaten all day, and I reach for another piece. "So the police came, and I was almost arrested, but then they figured out I was a biologist, and it was all just a misunderstanding, so they let me go."

When neither of them responds, I look up, cheeks chipmunk full, and look from one sister to the other. Both of them are staring like I've been speaking an entirely different language. "What?" I ask before digging into the second piece of bread.

Lucy puts a plate in front of me, her movements slow and deliberate, then lowers herself into the chair across from me. "Audrey. What famous person?"

I pick up my fork. "I don't know. Flint somebody? Am I supposed to know who he is?"

Summer's jaw drops. "You *don't* know who he is?"

Lucy's hands are pressed against her chest, and her eyes are wide. "Let me get this straight. You *trespassed* on Flint Hawthorne's property? As in, *the* Flint Hawthorne? Did you see him? Did you see his house?"

I take a big bite of pasta and groan. Forget crying over the bread. This pesto is unbelievable. I'm sure Lucy is an excellent nurse, and she seems to really like her job. But I still think she missed her calling in life.

"Audrey!" Summer practically yells, snapping my attention back to their question.

"I met him," I manage to say in between bites. "And I don't like him. He won't let me come back to photograph the squirrels, which is particularly irritating because now I know they're absolutely living on his property."

"So it was Flint Hawthorne who bought your research forest," Summer says, like this is some amazing revelation. She looks at Lucy. "We knew he moved back home. We probably should have made that connection."

I take a long swig of water. "Honestly, what's the big deal with him?"

"Oh my gosh," Summer says. She lowers her face into her hands. "You met Flint Hawthorne, and you don't even care."

Lucy scoffs. "Of course she doesn't care. This is Audrey. What else would you expect?"

"I mean, sure," Summer concedes. "Maybe I wouldn't expect her to win a game of 'Who's Who on the Red Carpet,' but we're talking about *Flint Hawthorne*. He's this generation's Tom Cruise."

"I do know Tom Cruise," I say unhelpfully. Just don't ask me to name any of his movies. Something with planes and missions, maybe? Oh! And the one where he was a sports agent. I watched that one on an airplane once. "But you still haven't answered my question," I say to my sisters. "How did you guys know some random actor was moving to Silver Creek?"

"He's from here," they say in unison.

"He's a *Hawthorne*," Lucy adds, emphasizing his last name. "Like, a Stonebrook Farm Hawthorne."

I recognize the Stonebrook Farm name—it's a commercial farm on the other side of town. But the last name doesn't mean much.

"He was a few years ahead of us in school," Summer says, "so we never met him. But he's like, the darling child of Silver Creek."

"He's younger than you though," Lucy clarifies. "I bet you went to school with one of his older brothers."

"You're forgetting I didn't go to high school in Silver Creek," I say. "And I don't remember anyone from middle or elementary school."

Summer waves her hands in front of us like this whole conversation is suddenly bugging her. Neither of my sisters has taken a single bite of their food. "We're missing the point," she says. "The most important thing here is that Flint Hawthorne is *here*, and you just met him. You need to tell us everything." She leans forward, her posture mirroring Lucy's. "What was he like?"

"What was he wearing?" Lucy adds.

"What did he say?"

"Did he smile? He's famous for his smile."

"Is he as gorgeous in person as he is in movies?"

My sisters are identical twins, but I can always tell them apart even without using the cheater butterfly tattoo Lucy has on the back of her neck just below her hairline. From their mannerisms to the way they style their hair, even just the way they carry themselves.

But every once in a while, there will be a moment like this one where they look so completely identical that if you took a freeze frame and only showed me their faces, I wouldn't be able to tell who is who.

I take a deliberate bite of food, chewing slowly, then take a long swig of water.

They watch and wait, their eyes tracking my every move. "Seeing as how I've never seen him in a movie," I finally say, "I'm not sure I could possibly judge."

"But he *was* gorgeous." Lucy says this like it's a statement, not a question.

I shrug. "I really liked his house. The outside, at least."

"She's face to face with Flint Hawthorne, and she notices the house," Summer says dryly.

"Come on, Audrey," Lucy says. "Try? For us? There has to be something you can tell us."

I pause, my fork hovering over my plate. All things considered, the man I met this afternoon *was* objectively handsome. Fit. Nice jawline. Nice hair. Blue eyes that I can conjure in my mind with very little effort. A smile nice enough to trigger a dopamine spike.

I put my fork down as a flush rushes through my body, warming my skin as I remember the way he looked at me when he asked me my name.

Lucy gasps. "Oh my gosh." She reaches over and grabs Summer's arm. "She's blushing. Audrey never blushes. What happened? What aren't you telling us?"

I roll my eyes. "*Nothing* happened." I grab my fork and shove a giant bite of pasta into my mouth. "Yes, he's handsome," I say.

"I noticed. Is that what you want me to tell you? He was wearing a T-shirt. Jeans. His hands were dirty like he'd been working in the yard. But he'd be more handsome if he would let me onto his property."

"He was working in his yard?" Lucy asks, her voice small and dreamlike. "That's so sexy."

I scoff and stand up from the table. "Is there more? If there isn't, you guys better start eating or I'm going to steal your plates."

"There's more," Lucy says as she protectively crowds around her food. "No stealing."

When I'm back at the table, plate heaped with a second serving of pasta, my sisters are both eating, but their eyes are still wide, like they're processing something unbelievable.

I don't get it. So the man is famous. It's his job just like biology is my job or the law is Summer's job. Why should we treat him any differently than we treat anyone else?

"I don't think you're understanding what we want, Audrey," Lucy says, her fork hovering in the air. "We need a play-by-play. Every single thing he said. Every single thing you said. All of it."

They can't actually be serious, but their expressions are sincere and earnest. I breathe out a sigh. "This is ridiculous."

"I fed you dinner," Lucy argues. "Indulge us."

"Fine, but it isn't a very exciting story."

I walk my sisters through a quick rundown of my interactions with Flint, even backing up enough to include our run-in at the Feed 'n Seed this morning.

The only thing I edit out is Flint's attempts to make me smile. It's probably silly, but in the back of my mind, I somehow know that if I imply a movie star was flirting with *me,* my sisters won't believe it. I might be as socially adept as an alligator snapping turtle, but I do have some pride. I'd rather not feel the sting of their disbelief or hear them laugh at such a ludicrous idea.

"And that was pretty much it," I finish. "We shook hands. He wished me luck. He said goodbye."

"*You touched him,*" Summer says dreamily. "You touched Flint Hawthorne."

"Who cares?" I say, even if the thought does make my gut clench the slightest bit. "It doesn't change the fact that now he *knows* I've been on his property, and he'll be looking for me if I go back." I slump back into my chair. "It would be a win for me workwise if I could find evidence of these squirrels. And right now, I need a win."

Summer frowns. "Have you still not heard from the foundation people about your grant?"

I shrug. "It's still under review, but my gut says they're going a different direction."

Even though I'm technically an employee of Carolina Southern University, my research is funded by grants—not the university itself. The university *did* own the forest—it was left to the school when some fancy alumni person died—but they weren't able to get an official state designation as a research forest, so after three years of trying, they sold it.

To Flint Hawthorne, apparently.

I'm not deluded enough to think that discovering white squirrels in Polk County would save my grant. But it would give me the chance to validate the research I completed for my PhD. And it *might* make it easier to find new funding, if (when?) it comes to that.

"You'll figure something out," Lucy says. "Even if you lose your funding, you can still teach."

"For a while. But a PhD with no research is like a doctor with no patients. The university won't tolerate it for long."

I think of the grad students I've worked with over the past few years. And the friends I've made at the forest service research lab. Carolina Southern has been leasing access to the lab so I have a home base for *my* research, and the forest rangers who work there have become good friends. It was one of them who first tipped me off about white squirrels in Polk County in the first place.

If I lose my funding, I'll lose them too.

A silence settles across the table, but I can tell by my sisters' starry-eyed expressions that they're still thinking about Flint and not my potential job woes.

"I still can't believe you actually touched him," Lucy says with a sigh. "I would have been a complete wreck."

"I would have cried," Summer says. "Big, fat, genuine tears. Either that, or I would have wet my pants."

I push my empty plate away and let out a tiny laugh. "It wasn't that big a deal. He seemed pretty normal, honestly."

"Ha! Normal," Summer says. "That's funny."

"I wish you'd been wearing something different," Lucy says, sitting up a little taller in her chair. Apparently, we're going to talk about Flint and only Flint for the rest of eternity. "Or at least had on a little bit of makeup."

I tense the slightest bit but quickly shake it off, giving my shoulders an easy roll. "Why? What would it have mattered? I wasn't there for him. I was there for the squirrels."

"Still. Stranger things have happened," Lucy says. "He's young, single..."

This makes Summer giggle. "Can you imagine? Flint Hawthorne asking out *Audrey*?"

I frown, hating that even with my earlier efforts to avoid the subject, we still wind up here. "Gee. Thanks."

"I mean, come on," Summer says. "I'm not saying that to insult you. You're gorgeous and brilliant and any man—even a movie star—would be lucky to be with you. But you hate movies. And you don't exactly dress like a woman hoping to catch a man's attention."

I'm momentarily stunned by the generosity of Summer's assessment. She thinks I'm gorgeous? But then my brain catches up with the rest of her words, and I glance down at my T-shirt. "What's wrong with my clothes?"

"Audrey," Lucy says, her tone level. "Most days, you dress like you're preparing for guerilla warfare, and we haven't seen you wear makeup in years."

"Since your PhD hooding ceremony," Summer adds unhelpfully.

"Guerilla warfare?" I scoff. "I dress to protect myself when I'm in the woods. There are any number of things that could hurt me. Copperheads, mosquitos, Toxicodendron radicans—"

"Toxico what?" Lucy asks.

I furrow my eyebrows. "Poison ivy."

"Then why didn't you just say poison ivy?"

"Because she's Audrey," Summer says to Lucy. "That's not how her brain works."

She does not say this like it's an insult because it isn't one. My sisters *do* know how my brain works. They might have gotten a larger share of fashion sense than I did, and they definitely got *all* the social awareness, but they grew up in the same brainy family, and their SAT scores were just as high as mine.

If our parents taught us anything, it was to appreciate the brains in our heads and use them to the best of our abilities. Summer and Lucy know better than to ever make fun of me for using mine.

Still, their observations about my wardrobe sting a little. Which is stupid. I *don't* dress to catch a man's attention. But *being* hopeless and knowing *they* think I'm hopeless aren't the same thing.

Summer leans forward and rubs her hands together. "Okay. So I'm thinking we find a few projects to do around the yard, ones that would require trips to the Feed 'n Seed, then we spend every Saturday there to see if Flint shows up again."

I stand and carry my plate to the sink. "Very funny."

"I'm not being funny," Summer says. "I'm totally serious. And I'm offering free manual labor, so I think you should take me up on it. I'm sure you can think of *something* you want to..." She hesitates because Summer spends as much time outside as I do at the mall. She's a brilliant attorney, but the only biology she knows is what she learned for the AP exam her junior year of high school. "Plant?" she finally finishes.

"You want to plant something, huh?" I purse my lips. "Like what?"

"*Flowers,*" she shoots back.

"Okay. What kind?"

She purses her lips. "Yellow ones are nice."

"They are," I agree. "But not nice enough to justify you stalking an innocent man just because he has a job that makes him famous."

"I thought you didn't like him," she says sulkily. "Now you're defending him?"

I lean against the sink, arms folded across my chest. "I'm defending his right to *not* be accosted at local businesses just because you've seen him in a movie. That's different from his ridiculous need to have seventy-five acres of *privacy*." I load my plate into the dishwasher, then move back to the table to gather the rest of the dishes.

"So what *are* you going to do about the squirrels?" Lucy asks. "Are you sure they're only living on his land?"

"Not necessarily. But so far, that's the only place I've seen them. I could start asking around, see if anyone else nearby has seen anything. But considering the proximity of his land to the Henderson County border, and assuming that's where they're coming from, his property makes the most sense."

"Will you try to go back?" Summer asks.

"I have to," I say, a little too quickly. I temper the vehemence in my voice. "It's my only option if I want to see how many squirrels there are and start tracking their movements."

Summer's expression immediately shifts from starry-eyed fangirl to grumpy, stern lawyer. Apparently, loitering at the Feed 'n Seed is *not* in the same arena as actual trespassing. "Audrey, a man like that has a lot of money to fight legal battles. He let you go this time, but who's to say he will next time if you trespass again? Especially if you no longer have the support of your university behind your efforts."

Spoken like a true assistant to the district attorney.

I purse my lips to the side. Her reasoning is sound. If Flint Hawthorne were to actually press charges, my university wouldn't back me for a second. In fact, I'd probably lose my job, though, if that's going to happen anyway, what do I truly have to lose?

"Trespassing only carries a fine. *Maybe* community service," I reason. "It's not like I'd actually go to jail."

"You *absolutely* could go to jail," Summer says. "Your sentence would be at the discretion of the judge, and with someone like Flint Hawthorne on the other side of the courtroom, I'm not sure *any* judge in Silver Creek would opt for leniency. It would only invite other creepers to Flint's property, make them think that if you got away with it, they could too."

"But I'm not a creeper," I say.

"Tell it to the judge, honey," Summer says.

I sigh, suddenly ready for this conversation—for my entire day—to be over. I move toward the hallway that leads to my bedroom. "I'm going to take a shower."

"Audrey," Summer calls, and I turn around, one hand propped on the door jamb. "Just be careful," she finishes. "No squirrel is worth losing your job."

What job? I think to myself, but if I complain any more than I already have, one of them will inevitably tell Mom and Dad, and the next thing I know, my parents will be racing up from Florida to plant their RV right in the middle of my driveway, *just in case* I happen to need them.

I love my parents. I do. But this isn't a problem they, or my sisters, can solve.

Finally alone in my bathroom, I turn on my shower and drop onto the closed toilet seat to wait for the water to warm up. I turn on my favorite classical playlist, then tap my phone against my knee.

I don't *really* care that Flint Hawthorne is a movie star. I didn't care when I met him earlier, and I don't care now. But my sisters have made me curious.

I open Google and search for a celebrity's name—something I have literally never done before.

Oh my.

There are a lot of hits.

I click over to images.

And so. many. pretty. pictures.

Flint posing with his shirt off.

Flint on the beach.

Flint beside stunningly beautiful women.

Flint beside *multiple* beautiful women.

Flint on a horse.

Oh, this is ridiculous. A horse?!

I'm about to close out the search when my eyes snag on a picture of him arm in arm with three men who all look enough like Flint, they must be his brothers. I click on the picture. If my sisters are correct, one of these men went to elementary school with me. Middle school, too.

I read through the caption, noting the names of each brother. Lennox Hawthorne is the only name that triggers my memory, but I can't remember anything concrete, though that's not all that surprising. Middle school wasn't exactly an easy time for a nerdy kid like me. A lot of memories I blocked on purpose.

I stand up and put my phone on the bathroom counter, then look in the mirror, taking in my bare face. I reach up and pull out a twig that's lodged in my hair, just above my ear.

What did Flint truly see when he looked at me today? Was he genuinely interested in seeing me smile? Or was it just a game? Is flirting something he does because he can? Because he's so used to women fawning all over him?

Lucy's laugh from earlier echoes in my mind.

Either way, she's right. Whatever his motive at the Feed 'n Seed, whatever made him look *once,* I am *not* the kind of woman a man like Flint Hawthorne would look at twice.

A gnawing discomfort settles in my chest.

I'm a biologist. Dedicated to science and research and way too enthusiastic about most forms of wildlife.

Most of the time, it's enough.

But every once in a while, something reminds me that I'm more than just a brain. I have a beating heart, too. And right now, it's aching in a way that feels foreign and disconcerting.

It takes a moment of careful thought to figure out what the feeling is.

I'm lonely.

And I have no idea what I'm supposed to do about that.

Chapter Four

Flint

I LEAN AGAINST THE counter in the middle of my kitchen, my arms crossed over my chest. Nate and Joni sit on the opposite side of the island, while my publicist, Simon, and my agent, Kenji, both back in LA, are on a video call connected through Joni's iPad, propped up in the center of the island.

It's a relatively small group, and that's just the way I like it. The longer I'm in this business, the happier I am with as few people as possible involved in my career. A few years ago, it was thrilling to travel with an entire entourage, knowing they were all there for me. But now, the simpler my life is, the better.

"What if we come up with some credible reason for him to skip the premiere?" Joni says. "A family issue, maybe?"

"He's the lead," Simon says. "His attendance isn't negotiable. Unless someone is dead or dying or in need of a life-saving kidney only Flint can provide, he's *going* to the premiere."

"Of course I'm *going*," I say. "But there has to be a way we can preemptively manage this."

And by this, I mean *her*.

Claire McKinsey.

Hollywood darling. *Turning Tides* co-star.

And my ex-girlfriend.

It wasn't a long relationship. But you wouldn't know it for how much she's milking the few months we spent together whenever she's in front of the press.

"It's like she's honed it down to a science," Joni says. "It's honestly impressive how she manages to say just enough to keep people guessing but not enough to actually *declare* anything outright."

"Kenji, were you able to make any headway with Rita?" I brace my hands against the cool countertop, wishing this entire conversation could be over. This is the part of my job I'm really starting to hate.

"Rita. That's Claire's manager?" Nate asks as he reaches for one of the sugar cookies I brought home from the feed store.

Joni nods and picks up her own cookie. The icing on hers didn't set quite right, and my nose has three nostrils. When she holds it up to show Nate, they both start to giggle.

"We talked last week," Kenji says, his voice all business, despite the circus clowns hanging out in my kitchen. "I kept things casual. Like we were just catching up. But I did make a light *suggestion* that Claire tone down the storytelling. Rita seems to think the gossip Claire is generating is only going to help the movie. I could try again, make the request feel a little more official, but I don't think Rita is our ally in this."

I sigh and run a hand through my hair. Maybe I'm the one who needs a cookie.

Claire was sweet at first. But she was hungry, too—*Turning Tides* is her first major motion picture role—and her attempts to piggyback off my fame and thrust herself into every possible spotlight quickly led to our relationship's demise.

At this point in my career, I'm ready to get *out* of the public eye when I'm not working. She's looking for the opposite.

"Okay, hear me out," Simon says, and my jaw tenses. This isn't the first time we've talked about the Claire problem and last time, Simon agreed with Rita.

"What's truly the harm?" he argued. "Claire is the kind of star America is going to love, and they already love you. If she's getting people talking about the film, who cares if she's telling the truth?"

To a point, I understood where he was coming from. I learned a long time ago that I can't react every time someone says something about me that isn't true. But this time, Claire's antics are hurting more than just me. *Turning Tides* will be the directorial debut of Lea Cortez, who happens to be a good friend of mine. Back on set, she expressed concern that Claire's starlet behavior might detract from the seriousness of the film. Claire and I were dating at the time, and I assured Lea everything would be fine.

I want those words to be true. But more than that, I don't want Claire to overshadow the work Lea did on the film. If Claire keeps this up, it's all the press junket will focus on. We won't talk about my acting. About Lea's directing. Every single question will be about whether I noticed Claire's latest Instagram post and do I really have plans to meet her in Fiji next week? Lea deserves to have her work celebrated, not overshadowed by an upstart's attempt to steal the show with a false narrative. That's the last thing this movie needs.

When no one protests, Simon clears his throat and dives in. "As I made it clear the last time we spoke, I don't actually disagree with Rita. Be that as it may, *you* are my client, so I've come up with a potential solution that should, if executed correctly, get Claire to shut up."

My eyes lift to Joni's. She doesn't love Simon, and I trust her instincts. But he's too good at his job for me to let him go. Hollywood is a multilayered web of connections—someone who knows someone else who knows that one guy who knows the casting director for the movie you really want to work on. Simon is neck-deep in connections. I don't want to need him, but there's no escaping how much I do.

Joni lifts her shoulders as if to say there's no harm in hearing him out, and I nod.

"Okay, what's the plan?" I ask.

"Fake a relationship," Simon says bluntly. "Drop a few photos of you with someone else, someone who *won't* talk to the press, and make it clear you're *really* enjoying your time with this woman. Then bring her with you to the premiere."

I'm already shaking my head. This is exactly the kind of Hollywood drama I was trying to get away from when I moved. Joni's frown echoes mine, and she opens her mouth, but Kenji speaks before she can. "I'm guessing you already have someone in mind?"

Kenji is a few steps ahead of me, but *of course* Simon has someone else in mind. He's a publicist with multiple clients. If he can work this so it benefits someone else as well? He will.

"I'm not faking a relationship," I say before Simon can mention any names or provide even one more detail of his ridiculous plan. "Especially not with any actresses."

"Not all actresses are like Claire," Simon says, his tone annoyingly gentle, to the point that he sounds like he's patronizing me. "We'll choose someone discreet. Someone experienced with the media."

I turn and open the fridge, pulling a water bottle from inside. "I don't disagree with you," I say as I twist off the top. "Not all actors are like Claire. But the ones who have the discretion and the media experience to pull off what you're suggesting are *not* the ones who need to fake a relationship to get ahead in their careers."

"You're too generous," Simon says dryly. "Just let me mention a few names—"

"No." I toss the water bottle lid onto the counter, and it clatters into the phone. "I won't do it. I already told you I want my personal life to be off-limits. It's why I moved. I don't want to play these kinds of games anymore. Even to shut up Claire."

It wasn't all that long ago that I milked the media as much as the next guy, as much as Claire, even, taking every leg up the extra attention would give me. But I don't want that life anymore. I want to take myself seriously enough to believe I can maintain my career because I'm good at what I do, not because TMZ won't stop speculating about who I'm dating. Others have done it. Separated their personal lives. Made their public persona about their *work*. I have to believe I can do the same thing—that I can take back control before I lose control altogether.

"I admire your idealism," Simon says, "but what other solution is there? Either you control the narrative, or Claire does. It's your choice."

"What I want is for Lea to control the narrative. She doesn't deserve to have her directorial debut overshadowed by the personal drama of a bunch of idiot actors."

"We don't always get what we want, Flint. Ideals are nice, but it doesn't change the reality of the situation. Just think about it," he says. "We can circle back next week. In the meantime, I'll have the details of the Oakley thing within the week. I'll send them to you and Kenji as soon as I have them. All right. That's it from me. I'm out." Simon disappears from the call, and I look at Kenji.

"The Oakley thing?" I ask.

"Sunglasses," Kenji says. "You're doing their spring ad campaign."

"I am?"

Joni exchanges a quick glance with Nate, then looks back at me. "They came to see you in Costa Rica."

Details flood my memory. The Oakley people *did* come to see me. We had dinner at a little cantina on the beach, and they plied me with alcohol and showered me with compliments, and I guess...here we are. "When? And how long will it take?"

"Not until November," Kenji says. "And it shouldn't take more than a couple of days. One for the photoshoot, another to film the commercial. Those are the details we'll have from Simon this week."

I nod. "Fine. But it can't conflict with Thanksgiving." It's been years since I've spent the holidays with my family. I've had to modify my expectations somewhat since getting home—I'm not spending nearly as much time with my brothers as I thought I would—but the holidays are different. That's when we're *supposed* to be together.

Joni's expression softens. With the angular cut of her straight blond hair, hitting right at her chin, her look generally says *I'm perfectly capable, thank you,* with a side of, *So you'd better get out of my way.* But right now, her face is saying something else entirely. She's either touched that I'm trying so hard to do things differently now, *orrrrr* she feels sorry for me because my brothers are not the bachelors they used to be, and they spend their time accordingly.

Not that I blame them. If I had the option to snuggle up on the couch with a beautiful woman, I wouldn't want to come over to drink beer with me either.

"Of course it won't conflict with Thanksgiving," Joni says. "We'll make sure of it."

"All right, I'm out," Kenji says. The sounds of Los Angeles suddenly come through the phone, and I can imagine him pushing out of his office, tugging at the sleeves of one of his impeccably tailored suit coats. "I'll reach out to Rita one more time and make the point about Lea's directing and see if that sways her. It can't hurt to try, anyway," he says.

"Thanks, man," I say, but I don't have a lot of confidence in Rita. I've met her. She's as fame hungry as Claire.

Kenji disconnects and Joni closes down her iPad, a welcome silence filling the room.

I'm suddenly very tired. And very grouchy. And I definitely need a cookie.

I reach for one and rip off the cellophane, only to notice this one has a tiny mustache drawn above my lip, the ends long and curly.

Wait a minute.

I look up to see Nate, lips pressed together like he's trying to hold in his laughter. I reach for the bag of cookies and dump them onto the counter. Every single one is slightly different. A beauty mark on my cheek. A third eyeball in the middle of my forehead. An impressive array of different mustache and goatee styles. But the most impressive thing is that the cookies are all still *sealed*. Somehow Nate—because it was *definitely* Nate—managed to graffiti every single one of my cookies and then *reseal* them into their packaging.

"Dude. You've got too much time on your hands."

He bursts out laughing. "This one is my favorite." He pulls out a cookie from the bottom of the stack and slides it toward me. On this one, one of my teeth is blackened out, and a long feather earring dangles from my ear. Honestly, I'm impressed with the artwork. I had no idea Nate had it in him.

"How did you even know how to do this? Can we still eat them? This isn't sharpie or anything, is it?"

"Ann taught me," Nate says. "And they're fine to eat. I used edible ink."

"I still think it was totally unfair for you to ask Ann to help when you wanted to deface *her* cookies," Joni says. "She never would have answered your questions if she'd known what you were up to."

Nate waves his hand dismissively. "Pretty sure she figured it out. Either way, she had a fresh batch of cookies out on the counter. Who cares what happens to the ones she already sold?"

"Wait, she has new cookies out?" I ask. "She made more?"

Nate nods. "She sold three while I was waiting in line. Only person who didn't buy one was the trespassing biologist lady."

"Audrey?" I ask. "She was there?" My heartrate ticks up the slightest bit at the thought, which is dumb. I probably won't ever see her again. Her bright blue eyes flash through my mind's eye, and a twinge of disappointment pushes through me. "She saw the cookies?"

Nate nods, and the feeling in my chest tightens, then shifts to embarrassment. This should not matter even a little. But the thought of Audrey seeing those cookies, maybe even thinking I had something to do with them, makes me uncomfortable.

"Did she say anything to you?" I ask, trying to keep my voice neutral.

"Nah. She waved," Nate says, "but she didn't look very happy to see me."

"Because you almost had her arrested," Joni says. "And you're the size of a tree." Joni leans over and kisses Nate on the cheek.

"Sometimes you intimidate people, baby." She grabs her phone off the counter and slides it into her pocket. "Are we done here? I've got a million emails to sort through."

"Yeah, go," I say, waving her off. "Just keep thinking about possible solutions to this whole Claire situation."

Joni nods. "Will do." She steps away from the counter, then pauses and spins back around. "Flint, have you thought about just taking a *date* to the premiere? Not a fake one, like Simon suggested, but just...a date."

I furrow my brow. "A real date? *Who*? I'm not seeing anyone."

"We could easily figure that part out," Joni says. "Just think about it. If you have a beautiful woman on your arm, looking all cozy and comfortable, people aren't going to be asking about Claire."

"No, they'll be asking about the mystery woman on my arm. Besides, the press junket is *before* the premiere. That's when people will be hounding me the most."

Joni frowns. "That's true. But if you *did* have a date, maybe we could do something before that makes it clear you're with someone. Simon was right about that part, at least. If you're seeing someone new, it would put *you* in control of the narrative."

"And you won't feed the flames like Claire does," Nate says. "You can just say you want to keep your personal life private, and then move on to the next question."

"*Exactly,*" Joni says, her eyes sparkling. "Claire will know that if she keeps talking about meeting up with you, dating you when you've clearly moved on, she'll only look desperate."

"And stupid," Nate adds. "She won't want to look stupid."

I reach for my water and drain half the bottle. I still don't love the idea, but it's slightly more tolerable than Simon's. His plan felt like a publicity stunt. This feels more like a decoy.

I run a hand through my hair. "Ya'll are talking like I could just head down to the Feed 'n Seed and pick up a girlfriend on aisle four." Audrey's eyes flash through my mind one more time, and I quickly shove the image away.

"If anyone could, it's you," Joni says. "Just mention it to Ann. I bet she'd have a dozen women lined up in an hour, ready to date you."

I appreciate Joni's confidence, but I'm not half as certain. Besides, women lining up to date me because I'm *Flint Hawthorne*, famous actor, is a lot different than a woman wanting to date me because I'm...*me*. A lot less appealing, too.

"I'll think about it," I say, suddenly restless to be out of this room, away from the drama that drains the fun right out of my career. I look out the window at the late afternoon light. It's already past four, but that doesn't mean much. It'll be almost nine before it's fully dark. "I'm going to go work on the trail."

Nate perks up. "You want me to come with you?"

"Nah, man. I need solitude. But I'll keep my phone on me."

I head toward the garage, but not before Joni yells out, "Please be careful with the machete, Flint. Your face is worth a lot of money!"

I pause, sensing that what Joni really needs is some sort of indication that I'm okay. That despite the tension of our conversation, I'm not going to drive off into the wilderness and never come back.

I pause and lean back into the kitchen where she can see me, offering her a wide grin. "I'm not worried. A few scars will only give me more sex appeal."

She rolls her eyes, but I don't miss the relief moving across her expression. Her voice follows me as I disappear into the garage. "Flint, I'm serious!"

"Love you, Joni!" I say in reply.

I appreciate my manager's concern. I really do. But I'm stressed as all get out at the moment, and any man with blood pumping through his veins would agree. There are few frustrations in life a little time with a machete won't cure.

Chapter Five

Flint

LATE AFTERNOON SUN WARMS my shoulders as I drive a four-wheeler down the roughly cleared trail I've been working on the past few weeks. Eventually, it'll meet up with the old forest service road that runs along the west edge of my property, and I'll be able to *mostly* make it around the entire perimeter. I don't have a particular purpose in connecting to the road, other than it seems like a good idea to have access to all the acreage I bought.

Plus, it's not like I have anything else to do. Not unless I want to go hang out with one of my brothers like some kind of lost puppy. None of them would truly mind. But I'm only comfortable being a third wheel for so long.

I drive the four-wheeler as far as I can, stopping a few yards shy of where I stopped clearing. There's a thick stand of rhododendrons just in front of me, which is going to require more than just a machete.

I smile to myself. I get to use the chainsaw.

An hour later, I'm covered in leaves and dirt and sweat, but I've made a hundred yards of progress, and I've finally reached the shallow creek bed that runs down the mountainside to meet the Broad River. I crouch down and scoop up a handful of the icy spring water and splash it onto my face, then toss another onto the back of my neck.

I'm tempted to take a drink. There are multiple springs in the mountains that are fully potable, but until I can test the water to be sure, I won't risk it. I've experienced firsthand what happens when you *do* risk it, and it's definitely not worth it.

Back at the four-wheeler, I slide the machete into its sheath and lower the chainsaw into the cargo basket on the back. Sweat drips down my brow, so I lift the hem of my T-shirt to wipe off my face, pausing when I hear what sounds like a gasp.

I freeze as my heart rate climbs, my eyes roving over the surrounding woods. I don't hear anything else, but all the hairs on the back of my neck stand up.

I'm *not* alone out here—I'm sure about that.

Off to the left and up the mountainside a ways, a bush shakes and then settles.

I narrow my eyes and step closer.

Suddenly, everything becomes clear.

The bush isn't a bush at all. It's a person disguised as a bush. A *familiar* person disguised as a bush.

I fold my arms across my chest, my lips twitching into a smile. "Hello, again," I say dryly.

Audrey doesn't move, but she's absolutely close enough to hear me. Does she think I'll just leave her alone if she doesn't respond?

"You can't sit there all day, Audrey," I say. "I *know* you're there. You might as well come out now."

The bush shakes one more time, and Audrey stands up.

I can't help it. I burst out laughing.

Her get-up is absolutely ridiculous. It's also kind of ingenious. Leaves are sewn down the sleeves of her shirt and across the top of her hat, and her camouflage shirt and pants blend into the woods around her. Had she not made a noise, I probably wouldn't have seen her at all.

But she *did* make a noise, and I'm pretty sure she made it when I lifted my shirt to wipe my face. Is it possible she was actually checking me out? After the way she dismissed me at the Feed 'n Seed, she was more likely startled by a chipmunk or suddenly surrounded by a swarm of mosquitos. She definitely wasn't impacted by the sight of my abs. *Was she?*

Audrey slowly moves down the mountainside, her camera in hand, and stops on the trail behind me. She doesn't look even a little bit repentant even though she's obviously trespassing. *Again.*

I nod toward her clothing. "That's an awful lot of trouble to go to just to hide from me."

"I'm not hiding from *you*," she says, like that's the most absurd thing she's ever heard. "I'm hiding from the squirrels."

"Oh, right. The squirrels." Her expression is so serious, I hate to keep smiling. But this woman clearly has no idea how adorable she looks with leaves sewn onto her hat. I *can't* take her seriously. Not really. I scratch my jaw. "Tell me again why the squirrels at your house aren't good enough. Why is it you have to risk going to jail to see the squirrels over here?"

She winces the slightest bit when I say jail, but she quickly regains her composure. "The squirrels at my house are just regular eastern gray squirrels," she says, her words measured and slow like she's trying to explain trigonometry to a six-year-old. Or maybe like I'm a guy who just doesn't understand squirrels. "But the squirrels over here are white." She takes her hat off and tucks it under her arm while she pulls out her ponytail and shakes out her hair. It's long—longer than I expect—cascading over her shoulders in dark waves.

I swallow. *Focus on the squirrels, man. Squirrels.*

I clear my throat. "I remember you mentioning that. But why does that matter? Are they albino?"

She shakes her head as she regathers her ponytail, talking around the hairband she's holding with her teeth. "It's called leucism." She pauses long enough to grab the hairband and secure it. "It's a condition characterized by reduced pigmentation linked to a recessive allele. You can tell them from albino squirrels because they still have dark eyes and skin. Just white fur."

I study Audrey closely, noting the way her eyes brighten as she talks. Her posture is confident, her tone steady, her words punctuated with an air of certainty. I'm positive, even just from those few sentences, there isn't anything I could ask about squirrels, probably about these woods in general, that she wouldn't know. It's a weird thought, considering she's dressed like a bush *and* she's trespassing on my land, but her confidence, her knowledge—it's kinda sexy.

I take a step toward her, but she immediately steps backward, and I lose the ground I gained.

Okay. Sexy and still entirely uninterested.

If only *I* had white hair and a little brown nose.

"I think I saw one of those the other day," I say.

If Nate were listening, he would not be happy. Mentioning the squirrels I saw outside my kitchen window is only going to make Audrey want to see them. And that's going to make her ask me if she *can*, and then I'm going to have to say yes. Because *of course* I'm saying yes.

Her expression visibly brightens. "Just one? Or more than one? Where? Were you near your house?"

I chuckle at her enthusiasm. "There were two. And I was *in* my house. They were on the lawn beside the pool."

"That's the first time you've seen them?" she asks.

"First time. Though it's possible I saw them and just didn't notice until you showed up and told me it was a big deal."

"Right. That makes sense." She lifts a hand to the back of her neck, her eyes glazing over the same way Brody's do when he's doing high-level math in his head. "There were two of them?" she finally asks.

I nod, and she moves her hand from her neck to her forehead, her expression disbelieving. "Two. That's—that means this isn't just a fluke but an actual migratory event."

"Slow down, Dr. Doolittle."

She looks up, meeting my gaze, and I grin. Her eyes are so incredibly blue, it's really hard not to stare.

"How about you try again in English?" I say gently.

A slight blush tints her cheeks, but she nods like this is something she's been asked before. She's used to communicating with people who aren't as smart as she is. "For over a century, white squirrels have only been native to a very small part of Western North Carolina. But now, apparently, they live in other places, too. The population is growing—*moving.*"

I move over to the four-wheeler and pull a water bottle off the back. I screw off the top and offer her a drink, but she declines, picking up a straw that's connected to the shoulder of her backpack. "I have a Camelbak," she says.

Of course she does.

I have a feeling she could live out here for days and probably be just fine, living on the land, mapping her location using her shoestrings and the clouds overhead. I take a long swig of water. "You said something about your PhD the last time you were here. You're a scientist?"

"Wildlife biologist," she says. "I wrote my dissertation for my PhD on the migratory patterns of the class Sciuridae as a result of urbanization and suburban sprawl, so the fact that these squirrels are moving—it's incredibly relevant to my research. You have no idea how thrilling it is to discover it happening."

Okay. Her brains are *definitely* sexy. No *kinda* about it.

Audrey studies me for a long moment before she steps forward, her expression pleading. "Look, I know I'm trespassing. But I swear I'm only here for the squirrels. Can you just..." She bites her lip, and I'm momentarily distracted by the way her teeth press into her skin.

I prop my hands on my hips. "What, give you permission?"

She nods. "Obviously, I wouldn't go near your house. Or, at least not *in it.* If you saw them by the pool, they're probably nesting nearby, which means I'd have to get close enough to take pictures. And I'd need to find their nest. See if I can date it and determine how long they've been living there."

"Date their nest? You can do that?"

She levels me with a look. "We can carbon date trees that lived over fifty-thousand years ago. You don't think I can guesstimate how long a squirrel has been nesting in a certain spot?"

I can't help but smile. There's something endearing about her fascination with a subject that is so patently boring to everyone else. But then, what do I know about what's boring? I've been standing here talking about squirrels for at least five minutes, and I'm thoroughly invested. I suspect that has more to do with *who* I'm talking to than *what* we're talking about.

The truth is, now that I'm certain she really *is* only interested in squirrels, in my mind, there's no reason she can't come back no matter what Nate says.

I've seen some paparazzi go to a lot of trouble to disguise themselves and get close to celebrities. But there's no way someone could fake Audrey's knowledge or enthusiasm. This woman is harmless.

A little odd.

But harmless.

Though, I'm kidding myself if I think I'm *only* letting Audrey come back because I think she's harmless.

I also want a reason to see her again.

"How long would you need?" I ask, my eyes focused on the gear in the cargo box on the four-wheeler as I make sure everything is securely strapped down. If I look straight at her, I might scare her off with *my* enthusiasm.

"A week? Two, tops," she says, hope infusing her voice.

"Two weeks to take a few pictures?"

"And gather the necessary data," she says. "But you won't even notice me. And I promise. No photographs of you, or the house, or anything that might identify where the squirrels are specifically located."

"Would you be willing to sign an NDA?" I won't make her sign one, not for something as harmless as this, but it's a good test anyway.

"Absolutely. Whatever you need. And I'm happy to send over proof of my credentials. And a copy of the research grant currently funding my research."

"Credentials?"

She clears her throat and steps forward, holding out her hand like she's introducing herself. I finally look into her eyes as she slips her hand into mine. "Dr. Audrey Callahan," she says. "Wildlife biologist, professor at Carolina Southern University, and published author. Google me."

My gut tightens. I don't need more reasons to be impressed with this woman, especially when she doesn't seem all that impressed with me. But hearing her name like that—*Dr. Audrey Callahan.* And she's a published author? I'm falling into full-on *crush* territory. Except, somehow, this crush feels bigger—different from anything I've ever experienced before. Maybe because Audrey is different. *Better.*

I study her for a long moment, this time letting myself fall into the pale blue of her eyes. They're ringed in dark navy, but near the iris, they're the color of the early morning sky.

Audrey doesn't flinch under my scrutiny. She may be young to have accomplished so much, but she knows how to hold herself, how to go after what she wants. Which makes *me* want *her.*

"All right, Doctor Audrey Callahan. I'm going to make a deal with you. I'll give you access to my property so you can study your white squirrels on one condition."

She nods. "Anything. I'll do anything."

"No more hiding," I say. "At least not from me. You use the main driveway. You check in with Nate. And you let us know where on the property you're going to be."

She cocks her head to the side. "I already told you I wasn't hiding from *you.*"

I motion toward her outfit. "You're saying when you got dressed this morning, you didn't hope, even for a moment, that your disguise would keep you out of sight from me?"

"It *would* have kept me out of sight if I hadn't *gasped.*"

I raise my eyebrows and lean forward the slightest bit. "That's true. Why *did* you gasp, Audrey?" I ask, my tone playful.

She folds her arms across her chest. "I felt a bug run across my shoe."

"I bet." I mirror her stance. "You *really* seem like the kind of woman who is freaked out by bugs."

Her shoulders drop and she moves her hands to her hips, the leaves sewn down the seam bouncing as she does. "*Fine,*" she finally concedes. "Yes. I *gasped* because I was not prepared to see twelve inches of your exceptionally defined abdominal muscles. Is that what you wanted me to admit?"

I turn on my famous smile—the same one she completely ignored when we first talked in the feed store parking lot. "I'm just having a conversation, Audrey."

I can't explain why this is so fun for me. Except, maybe it's not all that complicated. I haven't had to *work* to get a compliment out of a woman in years. And this one seems utterly and completely unimpressed. Well, by everything except my abs. "Now, do you agree to my terms or not?" I say.

She purses her lips. "Right. Your terms. So I'll come to the main driveway, check in with your scary hulkish bodyguard, and then I can go wherever I please?"

"As long as you tell us where you're planning to be. And Nate's harmless. I promise he'll be nice."

"Oh, I'm sure," she says dryly. "He was *so nice* when he was flashing his gun at me and threatening to take away my camera."

"He thought you were taking pictures of *me*," I say, enjoying the way she's bantering with me. "And considering the fact that I was mere moments away from stripping down to nothing and diving in my pool when he picked you up on our security cameras, I'm glad he reacted the way he did."

Her gaze drops to my torso, sliding up to my chest and shoulders before she lifts it back to my face. "You swim naked?" she asks, her voice small.

I smile playfully, lifting my shoulder in an easy shrug. "There are some perks to living alone."

She shakes her head, like she's breaking out of some sort of trance, then clears her throat. "Fine," she says haughtily. "*For the squirrels,* I agree to your terms."

I don't miss her emphasis on squirrels. She really wants me to know she isn't here for me, which somehow feels like both a good thing *and* a bad thing. "What's your number? I'll have my manager text you, then you can work out the details with her."

Audrey holds out her hand. "Here. I can just plug my number in and send myself a text."

I pull my phone back, away from her reach. "Nope. Then you'd have *my* number."

"So?"

"So...you might feel tempted to share it or sell it or who knows what else with it." Sadly, I'm only half-joking. I've been burned before, and changing my number is too tedious for me to want to do it again. Also, Joni would kill me if I gave my number to someone I've only known as long as I've known Audrey.

Audrey blinks in surprise. "You really think I'd do something like that?"

Her question is serious, so I give her a serious answer. "I don't. Mostly, I'm just trying to avoid getting in trouble with my manager. She's as much of a guard dog as Nate and takes protecting my privacy very seriously."

Audrey shakes her head. "People bother you that much?"

I shrug. "You'd be surprised how far some people will go."

She nods. "Right. That makes sense. You *should* be cautious. You don't really know anything about me."

I playfully tap my phone against my palm. "I don't know if I'd say *that*."

She tilts her head to the side. "What would you say?"

"I'd say I know you're serious enough about your work to trespass not once, but twice. Also, you have an uncanny ability to blend into the wilderness, and you know more about squirrels than any person should. Also, I'm pretty sure you have a thing for rock-hard—"

She cuts me off. "If you say one thing about your abdominal muscles, I swear, Flint Hawthorne, I will..." She hesitates, her eyes darting around like she's trying to find an appropriate threat.

I lift an eyebrow. "You'll what?"

"I don't know what I'll do," she says, her tone snobbish, which is hilarious, considering she's currently dressed like a bush. "But it won't be good."

"Well, now you've got me worried."

She holds my gaze, and for a second, I think she might smile. I'm filled with a sudden craving for the sight of it, and that same certainty I felt the first time I saw her settles into my soul.

If this woman smiles at me—*because of me*—I think I'll be done for.

Audrey rattles off her phone number, then glances up at the quickly darkening sky. "When can I start?" she asks as she rearranges the strap on her camera bag. "Is tomorrow too soon?"

I almost say yes, but I don't want to sound too eager. This woman has already made her lack of interest perfectly clear. I don't want to scare her off. "Just work it out with Joni," I finally say. "She knows my schedule better than I do. I'll make sure she reaches out tonight."

Audrey nods. "Okay. Perfect. Sounds good."

I tilt my head toward my four-wheeler. "Do you need a ride?"

She looks over her shoulder, toward the creek. "I don't think your trail goes far enough. But I'll be okay. My truck isn't far from here."

I nod. "Okay. Then I guess I'll see you when I see you." I move to my four-wheeler and climb on, then reach forward and crank the engine until it hums to life. I look back one last time and watch as Audrey takes a few hurried steps toward me.

"Flint, I just..." She licks her lips. "Thank you. You have no idea what this means for my research."

If this were anyone else, I might laugh. We're talking about squirrels, after all. But after meeting Audrey and really talking to her, I have to respect someone who has so much passion for her work, who takes her job so seriously.

"Also, I know how important privacy must be to you," she continues. "I want you to know I won't tell anyone about this—that you're letting me come here. Not anyone."

"I appreciate that," I say. Nate *is* going to protest, but I believe Audrey, and weirdly, even though we just met, I also trust her. She isn't going to cause any trouble.

I lift a hand in a final wave, then ease my hand off the brake and head toward the house. Just before I pull into the garage, a white squirrel darts across the driveway and into the woods.

I grin, feeling invigorated in a way I haven't in years.

Maybe it's all the physical labor I'm doing. Maybe it's being back home in the mountains.

Or maybe—just maybe—it's the squirrels.

Chapter Six

Flint

"SO LET ME GET this straight," my oldest brother Perry says, his expression disbelieving. I follow his gaze through the kitchen window and out to the lawn beside the pool where Audrey is sitting in a camp chair, scribbling something down in a small, leatherbound notebook. "You've given a complete stranger access to all of your property because she wants to take pictures...of squirrels?" He leans across the counter and grabs a cracker and a slice of cheese.

It is not surprising that Perry is the one asking the hard questions. He's the oldest and the grouchiest and definitely the one most likely to point out potential problems.

It *was* surprising when my family descended upon the house, laden with groceries, for what they claimed was a "random family gathering." Perry said it was because his son Jack wanted to swim, but I'd put money on this having something to do with the conversation Brody and I had a couple of weeks back. Brody thinks I'm lonely. And now he's made the rest of my family think I'm lonely too.

To be fair, Jack *is* swimming—he and Perry's wife Lila are outside by the pool with everyone else. Still, I know my family well enough to recognize their meddling for what it is.

It makes me itchy to know they're all talking about me, worrying about me. At the same time, I *do* wish I got to spend more time with them, so I can't really complain about them all coming over. Especially since they brought food. My brother Lennox and his wife, Tatum, both chefs, took over my kitchen the minute they arrived, setting out appetizers and commandeering the grill for what they swear are going to be the best hamburgers any of us have ever eaten.

I have to wonder what Audrey thinks about my family. Or if she's even noticed the people for all the squirrels.

As I watch, Audrey stands and moves toward the sugar maple at the edge of the lawn. Conveniently, the squirrels have a nest somewhere in its branches, though Audrey told me it's not all that uncommon for squirrels. Living closer to people means encountering fewer predators.

"She isn't a complete stranger," I say, finally answering Perry's question. I got so distracted watching Audrey, I almost forgot he asked. "And I promise she's harmless. I'm good at sniffing out people with ulterior motives, and she definitely doesn't have one."

"Just like you sniffed out Claire McKinsey's ulterior motives?" Perry asks, his brows lifted.

I frown. Sometimes I hate how much my family knows about my life. "This is different. Audrey is nothing like Claire."

"Did she grow up around here?" My sister Olivia leans backward in her chair so she can see Audrey through the window. "She doesn't look familiar."

"No clue," I say. "But Joni checked her out. Verified all her credentials. She's got a PhD. Publishing credits. She's legit."

"I've never seen a white squirrel," Mom says as she walks over to lean on the counter. "I didn't even know they existed." She moves to the fridge and pulls out a water bottle, holding it out to me. "Here. Take this out to Audrey. She looks thirsty." Her expression turns sly. "She might be hungry, too. Maybe you could invite her to join us for dinner."

I take the water bottle but lift a finger in warning. "Mom? That's not what this is."

She shrugs. "It might be. How will you know if you don't try?"

"Trust me. I know." *And it's not for the lack of trying.* "I am not that woman's type—not by a mile."

"It pains me to say this," Olivia says, "but you're Flint Hawthorne. Doesn't that make you everyone's type?" She bounces her daughter on her knee.

"Not hers," I say. "She didn't even know who I was the first time we met." And she hasn't been impressed with me *any* of the times we've interacted.

"Well, that sounds perfect," Mom says. "You don't want someone who's only interested in you for your celebrity. Maybe you've finally found the one woman on the planet who isn't."

I love the idea of a woman not into my fame, but no matter how I shake it, my fame *is* a part of the package. I'm working on making my private life more private, but the acting, the need to perform, the way I thrive in the spotlight—those characteristics are a part of what makes me *me*. And it seems in direct contrast to what might make a serious wildlife biologist interested in a relationship.

I move toward the patio door. "Please don't make this a thing. It's not a thing. She's here for the squirrels. Period."

I push outside and slide my sunglasses onto my face. I should have expected the matchmaking, especially from Mom. Audrey has a pulse, and she doesn't live in California—as far as Mom is concerned, that's all she needs to qualify.

I study Audrey as I approach, water bottle in hand. She's back in her camp chair now, leaning over her notebook, her pen flying across the page. Her hair is pulled back into a simple ponytail, and her expression is serious. Focused.

She's nothing like the women I've dated in the past, but she's pretty in a simple, natural way that I appreciate. I once had a girlfriend explain to me that looking *effortless* actually requires quite a bit of effort. Wearing just enough makeup, but not too much. Having hair that's polished but still totally natural. But that's not what's happening with Audrey. I think her beauty really *is* effortless—in a way that probably makes women who work a lot harder to get similar results feel irritated.

"Are you thirsty?" I say when I'm a few feet away.

Audrey looks up, and it takes a moment for her eyes to focus. "Oh," she finally says. "Thank you. That'd be nice."

I twist the top off the water bottle and hand it to her. My eyes trace her slender fingers, smudged with dirt and ink, as she wraps them around the bottle and takes a long drink. The only thing more distracting is the long curve of her neck as she swallows.

I clear my throat and look away. I have *got* to get a hold of myself. "How's the data collecting?" I ask, my voice a little too loud.

Audrey's expression brightens. "Amazing. Incredible. I've identified a female and three younger squirrels I believe are her offspring and they're—" Her words stop short, and she holds up her free hand. "Sorry. My sisters are always telling me how *not interesting* my research is. But things are good. Thanks again for letting me be here." She looks over her shoulder and bites her lip. "Especially during a party."

"It's just my family," I say. "Nothing fancy."

"All these people are your family?"

I turn and look over the collection of people hanging out around the pool, then drop onto the grass beside her, extending my legs out in front of me and crossing my ankles. "The guy on the diving board, that's my brother, Brody. He teaches chemistry over at the high school. And whitewater kayaking on the Green River during the summer." I lift a hand and point to Kate who is lounging under an umbrella with their daughter, River. "That's his wife, Kate, and their baby, River." I look at Audrey and lift an eyebrow. "Yes, they did name their baby after the river, and no, none of us were surprised."

She smiles, and the sight tugs at something deep in my gut. I was right. Her smile *is* going to be the end of me.

"The guy coming through the door—that's Perry. He's the oldest. He and my little sister, Olivia, she's the youngest of all of us, run Stonebrook Farm together."

She nods. "I've heard of the farm. Apples, right?"

"Mostly. And strawberries. They grow a little bit of everything. And host events. Weddings, reunions. That kind of thing." I point at Lennox and Tatum, who are standing by the grill. "That's Lennox, and his wife, Tatum. They're both chefs. They've got a baby now too, but I don't know where she is. Oh—right over there with my dad. Her name is Hannah, after my mom. And there's Olivia and her two kids, Asher and Maggie, right there, getting in the water. Her husband is out of town, so he's the only one not here, and that's my mom sitting by the door."

"Wow." Audrey's eyes are wide. "I hope you aren't going to quiz me later because I'm not going to remember anyone's names."

"There will absolutely be a quiz," I say. "If you want to study the squirrels, I expect first names, last names, ages, occupations. All of it."

She nudges my shoulder with her knee. "Shut up."

I look up and grin. "No quizzes, I promise."

"Do they all live in Silver Creek?" she asks.

"Believe it or not. It's the biggest reason why I moved back. Couldn't stand the thought of them all being together without me."

"I can't imagine," Audrey says. "I live with my two younger sisters, and sometimes even just they feel like too much. This is..."

"A lot," I finish for her. "For sure. But most of the time, they're worth it."

"I guess you don't really need friends when you have a family like this."

"No, I guess not," I say, but as I survey the scene, it's not lost on me that I *do* need something else. In a family where everyone has someone, I'm the only one still alone.

I'm working on being okay with this. My life has always been different from the rest of my siblings, but before, it was always because of my career. Now, it's different for other reasons. More personal reasons. And they somehow feel so much more substantial. I've never been particularly opposed to meeting someone and settling down. But now, seeing my siblings so firmly entrenched in family life is only making it obvious how much I want the same thing.

With someone *not* like my fame-hungry ex.

I lift an eyebrow as my gaze turns back to Audrey. She couldn't be more different from Claire. "Hey, what's your favorite movie?" I ask.

She leans back like the question surprises her. "Me?"

"I'm not talking to the squirrels," I joke.

She looks up, her eyes scanning the trees. Apparently, the very mention of her squirrels requires her to look for them. She looks back at me with a sardonic expression and pulls her dark ponytail forward so it's hanging over her shoulder. "I guess I don't have a favorite. I don't really watch movies."

I stare. She doesn't watch movies? Who doesn't watch movies? "Like, ever?"

She grimaces. "I realize that might be an insult to you, considering your profession. I just...I don't know. I have a hard time giving up two hours to do something so...pointless?" This last word she says like a question, almost like she senses it might not land well.

"Pointless," I repeat. I'm not exactly offended. I don't need everyone in the world to like movies. I'm just surprised. And maybe a little disappointed since, so far, I've liked everything about this woman. "The point is to relax. To be entertained. To feel...I don't know. Happy."

"There are other things that make me happy," she says, like that alone is enough to disqualify my argument.

"Like what?"

She takes another sip of her water. "Sometimes I read."

"Science books?"

She rolls her eyes. "Not *always*. I read novels, too."

"Novels about science?"

"Or nature, or—" She huffs and sits up a little taller. "You know what? It's okay if I like different things."

"Sure. If you liked different *kinds* of movies. But to not like movies at all? I don't know that I've ever met *anyone* who doesn't like movies."

"Leave it to me," she says dryly. "But don't worry. Being the odd woman out is a feeling I know well."

Audrey's words ring with a note of truth that makes my heart twitch, and I feel a weird compulsion to invite her to everything. *Include her* in everything.

Across the yard, Mom and Olivia wave from where they're standing near the house. Their smiles are wide, their waves much more enthusiastic than the situation warrants. It's probably taking all their resolve not to come over and join the conversation. I shift my body so more of my back is facing them and turn all my attention to Audrey. "What if you're just not watching the right movies?" I ask.

Audrey reaches down and scratches her ankle, her fingers dipping inside the top of her very utilitarian hiking boots. "Trust me, my sisters have tried," she says. "But my brain—it takes a lot for it to slow down. Now, you want to watch a nature documentary? I'm here for it."

"I narrated a nature documentary last year—the one about the orca whales."

She brightens. "I loved that one! That was you?"

I clear my throat, then drop my voice into the baritone I used when narrating the documentary. "The orca whale, known colloquially as the *killer* whale, is the largest member of the oceanic dolphin family."

"It *was* you!" she says, her smile wide. "You did an excellent job."

I can't help but grin. The power of that smile—I don't even care that she doesn't like movies. That, of all the work I've done, the only thing familiar to her is a nature documentary that's barely a blip on the map of my career.

"Maybe I should have talked a little more when we first met," I say. "Then you might have recognized me."

She closes her notebook and notches her pen on the outside. "Did it really bother you that I didn't know who you were? I mean, admitting I don't watch movies—that has to ease the sting a little bit. There aren't many actors I *would* recognize."

"It didn't bother me at all," I say. "Honestly, it was kind of nice. And it worked to your advantage because your indifference was a big part of why I was okay with you coming back."

She barks out a laugh. "Ha! It would kill my sisters to hear you say so. They're constantly teasing me about being too nerdy for my own good. If only they knew."

"They don't know?" I ask.

"They know we met. But they don't know I'm coming here to research," Audrey says. "I told you I wouldn't tell anyone."

"Right, but, I mean, they're your family."

"Maybe, but they're...let's just call them fans. I'd rather not have them begging for a play-by-play of our interactions every day. Also, I'm pretty sure they wouldn't be able to keep from mentioning it on Instagram. Trust me. It's better they don't know."

"Well, then I appreciate your discretion." We're silent for a beat before I ask, "Did they really make you give them a play-by-play?"

"Tell us everything he said," she says, her voice breathy and light. "And everything he did. What was he wearing? Did you touch him? Did he touch you?"

I chuckle. "You probably hated that."

She eyes me curiously. "You're figuring me out, Flint Hawthorne."

If I'm figuring *anything* out, it's that this woman is unlike anyone I've ever met before. She's smart—there's no denying that. But she's got this steadiness about her that makes me envious. Audrey Callahan doesn't seem to care the slightest bit what other people think of her. *Authentic.* That's the right word for it. She's unapologetically who she is. And it's *fascinating.*

I nudge her knee. "You know what I think, Audrey?"

She smiles a little shyly. "What's that?"

"I think you're watching the wrong kind of movies."

She wrinkles her brow like she disagrees with me. "I doubt it. But if you come up with something you think I'd like, I'll happily give it a try."

"Challenge accepted," I say. "I'll start researching tonight." I hold out the cap to her water bottle, which I've been holding this whole time. "Hey, are you hungry?"

Audrey takes the cap, her fingers brushing against mine. They linger a beat longer than necessary before she yanks her hand back, drops her eyes, and quickly twists the lid onto the bottle. She clears her throat. "What?"

"Are you hungry?" I repeat. "The food will be ready soon, and there's plenty. You're welcome to come grab a plate."

She visibly swallows, her eyes darting from me, over to the pool, then back again.

"I promise my family won't bite. They're good people. Silver Creek people."

She nods. "I think I went to middle school with Lennox."

So she's older than me. I file this information away, adding it to the quickly growing collection of *Things I find sexy about*

Audrey Callahan. "You didn't go to high school in Silver Creek?"

She shakes her head. "I went to NCSSM. In Raleigh."

"That's the North Carolina…"

"School of Science and Mathematics," she finishes. "I really was the biggest nerd, Flint."

"Really?" I say. "I hadn't noticed."

Her cheeks flame, but the smile that spreads across her face tells me she doesn't really mind the teasing.

"For real. Come eat with us. Brody's a total math nerd. If nothing else, there will at least be one person at the table who speaks your language."

She nods. "Okay. If you're sure your family won't mind."

They won't mind at all. In fact, they'll eat this up. But I've got more important things to think about.

Like what movie might turn Audrey Callahan into a believer.

Chapter Seven

Audrey

I SMILE AS FLINT's mother, Hannah, lowers herself into the chair on the other side of the long patio table next to the house. "How was the burger?" she asks as I polish off the last bite.

I pick up my napkin and wipe my fingers. "Honestly, it might be the best I've ever had. What was so different about it?"

"Oh, tons of things, probably," Hannah answers. "Lennox is always trying something new. But I'm pretty sure the truffle butter is what made it so good this time."

Somewhere in the back of my mind, I realize that what's happening right now is a very big deal.

I'm having dinner at Flint Hawthorne's house.

With Flint Hawthorne's family.

Even if I'm not particularly wowed by celebrity, I'm not so clueless as to ignore how much these circumstances would blow away the average thirty-year-old woman.

Ugh. Thirty.

I'm still not used to the sound of it. I mean, my sisters tell me I've been sixty-five since my seventh birthday—that I have an old-person vibe. But having an old-person vibe is very different than having an old-person body. And my thirtieth birthday has sent me into a spiral of worry about that very thing.

I'm a scientist. I know how these things work. I know the ovaries in my body are already holding all the eggs they're ever going to hold, and every year that passes makes those eggs less and less viable.

Don't get me started on how unfair it is that men can father children until they're ninety-five as long their equipment is still working. But women? Nope. We get to have it all, sure. The careers. The education. The leadership positions. But if we want to have a family? Well, better fall in love before you hit thirty-five. No pressure. It's not like it takes a long time to get a PhD. It's not like your life when you're in grad school is basically nonexistent. There's time! Women can have it all!

Sometimes I feel like screaming.

Women *can't* have it all. Not without making some major sacrifices. Which is a problem because I *do* want it all. I love being a scientist, but I think I'd also love being a wife. Maybe even a mom if my eggs can hang on long enough.

I look around Flint's backyard, where his siblings are sitting, eating, bouncing babies. Olivia, his sister, runs Stonebrook Farm with Perry, so she's managing to do both. And Tatum—I think she's the chef? Maybe it's just about timing instead of being an either/or situation.

And maybe my sisters are right when they argue that if I spent more time with people instead of animals, my prospects wouldn't look so bleak.

Hannah looks over my shoulder and smiles as she points. "Look. That's why you're here, isn't it?"

I turn and see a couple of white squirrels running across the grass beside the pool before darting up the trunk of a nearby tree.

"They're pretty fun, right?" I shake my head. "Or, not fun, I guess. Not for everyone else. They're just squirrels. I know they're just squirrels. It would be so silly for people to care—"

She reaches over and touches my hand. "Honey, there's nothing wrong with being passionate about your work. I make goat's milk soap, and I treat my goats like they're my children. My kids tease me all the time for it, but it makes me happy. And it's good soap, too."

Flint drops into a chair across from his mother and directly beside me. "It *is* good soap," he says. "I ordered it in bulk when I was living in LA."

Hannah rolls her eyes. "You know I'd have just sent you a box. You always had to be so official, with Joni placing orders."

"If I'd had you send me a box, you wouldn't have let me pay for them."

"It's just soap, baby."

"It's just money, *Mom*," Flint says, his eyes full of warmth. "And you know I like to support the farm."

Hannah looks at Flint for a long moment, and I get the sense they're having a wordless conversation. About money? About soap? About the farm? I don't know these people well enough to judge.

Hannah finally chuckles. "As if the soap really matters after everything else you've done."

My eyes move from mother to son, then back again. There *is* something going on here, and I find myself desperately curious to know what it is.

Flint rubs a hand across his face as he looks away, but I don't miss the tips of his ears turning slightly pink.

"Tell me, Audrey," Hannah says, steering the conversation back to me. "What is it that makes you so passionate about your work?"

Something about the way she says *passionate* makes me think she probably knows about the trespassing. My eyes dart to Flint, who seems to have recovered from whatever embarrassment his mom caused and is looking at me, his lips lifted into a playful smirk.

"Yeah, Audrey. What makes you passionate enough to hike *miles* into the wilderness, property lines and giant security guards be damned, in pursuit of the elusive white squirrel?"

I roll my eyes, but I'd be lying if I said I didn't like the way he's teasing me. "To be fair, your property belonged to my university before you bought it. It was my research forest—connected to my lab—and I've been visiting all my research locations for months without anyone caring or knowing."

"So you admit you've been trespassing for months?" Flint says, his tone light.

I wince and offer a placating smile. "Yes? But relocating my experiments would have compromised so much data!"

"Does the university know about this? About your surreptitious forest use?"

An actual jolt of panic shoots through me. They *don't* know, and they wouldn't be happy about it. "Oh, well, I mean..." I swallow.

"Hey." Flint touches my wrist, his fingers triggering an eruption of goosebumps across my arm. "I'm just teasing. I'm not going to tell anyone."

I nod, grateful for the reassurance. "Causing trouble is the last thing I need to be doing right now. I've been using the same research grant for the past three years from this foundation over in Asheville. But I've gotten the sense lately that my funding might not come through for another year."

"Which means what?"

"A lot more work for me. Writing new grant proposals, schmoozing, networking. It's the part of my job I don't like. There's research money out there. It's just not always easy to find it."

He frowns. "That's too bad."

I shrug. "It's the way it goes sometimes. I'm determined not to stress about it until I have more reason to think I should."

"You know, Stonebrook is almost twice as big as Flint's place," Hannah says. "We don't have as much forest land as this"—she motions around us—"but you're welcome on our property any time if it would suit your research needs."

"I appreciate that," I say. "That's really generous of you."

She smiles warmly. "I'd still love to know what makes you love what you do."

I glance at Flint, his open, curious expression encouraging an honest answer. "It isn't *just* about the squirrels, really," I say, careful not to make my response too didactic. "So much of my research is about the way nature intersects with human life. Squirrels are very adaptable. They've taken to living among humans better than a lot of other species. But when we bulldoze entire stretches of forest, it still impacts their environment. We've gotten better at living alongside nature and respecting it, but there's still progress that needs to happen. I mean, I like research because it's cool to know stuff, but the greater purpose is to discover better ways to live *in* nature without destroying it."

I press my palms against my thighs, suddenly self-conscious. This is not the first time I've rattled on and on about things that are only interesting to me. I bite my lip. "Sorry. That was probably more of an answer than you bargained for."

"I love it," Flint says warmly. "I respect your passion and dedication. And I'm all for respecting nature, living among it instead of destroying it."

"I think you did that with your house," I say. "It feels like it belongs here. Like it's always been a part of the mountainside. I don't know if that makes any sense."

"No, it totally makes sense," Flint says. "And I appreciate you noticing. That's exactly what I was going for." He holds my gaze, steady and confident, until I have to look away to catch my breath. I'm not sure my lungs can fully expand when he's looking at me like that.

Hannah looks from Flint to me, then back to Flint again, a smile playing at her lips. "Well, I'll be," she says softly.

Flint's eyes jump to his mother, then he clears his throat and stands so quickly that his chair falls over behind him. He scrambles to pick it up, nearly tripping on his own feet as he does so. Once the chair is back on all four legs, he pushes it under the table and backs away.

"I'm going to get some more potato salad. Anyone else want more potato salad? No? Okay, then."

Hannah chuckles as he walks away. "I haven't seen that in a while," she says.

"What's that?" I ask, almost afraid of her answer because I know what I *want* it to be, and it's the most preposterous thought that has *ever* popped into my head.

Don't say it, I think to myself. *Just don't say it.*

"He's flustered," Hannah says. She looks at me coyly. "I think you did that."

I laugh much too loudly, even as the rebellious part of my brain rejoices that she thinks I could *ever* make someone like Flint Hawthorne flustered. "Ha! No. I'm not—he wouldn't—" I shake my head like a six-year-old trying to convince her mother she didn't steal the last cookie. "I'm just a girl who likes nature," I finally say.

She shrugs. "He's just a boy who likes movies."

Heat floods my cheeks, and I lift my palms to cover them, positive that Hannah—or anyone else who spares me a glance—will see how much the implication of her statement is getting to me. "Um, do you think Flint would mind if I use the restroom?"

I need a minute.

Or an hour.

Or maybe three days.

"Of course, honey. That door will take you to the kitchen, then just follow the hall to the left, and you'll find it."

I nod and quickly retreat to the cool interior of Flint's house. But good grief—if I thought this was going to help things, I was dead wrong. The outside of Flint's house is actually pretty simple. Rock and wood and earthy muted colors. But the inside is bright and modern and beautiful. Clean lines. Huge windows. Light everywhere, even in the fading evening hours.

The living room just off the kitchen looks warm and welcoming. The furniture is leather, but it looks incredibly soft, and every chair and couch is draped with cushy blankets the same color as the walls—a pale, dusky gray-blue. I pause before crossing the kitchen and tug off my boots, not wanting to track any dirt through this incredibly perfect house.

The action only reminds me of how ridiculously I'm dressed. Not that I knew I was dressing for a family barbecue. I'm dressed for *work.* I've never felt uncomfortable in my baggy cargo pants. They are incredibly practical. Lots of pockets for my notebook, my phone, extra memory cards for my camera, ChapStick. But my sisters have teased me enough for me to know that, especially when combined with an old baggy biology T-shirt from my undergrad days, they aren't exactly flattering.

I do not miss the fact that I have never cared about whether my work clothes are attractive. Who would I ever be trying to impress when I spend most of my time alone in the woods?

It shouldn't be any different now. Flint Hawthorne might as well be an oak tree, for all the likelihood there is that he would ever find me attractive. I mean, *yes.* He flirted when we first met. But that was probably just an actor thing. The way he is with everyone.

And okay, *yes,* his mother did just imply that he's flustered, and it can only be because of me. But she's probably just reading into things because she's his mom, and isn't that what moms do? Try to play matchmaker for their kids?

I leave my hiking boots next to the door and head down the hall to find the bathroom, and *oh good grief,* this room is just as gorgeous as the rest of the house. It has to be a guest bathroom, off the kitchen like it is, but there's a full shower tiled in smooth river rock and stacked stone. It looks like the inside of a waterfall, and I immediately want to use it. It's a stupidly impulsive thing to think. I'm not going to randomly take a shower in Flint's house. There aren't even any towels—*oh.* There *ARE* towels. Thick, fluffy gray ones stacked on the corner shelf. I reach out and touch one, but then quickly yank my hand away.

No, Audrey! No impulsive bathing!

I finish up in the bathroom without stripping down for an impromptu shower and head back down the hall. Based on the rest of the house, I'm itching to look around, open all the doors to see what the rest of the place looks like. It wouldn't be *quite* as bad as taking a shower, but it's still more than I'll let myself do. Except, just before I reach the kitchen, there's a room with a door that's already open.

There's nothing wrong with peeking into a room with an *open* door, is there? I step into the room, the plush carpet sinking under my feet, and pause in the doorway. This must be Flint's office. There's a desk on the back wall, a dark brown leather sofa on the other, and low bookshelves, about knee-height, circling three entire walls. But it's the wall decor that catches my attention.

I step back into the hall and peek around the corner into the kitchen to make sure I'm still alone, then tiptoe back into the room. It only takes a second to realize that the framed posters above the bookshelves are movie posters—and they are all movies Flint has been in. They're arranged chronologically, and I walk slowly past each one. Flint's picture isn't on every poster, especially not the early ones, but I make it a point to find his name listed at the bottom when he isn't a headliner. The farther I go into his career, the more frequently I see his face front and center. Action films. Dramas. Romantic comedies. Something about time travel?

"That was a really terrible movie."

I jump, a hand flying to my heart, and turn to see Flint standing in the doorway. "Geez, you scared me."

He's leaning against the doorframe with an easy confidence I envy. "Sorry. Didn't mean to." His tone is warm and friendly, like he doesn't care at all that he just found me snooping through his house.

I look back at the movie poster. "You were *in* this movie," I say. "Why would you make a terrible movie?"

He shrugs. "Sometimes you don't know it isn't going to work until you're already in it and it's too late. Sometimes you just need a paycheck, so you do it anyway." He moves into the room and stops beside me.

"Which was it with this one?"

"A little bit of both. I was in a bit of a dry spell, and the script seemed promising enough. My agent really wanted me to do it, so I did. But halfway through, I could already sense things weren't clicking. The chemistry was off, maybe, or...I don't know. Sometimes you can't really pinpoint what's wrong, only that something is. Sure enough, it tanked at the box office and was released for streaming less than two months later."

"That's not a good thing?"

He chuckles. "Not this time, it wasn't."

I continue my journey around the perimeter of the room, Flint following just behind. The next poster features Flint dressed as a soldier from what I'm guessing is World War II based on the style of his hair and uniform. "What about this one?"

"One of my favorites," he says. "I won a Golden Globe for that one. Nominated for an Oscar, too. But I didn't win."

"Quite a comeback after the last one, then."

"Something that every film critic felt they needed to point out," he says dryly.

"I'm sorry you didn't win the Oscar," I say, and Flint scoffs.

"Are you kidding? I was up against Matt Damon. I know it's what everyone says, but it really was just an honor to be nominated with someone like him."

I wrinkle my brow, hoping the name will jog something in my memory, but I've got nothing.

Flint frowns. "You don't know who Matt Damon is, do you?"

I grimace.

"*Good Will Hunting*?" he says. "Audrey, come on. It's one of the greatest movies of all time."

"I'm sorry!" I say through a laugh, and I really mean it. Could I possibly make myself any less interesting to this man? "Is that one I should watch? *Good Will Hunting*?"

"I mean, yes," he says quickly. "Everyone should watch that one. But..." He holds up a finger. "Not yet. I want to be more intentional when it comes to you."

My heart trips and stutters. He wants to be intentional *for me?* He's taking this whole movie thing much more seriously than I thought he would.

An image of me and Flint, snuggled up on the butter-soft couch in his living room watching a movie, suddenly pops into my brain, and my cheeks flush with heat.

I spin around, not wanting Flint to see, and press my palms to my cheeks. "What about this one?" I say, motioning to the next poster. "Should I start with this one?"

He's close to me when he responds, his voice just over my shoulder, and it sends another wave of goosebumps across my neck. "Not this one," he says, his voice low. "None of these, actually. To convince the woman who doesn't like movies to like movies? We have to go bigger than anything I've ever done."

It occurs to me that knowing Flint is *in* a movie might make me a lot more interested in sitting down to watch it.

But I'm not about to admit that to him.

I'm not sure I even want to admit it to myself.

I turn around, startling when I realize how close we're standing. There isn't six inches of space between us. I'm close enough to touch him—to lift my palm and press it against his chest.

Instead, I tuck my hands behind my back, just in case they get any ideas, and force a deep breath through my nose. "Bigger like what?"

Flint lifts his hands and wraps them around my shoulders, his fingers brushing along the hem of my sleeves. The skin-to-skin contact makes my heart rate spike even more than it already has, and my breath catches in my throat.

"Patience, Audrey," he says. "I'll find the perfect movie for you. But this isn't a process you can rush." He gives my arms a quick squeeze before his hands fall away.

Oh, he's good. Too good. No wonder all of America is in love with this man.

"Come on," he says, taking a step toward the door. "There's ice cream pie, and I'm not sure my brothers will save us any if we don't grab a piece while we can."

"Oh, I couldn't," I say quickly. "You've already been so generous. I don't need anyone to save me a piece of anything."

He shrugs. "Suit yourself. But you're here. And it's *really* good ice cream pie." He holds out his hand in invitation. "I wouldn't have offered if I didn't want you to have a piece."

I shake my head and slip my hand into his, letting him tug me into the kitchen. He doesn't drop my hand until we're halfway around the enormous kitchen island. "Is this how you treat everyone who trespasses on your land?"

"Only the biologists." He smirks and glances at my shirt. "Even if you do want me to *leaf you alone.*"

I smile, my gaze lifting to his blue eyes, which are sparkling with mirth. I shake my head, letting out a small laugh as I look down at my navy-blue T-shirt. There's a leafy sugar maple on the front and the very caption Flint just read: *Leaf Me Alone.*

Ninety-nine percent of the time, I *do* prefer to be left alone. I am nothing if not a solitary creature.

But maybe company isn't so bad.

Even if that company is a movie star.

Chapter Eight

Flint

CLAIRE MCKINSEY IS GOING to be the end of me.

Or maybe just the end of my career. I close my laptop, cutting off the latest video Kenji sent over. Claire is still talking. *Hinting.* Making it seem like some time apart was good, but now we're in a good place, and we're *very* excited about promoting *Turning Tides* together. She isn't being explicit enough for me to call her a liar, but the innuendo is strong, and right now she's dominating entertainment news. Every possible public event she could attend, she's attending, talking to the press every time they call her name. And don't even get me started on her Instagram feed.

My team is getting daily requests for comment on the status of our relationship. Simon is fielding those requests, but he isn't doing much else except irritating me.

"You look happy," Joni says from the doorway.

I turn to see her leaning against the door jamb, arms crossed.

"My life is stupid, Joni," I say, dropping back into my desk chair and closing my eyes. I hear her move into the room and sit down across from me, but I don't move or look up.

"Did you talk to Simon?"

I nod.

"What did he say?"

I sigh and look up. "Just more of the same. He doesn't think I have any reason to worry." I crack my neck, tilting my head from side to side. "Says I need to get off social media and try to *relax.*"

Joni rolls her eyes. "You know, there are other publicists."

I huff out a laugh. "Don't tempt me."

"I'm serious. He annoys you every time you talk to him. Why not cut your losses and let him go?"

"Maybe after the premiere," I say. "He's too involved with everything to cut ties before then."

Joni scoffs. "I think we would manage just fine without him. Most of the hard stuff is done already anyway. Did he push the fake relationship thing again?"

"He did. But he thinks I'd need to be back in LA to truly sell it. Says we would need to orchestrate a few well-timed appearances in public places with a woman who isn't Claire. I see his point, but honestly Joni, the thought of reviewing a list of names and picking one like I'm ordering a woman out of some sort of catalog, it feels so..."

"Misogynistic?" Joni says, her expression smug.

"I was going to say old-fashioned, but that works too. I just don't like it."

"You're right not to like it. But then, I don't like anything Simon suggests, so I'm not sure my opinion is relevant here. Have you given any more thought to taking someone from Silver Creek?"

"Like who? The only women I know are related to me, and I'm not sure that would have quite the same impact, do you?"

She considers me for a long moment. "Flint, what about Audrey?"

My hand jumps and knocks over a cup of pens, and I scramble to pick it up. When everything is back where it belongs, I take a moment to neutralize my expression before looking up. Joni knows me well, almost as well as my family knows me. She'll see right through me if I'm not careful. "What *about* Audrey?" I finally ask.

"Invite her to the premiere." Joni says this simply, but there is nothing simple about her suggestion.

"That's...no. That's not a good idea."

"Why not? I think it's a great idea. Audrey is exactly the right kind of woman. She's poised. She's confident. She's well-spoken. She won't get flustered when she meets other celebrities."

"She won't even know who the other celebrities are."

"Exactly! Yet another reason why she'd be perfect." Joni shifts on the couch, sitting a little taller, like she's gearing up to really hit me with all her reasoning and logic. It's a very *Joni* move—one I know well. "Listen. I know she might not be the kind of woman you can actually see yourself with long-term, but for this, she doesn't really need to be. You just need her to be your decoy. And I think there's something you can offer her in exchange that she won't be able to refuse."

I let Joni's words settle into my mind. I'm surprised by a couple of things.

One—as well as Joni knows me, I don't know how she hasn't noticed that I've got a thing for Audrey.

Two—I can't think of any possible incentive that would motivate Audrey to say yes to whatever scheme Joni is hatching. Audrey doesn't even *like* movies. Why would she want to attend a premiere for one?

Especially when she has no interest in spending any time with *me*.

For the past three days, whenever Audrey has been on my property, I've been distracted, preoccupied with her presence. It's ridiculous the number of reasons I've found to walk across my backyard.

Install a new garden hose? That definitely needs to happen today.

Cut the grass even though I already cut it four days ago? Absolutely.

Weed the vegetable garden? No time like the present!

Unfortunately, all that effort has resulted in exactly zero progress. Despite all my efforts to capture her attention, Audrey has been so focused on her work, she's barely taken notice.

If I speak to her, she always responds with kindness, but I am always the one who speaks first.

"Okay. I'll bite," I finally say. "What could I offer Audrey that she couldn't refuse?"

Joni smiles. "Access to your land."

I lift my eyebrows. "She already has access to my land."

"For one more week. Tell her she can come back for the rest of the summer. Whenever she wants."

"In exchange for her coming to LA with me and pretending to be my girlfriend on the red carpet? That's a big ask, Joni."

She shrugs. "Yeah, but Audrey really likes those squirrels. She might say yes."

I stand up and move to the window, my stomach grumbling as I go. It's already past seven, and I still have no idea what I'm doing for dinner. "You've clearly given this some thought."

"It's better than Simon's plan," Joni says. "I know it still requires some faking, but if we're honest with Audrey, explain the situation, I think she'll say yes. I mean, you could at least ask, right? What's truly the worst thing that could happen?"

"She could come with me to California, realize my life is an absolute circus, and run the other direction as fast as she can."

Joni's quiet for a long moment. "Oh," she finally says. *"Oh. You like her."*

I push my hands into my pockets and turn to face her, shrugging in acknowledgment.

Joni presses her palm to her chest. "Does she know?"

I huff out a laugh. "No. I—*no.* She's clearly not interested."

"What makes you say that?"

"I've seen her three days this week, and I've tried to talk to her every time. She's polite, but otherwise, she's totally indifferent. If I talk to her, she talks back. That's pretty much it."

Joni stares. "That's it? That's all you have to go on?"

"That feels like more than enough."

"Flint. Just because she isn't fawning all over you doesn't mean she isn't interested. She's a guest when she's here, which means she's probably trying to be respectful of your time and not demand any unnecessary attention. Anything more than that might seem presumptuous, and I get the sense Audrey is *not* the presumptuous type." She tucks a strand of platinum hair behind her ear and scoots forward on her seat. "I'm not saying she *does* like you," she says. "But I *am* saying you might have to give her a little more to go on if you want her to know you *do* like *her.*"

"Something like asking her to fly to Los Angeles and attend a movie premiere as my date?"

Joni shrugs. "It can't hurt to try."

"And you think this would actually *help* my cause if I want Audrey to like me? Exposing her to the press, the fans, the relentlessly rude paparazzi? This will sell her on the benefits of being with someone like me?"

"Well, when you say it like that, it sounds like a terrible idea. But Flint, that's not all your life is. It's a pretty small part, actually. And if she just gets to know you, she'll be willing to deal with all the attention and drama."

"Or she won't," I shoot back. "And then what?"

Joni's shoulders fall, and she frowns. "I guess that's true," she relents. "But if she's scared off by a single movie premiere, honey, she's not the woman for you anyway. Maybe this will be a good test."

I rub a hand across my forehead, suddenly feeling so tired. "I don't want a test. I want a normal relationship."

"I know you do," she says, her tone gentle. "But Flint, you haven't had a normal life in years."

I leave the window and drop onto the couch beside Joni with a weary sigh.

She's at least right about that much.

Without saying anything, Joni slides her iPad onto my lap. There's a long list of bullet points on the screen. "Just look it over," she says. "Give it some thought."

I sigh and pick up the iPad.

The plan isn't complicated. We would start with a couple of photos on my Instagram account of me and Audrey hanging out around the house, maybe swimming in the pool, but the photos would *not* show Audrey's face. She would just be an unidentified woman spending time with me. Over the next few weeks, up until the premiere, I'd post a few more times, making it clear I'm seeing someone, still without revealing Audrey's identity.

I like this part of the plan because it will keep Audrey out of the limelight as long as possible. Her life will continue as normal—something that wouldn't happen if the photos were to give any hint as to who she is. The internet wouldn't need more than her face to dig up everything there is to know about her.

Finally, Audrey would attend the premiere with me, and we would act very much like a couple.

"Who knows?" Joni says as I hand her back the iPad. "Maybe after spending all this time together, you won't even have to fake it on the red carpet. You can just *be* a couple."

"You know, when I moved back to North Carolina, I thought I was leaving all the Hollywood drama behind," I say.

"Claire's too persistent to just let you go, Flint," she says. "But I really think this plan will work. And it's so much better than Simon's idea."

"What's better than Simon's idea?" Nate asks as he ambles into the room. He hands Joni a plate holding the most beautiful tomato sandwich I've ever seen. "I brought you dinner."

"Did that tomato come out of my garden?" I ask, my stomach rumbling loud enough for both of them to hear.

Nate lifts an eyebrow. "Maybe?"

Joni takes a huge bite. She lets out a groan while she chews. "Oh my gosh, this is delicious." She grabs Nate's shirt and tugs him down for a kiss. "Thank you," she says, and I look away. Sometimes the two of them are sweet. Sometimes they're completely ridiculous.

"Okay, I need some food," I say as I head toward the door.

"You want a tomato sandwich?" Nate calls after me. "Sorry, man. I should have brought you one."

"Nah, I think I'm going to head out, actually."

Nate stiffens. "Where to?"

I sigh. My personal protection officer does not like it when I go places alone. Even in Silver Creek.

"Just to Lennox's," I say, deciding on the spot. "I'll be fine on my own. I promise."

I don't wait long enough for him to respond. Instead, I hurry out of my office and into my kitchen, where I grab my keys and a beat-up baseball cap from the hook by the garage door. I cram the hat on, then hurry out to my truck.

Is this really what my life has become?

Conversations about faking out the media and throwing off persistent exes?

Is it really too much to ask that I just *like* a woman, date her, then settle down without all this extra drama? I know there are actors in Hollywood who just *act,* who focus on their art without getting distracted by all the noise. Can I just *be* one of them? Can I let all this other stupid stuff go?

Ten minutes later, I pull up to the backside of Hawthorne, Lennox's restaurant, craving, more than anything else, a conversation about something besides my own stupid life.

The public parking on the opposite side of the restaurant was slam full when I drove past, and I don't love the idea of navigating a crowded dining room, so I'm hoping if I sneak in the back and find Lennox, he'll be able to feed me without making a scene.

I push through the back door and slowly make my way toward Lennox's kitchen. The Stonebrook Farm catering kitchen occupies the back half of the building, but it's quiet tonight, so there must not be anything going on at the farm.

I pause at the back of Lennox's kitchen. It takes me a minute to find him, but when I do, a burst of pride fills my chest. He's clearly in his element, doing something he loves to do. It's also clear that every single person in this room is tuned into him, listening to his instructions, paying attention to every single word that comes out of his mouth.

Until someone turns and sees *me.*

Awareness moves across the kitchen like a wave, and suddenly all is quiet as everyone turns to stare.

Lennox is the last to notice. "Hey, what's going on?" he asks, but then his eyes meet mine. "Oh. *He's* going on," he says dryly. He tugs a dish towel off his shoulder and drops it onto the counter. "Okay, let's all say hi to Flint together so we can get back to work, yeah?"

Laughter echoes around the room, then a few voices call out, "Hi, Flint."

I lift a hand, offering Lennox an apologetic smile. "Hey, y'all. Sorry to interrupt."

"Trust me," a female voice says from across the kitchen. "We *really* don't mind."

"Okay, that's enough," Lennox says. "Zach?" He gestures to a guy standing off to his left. "Cover for me?"

"You got it, Chef."

"Sorry," I say as soon as Lennox reaches me. "This seemed easier than trying to get a table out there." I motion toward the dining room.

Lennox claps me on the back. "No worries. Are you hungry?"

"Is that totally obnoxious? To just show up and expect you to feed me?"

"It *is* a restaurant, Flint."

"I know. But I don't want to cause any trouble. Or, I don't know. Expect special treatment."

Lennox looks at me funny, then grins. "Are you feeling okay? I kinda thought special treatment was your jam."

I roll my eyes. "Trust me. Sometimes it gets really old."

"Come on," Lennox says. "I'll take a break and eat with you. You can wait in my office while I make us plates."

"Sounds great."

"You want a menu?"

I wave a dismissive hand. "Whatever you have extra is fine."

Lennox leaves me in his office, and I kill time by pulling out my phone and checking my messages. I regret it the minute my phone is in my hand. Kenji has sent over another Instagram post from Claire. This one is a picture of the two of us. I recognize it immediately—we took it in Costa Rica when we were still dating and still filming *Turning Tides*. The background of the photo is dark enough that you can't really tell where we are, something Claire uses to her advantage because her caption makes it sound like the photo was *just* taken.

Kenji: She isn't leaving much room for debate, man. If you don't say something soon, you're as good as confirming your relationship.

Lennox pushes into his office holding two steaming plates and puts one down on either side of the desk. I drop my phone onto the desk and reach for the fork he just pulled out of his apron pocket.

"Baked salmon with mango creme fraiche, tropical chutney, and coconut lime rice."

"Sounds amazing."

He sits down across from me and shovels in an enormous bite. He motions toward my phone. "Who's the woman?" he asks around his food, his words almost too muffled for me to understand him.

"Don't get me started," I say glumly. I take my own bite, the flavors immediately exploding on my tongue. "Dude, this is amazing."

"One of my favorites," Lennox says. "Is that the squirrel lady? Audrey, right?"

"What? No. It's not—it's Claire McKinsey."

"Really?" Lennox takes another bite—the man is eating incredibly fast—then reaches for my phone. "Her hair's darker. I didn't recognize her. Did she just post this?"

"Unfortunately, yes."

"So she *is* still your ex."

I sigh. "Definitely. But apparently, she's happy to let the world think she isn't."

"That really sucks."

"Whatever. I don't want to talk about it. How are you? How's the baby?"

Lennox smiles wide. "She's great. Sleeping like a champ. You should come by and see her some morning. She's growing so fast, man. It feels like she's different every time I see her."

"Yeah? I'd like that."

Maybe this has been my problem. Instead of thinking like a bachelor, looking for nights out with my brothers, I need to think like a dad and show up for breakfast and playdates.

We eat in silence for another minute until Lennox drops his fork, his plate clean. He nods toward my phone. "So what are you going to do about Claire? Is this one of those situations where you'll get in more trouble if you respond?"

"Maybe. It's more complicated because of *Turning Tides*. I don't want to start something and have it reflect poorly on the movie."

"Who cares about the movie? She's yanking you around, and that's not cool. If it were me, I'd take back control however I could." He stands and motions toward my plate. "You finished?"

"Yeah, thanks."

He takes my empty plate, stacking it with his own, then heads toward the door. "I've got to get back to work, but seriously, come by anytime. You're always welcome."

He leaves me in his office, promising he'll send in dessert if I have time to wait around a few more minutes. I reach for my phone—I'm not about to turn down one of Lennox's desserts—and scroll back to the picture Claire posted.

Lennox is right. I can't let her keep doing this.

Making sure I'm logged in to my public Instagram account, I post a comment on Claire's picture. *I remember this night! We'd just filmed our last scene together for #TurningTides. So many happy memories! See you at the premiere!*

Then I text Joni and ask her to send over Audrey's address.

If this is ever going to work, there's one enormous hurdle I have to leap over first.

I have to get Audrey to agree.

Chapter Nine

Audrey

WHEN I FIRST HEAR my sisters scream, my mind automatically jumps to the worst possible scenarios.

Something is on fire. A murderer has broken in to kill us. A tree has fallen on the house and crushed our living room.

It only takes five seconds for my brain to decide that, knowing my sisters, it's something much less sinister. A giant spider. A wasp caught inside the kitchen. Or—I don't know. A mouse, maybe? This is a *really* old house.

But then my sister's screams turn into squeals and move down the hallway toward my bedroom.

"Oh-my-gosh, oh-my-gosh, oh-my-gosh," Summer says as she and Lucy appear in my doorway. Lucy has a hand pressed to her heart, and both wear matching expressions, their eyes wide.

I stay on my bed, where I've been reading for the past hour. They look happy, not worried, which means there probably isn't a murderer chasing them, so I don't see a reason for me to get out of my very comfortable cocoon. "What?" I motion between them. "What is this? What's happening?"

"Um, Flint Hawthorne's on the front porch."

"What? No, he's not." I still don't move, but my heart starts hammering in my chest.

"*Yes,* he is," Lucy says. "We just watched through the living room window as he climbed out of a very shiny truck, and now he's on the porch."

A quick knock echoes through the house, and both my sisters gasp, then start to laugh. "We're going to meet Flint Hawthorne," one of them says.

I'm no longer paying attention because there is only one person in this house who Flint Hawthorne actually knows.

He has to be here to see me.

I scramble out of my bed and move toward the door, but Summer catches me by the arm, swinging me back into the room. "What are you doing?"

"I'm answering the door?"

"Wearing that?" Lucy says, her voice too high. "You're braless, Audrey. It's totally nipple city in here."

I look down at my outfit—baggy sweatpants and a black tank top. "Oh, geez. You're right." I reach for a hoodie to pull over my tank top.

Summer grabs it out of my hands. "NO. That only makes it worse. At least in the tank top, you look like you have a shape. Just put on a bra."

Lucy tugs open the top drawer of my dresser and starts riffling through it. "Seriously? Do you have anything that isn't a sports bra?"

"They're comfortable," I say as I wrestle my sweatshirt away from Summer. "And it doesn't matter anyway because Flint Hawthorne is not here to see my boobs." I head down the hallway, and they scurry after me.

"But he might come *back* to see them if you let him catch a glimpse," Summer says, and I send a silencing glare over my shoulder.

"Stop it. Both of you. I don't know what this is about, but you're going to stay hidden until I find out."

"Hidden?" Lucy squeals. "You aren't going to introduce us?"

"Just go!" I whisper-yell and motion them back down the hallway. "Not a word."

I tug my hoodie down and adjust the hood, then take a calming deep breath that does nothing but make me realize how *not* calm I am.

This is not a big deal. I've met Flint before. We've had a couple of actual for-real conversations. I even had dinner with his family. I can handle this.

I swing open the door.

Flint is halfway down the stairs, but he swings around as soon as I call his name. He's wearing khaki shorts and an olive-green T-shirt, sunglasses, and a baseball hat pulled low on his head. The sun is setting behind him, casting an orange glow across his features. It's perfect lighting. Movie star lighting. And I suddenly wonder if he timed his arrival on purpose.

Though honestly, he doesn't need the lighting. I'm pretty sure he'd look good anywhere. Any light. Any situation. Any wardrobe. Put the man in a hotdog Halloween costume, and he'd still make it look sexy.

"Hey," he says. "I thought you weren't home."

"I'm home," I say. "Sorry to keep you waiting."

He looks me up and down, a smile playing at his lips. "You worried about a cold front coming through?"

I press my lips together, regretting the sweatshirt, but it's better than nipples, so I force a smile anyway. "My sisters like to keep the house cold. Um, do you want to come in?"

He climbs back up the steps so he's standing directly in front of me. I catch the scent of him—something clean and masculine that makes my toes curl into the wooden porch slats beneath my feet. "I'd love to come in if you don't mind. I have something I want to ask you."

"Okay. Sure." I step back into the house and hold the door open for him.

He follows me into the living room, where we stand awkwardly for a long moment. "Do you want anything?" I finally ask. I'm terrible at this. At hosting. At *socializing*. "Water? That's pretty much all I have."

"We have Dr Pepper downstairs!" a voice whispers from the hallway.

Flint's eyebrows go up, and I wince as I look toward the hallway where I know my sisters are hiding. I sigh. It's probably better to get this over with now, then I'll force them into the basement.

I look back at Flint. "My sisters," I explain. "They're nothing like me, so you might want to brace yourself." I walk to the hallway and grab my sisters' hands, pulling them into the living room. They stumble to a halt, and I step to the side, allowing them a full view of the movie star standing in my living room. "Flint, these are my sisters, Summer and Lucy."

Something in Flint changes just slightly. He smiles as he steps toward my sisters and extends his hand, but it doesn't seem fully genuine. But that's not quite right, because he doesn't seem fake either. He just seems like—the answer clicks into my brain with sudden clarity. He seems like he's performing. *Acting.*

I just watched him put on his Hollywood face.

"Nice to meet you, ladies," he says warmly.

I tune out my sisters as they babble at him, talking about their favorite movies, asking him about living in LA, what it was like to move home. My attention jumps back to the conversation when Lucy asks for his signature—I'm not at all confident she wouldn't offer up a body part—but she pulls out her journal, and I relax back into my careful study of Flint's behavior.

I do not think he minds the attention. I've told him I have sisters, and that they lived with me, and he came here willingly. If he wanted to avoid them, I'll be at his house tomorrow to finish up my week of research. He could have talked to me then.

But the way he's interacting with Lucy and Summer, it feels very practiced. When they ask for a picture, he agrees, but he seems very conscious of where he puts his hands—on their shoulders, with lots of space still between them. He answers their questions, but he doesn't really tell them anything significant. He maintains eye contact, smiles just warmly enough to make them feel seen, like they've had a personal interaction with him. But nothing about this feels personal for *Flint*.

It's fascinating.

And impressive.

"Okay, that's enough," I say to my sisters. "Time for you to go home."

"You're banishing us to the basement?" Summer says.

"I'm banishing you to your *apartment* that just happens to be in my basement," I say.

"It was nice to meet you both," Flint says, and it's this that finally makes them move. "Summer and Lucy, right? I'll remember that."

My sisters pause their awkward backward shuffle through the kitchen—an obvious attempt to get as much face time as possible on their way out. "You'll remember our names?" Lucy asks.

Flint shrugs easily. "You're Audrey's sisters, and Audrey is a friend. Of course I will."

Oh my gosh, the man is a master.

Summer makes a noise like she's trying to swallow a squeal while Lucy breathes out, "Flint Hawthorne is going to remember my name."

I clear my throat. "Goodnight, guys!"

Their sighs follow them to the basement steps, but the sound of them actually going *down* the stairs never follows.

"Door!" I call out, and they huff before the door finally clicks closed. I roll my eyes as I drop onto the couch. "I'm sorry about them," I say. I motion to the empty space across from me. "Want to sit? Oh. They interrupted before I could get you anything. Do you want water? I'm nixing the Dr Pepper idea because that would mean opening the basement door again, and I think that's probably a bad idea."

He smiles, and this one *is* real. The mask from moments before is gone. "I'm okay. But thank you."

A tiny ribbon of satisfaction unfurls in my chest. I'm not getting actor Flint. I'm just getting Flint. I didn't realize it was something I appreciated—something that even mattered—until right now.

I pull my knees up to my chest and wrap my arms around my legs. "That was pretty impressive how you handled them," I say motioning toward the kitchen and the basement door just beyond. "They can be a lot, and they're big fans."

"It's fine. I don't mind."

"Do you ever get tired of it?"

He shrugs, but I don't miss the way his jaw ticks first. "It's part of the job. And trust me, they were a lot nicer than a lot of people are."

"I don't know how you endure that kind of attention all the time. It would make me want to crawl out of my skin."

A flash of uncertainty crosses his features. "Why, do you think? Is it the crowds or talking to people you don't know, or...?"

I narrow my eyes, studying him. His question—or maybe the way he *asked* the question—feels very specific. Like he's looking for a particular kind of answer. "I mean, I'm not incapable. I defended my dissertation in front of an entire auditorium of biologists, and I've spoken at multiple conferences. I can handle attention. I just don't like it. And it drains my social battery pretty fast."

"Yeah, I guess that makes sense."

"Does that ever happen to you? A drained social battery?"

He grins. "My brothers would say no, and admittedly, it takes a lot. But yeah. It happens. Press junkets usually do it."

"I have no idea what that is," I say.

"Three days of hell," he says, but then he shakes his head and gives me another easy smile. "Or three days of interviews promoting a movie. All the actors and directors gather together in one place and journalists file through for back-to-back interviews."

"Sounds exhausting."

"It is exhausting." He runs a hand through his hair, then leans forward, his elbows propped on his knees. He fiddles with his fingers for a moment, and I get the strangest sense that he's nervous about something. "Actually, that's part of why I'm here." He looks up and meets my eye, his gaze serious. "I have an unusual favor to ask you."

I sit up a little taller and drop my feet to the floor, suddenly feeling like a serious question deserves serious posture. "Okay. Shoot."

"This is going to sound weird at first, I'm just warning you. And you're probably going to think—" His words cut off, and he clears his throat before he starts again. "Actually, let me give you some background information first. That's probably going to help."

The next five minutes are a blur as Flint walks me through the details of his new movie—and his last relationship. His co-star, Claire McKinsey. The way she's talking to the press about him. The problem this is creating surrounding the upcoming premiere in Los Angeles.

The longer he talks, the more confused I become. Because what on earth could this possibly have to do with me? All he could want is advice, and I'm the last person on the earth who would know anything about how to navigate a situation like this.

"If I were dating someone else, this would be easier," he continues. "But I'm not, and I don't exactly have a lot of time to sort that out before the premiere. But after talking to my publicist, and my manager, we're thinking that I only need to *appear* as if I'm in a relationship with someone else," Flint says.

"A decoy," I say, at least understanding this much. "That makes sense. If the public thinks you're seeing someone else, it will only make Claire look foolish if she keeps up her narrative."

He lets out a relieved breath, like he's grateful I understand. "Exactly."

"So you just need someone to pose as your girlfriend?" I tug at the drawstrings of my hoodie. "I'm not sure I understand what any of this has to do with me. Are you hoping I'll know someone who can help?"

My question seems to take him by surprise. "No, that's not—" He runs a hand across his face, and I notice a slight tremble in his fingers. "Audrey," he finally says, "I'm here because I want *you* to come with me."

Me.

Me?

Audrey Callahan posing as a movie star's girlfriend?

And that's when I start to laugh.

Chapter Ten

Flint

I'LL BE HONEST. THE laughing isn't doing much for my ego.

Audrey practically has tears coursing down her cheeks.

I sit patiently while she presses a hand to her stomach, actual guffaws coming out of her mouth. I mean, I realize I might not be her type, but is it really such a ridiculous thought?

Audrey sniffs and sits up a little taller. "I'm sorry," she says. "That was—" She wipes her eyes. "I promise I'm not laughing at you."

I chuckle lightly. "Thanks for the reassurance."

"Flint, I'm serious. I'm just—do you honestly think anyone in the world would believe you're dating someone like me?" She holds out her hands and looks down at her sweats.

Not that it's the only thing that matters—and Hollywood is full of attractive people, so I'm speaking from plenty of experience here—but does she not realize how beautiful she is?

I almost tell her I *would* date someone like her and that should be evidence enough, but I don't want to scare her off, so I stick with something simpler. "Audrey, I don't know what you're basing your opinion on, but you're beautiful. I can't imagine why anyone would question."

She scoffs. "I'm not—"

She doesn't finish the sentence, but I can fill in the blank well enough.

"Flint, I'm a scientist."

"I know."

"I haven't worn makeup in years."

"I know a few women who would kill for skin that looks that good bare."

Her cheeks flush, and she lifts her hands to cover them. She shakes her head, like she thinks I'm feeding her a line.

"Flint, it's a terrible idea," she finally says. "I'm not girlfriend material. Definitely not *movie star* girlfriend material."

She wouldn't be the first woman to assume I need a woman with special qualifications just because of my career, but she's wrong. Not that it actually matters, because it wouldn't be real in the first place.

"But are you *fake* movie star girlfriend material?" I joke.

She rolls her eyes. "What does that even mean?" She leans back and pulls her legs up to her chest, sitting like she was when our conversation first started. It almost seems like she's trying to make herself smaller.

This was a terrible idea. I've clearly made her uncomfortable. If just having the conversation is enough to do that, there's no way she'd ever agree to everything this would involve.

"Audrey, I'm sorry," I say quickly. "I'm realizing now this was a bad idea. This is not a problem for anyone else to solve. I'll just—" I push off my knees and stand. "I'll figure it out, all right? Forget I asked."

Before I can step away from the couch, she reaches out and grabs my arm, her fingers circling around my wrist. "Wait," she says. She slides her hand down to mine and I instinctively wrap my fingers around hers and let her tug me back onto the couch, this time sitting a little closer to her than I was before. "Just walk me through it. What all would this involve?"

A surge of hope pushes through me, but I still hesitate. If she's going to shut me down—and all signs point to her doing just that—this will be the moment it happens.

"It really is okay if you say no," I say, giving her fingers a reassuring squeeze.

She squeezes mine right back then slips her hand out of my grip. "I know," she says. "But at least let me know what I'm saying no to."

Here goes nothing.

"Okay, at first, it would just be a photo. The two of us together, but nothing that shows your face. I'll post the photo on Instagram, hinting heavily that I'm seeing someone new, maybe hint that it's someone I used to know growing up."

"That doesn't sound too bad."

"It wouldn't be, but that's the easy part."

She bites her lip. "What's the hard part?"

"I would need you to come to Los Angeles with me for the movie premiere."

Her face goes white. "To like, *go* to the premiere? Isn't that a big deal?"

"Pretty big," I say. "Red carpet. Lots of cameras. Questions, though they would only be for me. You wouldn't have to say anything." I keep going, hurrying through the worst of it all at once. "I would also need you with me during the press junket. You wouldn't be on camera then, but all the journalists interviewing the cast would see you there with me, and it would make asking about my relationship with Claire seem moot."

She breathes out a slow breath, a little bit of color returning to her face. "It sounds like you've given this a lot of thought."

"*Joni* has given this a lot of thought. But I know Claire well enough to know this is the only thing that might shut her up."

Audrey nods. "I get it. I really do, but Flint, I don't know the first thing about how to act on a Hollywood red carpet. I wouldn't know what to say. And I definitely don't have anything to wear."

"Don't worry about that. One email from my publicist saying my date to the premiere is in need of a dress, and you'll have three dozen in your hotel room by the time we get to LA."

She lets out a little disbelieving laugh. "Okay, but what about everywhere else? You've seen what I wear every day. That's basically my wardrobe. Work pants. T-shirts—"

"Don't forget the bush disguise," I add with a smirk.

She reaches over and smacks my arm. "Don't make fun of me! Sometimes I need to blend in when I'm working."

"I believe you," I say. "Audrey, don't worry about the clothes. I'll buy you a whole new wardrobe if I have to. You'll deserve it if you actually agree to go along with this crazy scheme."

"If I were one of my sisters, that's all it would take to get me to agree. But I just don't—"

"What if I give you access to my land for the rest of the summer?"

Her eyes go wide, but then they quickly narrow, like she's already two steps ahead of me. "*Just* for the summer?"

She's negotiating. That has to be a good thing. "To the squirrels living in my backyard, yes." I think about the various research sites she's told me about that fill the forest behind my house. "To the rest of the acreage, you can have access indefinitely."

She sits up a little taller. *I've got her.*

"For you, and any of your associates at the university," I add.

"You would do that?"

I shrug. "I wanted the woods for privacy and a buffer from any future development. But it won't hurt anything to have a bunch of biologists hiking around. As long as everyone steers clear of the house."

I can almost see the thoughts flying through her brain. She's probably already cataloging all the experiments she had to abandon but can now continue.

It occurs to me that had I known it would make her this happy, I would have offered her access to the land anyway. No strings attached. I'm a little disappointed that now I can't.

She laughs to herself as she drops back into the sofa cushions. "I can't believe I'm actually considering this," she says. "*Me.* Maybe I'll be able to convince a few journalists, but Flint, anyone who knows me is going to immediately know it can't be real."

I'm sure she doesn't mean for her words to be an insult, but *man,* this woman is giving my ego a beating. Who cares if I do like her? Audrey couldn't make herself any clearer. She'll never feel the same way about me.

"Good thing you're such a recluse, then," I say, defaulting to what comes easiest to me. When all else fails, I can always crack a joke. "What are we talking, here? Ten, eleven people?"

She rolls her eyes. "Shut up. I know more than eleven people. It has to be *at least* fifteen."

I grin. "I think those odds are good enough for us to take our chances."

She gives her head another shake. "Girlfriend to a movie star," she says, like it's the most preposterous thing she's ever heard.

"Maybe let's drop the movie star thing," I say, nudging her knee. "I'm just a guy, Audrey."

"A guy who *IS* a movie star."

"Just think of me as the guy who flirted with you at the Feed 'n Seed. The guy you met *before* you knew he was anyone famous."

She taps her chin. "Trouble is, that guy also had me hauled across the mountain by his Incredible Hulk bodyguard, placed in handcuffs, and interrogated by police." Her eyes sparkle with humor, pulling an automatic smile out of me.

"That's better than an actual rap sheet, right?" I ask. "And Nate's not as scary as he looks."

"When he's looming over you in the middle of the forest, he's *terrifying*." Audrey holds my gaze for a long moment, her clear blue eyes bright even in the fading evening light. "But you're right. He's definitely a big softie. Especially when Joni is around."

"I'll take credit for that," I say. "I set them up on their first date."

"Speaking of dates," Audrey says. "When is all of this supposed to happen?"

"The premiere is four weeks from Saturday. But we'd probably need to post a picture much sooner than that. As soon as possible."

"Four weeks." She licks her lips. "That's just before classes start for me. What happens after?"

"After, you're under zero obligation to do or say anything at all. We'll probably both deal with people around here—especially people who know us—asking questions. You can be honest with the people closest to you—all my family will know the truth because I don't lie to my family—but for everyone else, it will probably be easiest to just let them assume we dated and parted ways amicably when we realized you would never be happy dealing with all the crazy my life brings."

My words ring with truth—at least in my own head—but then Audrey nods, confirming them even further. "I definitely don't think I'm cut out for celebrity life."

Well. Glad we've got that cleared up.

This will be fake dating and *only* fake dating.

Hooray for me.

"So you'll do it?" I ask, and Audrey nods.

"I'll do it."

"For the squirrels?" I echo the qualifier she used when we first negotiated the terms of her research.

"For the squirrels," she says. "But also..." She bites her lip, blue eyes blazing, and my heart climbs into my throat. "Also for you," she finishes.

And those words carry me home.

Chapter Eleven

Audrey

I MEAN, IT'S NOT like I've never worn a swimsuit. But these very tiny scraps of fabric my sisters keep foisting on me are far, *far* outside of my comfort zone.

I toss a magenta string bikini onto my bed. I'm not even willing to try that one on.

"What if I'm just hanging out *beside* the pool in a T-shirt?" I ask. "Or I'll just wear this one." I grab the very practical speedo I wore when I was in grad school and swam laps three times a week.

"That one gives you the worst uni-boob," Summer says, yanking the suit out of my hands. "Please just try this one on. Once you see how good it looks, you won't be protesting nearly as much." She thrusts out her hands, the least offensive of the bikinis dangling from her fingers.

"Ohhh, yes. That one," Lucy agrees. "The halter will look great with your shoulders."

"And look at the butt." Summer drops the top and holds up the bottoms. "There's plenty of coverage."

I sigh. We've been at this for half an hour already, and I'm supposed to leave to go to Flint's in half that time. I took an entire afternoon off from work for this. I don't have time to waste. "Fine," I finally say. "I'll try it on, but if it doesn't look good, I'm wearing the Speedo, and there's nothing either of you can do about it."

"So help me, if you try and pose for a photo in *that* old thing—"

I slam my bathroom door, cutting off the rest of Lucy's sentence, and wiggle my way into the swimsuit. It's been three days since I agreed to pose as Flint Hawthorne's girlfriend. Three days since my sisters had the freakout of the century when I told them the reason Flint showed up at my door and offered me unfettered access to his property.

Lucy is convinced Flint is going to fall in love with me for real.

Summer is hopeful he'll discover he isn't in love with me, but one of the sisters he saw when he showed up at my house definitely caught his eye.

I'm still in shock that I agreed to go along with this.

The whole plan is completely ridiculous.

Utterly Laughable.

Totally—*wait.* I adjust the straps on the halter of the bikini top, tightening them the slightest bit.

Okay. This doesn't look half bad. I turn to the side and take in my profile, then shift so I can see how much of my butt cheeks are hanging out.

"Not bad, Callahan," I say softly to myself. "Not bad."

Summer bangs on the door. "How's it look?"

I take one last calming breath and swing the door open, then step into my bedroom.

Lucy's jaw drops.

Summer swears softly and lets out a disappointed sigh. "Okay. He's so going to fall in love with you."

I roll my eyes. "It's just a swimsuit. He's not going to fall in love with me over a swimsuit."

"But he might fall in love with you because of the body *in* the swimsuit," Lucy says. "I can't believe you've been hiding this." She waves a hand up and down my body, like she still can't believe it's me standing in front of her.

"Do you really think it looks okay?" I ask, one hand pressed against my bare stomach.

"You're smoking hot," Summer says. "Ridiculously hot."

I move to the mirror hanging above my dresser and take in my appearance one more time. Ridiculously hot is never a description anyone has ever used to describe me before.

I once overheard one of my TAs referring to me as *secret hot.* And the boyfriend I had during my master's program always told me I was pretty in a modest, understated way. (I have no idea what he actually meant by this. When I told my sisters, they seemed offended on my behalf, but I always felt like it was an honest, practical assessment.)

Which is why *ridiculously hot* feels like such a reach. "You're just saying that because you're my sister," I finally say.

"She's not," Lucy says. "I mean, you really need to tweeze and shape your eyebrows. And your skincare routine needs leveling up. But if you made an actual effort? Wore makeup? Bought clothes *not* from the men's section at Tractor Supply? Yeah. You'd totally be hot."

I reach for the nearest pair of pants. "Tractor Supply has a lot of really practical clothing."

Summer grabs the pants away from me. "None of which you are wearing today. You're going to the pool. Don't dress like you're out hunting for wild hogs. Hang on." She holds up her finger, then disappears down the hall. Less than a minute later, she's back holding a gauzy white sundress. "Here. Try this."

I pull it over my bikini and turn to look. It's loose and flowy, but somehow still flattering, which is a welcome surprise. In my head, clothes designed to flatter my shape are automatically clothes that will be restrictive and uncomfortable. But this isn't either of those things.

"You like it," Summer says proudly. "I can totally tell you like it."

I smile the slightest bit. "It isn't terrible," I say.

"Here. Shoes. Bag." Lucy drops a pair of strappy sandals onto the floor in front of me and holds out an oversized mesh tote. "I stocked it with everything you'll need. Towel. Sunscreen. I even grabbed that boring book off your nightstand."

"*Unseen Dangers* isn't boring," I say as I take the bag. "It's a realistic look at the worsening crisis the Southern pine beetle is bringing to North Carolina pine trees."

"And to think I've been wasting my time reading Emily Henry novels," Lucy says, her voice a robotic monotone. "I had no idea what I was missing."

"Whatever. I have to go." I push past my sisters but hesitate when I reach my bedroom door. I look back at them both. "Are you sure I can do this?"

Their expressions shift simultaneously into identical looks of confidence and compassion.

"Of course you can do it," Summer says.

Lucy nods. "Just remember. You're doing this for the squirrels."

I repeat those words the entire time I'm driving to Flint's house. He must have Nate watching and waiting for my arrival because I don't even have to press the call button before the gates are swinging open, admitting me onto the winding drive that cuts through Flint's acreage and leads up to the house.

Here, in front of the house, it's less woodsy and more just rolling pastureland. New fencing lines both sides of the drive, and I wonder if Flint is eventually planning to have animals. He grew up on a farm, after all—it probably wouldn't be outside his comfort zone.

Pondering this question distracts me until I'm parked in front of Flint's house.

I cut the engine but stay in my seat, hands still gripping the steering wheel.

This is stupid.

I am not sexy bikini material. Girlfriend material.

Definitely not Flint Hawthorne girlfriend material.

It's funny. A few weeks ago, that name didn't mean anything to me. And now, it feels like I see it everywhere. In the *People* magazines Lucy is always leaving all over the house. In my Apple news feed on my iPhone, though that probably has everything to do with the increased Google searching I've been doing lately. I *told* my phone to show me stuff about Flint because I looked him up a few (or ten...maybe a dozen?) times. I even saw his face on a cookie down at the feed store. Apparently, Ann has always been a fan.

The only thing I haven't done yet is watch one of his movies, for reasons I can't quite define. A part of me thinks I don't want to watch one, only to be disappointed. Considering my track record with movies, that feels like a real possibility. But a bigger part just wants to see Flint...as *Flint.* Not as the movie star he became when he was interacting with my sisters, but as the guy who works in his own backyard and invited me to eat with his family. If I watch his movies, he'll turn into a movie star for *me,* too. And I don't know that I'm ready for that to happen.

A knock sounds on my window, and I startle, one hand flying to my chest.

I look out to see Flint bending down to look through the glass. He's wearing sunglasses pushed back in his hair, a plain white T-shirt, board shorts, and flip-flops. He's dressed for the pool just like I am, but on him, the clothes look effortless and easy. Like he dresses like this every day.

"You okay?" he asks, his voice muffled by the window between us.

I nod and unbuckle my seatbelt. It's now or never, I guess.

He opens the door for me, offering his hand, and I slip my fingers into his, letting him help me out of my truck.

"Wow," he says, as he looks me up and down. "You look amazing."

"Oh." I look down at my clothes. "I—honestly, my sisters made me wear it. I wanted to come in the Speedo I swim laps in and a pair of sweats, but they refused to let me out of the house."

"You looked great in sweats the last time I saw you. But this is nice too," he says smoothly. He moves toward the front door, talking as he goes. "Thanks again for doing this. Joni and I have been talking about the best way to grab a few photos." He opens the door, holding it open while I cross inside. "I've got a few ideas, but please remember you have full veto power. Anything that makes you uncomfortable, we don't have to do. And of course, you'll see every shot before I post anything publicly."

I nod as I follow him through the kitchen and toward the back door that leads onto the patio. "Is there really a point to keeping my face hidden? If I attend the premiere with you, everyone will see me then anyway, right?"

"Yes. But we want the element of surprise on our side. If your face is visible now, before the premiere, odds are pretty good that someone will figure out who you are *beforehand.* Then we risk people showing up at your house or your lab, following you to the grocery store. I'd rather spare you that drama as long as possible."

"So, wait. Those things will happen *after* the premiere?"

He grimaces. "Probably. But we'll be prepared for it. As long as we both stay isolated for a few days, interest should die down."

"Stay isolated. What does that mean?" I ask.

He shrugs. "The easiest thing would be for you to stay here for a few days. That way you won't have to deal with people knocking on your door. And you'd be close to your squirrels so you could keep working."

My heart grows the tiniest bit when he refers to them as *my squirrels.* But also, he thinks I'll just stay here? At his house? With him?

Flint lets out an easy chuckle. "It's a big house, Audrey," he says. "I've got plenty of guest rooms. You can be on the opposite side of the house from me if you want."

I press my lips together.

Am I really so transparent? Or is this man just really good at reading me? "No, I know. I wasn't worried," I lie. "I'd be happy to stay here. You know. For the squirrels. But I'm sure we can figure it all out then."

He gives his head the tiniest shake, like he can't quite make sense of me, but then his easy smile is back, and he's tilting his head toward the pool. "So we're thinking something candid," he says, steering the conversation back to the here-and-now of what we're trying to accomplish. "Maybe we're in the water, your arms around me, the mountain view visible behind us, and I take a selfie that shows my face, but only the back of your head."

He's talking like he's reading a list of bullet points, which goes a long way toward keeping me calm.

"Whatever you think," I say.

He nods. "Then maybe one of just you—another shot from the back—of you leaning on the edge of the pool, looking off into the distance—" His words cut off, and his cheeks turn the lightest shade of pink before he shrugs. "I don't know. It sounds cheesy when I say it out loud, but I can see it in my head. If you're game, we can take a few different shots and see what happens."

"Okay. I trust you. Whatever you need, I'm happy to help."

I follow him onto the pool deck and drop my bag onto a chair. The pool sparkles in the sunshine, the water a deep, mesmerizing blue. At one end, the pool has no visible edge; instead, it cascades over a hidden rim, giving the impression that the water goes on forever, blending right into the horizon. Whoever designed this place knew what they were doing. The water in the pool, whether because of the deep blue tiles lining the deck or just sheer magic, is the exact same shade as the rolling Blue Ridge Mountains in the distance.

"Did you do that on purpose?" I say, pointing at the horizon. "You color-matched your pool to the mountains?"

Flint grins, then tugs his shirt off before dropping it onto a nearby chair. "I wish I were that good, Audrey. But that's just luck. And a trick of the light."

For a moment, I don't have words. I caught a glimpse of Flint's stomach that day he found me hiding in the bushes. And the internet has shown me *many* views of his physique, including a shot of his bare butt I possibly scrolled past four dozen times. But seeing him here, in person, only feet from me. He doesn't even look *real*.

I swallow against the lump in my throat and force my eyes onto Flint's face. His eyebrows are raised, his expression saying he's fully aware I was just checking him out, but he doesn't tease me about it. He steps toward the water. "Are you coming?"

The words sound like a challenge, and I'm not about to back down even if it means taking off this stupid sundress while I'm wearing this stupid tiny bikini.

I reach for the hem of my dress.

I'm not ready for this. Not even a little bit.

But there's no going back now.

Chapter Twelve

Flint

AUDREY IN A SUNDRESS, her shoulders bare and her hair down around her shoulders was one thing.

But Audrey in a bikini?

I am...*not prepared* when she pulls off her dress and drops it onto a lounge chair. She turns to face me, her hands pressed to her stomach like she's nervous.

I'm staring.

Of course I'm staring. Audrey is stunning. I'm used to being around women who spend hours with personal trainers every day, toning, tightening, perfecting. But Audrey feels different. Not that she's any less gorgeous. She isn't. Long legs, subtle curves. She just looks...*real.*

I pull my eyes away, somehow sensing that if she realizes I'm staring, it's going to make her uncomfortable. So I do the first thing that pops into my mind. I run toward the pool, shout "Cannonball!" at the top of my lungs, and jump in.

When I emerge from the water, Audrey has made her way to the edge of the pool. She has a towel and a bottle of sunscreen in her hands, and the expression on her face says she has no idea how she wound up here.

I don't know how she wound up here either, but I'm so glad she did.

Despite the impression she's given me that there will never be anything real between us, I can't quell my desire to impress her—to charm her.

I want Audrey Callahan to like me.

The challenge of that—of realizing those feelings aren't a guarantee—I could get high on it.

It makes this small slice of my life feel normal, and right now, I need all the normal I can get.

I swim toward Audrey, standing when the water is shallow enough for me to touch the bottom. I don't miss the way her eyes drop to my exposed chest and biceps, and I barely resist the urge to flex. Something tells me that kind of blatant display would only irritate Audrey.

She squirts a little sunscreen into her palm, then holds out the bottle. "Care to make yourself useful?" she asks. "Fifteen minutes without sunscreen, and I'll turn into a tomato."

She rubs the lotion into her arms and shoulders, then turns slightly, showing me her back.

Okay. No problem. I can totally handle this. I'm a grown man, not a fourteen-year-old boy high on hormones.

I swallow against the lump in my throat. "Well, we wouldn't want that." I lift myself out of the pool and sit on the deck beside her, then dry my hands on the towel she offers me.

I hold out my palm while she fills it with sunscreen, then rub my hands together before slowly sliding them across her shoulder blades. Goosebumps break out across her skin, and she sits up a little taller, almost like she's trying to compose herself.

I smile to myself, glad whatever this feeling is goes both ways, and slow my movements, prolonging the contact as long as possible.

Audrey tilts her head, looking at me over her shoulder. "So, what? Are you one of the lucky ones who just turns brown in the sun?"

"Not at first," I say. "But I got enough of a tan down in Costa Rica that I do okay now. If we were going to be outside all day, I'd probably put some on."

"How long were you there?" she asks.

My hands move down her back until I reach the top of her swimsuit bottom. I let my fingers linger there, sliding around until my hands are on either side of her waist. I might be making things up, but it feels like she leans into me the slightest bit before I move my hands back to her shoulder blades and clear my throat. "Six months shooting on location," I say.

"Sounds like a tough gig."

"You might feel differently if you saw the spiders."

She perks up, looking at me over her shoulder. "Goliath bird eaters? Did you actually see one?"

I chuckle. "I forgot who I'm talking to. Only you would get excited about a spider the size of my palm." I rub in the last bit of sunscreen just under the strap of her top. "That should do it," I say.

She turns back to face me. "Thanks." She drops her feet into the water, swirling them around a little. "I *would* be excited to see one. I mean, I'm not saying I want to find one in my bed, but they're fascinating. Theraphosa blondi. They're a part of the tarantula family."

"Are they the big ones the Costa Ricans roast in banana leaves and serve as a delicacy?"

Her expression brightens. "Please tell me you tried one."

I sink down into the water, letting it lap against my shoulders. "Only because I had to. It was in the script. But we just referred to them as big-ass spiders. I never knew the official name."

She grins. "We should petition for an official name change."

"Trust me. It fits."

"What did it taste like?"

"The only thing I tasted was the whiskey I downed before and after every take. There was no way I was eating one of those things sober."

She rolls her eyes and kicks a little water toward me. "Come on. Was it really that bad?"

I lift my foot and splash her right back. "It tasted like seafood. Like shrimp, maybe? But lighter. Crunchier."

She nods, not at all disgusted. "Man, I need to travel more."

I shake my head. Who even *is* this woman? And when is she going to stop surprising me?

"So what's the movie about?" she asks.

I drop back into the water, and turn, leaning against the deck right beside her, enjoying the warm sun on my shoulders. "It's about an American named Paul who grew up in Costa Rica with his ex-pat parents. He's working as a lifeguard and a long-distance swimmer and has these crazy goals of competing in open-water swims all over the world."

"That's you? Paul?" Audrey asks.

I nod. "So then there's this woman on vacation—that's Claire—who gets sucked into a rip current, Paul saves her, and they fall in love. But the movie is about more than that, too. A hurricane hits and decimates the community where Paul has lived his whole life, and he has to make some tough decisions about where he truly belongs, whether he wants to leave Costa

Rica, for swimming, *or* for the woman who just turned his life upside down."

"I'm assuming you spent a lot of time in the water," Audrey says.

"Both before and after we started filming. Apparently, I swam like an erratic helicopter before." I grin. "My stroke needed some work."

"But it's better now?"

I splash her the tiniest bit. "Come in and judge for yourself. Are you a swimmer?"

"Not a fast one, but I swam laps when I was in grad school to keep myself sane." She moves like she's about to get in the water, but then she pauses, looking back toward the lounge chair where she left her things. "That's my phone," she says, the ringing distant but audible. "Um, just give me one sec," she says. "That's the ringtone assigned to my parents."

"Take your time." She walks back to the chair, and I do my level best not to stare as she goes. I sink into the water, letting it cool my face, but it doesn't come close to cooling my attraction. If this is the way things are going to be whenever I'm around Audrey, it's going to be a long month of faking.

"Mom, I need you to calm down," Audrey says, as soon as my head is out of the water, and I immediately stand up, a sense of alarm racing through me.

Audrey must see me, because she waves her hand and smiles, her expression saying there isn't a *real* emergency going on. She listens for another moment, then bites her lip like she's trying to control her laughter. "No, I understand," she says. "But I promise it isn't going to hurt you. It's just as scared as you are."

Slowly, she walks toward me, then lowers herself back to the pool deck, sitting like she was before with her feet in the water.

She lifts her finger to her lips as if to shush me, then puts the call on speaker phone.

"...it just climbed right through the window!" her mom says. "Ohhhh, Audrey! It's on the bed. It's on our bed! We're going to have squirrel poop on our bed!"

"Get out of the way and I'll catch it," a man's voice says. This must be her dad. "I've got the oven mitts on."

"Dad, please don't try to catch the squirrel," Audrey says. "Even with oven mitts on. The RV isn't very big. If you both just calm down and leave the windows and doors open, I promise it'll find its way out on its own."

"Can squirrels give us rabies?" her mom asks. "This one has angry eyes. Oh! It's on the curtains! It's climbing the curtains!"

"Squirrels don't carry rabies," Audrey says, her voice unflappably calm. "Is the window open next to the curtains it's climbing? I'm sure it's looking for a way out."

"Derek!" her mom whisper yells. "Take off the oven mitts and open that window."

Several thumps and bumps sound, followed by a loud crash. "It's just you and me now," Audrey's dad says, his voice low. "Now head on out that window, or else I'll swap the oven mitts for a baseball bat, and we'll have ourselves some nice squirrel stew for dinner."

I bark out a laugh, quickly lifting my hand and pressing it to my mouth to cut off the sound. Audrey's eyes widen—she made it clear I'm supposed to be silent—but she's just as close to laughing as I am. And rightly so. Audrey's parents are hilarious.

"Dad! Don't you dare get the baseball bat. Mom, do you have any nuts? Walnuts, maybe? Or pecans?"

There's some rustling, then Audrey's mom whispers, "I have walnuts. And peanuts."

"Go for the walnuts. You and dad get out of the RV, then leave a few walnuts on the floor leading to the door, and a few more on the ground outside. Then just relax for a minute. I promise that squirrel is no more excited about being trapped in your RV than you are about it being there."

"Right. Nuts. I can do that. Gah! It's coming at me! Derek! Get out of the way, you oaf!"

Audrey shoots me another exasperated look, and I press my lips together, still fighting laughter.

"He took the nut!" her mom whisper-yells. "Audrey! He took it!"

"That's good!" Audrey whispers back. "Are you outside?"

I love that Audrey is whispering too.

"We're outside," her dad says. "Are you sure I can't use this bat?"

"I'll never forgive you if you do," Audrey says.

Her mom squeals. "He took another one! It's working!"

A few seconds of silence pass, then her mom cheers into the phone! "He's free! Ohhh, and look. He seems happy to have something to eat."

"Mom, please don't start feeding the squirrels, all right? This is a one-time deal. Is everything okay now?"

"Thanks to you," her mom says. "How are *you*? Everything going all right?"

"Everything's great, but I'm not really in a place where I can chat. If you're okay, can I call you later?"

"Oh, of course. Squirrel crisis averted!" her mom says. "Call us anytime. Love you, Auds!"

Her dad's voice echoes her mom's. "Love you! Tell your sisters hello!"

Audrey ends the call and drops the phone onto her towel. "So that was my parents," she says, her eyes still laughing.

"They sound fun," I say.

"They really are. You can follow them on TikTok if you want. They're traveling the country in an RV, documenting their adventures, and they've gained quite the following."

"Really? That's awesome."

"They're pretty adorable. They were both music professors at UNC-Asheville until they retired together last summer and decided they felt like traveling."

"I love that."

She smiles, her expression warm and genuine in a way that can only mean the relationship she has with her parents is a good one. "Mom plays the cello, and Dad the violin. They have their instruments with them, and wherever they stop for the night, they have these impromptu concerts. Mostly in RV parks. But they've done them in the lobbies of hotels, in restaurant parking lots, in public parks." She reaches for her phone. "Here. Look. I'll show you the one that went viral."

She scrolls and clicks a few times before she holds it up, the video already playing. I move through the water to get close enough to see, stopping just in front of her and dropping my hands onto her knees. She doesn't flinch or move away, so I assume it's okay.

Her parents are sitting in the middle of a gravel road, her mom sitting on a small stool while her dad stands behind her with his violin. They're wearing Tevas and casual clothes and floppy sun hats, and there's a small playground and a giant sign behind them that reads "Frank's RV Park and Campground." The music though—it's polished and refined and a complete contrast to the casual surroundings. "That's Bach, right?" I ask. "His Two-Part Inventions?"

Audrey's eyebrows shoot up. "You know classical music?"

"Little bit." I hand back her phone. "Your parents are great. I'm not surprised they've gained a following."

"Hold up," Audrey says, setting her phone down behind her. "People who know *a little bit* of classical music recognize Pachelbel Canon. But Bach's Two-Part Inventions?"

I grin. "Maybe I know more than a little? It's the only thing I listen to when I'm getting in character for a role."

She studies me for a long moment, her lip clasped between her teeth, and I resist the urge to reach out and tug her into the water just to have her close to me. "It's what I listen to when I'm working," she finally says, "and it's pretty much all we listened to growing up." She kicks the water lightly, splashing my chest.

"Are you ever coming in?"

She nods, then pushes off the deck and slides into the water. She gasps as the cold hits her skin, but then she drops all the way into the water, her head disappearing for a moment before she rises back up like some sort of ethereal water goddess, no care for what the water might do to her makeup—pretty sure she isn't wearing any—or her hair.

I've been around women angling for attention, and that isn't what Audrey is doing here. She isn't trying to be sexy, but she *is* sexy. Maybe even sexier because she has no idea what she's doing to me.

She runs her hand over her face and down her wet hair. "Do you have a favorite composer?"

I love so much that she seems to have forgotten that she came here for a purpose. We're just talking, getting to know one another, and it really seems like she's enjoying herself.

"I love Copland," I say. "And Dvorak. And Eric Whitacre. He's contemporary, though. What about you?"

"Bach, probably," she quickly says. "Because he's so familiar, but there's also something about the intentionality of his work that appeals to my scientific brain."

Once, after wrapping a particularly difficult scene in *Turning Tides,* Claire found me out on the beach, headphones on, listening to my favorite classical playlist. She stole my headphones, listened for a few seconds, then rolled her eyes, declared my music boring, and asked me to go skinny dipping.

"I like Bach, too," I say, loving that Audrey and I have this in common. "I get what you're saying about intentionality."

Audrey holds my gaze, her head slightly tilted, then she shakes her head and sinks into the water, her palms lifting to her face. Her expression looks disbelieving, but why?

The fact that we both like classical music?

Or is it more than that? Is she feeling this too? This tension?

If she's feeling even half the attraction that I am, she's gotta be overwhelmed, because I'm nearly out of my mind.

Wanting her like this—it's torture and bliss. Agony and ecstasy. But I don't even care. Even if this goes nowhere, I'll take the sting of that disappointment if it means even a moment of the pleasure that comes from her company.

Audrey Callahan has me hooked.

Chapter Thirteen

Flint

"So how are we doing this?" Audrey asks, her expression serious. "Where do you want me?" She's several yards away from me in the water, her hands propped on her hips.

I can think of a lot of places I want her, but I force my mind to focus on the task at hand. "Um, right. Let me just, uh, grab my phone, and we'll figure something out."

I climb out of the pool and walk to the long patio table where I left my shirt and phone. I grab a towel off a stocked shelf by the door and dry my hands before picking it up.

Joni and I discussed the possibility of her being here, either to take the photos or just to offer her opinion on what she thinks will work best, but we ultimately decided Audrey would be more comfortable without an audience. Now, I'm wondering if an audience would have been helpful if only to help me behave myself. This woman is only *pretending* to be my girlfriend, and I can't stop thinking about the way her skin felt under my palms when I helped her with her sunscreen.

I walk back to the pool, phone in hand, and use the stairs to get back in the water. My phone is waterproof enough, or so the manufacturer claims, but I'd rather avoid testing it out if I can help it. Audrey has moved to the infinity edge of the pool, her arms resting on the edge, her long dark hair trailing down her back.

Without pausing to think about it, I pull up my camera and snap a picture. I move a little closer, grabbing a few more before she turns and looks over her shoulder, an easy smile on her face. I snap one more photo. I won't be able to use this one, but she looks too amazing not to try and capture the moment.

"I could get used to this view," she says easily, turning back to face the mountains.

I leave the phone on the concrete pool deck and move up next to her. "Sometimes I forget how pretty it is here," I say. "Living other places. Traveling all over. Then I come home, and I'm surprised, you know? That I got to grow up here, enjoy views like this every day."

"I've never lived anywhere else," Audrey says. "But I'm still convinced this has to be the prettiest place on earth."

"You've really never lived anywhere else?"

She shakes her head. "I mean, high school at NCSSM in Raleigh, then college. But I was still in North Carolina for that. App State for my undergrad, then Carolina Southern for both my master's and my PhD."

"That's right over in Hendersonville, right?"

She nods. "That's where I teach. I'd love to do some traveling eventually, but I love it here, too. And my research is rooted in these mountains. To go anywhere else would be like starting my career over."

I turn and lean my back against the edge of the pool. "And you grew up in Silver Creek? I still find it hard to believe I never saw you. Never met you."

"But I wasn't around for high school, remember? Just home for the summers. But trust me. Even if you had run into me? You wouldn't have noticed me."

I look at her pointedly. "I find that hard to believe."

She flushes the slightest bit, then laughs as she looks away. "I'm serious. Every nerdy stereotype you can imagine, I was all of them. Braces. Big hair. Enormous glasses."

"Whatever. We were all dorks in high school."

She scoffs. "Nope. *I* was a dork in high school. The internet told me what you looked like in high school, and you were anything but a dork."

"Are you admitting that you Googled me, Audrey? Is that what's happening here?"

"You think I would agree to fly all the way across the country posing as your girlfriend if I hadn't Googled you? I'm a researcher, Flint. Of course I Googled you."

It doesn't surprise me that she looked me up. But the internet isn't always the kindest place for celebrities. "That's fair. Just as long as you're checking your sources. You know most of what the internet says about me isn't true."

"I hope so," she says without missing a beat. "Otherwise, explaining my presence to your alien wife is going to be tricky."

"Alien wife, huh? I must have missed that article."

"Oh, it's worth looking it up. They had pictures of your children and everything. And they didn't look photoshopped. In one shot, you're holding this tiny green baby close to your chest. Pretty compelling stuff."

I frown, suddenly uncomfortable with whatever level of photoshopping was required to make images like that. Did they use actual pictures? Have I filmed any movies with babies lately? Do

I need to call Simon and see if this is something I need to concern myself with?

But then Audrey smirks. She's messing with me. And it totally worked.

"Oh, that was mean," I say. "Alien babies? For real?" I push my hands through the water, sending a tiny splash her way.

She screams and darts away from the spray, then uses her legs to kick water toward me, fighting back with splashes twice as big.

"Oh, it's on," I say, darting after her. I catch her quickly, wrapping my arms around her waist as I tug her against me, her back pressed against my chest, and pull us both under the water.

She wiggles free, then jumps onto me, her hands pressing onto my shoulders until I'm back under the water again.

We keep going, tugging, pulling, dunking, chasing. I don't know if Audrey is thinking the same thing I am, but for me, every tease is a reason to touch her, to hold her against me, even just for the short seconds it takes me to dunk her under the water.

I can't get enough of this touching. Her skin against my skin. Her warmth seeping through my fingers, contrasting the cool pool water surrounding us.

After a particularly good dunk, she comes out of the water, spluttering, her smile wide, and lunges after me. Her hands land on my shoulders, and I catch her, tugging her against my chest. But this time, instead of splashing her or pushing her under the water like I have all the times before, I hold her, my hands around her waist, her body flush against mine.

Her breathing is labored, her chest rising and falling with each breath. Drops of water cling to the end of her nose and the tips of her eyelashes, and a dozen new freckles are visible on her cheeks.

I lift one hand from her waist and slide it across her cheek-bone. "You have new freckles," I say softly.

She lifts her hand to her cheek, touching the same spot. "Do I?"

I nod, sliding my hand back into the water. This time, I clasp my hands behind her back, tugging her even closer. It's how we'll need to stand for the other picture we need to take anyway. Might as well get used to it.

She settles against me in a way that sends a shot of warmth right through me. Like she likes it here. Like she *wants* to be in my arms.

My eyes drop to her lips.

It would be a bad idea. Wouldn't it?

Before I can deliberate further, Audrey pushes away from me, taking a giant step backward. "So about those pictures," she says, her voice full of artificial cheer, and the tension building between us pulls and snaps.

I don't know what just happened, but I'd put money on Audrey having felt it too.

"Right. Pictures." I swim back across the pool and grab my phone. "I already took a few of you that I think will work. So we just need one of the two of us together."

She nods and swims toward me.

I gesture to the infinity edge of the pool. "Maybe over here?"

She follows me, waiting while I position myself against the edge of the pool and flip my camera around to selfie mode. I reach for her hand. "So, maybe something like this?" I tug her toward me, and she slips her arms around me like it's the most natural thing she's ever done. I curl my free hand around her waist, holding her against me. She lifts one hand to my neck, but keeps her head turned, like she's looking out at the view behind us. I frame the shot so enough of my face is visible for people to know it's me and take a couple of shots, then take a few more of me looking down, my gaze trained on Audrey.

The curve of her jaw is visible, and the tumble of her dark hair down her back, but there's no way anyone will know, just from this picture, who she is. She looks freaking amazing though—like a goddess in my arms.

Selfishly, I keep my arm around her while I scroll through the shots. I'll want to run them past Joni, and Simon now too, since Joni filled him in on our slightly modified version of his plan, but I think they'll work.

Audrey turns to face me, lifting her chin from where it's been resting on my shoulder. "Did you get what you need?"

She's so close. Close enough that I would only have to lean an inch or two to press my lips to hers. My pulse pounds in my throat as Audrey leans in the slightest bit, and my arm around her waist tightens.

She takes a stuttering breath and closes her eyes, but then she moves the opposite direction, just like she did last time, sliding out of my arms and swimming several yards away.

I hold up my phone. "I did. Do you want to see? I won't post them unless you approve."

"Um, actually, could you just text them to me?" She takes a few backward steps. "Or have Joni text them, I mean. Since she has my number."

Okay, then. "Sure. Are you heading out?"

"Yeah, I, um, I just remembered something I have to do at the lab this afternoon." She taps the side of her head. "Me and my brain. Always forgetting things."

Something tells me her brain never forgets anything, but she clearly wants to get out of here, and I won't argue with her.

"Okay. Sure. I'll send them over later." *I* will send them. Not Joni. Joni's rules about me protecting my cell number no longer apply to Audrey.

"Perfect," Audrey says as she scrambles out of the pool. "Totally perfect."

She's flustered. Fleeing. Obviously uncomfortable.

Did I push things too far? Hold her too closely?

"Audrey, wait." I swim after her, climbing out of the pool just as she reaches her towel. "Are you okay?"

She wraps her towel around her and reaches down to pick up her shoes. "Of course I am. Why wouldn't I be?"

I stop where I am, my hands resting on my hips, sensing that any sudden movements might make her bolt even faster. "It just...feels a little like you're running away. Did I do something wrong?"

She starts to laugh—but not like she thinks something is funny. It's more like she's barely keeping it together and laughing is the only way she knows how to cope. "I'm fine," she says, her voice too high for me to believe her. "Totally fine."

I nod, resigning myself to letting her go. It's the only thing I *can* do. "Okay. Well, thanks again for everything. I had a lot of fun."

For a split second, whatever mask she put on when she decided to flee falls, and I see a flash of real emotion cross her face. Then she smiles tightly and disappears into the house.

I don't follow her. *I can't.*

Because the last thing I saw flashing in her eyes was fear.

Chapter Fourteen

Flint

JONI LEANS ON THE counter in my kitchen, my phone resting in front of her. She swipes through the photos of me and Audrey, studying each one for a quick moment before moving on. "I really think they'll do the trick," she says, but then she pauses on the last photo, the one I took with Audrey in my arms. "Holy cow, Flint. Has Audrey seen this yet?"

It's only been an hour since Audrey left, and I'm still reeling. Still *processing*. Spending an hour in the pool with her was so much more than I expected it to be. For the first time in a very long time, I forgot who I was. Forgot about Claire and the lies she's telling. I forgot about everything except how much fun it was to be in Audrey's company.

"She hasn't seen them yet. Why?" I ask, though I'm only trying to buy some time. I know exactly why Joni is asking. In the last photo, I'm looking right at Audrey. And the expression on my face is less carefree and easy and more *I'd like to eat you for breakfast.*

"Look at your face," Joni says, reaching over and tapping the phone screen before she straightens and props her hands on her hips. "If she sees this photo, she's going to know you aren't acting."

"Or maybe she'll think I'm just a *really good* actor."

"Honey," she says, turning on her mom voice. Joni isn't quite old enough to be my mom. More like an overbearing older sister. But that doesn't stop her from mom-ing me every chance she gets. "I really think you need to be straight with her. Tell her you like her."

"I *can't* tell her. Asking her to fake it is already something outside her comfort zone. If she knows I'm *not* faking, she'll back out, if only to spare my feelings."

"So you're just going to suffer in silence?" Joni says. "Fall more and more in love with her only to have her walk away when all this is over?"

I raise my eyebrows. "Dramatic, much? I'm not going to fall in love with her. We'll have fun, we'll get through the premiere, then we'll continue as friends. This isn't a big deal."

Joni huffs out a laugh. "Tell that to the man in this photo."

"The man in the photo is telling you *I'm fine,*" I lie. "Now, can you please send me Audrey's number so I can text her these photos and make sure she approves?"

Joni's eyebrows shoot up. "You already have it. It's in the text message you sent *me.*"

Oh. Right. I scroll through the message thread between me and Joni. "Geez. We text a lot."

"Your life needs a lot of *managing,*" she says. "You do know if you text her, she'll have *your* number, right?"

"And I trust her with it. It's fine. I told her I'd text her before I posted the pictures."

I don't fault Joni for being cautious. It's her job to protect my privacy—to be wary of anyone who gets close to me. But I'm not worried about Audrey.

"Here, stop scrolling. I'll just send it to you." Joni pulls out her phone. Seconds later, mine vibrates with an incoming message sharing Audrey's contact information. "Okay. Done." She grabs her bag off the bar stool beside her. "Let me know if there's anything Simon needs me to do once the pictures go live." She moves toward the front door, and I follow her. "Have you talked to your family about this yet?"

Oof. My family. I knew there was something I was forgetting. I grimace. "Not yet. But I will."

"Before you post the pictures, Flint. You know your mom follows your Instagram. She'll lose her mind if she sees those pictures and you haven't explained to her what's really going on. She'll be knitting new baby blankets before the end of the week."

"I get it. I'll call her." She opens the front door, and I look past her into the fading evening light. "Where's Nate? Is he really making you walk home by yourself?"

She rolls her eyes. "It's not even fully dark yet. And what's going to get me? A white squirrel?"

"How about a bear?"

She pulls a can of bear spray out of her purse. "What do you take me for? It's less than a hundred yards to my house, Flint. I'll be fine." She steps off the porch and starts down the driveway. "Call your mom!" she yells over her shoulder before she gets too far away. "I mean it, Flint."

I give her one last wave before moving back into my very empty house. It's not that my house in Malibu was any less empty. I lived alone there, too. But it's hard to ever *truly* feel alone when you live in Southern California. A hundred steps outside my front door in any direction, and I could find people, whether I wanted to or not.

Solitude means something entirely different out here.

I use my phone to turn on some music then drop onto my living room sofa. I call my mom first and talk her through the situation with Audrey, including all my reasons for deciding a charade is necessary in the first place.

Mom is, as I expected her to be, hesitant to think pretending is ever a good idea, but we still end the conversation on a good note. "I trust you, Flint," she says. "If this is what you need to do, then do it. But be careful, all right? I don't want either of you getting hurt. Though, I can't say I'd mind if you happened to fall in love for real."

"Thanks, Mom," I say. "I'll keep you posted."

I text Olivia and give her a quick update, then I pull up Audrey's number and create a new message. Nerves jump in my gut as I scroll through the pictures, picking out the best ones. Actually, the best ones are the ones where I can see Audrey's face, but I can't post those, so those are just for me.

I finally decide on three, one of Audrey looking out at the mountains, and two more of the two of us together, including the one that Joni thought was such a big deal. If I'm going to really sell this, that picture is my best bet. I send them over, adding a message after all three photos go through.

Flint: What do you think? Are you okay with me posting these?

I tap my phone nervously against my palm, then send one more message.

Flint: Hope it's okay that I'm texting instead of Joni.
Flint: I figured that would be easier considering all the time we're about to spend together.

I sit and stare at my phone for what feels like an hour but probably isn't more than a few minutes. Either way, Audrey doesn't respond.

I double check the number, making sure I didn't mess it up somehow when I saved it into my phone, but the numbers all match.

I'm being stupid. Just because she hasn't responded doesn't mean she *won't* respond. She could be away from her phone. On a walk. Taking a shower. Watching a movie with her sisters. Or *not* watching a movie—this is Audrey we're talking about—but there are a hundred different reasons why she might not be available to respond immediately.

Also, when did I become so insecure about a woman texting me back?

What even is this?

Grumbling, I pull up the ongoing text thread I've shared with my brothers as long as we've all had cell phones. One of them is bound to respond right away and clearly, I could use the distraction.

Flint: Hey. Just a heads up. Claire won't stop talking about the two of us getting back together, and it's becoming the THING people want to talk about instead of the actual movie we were in. My publicist suggested it might be good to give the impression I'm seeing someone else.

Brody: What does that even mean? How do you do that if you aren't actually seeing someone?

Perry: Photoshop?

Flint: Not photoshop. I'm not that desperate.

I pull up the photo of Audrey and me and send it to my brothers.

Lennox: Dude. That's a real woman in your arms. Care to explain?

Flint: It's Audrey, and she's in on it. She came over this afternoon and posed for a couple of photos.

Brody: Audrey agreed to pose as your girlfriend?

Flint: Is that really so hard to believe? She's also attending the premiere with me in a few weeks.

Brody: Also as your girlfriend?

Flint: Fake girlfriend.

Unfortunately, I think to myself, but I'm not about to admit that to my brothers. It's bad enough they're all enjoying their happily married lives. They don't need another reason to feel sorry for me.

Flint: I just need a buffer from Claire. If I go alone, she'll corner me and force me into a compromising position.

Brody: And then, GASP, you'd have to marry her to save her reputation.

Lennox: Let me guess. Kate is making you watch *Bridgerton.*

Perry: I watched it with Lila. Season two is better.

Flint: It's MY reputation I'm worried about. And the director's. She worked hard on this film, and Claire is hijacking everything.

Flint: We're hoping if it's obvious I'm with someone, she'll lay off. And then the press can talk to us about the actual movie instead of my nonexistent love life.

Brody: Except, won't they want to talk to you about your new mysterious girlfriend?

Flint: They'll ask questions, sure. But I don't have to answer. And Audrey isn't a celebrity. They won't care about her as much as they would if I were with Claire.

Lennox: I'm surprised the movie people aren't making you and Claire pretend to be dating, seeing as how you fall in love in the actual movie. Isn't that the kind of PR thing movie studios love?

Flint: If it were really happening, they might be willing to capitalize on it. But they wouldn't make us pretend. That kind of thing only happens in books.

Perry: Says the guy who is literally taking a fake girlfriend to a movie premiere.

Flint: Shut up.

Lennox: I'm surprised Audrey agreed. How much did you have to offer her?

Perry: No. Please tell me you aren't paying her.

Flint: I'm not paying her. I'm giving her access to my land so she can continue her research.

Brody: Wait. Is that a euphemism? Or...please tell me it isn't a euphemism.

Flint: My actual LAND. It used to be owned by Carolina Southern. Apparently, there were all kinds of research things happening closer to the river.

Lennox: So you ARE paying her.

Flint: More like...we're exchanging services. It's fine. She's fine with it. I'm only telling you because I don't want you to see the post and think we're dating for real.

Perry: It's so cute you think we follow what entertainment news says about you.

Flint: I'm posting the pictures on my Instagram account.

Lennox: It's so cute you think we follow your Instagram account.

Flint: You're all idiots.

Brody: Kate says she follows you.

Flint: Tell Kate I like her more than you.

Brody: She also says she really likes Audrey and thinks you should date her for real.

Yeah. She and I both.

Flint: That's not what this is. It's a business arrangement. Audrey is way too grounded and practical for it to turn into anything else.

Lennox: That's the second time you've told us how SHE feels about it. How do YOU feel?

Flint: What do you mean?

Lennox: I mean, your expression in that picture looks like you're really into her.

Flint: Yeah? Maybe I should go into ACTING or something.

Lennox: Okay. Point taken.

Deny, deny, deny. That's the game here. I just have to convince myself my feelings aren't already involved.

I'm not invested.

I'm perfectly fine knowing this thing with Audrey isn't ever going to be real.

As I field a few more of my brothers' idiotic responses, my brain is fully on board. *It's all pretend. It's only going to be pretend.*

But when a new text pops up, this one from Audrey herself, the way my heart jumps clean out of my chest tells an entirely different story.

Chapter Fifteen
Audrey

It takes me about fifteen seconds to figure out that the pictures that pop up on my phone came from Flint himself, and not Joni.

It shouldn't be a big deal. But he made such a point of not giving me his phone number. What changed? What made him suddenly okay with texting me directly?

The bigger question. Why am I so happy about it?

I scroll through the three photos he sent over with trembling hands. They're better than I expected. He must have run them through a filter because they look more artistic than just a regular snapshot. The shadows are heightened, and it looks like he deepened the contrast in a way that really emphasizes the distant mountains behind us.

I zoom in on the photo of me, looking for anything that might identify who I am.

The woman in the photo could be anyone. The one of us together shows a little more of me—the line of my jaw, the bend of my arm, my palm pressed against Flint's chest.

My sisters might be able to look at it and tell that it's me, but no one else could. Especially without any context.

A pulse of anxiety pushes through me as I think about all 56 million of Flint's Instagram followers seeing photos of me.

Yes—56 million. Ten minutes ago, I thought he might have a few hundred thousand followers. A million, tops.

When I said as much out loud, Summer laughed until she cried real, actual tears, then she pulled up his account and showed me how far off I was.

I understood that Flint was famous.

I didn't understand *how* famous.

I click out of the photos and drop my phone onto the bed like it's too hot to touch. A part of me feels like it was a different person in the pool with Flint today. The woman in the photos—it's not me. It *can't* be me. If someone sat me down right now and explained that I was a part of some cutting-edge experiment in which someone else borrowed my body for the afternoon to frolic through the pool with Flint Hawthorne, I would believe it.

And then I would feel relief because it would mean I get to go back to my regularly scheduled life. My work. My research. The woods I know as well as I know my own name. The occasional run-in with my sisters when they insist I need to take off my cargo pants and socialize with humans instead of wildlife every once in a while.

I lean back on my bed and stare at the ceiling.

The only trouble with that scenario is that I actually *enjoyed* swimming with Flint today. I know my sisters think the man walks on water just based on how beautiful he is, and I'll be the first to admit it—I definitely enjoyed the view he gave me today.

But aside from the abdominal muscles and the nicely sculpted shoulders and the biceps—I definitely have a thing for biceps—he was also really fun to be around. He paid attention to me. Made sure I was comfortable. Teased me in a way that immediately put me at ease. Had the afternoon not ended with the whole *snuggling up against him for a picture* thing, it might have just felt like a fun afternoon with a friend.

That's what he said, after all.

I had a lot of fun.

Sure. Fun. Until his touch lit my skin on fire and turned my heart inside out.

But was it Flint that did that? Or just the fact that I was being touched by anyone at all?

It has been a very long time since a man has touched me in any kind of intimate way. Since that much of my skin has been in contact with that much of someone else's skin.

Snatches of sensation flood my mind in rapid succession. His hand curved around my waist. His sun-warmed skin under my palm. The press of his thigh against mine as he pulled me close.

I groan and grab my pillow, using it to muffle the sound as I grumble out my frustration. This is fake. *Only fake.* I shouldn't be frustrated about anything.

A knock sounds on my bedroom door. "You okay in there?" Summer calls. "Do I need to call for help?"

I sit up and lunge off the bed and across the room where I yank the door open.

"Whoa. Hey," Summer says. "What's with the crazy eyes?"

"Flint told me he had fun this afternoon."

She lifts an eyebrow. "Okay? That's a good thing, right?"

"And I *also* had fun."

"Still not seeing the problem," Summer says.

I grab Summer's wrist and pull her all the way into the bedroom, then tug her down on the bed beside me.

"Summer, it felt...I felt...I liked being with him today."

She gives me a dry look. "Honestly, I think I'd have you committed if you felt anything else."

"Stop with the movie star stuff. I didn't like it because he's a movie star. He could be a normal guy, and I still would have had a good time."

"Okay, but to clarify, would the normal guy version of Flint Hawthorne include the pool and the house and all the muscles?"

I breathe out a huff of frustration. "You're missing the point."

"Then make your point more clearly. What are you trying to say here, Audrey?"

I groan and drop back onto my bed. I have a feeling I'm going to get awfully familiar with the blades of my ceiling fan over the next couple of weeks.

Summer taps my knee. "Okay. Let's treat this like a research project and start with what we know. What are the facts?"

I sit up. I can do research projects. "The facts," I repeat.

Summer nods encouragingly.

"I am *pretending* to be in a relationship with Flint Hawthorne."

"Right. Good," Summer says. "What else?"

"In exchange for my presence in his photos and my attendance at an event later this month, I'm gaining access to his land so my research may continue indefinitely."

"Yes. Fake dating. Land. Got it."

"I have been given no indication that our relationship is now or ever will be anything but strictly professional."

Summer lifts her hand in slight protest, like she's not quite comfortable with my last point.

"What?" I ask. "That's a fact."

"No, I know," she says. "I was only protesting the use of the word professional. Is there really *anything* professional about paying a woman to be your date?"

"He's not paying me. That's not what this is."

"It is what this is. He's not paying you with *money,* but he's still paying you."

"But he's—"

She cuts me off. "I didn't say I have a problem with it. I'm just calling a spade a spade. As long as he isn't paying you for sex, you're fine."

"Sex?" I squeak out. "You don't think—surely he doesn't—" I press a hand to my stomach. "Oh, man. I don't feel so good."

"Whoa, whoa, whoa." Summer reaches over and grabs my shoulders, giving me a little shake. "We're getting off track. And I'm positive Flint Hawthorne is *not* expecting sex."

"Right. Of course not. Because that would be ridiculous."

"Totally ridiculous," Summer repeats, but my thoughts are moving so fast, I barely hear her words. It's like the minute she mentioned sex, my brain lost a gear and spun completely out of control.

Summer lets out a little laugh. "Still, can you imagine?" Her expression turns sly, and she bites her bottom lip.

All at once, my jumbled thoughts coalesce into something potent and sharp, and I reach out and smack Summer's knee. "Stop imagining sex with my fake boyfriend right this second."

Her eyes widen, and her mouth stretches into a wide smile. "Oh my gosh."

She jumps up and runs to the door. "Lucy! You'd better get in here."

"What! Why?" I demand. "Why are you getting Lucy? And why are you smiling like that?"

"What? What's happening?" Lucy bursts into the room, her apron on and a wooden spoon in her hand.

"Audrey likes Flint," Summer says.

"What?" Lucy and I say at the same time.

"That's why you're so freaked out right now," Summer says. She turns to Lucy. "I made a comment about imagining sex with Flint, and Audrey immediately turned into a jealous she-bear and practically pushed me off the bed."

I roll my eyes. "I did not push you. I smacked your knee. And I'm not jealous, because I do not like him. Excuse me for thinking it's wrong for you to sit there, thinking about him like he's some sort of—"

"World-famous movie star?" Summer says. She lifts a hand to her chest in mock exasperation. "How dare I?!"

"He might be a movie star, but he's also a person," I say. "Why is it okay for people to think of him like an object just because he's famous?"

"It's a fair point," Lucy says. "But if that's the way you feel, definitely *do not* Google Flint Hawthorne fanfiction."

"Fanfiction?! What is fanfiction?"

Lucy and Summer exchange a look.

"Nothing for you to worry about," Summer says. She scooches over and makes room for Lucy on the bed. "You know, it wouldn't be a bad thing if you *did* like him, Audrey. You're great. He seems great. Why not be great together?"

"I don't know that he is great. I barely know him. And you only think he's great because you've seen him in movies. It's not the same thing."

"And interviews," Lucy adds. "We've seen him in tons of interviews, and he's very charming in interviews."

"Ohhh, the Graham Norton interview!" Summer says. "When he talks about his mom and all the little baby goats on the farm and then they bring out an *actual* baby goat, and he totally knows exactly how to hold it and feed it like he's a total pro."

Lucy sighs. "Or the one where he goes into the coffee shop wearing a headset and he has to repeat everything that Ellen Degeneres says, and the barista gets so flustered that she starts to cry, and then he gives her a hug and goes to all this effort to make her feel better."

"Seriously? You guys have been watching these videos all along and never thought to share them with me?" I make a mental note to do some Googling as soon as I'm alone again. Which—am I ever alone these days? Lately, it seems like my sisters are spending less and less time in their actual apartment. Or maybe it's just that I'm spending less time in my lab.

Ever since Flint, nothing has been the same.

"Share them with you?" Lucy says. "Are you kidding? Audrey, a month ago, you would have laughed in our faces if we tried to share celebrity news with you. The fact that you've somehow evaded the magic of Flint Hawthorne all these years is totally on you."

"We're still missing the point." Summer holds up a hand like she's trying to regain control of the conversation. She looks at me pointedly. "You said you liked hanging out with him today. If you don't like him, then what's going on? Why are you freaking out?"

"I'm not freaking out."

"You were groaning into your pillow like you got dumped the night before senior prom."

"Terrible analogy," Lucy says.

"Like you accidentally deleted all your white squirrel pictures," Summer amends.

"*Better* analogy," Lucy says.

"I think I'm just worried about how I'm supposed to gauge what's real and what isn't. He told me he had a lot of fun today. And even though he originally told me Joni was the one who would communicate with me about stuff, he's the one who texted me the pictures."

Summer takes a slow breath and closes her eyes. "I will not freak out that you have his number in your phone. I will not freak out that you have his number in your phone."

Lucy nudges Summer, then shoots her a *shut-up* look before she turns her attention back to me. "Audrey, I think you're overthinking it. So you both had fun. That's a good thing because you're going to be spending a lot of time with the guy over the next couple of weeks. And so what if he's the one who texted you? People text each other all the time."

"She's right," Summer says. "But you still raise a valid question about discerning what's real and what's not. Have you guys talked about it at all? Set boundaries? Talked about expectations? About the rules?"

My mind drifts back to the sex conversation I had with Summer before Lucy showed up. "That all sounds very official."

"You said yourself this was a professional arrangement," Summer says. "It should be official."

"Totally," Lucy adds. "Like, you're going to walk down the red carpet with him, right? But will he expect you to hold his hand? Kiss him?" Luckily, Lucy's questioning doesn't go quite as far as Summer's did, but I'm still feeling like I need a break anyway.

I swallow against the tightness in my throat. "I'll ask him," I finally say. "I'll make sure we talk about it."

Summer squeezes my knee. "And otherwise, you'll just try to have fun, right? You'll stop overthinking."

I stand and stretch, feigning a confidence I don't really feel. "Me? Overthink? Never."

"Did you say he sent you the pictures?" Lucy asks. "How did they turn out? Can I see?"

I grab my phone and take it over to my dresser, where I plug it in to charge. "You can see them once he posts them. Aren't you cooking something right now? Do I smell something burning?"

"Oh, geez." She jumps up and runs from the room, yelling as she goes. "Summer, make her show us the pictures!"

Summer lifts her hands in surrender. "I'm not making you show me anything. I'm surprised you've lasted this long, with all the talking we've made you do. I'm willing to cut my losses and see the photos with the rest of the world."

"Thanks," I say, feeling a surge of gratitude for my little sisters. There are a hundred things I don't love about their nosy, bossy presence in my life—especially when they are so completely different from me. But I'll be the first to admit it: the good definitely outweighs the bad.

The minute Summer is gone, I close and lock my door and grab my phone, returning to my bed.

I have some Flint Hawthorne interviews I need to Google, but I also need to respond to his text.

I look over the pictures one more time, then slowly key out a response.

Audrey: They look great. I'm fine with you posting these.

The message feels entirely too boring and bland, but what else can I possibly say? Before I can overthink it—you're welcome, Summer—I send the message and collapse back onto my pillows like I just ran a marathon and finally get to rest.

I close my eyes, half-expecting Flint not to respond at all, but my phone buzzes before even a minute goes by.

Flint: Great. I'll post them tonight. Can I give you a word of advice?

Audrey: Sure.

Flint: Don't go looking for the pictures. If you have an Instagram account, don't like the post. And most importantly, don't read any of the comments. Lots of people have opinions, but I've learned that the ones I value will never be left in a public comments section.

Audrey: I don't have an Instagram account, so this won't be difficult, but I appreciate the tip. Do you mind if I ask you a question?

Flint: Anything.

Audrey: Should we talk about parameters for how this whole situation is going to work?

Flint: Parameters?

Audrey: For when we go to California.

Flint: Right, so like, how long we'll be gone. What events I expect you to attend?

I take a deep breath. That information will be valuable, but that's not truly at the heart of what I'm asking. I muster my courage and try again.

Audrey: Sure. But also, what will you expect from ME? Hand holding? Public hugging?
Flint: I like public hugging.

He adds a winking emoji at the end of his message.

Audrey: Are you making fun of me? I feel like you're making fun of me.
Flint: I'm not! It's a valid question. Can we talk about it in person? Joni has a mile-long list of things to discuss with you. It might be overwhelming if we try to cover it all via text.

Before I can respond, a second text pops up.

Flint: Are you free on Saturday?

I drop my phone onto my chest, my hands trembling. But this is no big deal. I'm not overthinking. Spending Saturday with Flint will be No. Big. Deal.

Audrey: I'm free.
Flint: Perfect. I'll pick you up at 9.

I glance at my watch. Oh great. That's only...thirty-eight hours to *not* freak myself out.

An hour later, Summer bursts into my room holding her phone.

"He posted them! The photos are live!" She looks down at her phone. "Oh my gosh, Audrey. You look so gorgeous."

"I do not," I say even as I put down my book and scoot closer to the edge of my bed. "You can't even see my face."

"But look at your hair!" Summer says. "And your back looks amazing."

I push up on my knees and look over her shoulder. "My back looks like a back. There's nothing amazing about a back."

"Sure there is. No weird rashes or bulges. You look good."

"Let me see," Lucy says, pushing into the room. "My phone just died so I can't pull it up." She pulls Summer's phone out of her hands. "Ohhh, you do look good. And look! Already ten thousand likes."

Ten thousand likes. He posted the picture minutes ago, and it already has ten thousand likes.

"What do the comments say?" Lucy says.

"No! Don't read the comments. Flint says I shouldn't."

"I'll only read the good ones out loud," Summer says as she starts to scroll. I scoot back on my bed and lean against the headboard, pulling my pillow tightly to my chest. I watch as Summer's eyes dart back and forth over the screen. I shouldn't be curious. I know better than to be curious. But I can't help it.

"Ohhh, listen to this one." She clears her throat. "'WHAT? Flint Hawthorne is off the market? Crying for the rest of my life.'"

"How about this one?" Lucy says. "'Did Claire McKinsey dye her hair brown? Could they actually be back together? #clairandflint'"

"Umm, we hate *that* hashtag," Summer says.

"Wait, they think I'm Claire?" Flint and I didn't talk about that potential assumption, but it makes sense. You can't see my face. If the woman in his pictures could be anyone, why not Claire McKinsey?

"He makes it clear in the caption he's with someone from home," Lucy says. "And there are already a billion replies to that one comment saying it's absolutely *not* Claire in the photo."

Still, I feel like Flint needs to know even *one* person is making the assumption. I grab my phone from where it's charging on the nightstand and send him a quick text.

Audrey: So, I know you said not to read the comments, and I'm not. But my sisters are, and they say people are speculating about whether the woman in the photos is Claire. Is that a reason to worry?

His response comes through almost immediately.

Flint: People will speculate about everything. But we've added an element of doubt. That should be enough to keep the story under control.

Audrey: Okay. I won't worry if you aren't worried.

Flint: I'm not worried.

Flint: But Audrey? Don't even let your sisters read the comments.

Audrey: Clearly, you don't know my sisters.

Flint: Then don't let them read any of them to you. Promise me?

I look up at my sisters who are both staring at Summer's phone like vultures hovering over a dead raccoon on the highway.

"Okay," I say. "Time for bed." I stand up and usher them toward the door.

"No, no, wait, you need to hear this one!"

"I don't need to hear anything," I say. "I promised Flint I wouldn't read them, and that means not letting you read them either. At least not to me." Well, I *will* promise Flint. Just as soon as my sisters have left me alone.

Summer clutches her phone to her chest. "He made you promise? That's so sweet."

I nudge Lucy's shoulder, making her walk backward to the door. "I guess if you can text the *actual* celebrity, there's less thrill in reading comments about said celebrity," Lucy says.

"Exactly. So if you'll *excuse* me, I'm going to text him right now."

They pause in my doorway, twin images of wide-eyed wonder. "I can't believe this is your life," Lucy says.

I smile and start to close the door, pushing gently until they finally get out of the way and I hear the click of the latch. "Goodnight!" I call through the door, locking it for good measure.

Back on my bed, I snuggle under the covers and pull up the text thread to Flint. He texted again in the time it took to kick my sisters out of my room.

Flint: Audrey? Don't make me come over there and talk to your sisters myself.

Audrey: They would be thrilled if you did. But all is well. I kicked them out. And I promise—I won't let them read me any more comments.

Flint: You really don't have your own Instagram account?

Audrey: I really don't. I've never felt like I needed one.

Flint: How do you stay in touch with people? Keep up with what everyone is doing?

Audrey: I'm sure it will shock you, but as someone who mostly prefers the company of wild animals to people, I haven't exactly accumulated a lot of people to keep up with.

Flint: Come on. Everyone has people.

Audrey: I have my sisters. But I live with them, so I don't need to follow them on social media.

Flint: But you have TikTok, right? To follow your parents?

Audrey: ONLY to follow my parents. And watch cute dog videos.

Flint: *Makes note to self about sending Audrey cute dog videos*

I smile and bite my lip. I like flirty Flint, even if there's a possibility it's only *fake* flirty Flint.

Flint: What about college roommates?

Audrey: My freshman roommate was awful, but after that, I lived with my lab partner from my first biology class. We're still friends. We talk on the phone once a month.

Flint: Old school.

Flint: I like it.

Flint: Sometimes I wish I didn't have social media at all. But I do love seeing all the pictures my siblings put up of their kids. I have a private account that I use with my family. It's nice.

Audrey: With a family as big as yours, I can understand the appeal. That's a lot of people to keep up with.

It's another minute or two before another message pops up, and this one nearly makes my heart stop.

Flint: So, are you ready to talk about movies? I've been doing my research, and I've got a couple I want you to try. Maybe we can watch a few together?

I lean back into my pillows and smile, positive I won't actually be able to sleep anytime soon.

Audrey: Bring it on.

Chapter Sixteen

Audrey

"OH MY GOSH, HE'S IN A LIMO!" Lucy spins around from where she's spying out the front window, her eyes wide. "Audrey, he's picking you up in a limo!"

I press a hand to my stomach. A limo is fine. A limo is *no. big. deal.*

Seconds later, a knock sounds at the door. I nudge Summer out of the way and open it with trembling hands. It isn't Flint on the other side, but a serious-looking man in a dark suit with a thick, white envelope in his hand.

"Audrey?" he says.

When I nod, he hands over the note. "From Mr. Hawthorne. Regrettably, he's unable to join you this morning, but he hopes this will make up for it."

I ignore the disappointment blooming in my heart and yield to the curiosity urging me forward as I open the envelope and pull out a gold-edged notecard.

Beside me, Summer whispers, "Do you see that? Even his stationery looks rich."

I roll my eyes and tilt the card so only *I* can read it.

Audrey, So sorry I'm not there this morning. Something came up—an urgent production meeting for my next project—and since I'm signing on as a producer for this one, it seemed risky to ignore it. In the end, the women in my family assure me it's better this way, and you'll enjoy what I have planned more without me tagging along. I hope they're right, but I still don't want to spoil the surprise, so if you'll allow me this one indulgence, will you trust Charles and get in the car with him? (Older, balding, wearing a dark suit? If anyone else handed you this envelope, do not, under any circumstances, get in the car.) If your sisters are free, they're welcome to join you. If they already have plans, don't worry. My sisters are waiting for you at your destination. I hope it's a great day. And Audrey—please don't protest. After all you're doing for me, this is the least I can do in return. —Flint

I look up and meet Charlie's eye. "You're Charlie?"

He nods.

I look at my sisters, nervous excitement making me trembly and unsteady. Lucy's eyes drop to the quivering notecard. She steps forward and reaches for it. "Can I?"

I nod, and she pulls it from my hands. Summer steps up beside her, and they read it together. "Oh, wow," Lucy finally says. "How are you feeling, Auds?"

"I don't know." I press a hand to my stomach. "Overwhelmed?"

"K, listen," Lucy says, slipping an arm around my waist. I'm not generally great at surprises, something that has been true long enough for my sisters to have seen me freak out more than once. It's not a huge deal. I usually just need a minute to adjust. "It's a surprise, yes," Lucy continues. "But it looks like Flint has done every possible thing to make sure you're comfortable." Summer appears on my other side, bracketing me like my sisters so often do.

"Do you trust him?" she asks.

"I do," I say, realizing I don't even need to think about it. I *do* trust Flint. Maybe weirdly, considering how little I know about him, but I feel certain he wouldn't do anything to intentionally make me uncomfortable. He's been so cautious about all of this, about making sure he's not pushing me into anything. "I'm sure it's going to be okay," I say, as much to reassure myself as my sisters. "So, um, do you guys want to come with me today?"

"Are we leaving Silver Creek?" Lucy asks, though I don't know why she thinks I know the answer to her question. I don't have a clue what's about to happen. "I'm on call, but if we're staying in town, I could maybe come."

We turn together and look at Charlie. "You will not be staying in Silver Creek," he stoically says.

"Boo," Lucy says. "Then I'm out."

"I can't go either," Summer says. "I have hours of depositions to read. Though, if I stay up late tonight, I might could..." She cocks her head as if considering, but Lucy protests before she can say anything else.

"No!" she says firmly. "If I can't get out of work, you can't get out of work, either."

Summer scoffs. "That is not how this twin thing works."

"It is too how it works," Lucy says. "You don't get to have fun without me. Especially not movie star fun."

"It won't be movie star fun if Flint isn't even there," I say.

"It will be *planned-by-a-movie-star* fun, which can only mean it will be expensive and amazing," Summer says.

"And we'll hear all about it when Audrey gets home," Lucy says pointedly, and Summer sighs. "Fine. But if we didn't know Flint's family will be with her, I'd leave you in a second if it meant Audrey not being on her own."

"Of course you would. And I'd want you to go. But that doesn't matter now, does it? We're both staying home today."

"Fine, yes," Summer concedes. "We're both staying home today. Geez. Overreact much?"

I reach out and grab my sisters' hands. "Thanks for looking out for me, you guys." I smile, wanting to reassure them. There's still a slight edge to my nervousness—there always is when I'm facing the unknown—but the much larger part of me is excited. *Happy* excited. My sisters don't need to worry.

I look down at my jeans and the white, V-neck T-shirt I borrowed from Lucy because she insisted it was better than all the science pun shirts I tried to put on before she intervened. I lift my gaze to Charlie. "Do you know where I'm going today? Am I dressed okay?"

Charlie nods. "I was instructed not to give you any more information than what's on the card, but I believe your wardrobe is appropriate for the occasion."

I take a steadying breath and look from Lucy to Summer. "Okay, well, I guess I'll see you later?"

They both lunge forward and pull me into a group hug. "Whatever it is, it's going to be great," Summer whispers.

I hear her words, but I don't miss the concern hovering in my sisters' eyes. Not that I can blame them. Sometimes, I think my sisters forget what I'm capable of because I've intentionally made my world so small. But just because I don't *like* doing lots of people-y things doesn't mean I'm incapable.

"You guys. I'm fine. Please stop worrying about me."

"You *are* fine," Lucy says. "You've got this."

I give them one last hug, then follow Charlie to the limo which is really more like a stretched-out SUV. It's *enormous* and feels like a ridiculous expense to drive around one person, though I do feel slightly better when I see the eco symbol on the door telling me the car is fully electric.

I wait while Charlie opens the door for me, then I climb in. "There's chilled water and sodas in the fridge across from you," Charlie says through the still-open door. "And snacks in the basket next to you. Help yourself to whatever you like."

"Thank you, Charlie," I say, though honestly, I'm way too nervous to eat. It occurs to me, as Charlie pulls the limo onto the interstate heading toward Asheville, that the whole point of getting together with Flint today was so that we could talk about boundaries and expectations. I don't particularly love surprises, but even more, I don't love not knowing what to expect.

I pull out my phone, intent to text Flint and let him know he still owes me a conversation, but as soon as I look at my phone, I find a text from him already waiting for me.

Flint: Thanks for agreeing to go. Sorry again for abandoning you. Were your sisters able to join you?

Audrey: They're both working today, so I'm on my own. But thanks for inviting them.

Flint: I thought you might need your sisters to convince you to go at all. Now I'm even more grateful you said yes.

Audrey: Oh, I definitely needed them to convince me. I don't typically love surprises.

Flint: Noted. I hope you'll enjoy this one anyway.

Flint: Have a good day, Audrey.

Flint: I'll be thinking about you.

I lean back into the seat, keenly aware of the way my heart is fluttering. I don't have a lot of experience with this sort of thing, but Flint's texts feel...I don't know. Like *more.* Not quite flirting exactly, but like more than he would say to a casual acquaintance. But maybe I'm wrong. Maybe Flint is this thoughtful and solicitous with everyone he texts.

I take a couple of screenshots of our last few texts and send them to my sisters.

Audrey: Give me your thoughts.

Summer: Ummm, he's totally into you.

Lucy: Yep. Agreed.

Audrey: But is he really? How am I supposed to know what's real when our relationship is fake?

Lucy: I mean, you'll only be faking it in public, right? Why would his text messages be fake?

Summer: I agree with Lucy. I think he's into you for real. But you still have to talk to him. You need rules, woman.

My sisters can't be right.

I've lost sleep over the idea of being a *fake* movie star girlfriend.

I wouldn't know the first thing about being a real one.

Still, as I look at the basket sitting next to me and pull out a bag of chocolate-covered almonds, I let myself indulge in a frivolous, ridiculous thought: *A girl could definitely get used to this.*

⁓

Oh my. If I thought limo service directly from my front porch was nice, I don't even know *what* to think now.

Because we're at the Asheville airport. On the tarmac. Beside a private jet.

No lines. No ticketing agents. No security checkpoint. Just me, Charlie, and a set of stairs leading onto an actual airplane that is only here for me.

"This is not for real," I say out loud.

But then Olivia, Flint's younger sister, appears at the top of the stairs. "Audrey! You're here!"

Another woman appears beside her. Kate, I think? She's married to one of Flint's brothers, but I can't remember which one. She smiles wide and waves.

I look at Charlie, and he nods, as if he understands he needs to give me a nudge. "This is where I leave you," he says. "I hope you have a lovely trip."

Trip? Where on earth am I going? And for what?

"Come on!" Kate calls. "We've got places to go, baby!"

Olivia meets me halfway up the stairs and pulls me into a big hug. "How are you? Were you so surprised? Are you so excited?"

"Um, should I be excited?" I manage to say. "I still have no idea what we're doing."

"Oh, girl, you should absolutely be excited." She wraps an arm around me and pulls me onto the plane. Which is *not* like a plane. It's more like an upscale living room. Leather seats that swivel to face any direction. Sleek wood trim. An actual couch stretching along one side of the plane. Opposite the couch, there's a table holding a full spread of breakfast foods. Muffins, juice, quiche, five different kinds of fruit.

I look at Olivia. "Is this all for us?"

She nods. "Are you hungry? We've been waiting for you, but Tatum over there might eat her arm if we don't dig in soon."

"It's the breastfeeding," Tatum says. "I'm literally starving all the time."

"You remember Tatum," Olivia says. She leans a little closer. "This is the first time she's ever left the baby, so she might be a little emotional today. She's married to Lennox, who is two brothers up from Flint."

I nod, appreciating that she's including family ties in her introductions. I don't think I would have remembered everyone on my own.

"And Kate, she's married to Brody who is next up from Flint. And that's Lila, Perry's wife. Perry is the oldest. We love her because she tamed his grump and turned Perry into a big softie."

"Got it," I say. "And you and Perry run the farm, right?"

Olivia nods. "Yes! And Tatum's a restaurant consultant, Lila's a piano and voice teacher, Kate's a fancy magazine editor, and we really don't expect you to remember any of this."

I smile. "I'll do my best."

"I promise we're a forgiving bunch," Tatum says, standing and reaching for a plate. "Especially when we're fed."

"What about your husband?" I ask Olivia. "He wasn't at Flint's that night, was he?"

Olivia smiles, her expression softening. "Tyler. He's a video-grapher based in Charlotte, and he travels for work quite a bit, but he doesn't have any trips planned, so you'll totally meet him the next time we're all together. He's great."

I don't miss the way she so easily includes me—like it's just *assumed* I'll be with Flint whenever the family gathers.

I try not to read into it while we all fix our plates, happy chatter bouncing around the plane. It's hard to believe these women are just sisters-in-law because they sound a lot like my sisters do. Finishing each other's sentences, teasing each other with good-natured jokes. It seems incredibly lucky that, in a family with four sons, all their wives get along like this.

In an unusual beat of silence, I ask, "So what are you guys going to do if Flint marries someone you don't like?"

They all stare, their expressions curious, and I suddenly re-alize how random my question must sound without context. "Sorry. I just mean, you all seem to get along so well. You sound like actual sisters. At the very least, best friends. I just..." I shrug, feeling sheepish. "I was just thinking about how sad it will be if Flint ends up with someone who doesn't fit."

Lila shrugs. "You can love anybody if you try hard enough," she says simply. Her lilting Southern accent makes her words as soft and lovely as their meaning.

"Aww," Olivia says. "I love that. But also, if he picks someone we don't like, we just won't let him marry her."

Everyone laughs, but the sound quickly dies when a throat clears behind me. "Good morning, ladies."

Kate and Tatum are facing me, and I watch their expressions shift before I turn and look over my shoulder, immediately understanding their open-mouthed reactions. The man stand-ing behind me is one, clearly the pilot who will be flying us wherever we're going, and two, drop-dead gorgeous. Tall. Dark hair. Strong jawline. Beautiful brown eyes.

"My name is Captain Blake Salano, and I'm honored to be your pilot today."

We nod in unison, but no one says a word.

"The weather is clear between here and New York, so it should be an easy, relaxing flight. I'll leave you to your breakfast. I just wanted to assure you—you're in very good hands."

"I bet we are," Tatum says under her breath, and Kate snorts as she stifles her laugh.

The second the captain has returned to the cockpit, Olivia pulls out her phone as the rest of us start to giggle. "What on earth?" Lila says. "Where did *he* come from?"

"I feel like we need to be concerned about whether he's a real pilot or just one of Flint's actor friends *posing* as a pilot," Tatum says.

"We definitely need answers," Olivia says. "And I'm going to get them right now." She makes a show of calling Flint, then drops the phone onto the table where we're all sitting with our breakfast.

"Hey, what's up?" Flint asks. "Is everything okay? Did Audrey make it okay?"

My heart skips at the mention of my name, and Kate looks at me and presses a hand to her heart, like she can't believe how sweet it is that he asked about me.

"She's here, she's fine, and you're on speaker phone. We just thought we should call and make sure Captain Blake Salano is a *real* pilot and not someone you pulled off your last movie set."

Flint chuckles. "I thought you might like him."

"Looking at him, sure. But all your happily married sisters want to make sure he can get us to New York in one piece."

"Liv! Did you just spoil Audrey's surprise?" Flint says.

Her eyes lift to me. "Captain Salano already spoiled it, but she doesn't know what we're doing yet."

The *only* thing that distracted me away from asking about New York was Olivia calling Flint, but now the question is practically burning a hole in my tongue.

"Go ahead and tell her," Flint says. "She doesn't like surprises." Olivia's eyes jump to mine, and my heart squeezes, *again,* at Flint's efforts to be thoughtful, to remember what I told him. "I gotta jet," Flint says. "My meeting is about to start, but you guys take care of her, all right? Hey, Audrey?"

All eyes swivel to me. "Yes?" I say, proud of how *not croaky* my voice sounds.

"Try to have a good time, okay?"

I bite my lip. "I'll do my best."

As soon as Olivia's call disconnects, the sisters erupt in a round of gasps and sighs and squeals. "Girl," Kate says, gently shoving my arm. "What have you done to him?"

The more important question: *What is he doing to me?*

"So, do you want to know why we're going to New York?" Lila asks.

Olivia tosses a credit card onto the table. I lean forward and see Flint's name stamped onto the top of the card. "Brace yourself, Audrey," Olivia says. "We're going shopping."

Chapter Seventeen

Audrey

THE FLIGHT PASSES QUICKLY.

Too quickly, if I'm being totally honest.

Apparently, I'm supposed to get a whole new wardrobe, one fit for the red carpet and every other event I'll be attending with Flint.

Shopping has always been more of a utilitarian experience than an exciting one for me, so all this feels *very* overwhelming. At this point, the only thing keeping me together is the fact that Flint's sisters are all so happy to be here. To spend the day focusing on *me*.

If I can get past the discomfort of being the center of attention, this might end up being the perfect shopping scenario. There are four other women here who clearly know how to put together an outfit, and I'm positive they'll all be willing to give me their opinions. If I'm lucky, they'll just make all the decisions for me.

Tatum, Lennox's wife, drops into a chair next to me. Before she can say anything, Captain Salano's deep voice comes through the overhead speaker announcing our final descent.

"How are you feeling?" Tatum asks.

"A little overwhelmed? I've never been to New York."

"It's a lot," she says. She reaches down and buckles her seat-belt. "Well, it *can* be a lot. But it can be great, too. And the shopping is next level."

"I wouldn't even have anything to compare it to. I'm very practical when it comes to my clothes. The only dress I own is the one I wore under my graduation robes when I finished my PhD. And I only bought that one because my sisters made me."

She raises her eyebrows, but there's no judgment in her expression—just surprise. "Sounds like you're long overdue." She studies me for a second before she adds, "You know, Flint was *really* excited about doing this for you today."

I wave away her comment, ignoring the heat climbing up my cheeks. "Believe me, it's only out of desperation. He's seen the clothes I show up in every day. It's nothing fancy enough to ever wear into public with him."

"I doubt that's *all* this is about. If it were just about the clothes, he could have had a wardrobe hand-picked and shipped to Silver Creek." She grins. "I think he wants you to have fun."

I shake my head and lift my hands to my cheeks. "What is even happening, Tatum? What am I doing here?"

"All I know is Flint's instructions were to spare no expense. So whatever is happening, it's going to be amazing."

Ten minutes later, we're on the ground at LaGuardia walking across the tarmac from the plane to an awaiting helicopter. From there, we fly into the heart of New York City, land on the roof of a building I couldn't identify again if I had to, then ride an elevator down to street level before Olivia takes charge and ushers us into what I think is a Bloomingdales.

And that's when the whirlwind begins.

I don't know how to shop, but Flint's sisters *definitely* know. We start with the more casual things I'll wear when I'm *not* on the red carpet. Jeans. High-waisted pants that miraculously make my waist look tiny and my butt look better than I've ever seen it. And shirts that feel like regular T-shirts but are made of lighter, nicer fabric and look so much better. They keep their selections practical, picking out stuff I might actually wear even when I'm *not* posing as Flint's fake girlfriend.

At first, I try to minimize how much we're spending, but Olivia waves off my concerns, Flint's credit card clutched in her hand with obvious glee.

Three hours later, my feet are sore, I'm completely exhausted, and there are more bags between the five of us than we can easily carry.

Olivia just purchased *ten* new pairs of shoes for me, which feels utterly ridiculous and indulgent, but I've given up trying to argue with her. And let's be honest. The Frye ankle boots that I tried on last are possibly the most comfortable shoes I've ever put on my feet. *AND* they look amazing. Turns out, shoes that are both fashionable and comfortable *are* possible.

You just have to be willing to pay for them.

Olivia is currently negotiating with the store clerk about how to get all the shoes and the rest of the two dozen bags we've been hauling around delivered to the airport. I didn't even realize that was a thing we could ask for, but a no-limit AMEX card apparently goes a long way in this city.

"Perfect. Thank you so much," Olivia finally says before spinning around to face the rest of us. "Load him up, girls," she says, pointing back at the store clerk, a waifish man named Eduardo with bushy eyebrows and what looks to be a permanent frown. He opens a door behind the counter and holds it open with his foot while we hand him bag after bag. It seems awfully trusting, honestly. Olivia has been stingy with the receipts, not wanting me to see the total from each store, but I've been adding in my head as quickly as I can, and the number is...well, let's just say it's not an amount I'd feel comfortable losing to Eduardo.

"He won't just steal them, right?" I whisper to Tatum.

"Absolutely not. This kind of thing happens all the time," she assures me. We spent a little time on the plane talking about her childhood growing up as the daughter of a very famous celebrity chef, so I know I have every reason to believe her. But all this still feels so foreign to me.

"Okay," Olivia says, rubbing her hands together once we've given Eduardo everything we've purchased so far. "It's time for the best part."

Kate lets out a little gasp. "Evening wear?"

Olivia nods, her grin wide. "Oscar de la Renta, here we come."

"Oscar de la who?" I say as they usher me out the door.

"Oscar de la dream come true," Lila says. She loops her arm through mine. "Do you have any thoughts on color?"

"Is it awful if I tell you I literally have zero thoughts about evening wear?" We turn left and follow Olivia down Madison Avenue.

"Not even about style? Sleeveless? Sequins? Ruffles of any kind?" Lila asks, her tone teasing.

"No ruffles and no sequins," Olivia says, tossing a look over her shoulder. "Audrey needs something classy. Something sophisticated."

"Audrey needs something comfortable and easy to walk in," I say. "Anything to help combat the odds of me falling on my face."

"You'll have Flint to hold you up," Kate says. "He won't let you fall."

A wave of trepidation washes over me. He *will* be there to hold me up. Probably with an arm around me, or a hand pressed to the small of my back. It scares me to realize how excited I am about that.

Maybe it's just the exhilaration of the day. Or the acceptance and camaraderie I've felt from his sisters. Or it could be that Flint's fingerprints are all over everything we've done—he's done so much to make me feel special. But for the first time, the trepidation I've grown so used to feeling every time I think about what's coming shifts into something a little less frightening. It's more like anticipation—the good kind of anticipation. The kind that makes my stomach flutter and my heart pound out of my chest.

"Okay," Olivia says, pausing outside the door of Oscar de la Renta's New York store. "A woman named Remy is waiting for us, and she's handpicked several gowns for you to try that will compliment Flint's red-carpet look."

"Oh my gosh, this is so exciting!" Lila says from just behind me. "Have you ever worn a designer gown, Tatum? Is it as amazing as I think it would be?"

"It's pretty magical," Tatum says, and I frown. I don't even know what it means to wear a designer gown.

Tatum reaches over and squeezes my hand. "It just means you're wearing a one-of-a-kind dress instead of something off the rack."

"So, there's only one? What if it doesn't fit me?"

"They'll make it fit," Lila says. "Make whatever adjustments you need. Isn't that part of the magic?" She looks at Tatum, who has become our source for all things even tangentially related to celebrity life.

"Don't worry about the fit," Tatum confirms.

"Okay! Let's do it," Olivia says.

I fall in love with the first gown I put on.

It's ice blue—not far from the shade of my eyes—with a fitted bodice and a gentle flare that starts midthigh. A sheer sort of lacy mesh overlay with tiny flowers stitched on top (clearly, I have no idea how to talk about dresses) covers the entire dress, then extends over the chest and shoulders, making it look like the flowers are growing up and over my skin.

It's the most beautiful thing I've ever put on my body. I press my hands against my stomach as if the gesture will calm the riot happening inside.

"I don't think we'll need to alter it," Remy says, stepping up behind me and tugging gently at the fabric across my shoulders. "The fit is perfect."

"You look so amazing," Olivia says, and everyone else nods their agreement.

"Oh hey," Tatum says, picking up my bag from where it's sitting on a little bench behind the three-way mirror where Remy has me perched on a raised dais. "Your phone is ringing." She pulls the phone from the outside pocket and grins. "You want it? It's Flint."

A chorus of squeals erupts around the room, like this is some kind of middle school slumber party and I've just gotten a text from the boy I like. Which is a weird analogy to make because I was *never* that girl in middle school. I didn't get texts from boys, and I didn't have slumber parties. But right now, with all these women cheering me on, it's easy to guess what that might have felt like.

Tatum steps closer and hands me the phone, and I quickly answer it before the call cuts out. "Hey," I say, a little breathlessly. "Hi. Hello."

"Having fun?" Flint's smooth voice triggers a wave of goose-bumps to pop up across my skin, and my heart rate quickens. I lift my free hand and rub it across my bare arm as if the gesture alone will calm my racing pulse. I look up and see five sets of eyes on me. "I am, but...actually, hold on." I step off the dais and move toward the dressing room behind me. I look back at my ever-eager audience. "I'm just going to take this back here," I say. The heavy dressing room door won't provide a ton of privacy, but it's better than nothing at all.

"Okay, I'm here," I say, collapsing against the wall before remembering the very expensive dress I'm wearing and standing up tall again. "Sorry about that. How are you? How was your meeting?"

"Productive," Flint says. "I feel really good about the direction we're taking things."

"Good. That's good news."

"How has *your* day been? Have you gotten everything you need?"

"Flint, I've gotten so much more than I need. Olivia is relentless. You might hate me when you finally get your credit card bill."

"She was only following my instructions," he says easily. "And I'm not worried about the bill."

"I wouldn't be so sure. I bought a pair of jeans that cost half my mortgage payment. Do you know how stupid that is? How many children could be clothed with that kind of money?"

"I'll send over my charitable contributions for the year if it'll make you feel better," he says lightly.

"Just tell me it's more than what you're spending on me today. All of this just feels so...I don't know. Extravagant?"

"Audrey, you're worth a little extravagance."

I close my eyes, momentarily stunned by the thrill of hearing my name on his lips. Not to mention the words coming out of his mouth. *I'm worth a little extravagance? Be still my freaking heart.*

I press a hand to my chest. I should not be thinking like this. I should not be enjoying his attention this much.

"And I bet those jeans looked amazing," Flint says.

I smile, happy his sisters can't see the goofy expression on my face. The jeans *did* look amazing. Best my butt has ever looked, not that I've ever paid particular attention to how my butt looks in *any* pair of pants. The closest I've come is putting on jeans my sisters have thrown at me, insisting they'll look fine even if they *are* a little short in the inseam. It's possibly dangerous that I've discovered the magic of a pair of jeans made for *my* body instead of my sisters' much smaller frames.

"Maybe," I say through my grin. "Though, nothing is as amazing as the dress I'm currently wearing."

"I can't wait to see it. Has Remy taken good care of you?"

"Her and everyone else," I say, sensing in Flint's tone how much he wants this to be true. "Thank you for today, Flint. It's possible I might freak out tomorrow when I try to fit everything in my closet, but for right now? It's been a good day."

"Can we make it a good night too?" he asks, and I pick up on a tiny note of hesitation in his voice.

"What do you mean?"

"I was hoping you'd have dinner with me tonight. I owe you a conversation, so I was thinking you could come back to the house, I could order us some takeout, then we can talk. Maybe watch one of those movies I sent over since I'm positive you haven't watched any of them on your own yet."

I bite my lip, a faint flush spreading across my chest. "What makes you so sure I haven't watched?"

"Audrey," he says, his tone dry.

"Fine," I concede through a smile. "But I had to work late last night! I genuinely haven't had time!"

"I was also thinking we could take another picture to post on Instagram. Something to keep people guessing."

My heart sinks, hating the reminder that no matter how amazing this feels, it isn't real.

"Oh. Right. Yeah, that's probably a good idea."

"So you'll come?" Flint asks.

I glance at my watch. It's just past two o'clock, but, according to Olivia, I still have an appointment at a salon for whatever makeover-ing they decide I need. I *do* want to talk to Flint, though. As nervous as the prospect makes me, I'll feel better if I have some clarity about what to expect moving forward. Fancy clothes are nice, but they won't matter at all if I'm so overwhelmed by everything else that I'm in a constant state of panic.

"It might be late," I say. "We aren't quite finished with everything."

"I don't mind late," he says quickly, almost *eagerly*. "I'll wait up."

I agree to Flint's plan, we say our goodbyes, then I hang up the call, his words echoing in my mind the entire time.

I'll wait up.

I look at myself in the mirror and study my reflection. He'll wait up for what?

For me? For this woman looking back at me?

Once upon a time, I used to dream about being the kind of woman who wore fancy dresses. Or even just *regular* dresses.

Anything even remotely cute or moderately fashionable would have been a step up from the practical, mostly frumpy clothes I wore.

I figured out by middle school that I didn't have a very strong sense of style, but more than that, I figured out that I didn't have the social skills that seemed to go along with being fashionable. You couldn't just have *the look*. You needed the personality to go along with it. The confidence. I didn't have either of those things, something that was made even more obvious as my twin sisters grew up. It didn't take long to realize that everything I lacked, they had in spades.

That's when I really gave up trying.

What did I know about putting together a cute outfit? And where would I even wear it if I did?

Attending a magnet high school for the smartest math and science kids in the entire state didn't help my cause. By college, I was settled into my ways. My clothes were functional. Practical. As boring as my nonexistent social life.

But the woman I'm looking at now?

She looks different.

Still like me. But maybe a little more like the me who used to look at the oversized blazers everyone wore to school and think, *what would I look like in one of those?*

I think she's been in there all along.

Maybe I just needed a nudge—or, you know, a free shopping spree in New York City—to wake her up again.

Still, the fashion isn't really the problem, is it?

I'm not so shallow to think that a new wardrobe will turn me into a different person. And I'm mature enough to recognize that I don't really *want* a relationship with someone who doesn't like me for who I am—nerdy job, lack of social skills, and all.

But I've only been myself when interacting with Flint. I've been *dressed* like myself. He doesn't know a lot about my job, but he knows I was willing to sneak onto his property disguised as a bush.

Could he actually like me?

Or is this just part of the charade?

Either way, it shouldn't matter. Flint is a movie star. I know what his life is, and I'm not supposed to like him back.

Which is troubling.

Because I definitely already do.

Chapter Eighteen
Flint

I'VE BEEN WAITING FOR Audrey for hours, anticipating her arrival, and I'm still not prepared to see her standing on my doorstep, looking like some kind of vision ripped directly out of my private fantasy.

The first time I saw Audrey outside the Feed 'n Seed, I noticed her—her eyes, in particular.

Then I actually met her and got to know her a little bit, and she only became more attractive. Even in her cargo pants and T-shirts, her hair swept back in practical ponytails, her face completely bare. I even thought she was cute when she was dressed up like a shrub.

But now?

I don't know what to think. How to breathe.

I definitely don't know how to *talk.* "Hi," I croak out, my hand still gripping the front doorknob. "You look...*Wow.*"

I am a fumbling mess, and I don't even care. Any man in this position would be.

Audrey lifts a hand to her hair, which is down, falling around her shoulders in loose waves, and runs her fingers through the glossy strands. Her eyes drop to the floor, like she's nervous, or at least uncomfortable, and I do my best to rein in my reaction. The last thing I want to do is make her feel like new clothes and hair make her any more worthy of attention than she was before.

"That's not to say...I mean, you always looked..." *Oh man. Abort! Abort! This is not going well.* "I just mean you look nice. That's all."

I finally step back from the door and gesture into the house. "Come on in."

She follows me into the living room and drops her bag onto a chair. Her hands move to the skirt of her dress, smoothing it down, and I do my best to keep my eyes on her face and not her long, shapely legs. "It's fine if you say something about how different I look," she says, lifting her gaze to meet mine. "I looked in the mirror, Flint." She looks down at her dress and holds her arms out to the side, lifting them just slightly. "It's pretty drastic, right?"

I push my hands into my pockets. "You look beautiful," I say. "Truly."

She rolls her eyes. "You're just saying that because you have to," she says.

"Why would I have to?"

She waves her hands in front of her like she's trying to emphasize her point. "You know. The whole fake girlfriend thing. The charade. Telling me I'm beautiful—that's what a boyfriend would say."

I lift my eyebrows and look around the room. "There's not anyone else here for us to fool, Audrey."

She drops onto the couch with a tiny, adorable huff. "I know that. But I guess I figured you were just, I don't know, practicing?"

I sit down on the opposite end of the couch, angling myself so I'm facing her. "There are probably things that we *should* practice," I say. I lean forward and clasp my hands together, resting my elbows on my knees. "But Audrey, if we're alone, if there's no one else who can see us or hear us and interpret our interactions, it's important to me that you know—I won't lie to you. I won't pretend."

She nods and bites her lip. "Okay. That's good to know."

"I really do think you look beautiful right now."

She takes a deep breath. "My eyebrows are still sore from the torture they put me through at the salon. I'm surprised I have any eyebrows left."

I grin. "Does it make you feel better or worse about the suffering to know I thought you were just as beautiful before?"

She raises one of her perfectly sculpted eyebrows. "You really thought I was beautiful before? Even when I was wearing my bush hat?"

"Especially when you were wearing your bush hat."

She shakes her head and lifts her hands to her cheeks. "That feels like a lifetime ago. So much has happened since then. I mean, for me, anyway. It probably doesn't feel that way for you."

I hold her gaze for a long moment. "No, it feels that way for me, too."

There's a question in her eyes, and I wish I had some way to answer it. But I don't have any more clue what's happening between us than she does. I just know I really like sitting here across from her.

"Flint, thank you for today," she says, her voice soft. "It was pretty magical. And your family was amazing."

Heat spreads through my chest. "You're welcome. I'm glad you had a good time." My hand twitches with the desire to reach out and touch her, and I curl my palms into fists. If this keeps up, I might have to sit on my hands.

"So," she finally says, her fingers curling over the tops of her knees. "Do you want to take the picture first?"

"Right. Yes. Let's do that." I grab my phone off the coffee table, happy to have somewhere to direct the energy coursing through me.

It's just past eight, and the sun has finally disappeared, leaving a sky streaked with red, yellow, and orange. "Actually, this is probably the perfect time to do it. Look at that sky."

Audrey moves to the window. "It's beautiful."

"Wait. Stop right there. Can I take your picture?"

She turns and looks over her shoulder, her lips curving into a soft smile.

My heart might as well be out of my body and on the floor.

"Looking out the window?" she says, turning back to face the sunset.

"That's perfect."

I watch her a moment, and she lifts her hand to her hair, brushing it to the side so I can see the long column of her neck. One arm rests on top of her head, her hair cascading down from her hand, and I snap the picture. When I pull it up to see if it works, I almost start to laugh. With the fading evening light, the sunset view over the mountains, and her silhouette in front of the window, it looks like a shot out of a magazine.

I walk over and stand beside her, showing her the photo. "You're a natural."

She takes my phone. "What? That's not me. How did you even do that?"

"You did it," I say, taking the phone as she hands it back. "All I did was push the button." I pull up my Instagram account. "Are you okay if I post this?"

She nods, so I upload the photo and add a quick caption. *"Enjoying the view of her enjoying the view..."* I say out loud as I type. I show it to her. "Does that work?"

She lets out a tiny chuckle. "I like the hint of word play." She licks her lips, and I force my eyes away from them. I can't start thinking about kissing this woman. Not when we still have so much that we need to discuss. *Including kissing.* Will she be willing? Do I even want her to be if it isn't real?

"There. Posted." I toss my phone onto a nearby chair, determined not to touch it again. Simon will see the post and know how to field any questions or inquiries it triggers. For now, my part is done.

"Now what?" Audrey asks.

"Now we talk details."

She nods and follows me back to the couch. I start by going over the schedule in detail, using the outline Joni dropped off earlier. The plan now is that we'll fly into LAX together and make sure we walk through the airport holding hands. Simon will tip off a couple of photographers about when we'll be arriving just to make sure my presence—and the fact that I'm not alone—is noted by the press. The press junket will start early the following morning with a round of interviews, followed by the premiere that evening, then a panel discussion with the entire cast, hosted by UCLA and open to the press, the following morning. "We'll make sure you're around during the junket," I say. "Visible to reporters, but not on camera. I'll decline to comment directly on our relationship, but we'll make it clear through our interactions that we're together."

"Right. But what does that mean, exactly? *How* will we show them?" She fidgets with the hem of her dress, folding it up accordion style, then smoothing it out again.

"We don't have to do anything that makes you uncomfortable, but I was thinking we'd just touch each other a lot, hold hands. Maybe I'll whisper things into your ear every once in a while."

She nods, but she doesn't look up.

I wait, sensing she wants to say something, but nothing comes.

"Hey." I reach over and touch her knee, my fingers lingering just long enough for me to notice the silky softness of her skin. "It doesn't have to be that way. If anything makes you uncomfortable, it's off the table. You could tell me you've changed your mind altogether, and I'd say okay, no questions asked."

She lets out a little laugh. "You just spent a billion dollars on me today. I'm not backing out."

"Not quite a billion dollars. But okay. Then tell me what works for you."

She's quiet for a long moment before she stands up and holds out her hand.

I slip my fingers into hers, and she tugs me up so we're standing directly across from each other, no more than a foot of space between us.

"Show me?" she says, her voice soft. "If I just try to imagine what this is going to be like, my brain will spiral and come up with all kinds of uncomfortable possibilities. But if you show me, I'll know exactly what to expect."

"Show you how we'll touch?"

She nods, her expression serious. If she were any other woman, I might think she was trying to take advantage of the moment, but Audrey isn't messing around. She really wants to know. More than that, I think she *needs* to know.

I reach over and slip her hands into mine, entwining our fingers. "So, we might hold hands like this," I say, my voice low. "And whenever we're together, we'll stand close, like there's some sort of magnetic pull constantly tugging us closer."

That feeling isn't hard to imagine at all because it's what I *actually* feel every time Audrey is near. But I don't say that out loud. Something tells me that particular truth would make her run out the door and never look back.

"Okay, what else?" she says.

I lift her hand and press it to my chest, flattening her palm just over my heart. "You might put your hand here, while we're talking, or place it on my shoulder."

She slides her hand up, but then she keeps going, moving it up and around to the top of my neck where her fingers tangle in my hair. "How's this?" she asks on a whisper.

I swallow against the knot forming in my throat. "Yeah, that's—that works."

I lift my free hand to her waist and slip it around to the small of her back, tugging her against me. She drops my other hand and lifts hers to my shoulder, sliding it around until her fingers are clasped behind my neck.

We're standing *so close,* our bodies practically flush, and I'm about to completely lose my mind. She's all I can see, all I can smell, all I can feel.

I want her.

The feeling is sharp—a burning intensity that rushes through me like a roaring forest fire but then quickly settles into my heart with a frightening certainty.

I want her, but more than that, it feels *right* to want her. To hold her like this.

It feels like we belong together.

Audrey looks up and meets my eye. I don't know a lot about makeup, but whatever she's wearing, it makes her eyes look twice as big and twice as blue.

"Will I need to kiss you?" she asks. "Will that be part of what we do to convince everyone we're together?"

If it's even possible, my heart starts pounding even faster. "Would you be okay with that?"

She bites her lip, and her eyes drop, a light flush climbing up her cheeks. "I don't know how to kiss a movie star, Flint."

I tighten my hold on her, and she yields willingly, her body melting against mine. "Don't think of me that way. Just think of me as a guy who likes to landscape his yard and work in his garden and hang out with his siblings. Think of me as an uncle who really loves his nieces and nephews and a son who still calls his mom once a week."

Her gaze drops to my lips, but I don't move. There's still a question in her eyes—a question that I don't have. I'm all in. Ready to kiss her *for real.* But if this is going to happen, it will happen because she chooses it. Because she wants it.

She leans up, her head tilting just slightly, and I bend down to meet her. My nose brushes against hers, a whisper of a touch, but then she sucks in a deep breath and pulls away. Her hands fall from my body, and she backs up before turning and pacing across the living room, one hand pressed to her stomach.

She spins back around to face me, fire blazing in her eyes. "What are we doing, Flint? What was that?" She shakes her head, like she can't make sense of the situation, but then words start to tumble out of her. "We were *practicing.* You were showing me how things were going to be when we're *faking* a relationship." Her hands lift to her hips. "And then we almost...and we can't. That's not..." She props her hands on her hips, and I get the sense that wherever she's going, I need to let her get there before I interrupt.

"You're telling me to think of you as just a normal guy, but this isn't a normal situation. We're going to *Hollywood* so I can pose on the red carpet as your *fake girlfriend*. There's nothing normal about that."

I brace my hands on the back of the couch. She's right. But nothing about almost kissing her was fake. At least not for me.

"I know you aren't *just* a movie star. I do," she says. "But I have to think of you that way. It's the only way I can protect myself." Her shoulders slump, and she wraps her arms around her middle, hugging herself. I barely resist the urge to go to her, to pull her into a real embrace. But her words stop me in my tracks.

She wants to protect herself? From me? From having feelings for me?

"You have fifty-six million Instagram followers, Flint," she says. "Everywhere you go, people recognize you."

"That's true," I say slowly. "But Audrey, it isn't who I am." I wince at the words because even as I say them, they don't quite feel true. I hate it, but it's the truth whether I like it or not. "It isn't *all* I am," I correct, but even this amendment doesn't feel like enough.

"I get that," she says softly. "And I believe you. But that doesn't change your reality. The people, the paparazzi, the attention. I spent some time watching videos last night. Interviews you've done. And the crowds, the way everyone screams at you, clamors for your attention. I don't know how you do it. I'll get through the premiere, and I'll be fine. Because I'll know what to expect. I'll know what's at stake. But it will probably take me a week to recover. You'll see what I mean. I'm not...*equipped*."

I've made a career out of studying body language, paying attention to the tiny nuances, the almost imperceptible movements that tell a story ten times more powerful than the actual words we say. And what Audrey's body language is telling me now is that she's afraid.

But afraid of what? My fans? My feelings? Or is it her *own* feelings?

"You're not equipped to have a *real* relationship?" I ask slowly, wanting to make sure we're on the same page.

She shrugs. "Did I misread what that was? Almost kissing you. That didn't feel fake to me."

The fact that she's willing to own it, admit it, instead of hiding her feelings makes me like her even more. Which sucks since she's in the process of telling me that, despite whatever connection we clearly have, she doesn't want to give us a shot.

Still, there's no point in denying that I'm picking up on it too.

"It didn't feel fake to me either." I move to the couch and sit down. "So where does that leave us?"

She drops down beside me. "We get through the premiere. Play our parts. Silence Claire. Save your movie."

I nod, chuckling over her very frank summary. I lean forward to prop my elbows on my knees. "Then what happens?"

She shrugs. "Everything goes back to the way it was before. You go back to your life, and I go back to mine."

"What about your squirrels? You won't ever come back to check on them?"

She breathes out a weary sigh. "I'm not saying we'll never see each other again; I'm just saying we can't...that I don't want..."

I move a hand to her knee. "Hey. It's okay," I say gently. "I get it."

She lifts her eyes to mine. "You do?"

"I won't pressure you into anything you don't want, Audrey. That was never my goal."

She wraps her arms around her waist, and for a moment, it almost looks like a flash of disappointment crosses her features. "That's good. Great," she says. "I appreciate that."

"Are you sure you're still comfortable coming to California with me?"

She nods. "Of course I am. I made a commitment. And everything we—" She waves a hand in front of her, and I notice a slight tremble. "All of the touching. All of that is fine." She lifts her chin. "And kissing too, if we need to. I can—we can—whatever we need to do."

"I don't think we will *have* to, necessarily," I say, trying to keep the disappointment out of my voice. "But it would probably help."

"Let's plan on it, then," she says, her tone growing more and more business-like.

If I could see inside her brain, I'm pretty sure I'd find an army of construction workers building a brick wall, thick and impenetrable, its sole purpose to separate *me* from Audrey.

It occurs to me that even if she's willing, I'd rather *not* kiss Audrey than only kiss her because we're pretending. Now that I want to kiss her for real, anything else somehow feels cheap. Not to mention torturous. Nothing like having a small taste of something you really want but can't actually have.

"If it's absolutely necessary," I say, knowing I'll do everything in my power to make sure it isn't.

Simply put, I like her too much.

We're quiet for a long, awkward moment—so awkward that I expect Audrey to flee at any time. There's dinner in the kitchen, and a movie cued up for us to watch after we eat. But something tells me Audrey isn't going to want to stay. Not unless I do something to recover the mood and steer us back onto "friendly" ground.

A part of me wants to just let her go. Give myself the chance to wallow and lick my wounds. I didn't come right out and tell Audrey how I'm feeling, but I definitely implied it.

But a bigger part of me—probably the stupid part—still wants her to stay. This is a big and stupid lonely house, and I like Audrey's company. I just need to reframe how I see her. Somehow knock her back into the friendship zone.

It'll take some acting. Luckily, I have some experience with that.

I give my shoulders a little shake and nudge her knee with mine, willing my expression into something light and friendly. "Hey," I say, reaching out and giving her shoulders a gentle squeeze before dropping my hands back to my side. "It's okay," I say. "I'm okay. I'm grateful you're willing to do this, and I'm happy to do it as friends." I hold her gaze. "*Just* friends."

"I think that would be best," she says softly. "I'm glad you understand."

I lift a shoulder. "Actually, I think you're probably right," I lie. "Our worlds are completely different. We're probably saving ourselves a lot of trouble by getting this sorted out now."

She nods, but she's still frowning. "Right. Definitely."

I look over my shoulder toward the kitchen. "I promised you dinner," I say. "Will you stay? I was thinking we could eat while we watch a movie."

A flash of trepidation crosses her features, and her eyes cut to the front door before darting back to me.

"As friends, Audrey. I promise. I have no ulterior motive here. I just enjoy your company, and I'd like you to stay." My words sound so convincing, I almost believe them myself.

Except that isn't quite good enough. I have to make myself believe them. Find a way to be content if Audrey is only ever my friend.

She nods. "Okay. I'd like that. I like the sound of *friends*."

I lead her to the kitchen, willing, even if begrudgingly, to make this new dynamic work. Things are awkward at first, but then we both start to relax, falling into the same easy pattern we had when we were in the pool. Conversation comes easily, energy buzzing between us, and Audrey's smiles come quickly and frequently. We eat sitting at the island in my kitchen, our knees close together under the bar, and every time Audrey gets up—to get a napkin, to refill her water glass, to grab a second piece of bread—she touches my shoulder as she passes by. I'm not even sure she realizes she's doing it. Either way, it confirms my earlier suspicion. She might be afraid, fighting whatever this is, but it *is* something. She feels the pull, too.

And that thought fills me with a potent (and dangerous) emotion. At least when it comes to Audrey.

Hope.

Chapter Nineteen

Audrey

I DON'T EVEN KNOW what happened.

One second, I was inches away from kissing Flint Hawthorne, from letting my heart give in to whatever was happening between us. Then the next, I was caught in a nearly blinding panic.

Suddenly, all I could see was a future of photographers scrambling to take Flint's picture everywhere we went. Of fans wanting to talk to him, touch him, write *fanfiction* about him. Then I spiraled into thinking about what those fans might think of *me*. Would they judge me? Criticize my hair? My wardrobe? My career choices? Would they dig up old pictures from my high school yearbook and wonder why Flint Hawthorne was dating someone so completely nerdy?

The thought of all that attention, all that *noise* in my life. It was too much.

So I pushed away.

And it was the right thing to do.

Wasn't it?

I do not want to date a man well-known enough for Ann down at the Feed 'n Seed to put his face on a cookie.

I want a normal life. A *simple* life.

I mean, yes. I actually *did* have a good time on Saturday night. Once we decided that our evening wouldn't involve any kissing.

We ate, we laughed, we talked for an hour before we finally settled in to watch a movie, a drama about a wildlife biologist who gets trapped in the Amazon and survives on her own for three weeks before she's rescued.

Flint was right. I *did* like the movie. From beginning to end. It was thoughtful and informative and, according to the research I did after I came home, mostly historically accurate. I mean, I'm not fully converted. But I'm at least willing to acknowledge there might be *some* movies out there that aren't a waste of my time.

Though, let's be honest. I could have sat on the couch and watched *Sesame Street* for two hours as long as Flint was beside me.

Which is why all of this feels so complicated.

I don't want to like Flint.

I shouldn't like Flint.

Everything logical and practical and smart tells me that liking him would be a *very* bad idea.

But I *do* like him. When I'm around him, none of those practical reasons seems to matter.

I've seen him half a dozen times in the five days that have passed since last Saturday—don't judge, those squirrels are *really* interesting—and every time, it's harder and harder to see him as anything but a normal guy. Well, not normal exactly. He's much too charming to be normal. Charming, handsome, funny, thoughtful. He's basically perfect. And *perfect* and *normal* don't feel like they belong in the same sentence. I just mean it's hard to think of him as a celebrity. Because around me, he really doesn't act like one.

I zip up my last suitcase and slide it off the bed, setting it by the door. Joni came over to help me pack earlier this morning and *good grief* she has me bringing way more than I actually think I'm going to need. The only thing I didn't have to pack was my gown for the premiere, which Remy promised me would be pressed and perfect and hanging in my hotel room by the time I arrive.

My sisters swooned over my new wardrobe for hours, begging and bartering for the chance to borrow the things they love the most. I'm taller than my sisters. I have broader shoulders and bigger boobs, but there are a few things, the dresses and a couple of the jackets, that will work for them.

They didn't even really need to beg. It's not like I'll spend a lot of time wearing these things anyway. At least not after this weekend. Last time I checked, my grad assistants, and the state forest rangers who share my lab space don't care what I wear to work.

The squirrels definitely don't.

I just have to get through the next few days. Attend the events. Fake it with Flint. Then come back to Silver Creek. To my normal life in my normal town.

Let's not talk about the fact that I'll probably still *see* Flint after this week. He lives here, after all, and if I'm ever in the forest, there's a good chance I'll run into him.

But he can't stay in Silver Creek forever. Eventually, he'll have another movie to film. He'll jet off to some faraway location where he'll fall in love with a Brazilian bombshell who loves the limelight and would like nothing more than to bask in his celebrity for the rest of her days.

A pulse of irritating jealousy rushes through me. Which is just *stupid*. I'm not even supposed to like the man, and I'm jealous of a woman my brain just created all by itself?

Maybe I'm worse off than I thought.

"Hey, you ready to go?" Summer says from the doorway of my bedroom. "Flint just pulled up outside."

"He's driving?" I ask.

"Yep. His very pretty truck. Looks like he's alone."

"Well, we aren't traveling alone, so that's weird."

Summer shrugs. "Maybe you're meeting the rest of his team at the airport?"

Summer seems so calm about this. Talking about Flint's *team* like it's perfectly normal for someone to travel with an entourage. In the week since I had dinner with Flint, or as my rebellious body likes to remind me, the night when we *almost* kissed, my sisters have grown more comfortable with the idea of me spending so much time with a movie star. Or maybe they just got tired of my shutting down their attempts to talk about him *constantly*.

Either way, I'm glad today doesn't feel like some ridiculous send-off. I'm just a girl going to the airport. That's all.

"I'm ready," I say, picking up my shoulder bag, some butter-soft extravagance that I picked up in New York.

The only reason I caved and let Olivia add it to the stack of clothes I was already embarrassed to be buying was because it's vegan leather. I'm not anti-leather. But I maybe *am* anti-leather-that-costs-two-thousand dollars. This was a fraction of that amount, but it still feels soft and luxurious and, bonus, it's pretty practical. Big enough to hold a book and my water bottle and my iPad, should I have any need to work or do research while I'm gone.

Summer grabs my suitcase, which is also new (don't judge—I know it's ridiculous), and I grab my carry-on, following her to the living room. By the time we open the front door, Flint is already on the porch.

Summer lets out a little gasp when he smiles at her. "Summer?" he clearly guesses—there's no way he can tell my sisters apart—and Summer grins.

"Excellent guess," she says.

"I figured I had a fifty/fifty chance," he says easily. He turns to look at me. "Hey," he says easily. "You look good."

"Thanks. Are Nate and Joni not coming?"

"They're already at the airport. There was some sort of trouble with our connecting flight, and Joni thought she'd have an easier time working out the details in person."

"Oh. We're flying commercial?" The question sounds so completely pretentious, it almost makes me wince, but we definitely didn't fly commercial on our way to New York, so I'd expected it would be the same this time, too. "Not that I mind," I quickly say. "Of course I don't mind. Seeing as how I've flown on a private jet exactly one time, I don't exactly have grounds to simply *expect* it. Who even does that? Just assumes they get to travel on a private jet—*annnd* I'm rambling," I say. "I'll shut up now."

Flint reaches for the biggest suitcase.

"Be careful, that one's heav..." Summer's words trail off as Flint lifts the suitcase like I packed it with feathers and slides it into the back of his truck. "Or not so heavy," she says under her breath.

"I almost always fly commercial." He comes back for my carry-on bag. "All those CO_2 emissions for one guy feels a little excessive."

Summer grabs my arm and gasps. "Audrey! He speaks your language."

I shrug out of her grip and shoot her a look that says *shut up right now or I'm evicting you out of my basement,* but only because that's an easy distraction from the fact that Flint Hawthorne actually cares about CO_2 emissions, and that's doing crazy things to my heart.

"The private jet was a luxury just for you," he says, and Summer sighs. "Now he's speaking *my* language."

I grab the last of the suitcases and follow Flint. "Tell Lucy I said goodbye?" I say over my shoulder, ignoring her last comment. "I'll text you both and let you know I've arrived safely."

Summer shrugs. "Sure. But don't worry. If we don't get a text, we'll just turn on TMZ and wait for you to show up."

"TM-what?"

"It's a gossip—you know what? Never mind. Just text us," Summer says.

I'm buckled into the passenger seat, my bag at my feet, before Flint and I speak again. He looks over at me, and I reach over and press a hand to his cheek. "It's really growing in."

His facial hair has been a hot topic lately. He hasn't shaved all week, his attempt to disguise his face for our trek through the airport. At first, I didn't understand. The whole point of our trip is for us to be *seen*. But Flint assured me we'll be seen regardless of facial hair. "Lots of people will recognize me no matter what," he told me. "But we still have to make it through security and walk through the airport without getting mobbed. It's all about balance."

"It's itchy," Flint says. "I'm shaving the second we get to LA."

"I really like it," I say. "I think it makes you look mysterious."

His lips lift into an easy grin. "My brothers say it makes me look like I'm trying too hard."

"They do not."

He shrugs as he backs out of my driveway. "They like to keep me humble."

"They're crazy. It looks really good on you," I say, because it really does. He's got a good jawline, so he's ridiculously handsome either way, but as a woman who loves the outdoors, this slightly more rugged look on Flint is really doing it for me.

"Yeah?" He looks genuinely pleased by this, which surprises me but still makes me smile.

Before this summer, I'd never given a thought to what it might be like to be a celebrity, but after meeting Flint, finding out about his fame, his money, the never-ending attention that's thrown his way, I somehow assumed he must never feel insecure or lack confidence. With so much evidence of his success constantly surrounding him, how could he? These tiny moments, when he seems less superstar and more human, are nice to see.

Which is funny, really. When we first met, and my sisters completely freaked out, I was the one who insisted that he's just a man. I don't love how little it took to make me forget. One private plane ride to New York City, and I started seeing a *movie star* too.

An uncomfortable feeling niggles at the back of my mind.

Is that what I did when I pulled away from him last weekend? When I stopped him from kissing me? I saw him as a celebrity instead of a man?

"Flint, is it hard?" I blurt out, and he tosses me a quick glance before turning his eyes back to the road.

"Is what hard?"

I shrug. "I don't know. Living like this. Growing a beard to make it through the airport without getting mobbed. Spending a small fortune to outfit a woman just so she can pretend to be your girlfriend?"

He smiles. "Geez, Audrey," he says, his voice teasing. "Want to make me sound a little more desperate?"

I grin, glad that he's at least willing to joke about it. "If it matters, I *really* love my new wardrobe."

"That does matter," he says. "I'm glad you do."

"I do feel obligated to tell you that we'll have to stay in California for at least three weeks for me to wear every single thing Olivia bought. Or, *you* bought. As it were."

"I figured. I knew what I was doing when I asked my sisters to go along."

"That was really sweet of you. I think I would have been overwhelmed doing all of it by myself. But what I meant was, is it hard being famous?"

He shrugs. "Yes and no. I'm kind of built to like the attention—it's just the way my personality is—but sometimes the lack of privacy is tough. It's why I moved back home. Things are infinitely easier in North Carolina than they are in LA. But I try not to dwell on the negatives. I get to do what I love. Not a lot of people can say that, so it doesn't feel right to complain."

"I feel that way about my job sometimes," I say. "Once, I was out early in the morning collecting water samples from the creek that cuts across the bottom of your property—this was before you bought it—and I saw a doe and two fawns cross the path in front of me. The sun was filtering down through the trees, and the air was still and quiet and peaceful, and I just thought, *this is my job.* I actually get paid to be out here, to experience this magic. I felt pretty lucky."

He's quiet for a beat before he says, "I really am sorry I bought your research forest out from under you."

I shrug. "The university would have sold it anyway. Better it went to you instead of someone building mountain condominiums or something else ridiculous. I know I was mad at first, but I definitely prefer what you've done."

"Oh hey, I almost forgot," he says. "I got a couple new pictures for you this morning."

I sit up a little taller. "Of the squirrels?"

He nods. "There was a fourth one with them this morning, and I don't think I've seen this one before. His tail looks a little bushier than the other two."

"You can tell them apart?"

He smiles. "I couldn't at first, but I like watching them. And the more I do, the easier it gets." He nods toward his phone sitting in the center console. "Here. You can just pull them up if you want. They're the most recent photos in my Favorites album."

I reach for his phone, then hold it up to his face to unlock the screen. It only takes a little bit of scrolling to find his photos and pull up his favorites.

"See how the one on the left has a tiny gray spot between his eyes?" he says. "I've been calling him Coal Dust. The one on the left I'm calling Colleen."

"Colleen? What kind of a name is that?"

"Are you kidding? It's a perfect name. She looks like a Colleen. Don't tell me you don't see it."

I chuckle as I swipe to the next picture. "And this is the new one?" This photo is of a slightly smaller squirrel with a much bushier tail.

"Yeah. I haven't named him yet. But he's new, right? Have you seen him before?"

"I'll have to compare to my photos just to be sure, but I don't think so."

I scroll through the photos one more time, but then I swipe one too many times, and a new photo comes up. My breath freezes in my throat. The photo is of me, clearly taken that day we were in the pool together, only in this photo, my face is visible. I'm smiling, one hand lifting my wet hair off my neck and holding it up in a makeshift ponytail, and I'm looking over my shoulder with an expression that seems just on the verge of laughter.

Flint looks over and must see why I've fallen silent. "Oh, geez, Audrey. I'm sorry. That—I should have asked before I kept it. I just thought—" His words cut off, and he lifts a hand off the steering wheel to run it through his hair. He swears softly. "I must look like such a creep."

I breathe out a chuckle. "I knew you were taking my picture, Flint. It's okay."

He nods. "I just—" He clears his throat. "I really love that photo of you."

I swallow. *He loves a photo of me?*

A rush of heat flies through my body, reaching all the way out to my fingertips and down to my toes. Logically, I know it's only a surge of adrenaline and norepinephrine that's making my skin feel tingly and hot. It's hormones, not logic, and I shouldn't let it influence my thoughts.

But the guy saved a photo of me on his phone. He likes the way I look enough to save it and add it to his *favorites*.

"Thank you," I say softly. I breathe in, hoping he doesn't notice the way my words tremble. "It's okay that you saved it."

He lifts his brows, his eyes flashing with something that almost looks like hope, which shouldn't surprise me. Flint told me he was interested.

Or, he *sort of* told me. He told me that wanting to kiss me wasn't fake. Now that I really think about it, those two things aren't necessarily the same thing. He could absolutely want to kiss me without wanting to have a real relationship. But that doesn't feel quite right either. Flint doesn't really come across as the kind of guy who is into meaningless flings. I could be wrong—but I would be surprised if I am.

We park the truck in an overnight lot in front of the airport where Flint's brothers will pick it up later. Before climbing out, Flint puts on a baseball cap, then pulls his hoodie up *over* the hat. He slides on a pair of sunglasses to complete the look.

I've got to hand it to him. If I didn't know it was him, I might not recognize him. But then, I'm probably not the best judge since a month ago, I didn't even know who he was.

He pulls my suitcases out of the truck, as well as one of his own, and I begin to wonder how we're ever going to get all of this inside. But before I can even ask the question out loud, Nate appears with a luggage cart.

"Thanks, man," Flint says before helping Nate load everything up. He holds out his hand to me as we start to move, giving my fingers a quick squeeze as he laces his through mine. "Just trust me, okay? I'll get us through everything."

I nod, realizing that I *do* trust him.

And I might be more scared of that than I am the paparazzi.

Chapter Twenty

Audrey

It's the weirdest sensation.

Everyone is looking at us.

Flint keeps my hand held tightly in his, and Nate is a mountainous shadow hovering a few steps ahead, so I don't feel unsafe. But all the eyes—it's the most disconcerting thing I've ever felt.

In line at security, Flint pulls me close. "Audrey, stop looking at people, all right?" His words are gentle, not at all like a scolding, but my cheeks flush with heat anyway, though that could just be from his warm breath skating across my ear. "If you make eye contact, it invites conversation. And it only takes one person to approach for the dam to break, and then *everyone* will approach us, and we'll never make it to our gate."

I nod. "Right. That makes sense. No eye contact."

He wraps his arm around me and tugs me against his chest. His warm, solid, deliciously amazing chest. "Just keep looking at me," he says into my hair.

Behind us, someone calls out his name. I flinch and start to turn—a force of habit—and Flint's arm tightens around me. "Don't look," he whispers, and I relax back into him, slipping my arms around his waist so we're facing each other. I press my forehead against his chest and let out a little groan. "It wasn't even intentional. More like a reflex. How do you keep yourself from responding?"

"Lots of practice," he says. "You're doing an excellent job selling the girlfriend thing, by the way." His hands cinch a little tighter around my waist.

"Am I?"

"Mmhmm. You've basically got *me* convinced, and I already know you're faking."

There is something easy about standing like this in Flint's arms, and I find myself feeling disappointed when I have to let go long enough to walk through the security scanner.

The TSA officer on the other side of the scanner asks for a photo with Flint and he graciously obliges, putting a loose arm around her shoulder and leaning in while her co-worker takes the shot.

As soon as he returns to me, he slips my hand into his, then lifts it to his lips, pressing a kiss just above my knuckles.

And he thinks *I'm* good at selling the girlfriend thing? I am putty in this man's hands.

It's almost time to board, so I expect us to go straight to the gate, but as we pass one of those frequent flyer private travel lounges, Flint and I veer off from Nate and Joni and duck inside. The lounge is mostly empty—maybe a benefit of the time of day?—and Flint immediately pulls back his hood and removes his sunglasses.

"Not in a rush to board?"

He shakes his head. "Nate and Joni will board first and let the gate agents know we're on our way, then they'll text when the plane is mostly boarded so we don't have to sit there while everyone walks past us."

"Man, the things you have to think about."

His lips curve into the easy grin I'm beginning to love. "Are you hungry?" He looks around. "There are usually snacks in these things. And bathrooms, too. Nice, when you don't want to get cornered coming out of the stall."

My eyebrows shoot up. "Has that ever happened?"

"More times than I can count."

We walk together to a table full of snacks and iced beverages. Just beyond the table, there's a bartender serving an older gentleman a beer.

Flint lifts his hands to my shoulders, giving them a gentle squeeze. "We only have a few minutes, so I'm going to hit the bathroom while I can. Will you be okay here?" His eyes dart around the room like he's legitimately worried about my safety.

There's no one else even here, aside from the guy at the bar, but I appreciate his concern anyway. "I'll be fine," I say.

He leans forward and presses a kiss to my forehead. "Be right back."

I close my eyes for the briefest second. It would be so easy to just give in. To soak up his attention and wrap it around my heart. To chase away the fear that's currently acting as a giant barricade, and just *see what happens.*

Could I do it? Could I actually—

"Oh my gosh. Are you actually dating Flint Hawthorne? That's him, isn't it? I swear, if it isn't, your boyfriend could play his twin brother." The woman appeared out of nowhere—could she have truly entered the lounge just in the time I had my eyes closed?   and is standing uncomfortably close to me. The look of expectation on her face is strange. She doesn't just want an answer, she almost looks like she's *entitled* to one.

I know the whole purpose of this is to be *seen* as a couple. But does that really have to happen right this second?

I take a step backward. "Yeah, funny. He gets that a lot."

She frowns. "So, it *isn't* him?"

From the corner of my eye, I see Flint emerge from the bathroom. I take another step backward, away from the lady in front of me and toward Flint. "Sorry. I've got to go now."

She looks from me to Flint, and her expression shifts. "Shut. Up." She steps toward him. "It is him!" she squeals.

I turn and walk quickly now, grabbing the hand Flint is holding out as soon as I reach him. He looks over my shoulder, makes polite eye contact with the woman, says a quick, "Hi, there," then tugs me right out the door.

"She literally came out of nowhere," I say as we walk. "And she didn't even say hello. She just asked if my boyfriend was Flint Hawthorne."

"What did you say?"

"I was like, 'Yeah, funny. People make the comparison a lot."

He chuckles. "That one has actually worked for me a few times."

We approach the gate, and Flint slows. They're clearly already boarding, but there are still people everywhere. "Come here a sec," he says. He tugs me toward the wall and spins me so my back is against it, then hovers in front of me, his big body shielding me from view to anyone passing by. I lift my hands and press them into his chest, reveling in the warmth coming off him.

"What are we doing?" I whisper.

He smiles down at me. "We're hiding."

"Hmm. Do you do this often?"

"It's a little more awkward when I'm traveling alone," he says. He wraps his hands around my wrists and tugs them around his waist. "A guy standing against the wall all alone? That's a reason to worry. But now?" He leans down and brushes his nose along my cheek. "Now I just look like I'm getting a really fantastic goodbye kiss."

"It isn't goodbye if we're already through security." It's a stupid thing to say. But focusing on the logistics of airport goodbyes is the only thing keeping me from kissing him right now, which is a very alarming realization. I am exactly two hours into this entire fake dating scheme, and I'm ready to abandon all restraint and jump in?

"True," Flint says. "Stupid TSA has ruined so many potential grand gestures with their rules."

"Grand gestures? Is that a romance movie term?"

He chuckles. "Oh, Audrey. I have so much to teach you."

We stand like this, all wrapped up in each other, for another few minutes. Finally, Flint's phone buzzes in his pocket, and he pulls it out. "Okay. Nate says we're clear to board."

We walk hand in hand to the gate, where the waiting ticket agent smiles so broadly, it looks like her face might crack.

"It's a privilege to have you on board, Mr. Hawthorne," she says, her voice a little breathless.

Flint smiles easily. "Thanks, Marcy. I appreciate that."

We aren't two steps away when she calls after us and asks for a photo.

Of course, Flint seems happy to comply.

Again, I marvel that he handles everything so effortlessly.

We settle into our *very* comfortable seats at the front of the plane, and I do my best *not* to make eye contact with the women sitting across the aisle from us, who are openly gawking. Flint is next to the window, so I angle my body toward him. If I'm staring at him, I can't look at anyone else, even if I can *feel* eyes on my back.

I give my body a little shake, even as all the hairs on the back of my neck stand up. It's the most uncomfortable sensation, like tiny worms wriggling all over my skin. "Flint, I can literally feel people staring at us. How are you not squirming right now?"

"I promise you get used to it." He pulls out his AirPods. "Here. Put one of these in. I was thinking we could watch a movie together."

I make a face. "What kind of movie? Because I brought the latest edition of Wildlife Biology, and there's an article on evolutionary behavior that I am very excited to read."

"Uh, let's definitely do that, then. You could read it out loud to me."

If I didn't notice the way his lip twitched, I might have thought he was serious. But I'm learning this man's tells. Good actor or not, right now, I'm reading him loud and clear. I reach over and swat his chest. "Very funny, Mr. Hawthorne. But evolution is a very important subject."

"I don't doubt it," he says, his tone more serious. "But come on. This will be fun. I spent over an hour searching for the perfect movie to keep you entertained on the flight. And I really think you'll like this one."

"Fine," I say. "But later, I'm going to make you listen to my article."

"Sounds like a perfect bedtime story," he says. "It'll lull me right to sleep."

I roll my eyes at his joke, only momentarily distracted by the idea of going to bed with Flint. I'm positive Flint has zero expectations on that front. He's given me control of whether we even kiss. But to maintain the charade, his PR guy Simon says we need to stay in the same room. At the very least, we need to appear as though we're using the same bathroom, sleeping in the same bed. Otherwise, hotel staff might talk.

Apparently, it doesn't take much to motivate a hotel maid to sell a few lines to gossip magazines. And "Flint Hawthorne's girlfriend is sleeping in a different hotel room" would make a very juicy headline.

At least according to my sisters, who have dissected this entire situation inside and out.

After a flight attendant takes our drink orders, Flint turns on the movie, leans into the corner of his seat, then pulls me against him so I'm leaning against his chest. Like this, it's easier for me to hold the phone, so I take it from him, making it possible for him to secure his arms around my waist.

Okay. So there are definitely worse ways to sit on an airplane, even if, from this position, I can see the ladies across the aisle staring us down.

The women can't be much older than I am, and one of them is so blatantly ogling Flint that it makes my blood start to boil. Feeling surprisingly bold, I intentionally meet her gaze, lifting my eyebrows in a *do you have something to say* gesture.

The woman leans back the slightest bit and drops her eyes.

Behind me, Flint chuckles, his chest vibrating against me. "Well done," he whispers.

Not sure *actual for real* jealousy is necessary for a *fake* relationship, but if it's going to help sell it, well, might as well lean into how I'm feeling.

I tilt my head up and back and press a kiss to his jaw.

I feel more than I hear Flint take a stuttering breath when my lips press against him. His beard is sharp against my lips, but it's a rasp I'll take over and over if it means kissing him again.

Desire sparks in my gut, spreading outward, making me feel hot and tingly. I do my best to rein it in, both for the obvious reason—here is absolutely not the place—and the not-so-obvious.

Even if the not-so-obvious reasons are getting harder for me to remember.

The flight from Asheville to Atlanta is brief; there, we change planes for a longer flight directly to LAX. We repeat the same process we went through in Asheville, hiding out in a lounge until the plane is mostly boarded, then jumping on at the last minute. Flint poses for another photo with the gate agent and another with the first-class flight attendant before we're finally in our seats.

"Do you ever say no?" I ask him, and he shrugs.

"Not usually. Enduring fifteen seconds of posing for a photo is easier than dealing with people going online and telling all of Reddit that you're rude."

"People do that?"

He nods. "'Always be polite, always be respectful, always be generous with your time and energy.' Those are Simon's words. Says abiding by them will make his job a lot easier and my career a lot more successful."

Fortunately, there are a couple of businessmen sitting across from us on this flight, both of whom look like they couldn't care less about who Flint is or what movies he's starred in. I guess technically that means we don't have to lean into the faking, but that doesn't seem to stop Flint.

He must touch me a thousand different times in the almost five hours it takes us to get across the country. A steadying hand on my back when we hit a bit of turbulence. A nudge against my knee when something funny happens in the movie we finish on this flight because we didn't have time to get through it on the last one. An arm around my shoulders when the flight attendant gets particularly bold and asks if he's dating anyone.

I mean, does she think I'm his sister or something? Has she not noticed the *many, many* times we've touched throughout the flight?

Flint handles it like a pro, deflecting the question with an easy, "I'd rather not talk about my personal life, Jessica. I'm sure you understand." But then his arm was around me, his expression pointed as Jessica nodded and excused herself. Every time she passes by, he makes sure we're touching, at one point even pulling me in for a soft kiss just below my earlobe.

"You know, it's nice having you here," he says just before the flight lands. "Normally I keep Nate beside me to help fend off overeager fans, but you're a much more entertaining shield."

"I'm so glad I'm useful," I deadpan, and he grins.

"You're a lot more than useful," he says. "This is the best flight across the country I've ever had."

The mood stays light until we land at LAX. As the plane taxis to the terminal, Flint sobers quickly. He pulls on his hat but leaves his sunglasses off. "You don't want the full disguise?" I say, and he shakes his head.

Joni answers for him, leaning forward from where she and Nate are sitting behind us. "No disguises this time," she says.

"We need the photographers to get a clear shot of your face. There can't be any doubt that it's you."

Flint nods. "Have you heard from Jasper?"

Joni nods. "He'll be just outside security."

"Jasper?" I ask.

"One of the less despicable photographers in the business," she says, looking at me. "Audrey, you'll stay with Flint the entire time, all right? *Don't* let go of his hand, no matter what happens. Nate will stay just behind you on your other side, but people will still try to get close. Too close. Don't stop moving, don't make eye contact. Don't answer any of their questions, no matter what they say."

"Got it. Keep moving. No eye contact. No answers."

"And don't let go," she reiterates. "A car is already waiting outside. Nate will stay with you until you're safely inside the car, then we'll both come behind you as soon as we have your luggage. But no getting out at the hotel—"

"Until you catch up," Flint says, rolling his eyes. "Just like always."

"I was filling in Audrey as much as I was reminding you," Joni says. "One of these days, you're going to be grateful for all my nagging."

"I'm already grateful for your nagging, Joni." Flint squeezes my hand. "You ready to go?"

"Absolutely not," I say without missing a beat.

He smiles warmly. "You're going to do great."

Funny. I almost believe him.

Chapter Twenty-One

Flint

IT'S NOT LIKE I haven't walked through the airport before. I've dealt with the crowds. Listened to the questions thrown at me as I pass by. I've heard the click of a thousand cameras as they grab shot after shot and seen the cell phones lifted to record me.

But I've never done it with another person beside me.

When it's just me, I don't worry. I smile. Maybe even sign a few autographs. But this time? All I want to do is move. Get out of here as quickly as I can and keep Audrey safe.

Audrey is all tension. Her shoulders are tight, her steps stiff. Her hand is gripping mine so tightly, I can't even feel my fingers anymore. We're about to exit the terminal, and the crowd outside security will be much larger than the one here, where we're only dealing with ticketed passengers who happen to recognize me.

Out there? We'll find the people who *came* for me.

I have no idea how many other photographers Simon tipped off, but word tends to travel fast. And if anyone who saw us on earlier flights posted on social media, it won't just be photographers who are waiting, but fans. I'll never understand the lengths people will go to, researching flights, scouring the internet for any random mention that might give someone a clue about where and when I'm going to show up somewhere.

Audrey stumbles beside me, tugging at my hand just in time for me to reach over and stop her before she hits the ground. "Are you okay?" I steer her over to the wall, and Nate quickly steps up behind us, creating some semblance of a barrier between us and the passing crowd.

Audrey nods, even as she lifts her free hand, holding it up in between us. It's trembling like a leaf in the wind. "Sure. Totally fine."

I grab her hand and pull it to my lips, kissing it once, then again.

I never should have asked her to do this. "Hey." I drop her hands in favor of cradling her face, urging her to look right into my eyes. "It's going to be okay. Breathe with me." She nods, and together we take a slow, deep breath. "I've got you," I say. "I'm not going to let anything happen."

"Okay," she whispers. "Okay."

We've only made it fifty feet outside security before the voices start. At first, it's just people calling my name. Then the questions start.

Flint, who's your friend?

New girlfriend, Flint?

Are you cheating on Claire?

How long have you been together?

What does Claire think about you dating someone new?

I look for Jasper in the crowd and immediately spot his trademark bright red baseball cap. We make eye contact, and I slow, leaning down to whisper in Audrey's ear. "Look up and to the left just for a second," I say.

She does, and hopefully that means Jasper gets a shot of us both.

The crowd moves with us as we make it outside, closing in, despite Nate's attempts to keep everyone back. Now, people are yelling questions at Audrey.

What's your name, sweetheart?

How did you and Flint meet?

Have the two of you slept together yet?

I hear her gasp after this question, and I tighten my grip on her hand, tugging her into my side and wrapping an arm around her waist. "Just ignore them," I say close to her ear. "We're almost there."

Kenji is waiting in a dark SUV at the curb, just like Joni said he would be. He jumps out as we approach and opens the door, tilting his body to create as much of a shield as he can. With him on one side and Nate on the other, we're able to slip into the car with relative ease. It's hard to believe, but Kenji is even bigger than Nate. He's got the shoulders of an NFL linebacker, but he's got as much aggression in his entire body as I have in my pinky finger. I've never seen the man get ruffled. It's why I like working with him so much. He just takes everything in stride. Once we're inside the car, Kenji jumps in behind us as Nate moves back into the crowd to find Joni and retrieve our luggage.

Audrey exhales, her shoulders sagging into the seatback. "That was insane," she says.

"More insane than usual," I agree. I look at Kenji. "What's going on today?"

"You're going on, man," he says easily. "Some big-time influencer posted a picture of you two snuggled up on the airplane, and it only took about five seconds to go viral." He leans over me and extends a hand to Audrey. "I'm Kenji. Nice to finally meet you."

"I've heard a lot about you," she says.

Kenji lifts his expression to me, an eyebrow cocked. "Don't worry. I only told her that you're bigger than a tree but sweeter than a kitty cat. I didn't reveal any of your scariest secrets."

Kenji shrugs. "Just so long as you remember that no matter how much dirt you have on me, I will *always* have more on you." He pulls up his phone and navigates to *People* magazine's website. The headline is big and bold, in bright red letters. *Flint Hawthorne in Love?* "If you wanted the world to know you have a girlfriend who isn't Claire McKinsey? Well, you've done it."

Kenji's tone isn't exactly judgmental, but it doesn't need to be. He was never in favor of this whole scheme, not from the first time Simon mentioned it.

As I look at Audrey's drawn expression, noting the dark circles under her eyes, I have to wonder if he's right.

Not for the first time, I wonder what would have happened—if *anything* would have happened—had I never asked Audrey to come to LA. What if I'd just asked her out? Expressed an interest and told her I wanted to take her to dinner?

Just like every other time I've asked myself the question, doubt roars up to squelch the idea. I may not like the idea of lying to everyone, but the reality is, Audrey wouldn't have said yes had all I done was ask her out. For exactly the chaos we've just endured. She would never choose this.

She would never choose *me.*

For that reason, I have to be grateful Joni took Simon's hair-brained idea and turned it into something I could actually swallow.

It's bought me time with Audrey, and I'll never regret that.

Whether it will make a difference in how the press handles the movie, that's still up for debate. The pictures of Audrey on my

Instagram account have put a stop to Claire's veiled comments and innuendo, but for how long? If this business has taught me anything, it's that you only have so much control over any story, and things can spin out of control at any moment. The best I can do is hold on for the ride.

"Oh, heads up," Kenji says. "Mark Sheridan will be at the premiere tomorrow night. His RSVP came in late, but he'll be there."

I sit up a little taller in my seat, angling my body so I can better look at Kenji—no small feat seeing as how he fills up half the backseat all by himself. "He'll be there? Should I take that as a good sign?"

Kenji shrugs. "I don't think it's a bad one."

"Mark Sheridan?" Audrey asks, leaning around me to look at Kenji. "He's the one who did the documentary on offshore drilling."

Kenji's eyebrows go up. "Most people know him for his multiple Oscars, but sure. Off-shore drilling."

"He actually *won* one of those Oscars for the offshore drilling documentary," I say, and Kenji lifts a hand in acknowledgment. "But the most important thing," I say, looking back at Audrey, "is that he's the executive producer for a movie I really want to work on. If he's here, I can only hope he's interested in meeting me in person."

"This isn't the one you just had a meeting about the other day? The one you're producing?"

I shake my head. "Something different. That one is already a sure thing."

She nods. "Sounds like a big deal."

"It's a great role. It's thoughtful. A little cerebral. And it's a *tough* character. But *gah*—when I read the script, it felt right in my bones, you know?"

Audrey reaches over and squeezes my hand, her lips lifting into a smile that sends a bolt of heat straight to my heart. "I like it when you talk about your work," she says.

I hold her gaze. "You do? You know my work is *movies,* right?"

She rolls her eyes and tries to tug her hand away. "You make me sound like such a troll. I've watched *two* movies with you now, and I loved them both. So there."

I grin and hold her hand a little tighter. She's not about to get away from me. "Two down, only thousands more to go."

"The point," she says, wagging a playful finger in front of my face, "is that you light up when you talk about acting. I can tell you really love it. I'm just saying that's fun to see."

"Well, we want him to light up for this role," Kenji says. "It's the kind that could land him another Oscar nod. Maybe even a win."

I settle back into my seat, loving the way Audrey leans into me, her body flush against mine. "Only if I do it justice."

"For now, just focus on making a good impression when you meet Sheridan," Kenji says.

I nod. "I can do that. What time do we start tomorrow?"

"Early," Kenji says. "Eight a.m. Interviews will run until four, then you'll have a couple hours free before you walk the red carpet at six p.m. sharp." He looks from me to Audrey, then back again. "You're going to feel jetlagged in the morning, and you always get puffy when you're jetlagged. Stay in tonight. Even if Simon asks. And no alcohol. Alcohol also makes you look puffy."

Audrey snickers beside me, and I nudge her knee with mine.

"Simon will definitely ask," I say, knowing my publicist well enough to sense exactly where his priorities are.

"He will. And he'll probably want you to show up somewhere Claire is going to be." Kenji looks toward Audrey. "Don't let him cave, Audrey. Simon is very persuasive. Keep him in tonight. Tomorrow's a big day. You both need to rest up."

Audrey nods, but Kenji has nothing to worry about. I can't imagine wanting to go anywhere when the alternative is staying *in* with Audrey.

I've been thinking way too much about all the time we're going to spend together. The *hotel room* we're going to share—not that I have any intention of trying anything. I won't even kiss her unless she asks me to, even if it takes every ounce of restraint to keep from doing so. I just want her to be comfortable, to be able to relax for one night before everything gets crazy tomorrow.

Beside me, Audrey sighs and drops her head onto my shoulder as she stifles an enormous yawn.

The contact sends that same pulsing energy through me. Every place she touches me crackles with electricity. I could light up all of Los Angeles with this energy, with the fire that sparks whenever her skin brushes against mine.

I lift my arm and wrap it around her shoulders, tugging her closer until her head is resting against my chest. It feels so easy. So natural to hold her like this.

She must think so too because she lifts an arm and wraps it around my waist. Whether intentional or not, her hand slips under the hem of my T-shirt and presses against the skin on my lower back. Her touch is whisper soft as her fingers trace tiny circles on my skin. I close my eyes, not wanting her to stop but knowing if she doesn't, I might lose my actual mind.

She's killing me with this. *Literally* killing me.

My phone buzzes from my pocket, but I don't dare move to grab it. Instead, I tilt my wrist and read the message notification on my watch. It's a text from Kenji, and it's only two words long, so it's easy enough to read the entire thing.

Kenji: Fake, huh?

I look up and meet his knowing expression. All I can do is shrug.

I don't know much right now.

But I know that nothing about holding Audrey in my arms feels fake.

—ell—

We take the long way to the hotel, some swanky place in West Hollywood, giving Nate and Joni time enough to get our luggage, then get to the hotel and do a security sweep to make sure everything checks out.

Kenji has already checked us in, so it's a relatively straight shot from the car, through the hotel doors, and to the elevators. From there, it's a quick ride up to the eighth floor, and suddenly, Audrey and I are alone.

For the night.

The suite is spacious—an open living space, a full kitchen, and French doors that open into a luxurious bedroom.

Our luggage sits near the foot of the bed, and there's a tray of fruit, cheese, and sparkling water on the table by the window. A text from Joni confirms that dinner will be up in an hour, which means we won't have to leave this room for anything unless we want to.

Audrey didn't protest when Simon demanded we stay in the same room, but I can't help but wonder how things are going to go tonight. Whatever it takes to make Audrey comfortable—that's my priority.

I watch as she slowly walks through the hotel suite, her fingers running across the back of the sofa. It's a little small, but if I end up sleeping out here, I'll manage all right.

I push my hands into my pockets. "Are you hungry?"

She picks up an apple from the tray on the table, then puts it back down. "A little," she says, but when she looks up at me, it doesn't look like she's thinking about fruit.

We've been touching all day, taking every excuse to have our hands on each other, but now that we're alone, we don't have a reason to pretend. That doesn't stop me from wishing I could pull her into my arms.

"Flint, will you kiss me?" Audrey blurts out.

Her words are like cannon fire throwing me fifty feet backward. I stutter out a laugh. "What?"

"I liked being in your arms today," she says. She wraps her arms around her middle, like she's trying to shield herself from the room. From me, maybe? *I hope it's not me.* "I liked it a lot. And I know I said I didn't want anything to happen between us, and I think I probably still feel that way. But I also feel like my limbs are going to spontaneously combust whenever you touch me." She licks her lips and takes a step forward. "It's hard for me to even say that sentence out loud because hyperbolic expressions like that always irritate me. But I don't know how else to describe what I'm feeling. When you're not touching me, I want you to be. When you aren't in the room, I can't stop thinking about when I'll see you again. It's illogical." She lifts her fists to her cheeks, then thrusts them down again. "It's maddening."

She takes a deep breath and drops her eyes, then gathers her hair and pulls it forward over her shoulder with trembling hands. "Last week, when we almost kissed, that was real, right? You wanted to kiss me for real."

I nod slowly. "I did."

"Do you still want to?"

I swallow, thinking of the promise I made to myself to only kiss Audrey if I'm kissing her for real. "Only if it's what you want."

She shrugs. "I asked, didn't I?"

She *did* ask, and that's all the confirmation I need. I close the distance between us with two long strides and sweep her into my arms, one arm wrapping around her and pulling her body flush against mine. I lift my other hand to her cheek and cradle her face, my thumb running across her bottom lip. "Audrey, I wanted to kiss you the day I met you. And I've wanted it every day since."

She closes her eyes and takes a stuttering breath, then she pushes up on her toes and presses her lips against mine, slowly at first, then with increasing pressure. I let her set the pace, wanting, above all else, for her to be comfortable. But then she nips at my bottom lip before pulling back long enough to say, "Please don't hold back, Flint. I'm not going to break."

I let out a low groan and pull her even closer, my lips colliding with hers, the air between us crackling as our movements grow more frantic. I slip my hands around her waist, under the blazer she's wearing, and she shrugs it off, letting it fall to the floor behind her. I pause, breaking our kiss long enough to take in the curve-hugging tank top I've been catching glimpses of all day. I skate my palms over the silken skin on her bare arms and shoulders and close my eyes. I want all of her, to claim her with my touch, my kisses, each one an echo of the feeling coursing through me: *mine, mine, mine.*

I slide my hands to her hips and hoist her up until her legs wrap around my waist, then I kiss her like she *isn't* going to break, with every ounce of the desire that's been building in me for weeks. Her tongue brushes against mine as her hands tangle in my hair, and I almost lose my mind.

This woman is everything.

The taste of her, the feel of her as she moves with me, against me, like our bodies are tuned together in ways even our words aren't.

I walk us backward to the couch—the bed's closer, but I don't want to give her the wrong impression—and sit down, leaning back until she's hovering over me, her lips still pressed to mine. My hands splay across her back, reaching under the hem of her tank top to feel her skin warm against my palms. Her movements slow and her kisses yield to something more languid than frantic but still just as passionate. She isn't in a hurry, and that's fine with me. We've got all night.

If I have anything to do with it, we'll have forever.

Except, somewhere in the back of my mind, I can't let go of Audrey's words, spoken just before we kissed. *I know I said I didn't want anything to happen between us, and I think I probably still feel that way*

I want her. But not until I know she wants *me.*

All of me.

Even my stupid crazy life.

Our bodies really must be in tune because Audrey pulls back, shifting until she's sitting on the couch beside me. She breathes slowly, deeply, until she finally says, "Flint, we can't."

I lean forward and run a hand across my face, my elbows propped on my knees, and take a minute to regulate my breathing. After the last ten minutes, it's no small feat. "You're right," I finally say.

"It's not that I don't want to," Audrey says, almost like she didn't hear me agree with her. "Obviously I want...wait, I'm right?"

I look up and meet her gaze, then reach for her hands, tugging them into mine. "I just want you to be sure, Audrey."

"About us?"

I lift a shoulder and nod. "I don't really do casual. Not when it comes to sex." I only need one hand to count the number of intimate relationships I've had, even if the tabloids like to assume otherwise. "If that's where we take our relationship, I want it to be because we're both ready. Because we both want something serious."

She lets out a low groan of frustration, pulling her hands free and scooching herself to the other side of the couch, putting a few feet of space between us.

I miss her warmth the second she's no longer beside me. "Did I say something wrong?"

She quickly shakes her head, her eyes wide. "The opposite. By telling me you don't do casual, you just made yourself infinitely more sexy. I didn't even think that was possible, but you did, and I might need to go sit on the other side of the room." She scrambles off the couch and walks through the open bedroom doors, turning to face me as she sits on the edge of the bed. "I definitely need to sit over here," she says. "This is better. You stay where you are."

I smirk. "What are you going to do tonight?" I joke, glancing back at the bed.

"I'll sleep in the bathtub." She looks toward the bathroom. "I'm sure it's big enough."

Or you could just choose me, I think, but I can't say those words out loud. Audrey has a lot more on the line here than I do. Choosing me will change her future indefinitely. Her privacy, her work, her anonymity. All of it would be impacted. Only she can decide if it's worth it.

"A pillow barricade might work," she says. "As long as we both promise to keep our hands to ourselves."

"I can handle a pillow barricade," I say. "I'd prefer that over either of us taking the bathtub."

"Or the very tiny couch," she says.

I nod. "Glad we agree."

She's quiet for a long moment before she walks back to the couch and stands between my knees, her hands hooked over my shoulders. I pull her into an embrace, my face pressed against her stomach, and she slides her hands up to my hair, rubbing her fingers over my scalp in a way that melts my limbs and relaxes me against her. "Oh, man. Please don't ever stop exactly what you're doing."

She chuckles. "Flint, I really like you," she whispers. "I'm still scared. But I'm trying not to be, okay?"

My grip around her tightens. "I really like you too. And I'm glad you're willing to try."

Glad might be the understatement of the century.

Scared or not, I'm already halfway in love with this woman.

I just hope that doesn't mean I'm halfway to heartbreak.

Chapter Twenty-Two
Audrey

AUDREY: HI, SISTERS. I have news. Are you awake?

Lucy: We're awake! Are you there? Are you safe?

Audrey: Safe and sound in a very posh hotel suite in West Hollywood. Hang on. I texted a picture. Did it come through?

Summer: I am jealous on so many levels. But I'm more interested in your news.

Audrey: I just wanted to tell you I watched *Good Will Hunting*.

Audrey: And I LOVED IT.

Lucy: Shut up.

Summer: What have you done with my sister?

Audrey: I'm serious. I've been too hard on you guys. Movies can be really fun.

Summer: I mean, yes. But were you watching with Flint? Because if you were, the only thing we know for sure is that you like watching movies WITH FLINT. That's not the same thing as just liking movies.

Audrey: I see your point. But I really did love the story. Did you know Flint was nominated for an Oscar against Matt Damon? He didn't win or anything, but STILL. Matt Damon. He's in *Good Will Hunting*, and he's so great.

Lucy: Um, yeah. We know. Welcome to the world of popular culture. So happy you're finally joining us.

Summer: So I need more details about this whole movie viewing situation. Were you snuggled up on the couch? Relaxing on the bed? Naked in the hot tub?

Audrey: Stop it. No naked talk. We were on the couch, in our hotel suite, eating dinner. It was all very civilized and polite.

Summer: BORING.

Audrey: If it makes you feel better, we did a lot of making out BEFORE dinner. So there's that.

Lucy: !!!!

Summer: You're joking.

Audrey: Not joking.

Lucy: For real kissing or fake kissing?

Audrey: Definitely for real kissing.

Lucy: Oh my gosh. Oh my gosh. Oh my gosh.

Summer: *breathes into paper bag*

Lucy: How are you feeling? Was it amazing? Are you okay?

Audrey: I feel good. A little overwhelmed, but in a good way.

Summer: This is so freaking amazing. Seriously. I don't even know how to process.

Lucy: So what happens now? Are you together?

Audrey: We haven't really talked about it. We're taking things slow, I think. I mean, I had a lot of reasons for not wanting a relationship, and those things haven't really changed.

Summer: Maybe not, but people do crazy stuff for love all the time.

Audrey: I don't know about love. But I know I like him. And I know he likes me. And we're finally being honest about that.

Lucy: The rest will work itself out. It will!

Summer: Love conquers all! Or...in this case, really like conquers all!

Lucy: I'm so, so happy for you, Auds. Seriously.

Summer: Have you told Mom and Dad?

Audrey: They know I'm in LA, but they don't know I'm with Flint. I'll give them an update once I'm home.

Lucy: You aren't worried about them seeing you on the news?

Summer: Do you even know our parents? They're less likely to watch entertainment news than Audrey.

Lucy: Fair point.

Audrey: I promise I'll fill them in eventually. I just don't want them to worry. And this whole scenario will make Mom worry.

Summer: That's true. You're making the right call.

Summer: You have to keep us updated though. Any new details, you'd better message us!

Audrey: I will. Promise.

Lucy: And Audrey, try not to overthink, okay? Just enjoy yourself. This is an amazing, magical thing happening to you. Just enjoy it. You deserve all the happy things.

Audrey: Thanks. I love you guys.

Summer: Love you too. Please tell your movie star boyfriend I would love to meet Ryan Gosling, please and thank you.

Audrey: Hahaha. I'll pass that along.

Summer: Tom Holland would also be great.

Summer: And Liam Hemsworth.

Summer: Oh! And Chris Evans. Does he know Chris Evans?

Lucy: Summer. STOP.

Summer: Chris Pratt! I would love to meet Chris Pratt.

Summer: And Bradley Cooper! Flint was in a movie with Bradley Cooper, right? He has to know him!

Summer: Why do I suddenly feel like I'm here by myself now?

Summer: FINE. I'm done now.

Summer: Just kidding. One more. Harry Styles. The internet says he and Flint are FRIENDS, Audrey. FRIENDS.

Lucy: Okay. You're safe. I stole her phone. Love you, Auds! Have fun!

Chapter Twenty-Three
Flint

THE CAST AND CREW of *Turning Tides* are set up in three different hotel rooms, with a fourth room available to us when we need coffee or food or just a break away from the reporters who will be cycling through in ten-minute intervals.

As expected, I'll be interviewed with Claire. We're the stars of the movie, so it only makes sense, but I'm not looking forward to an entire day sitting right beside her. At least Audrey will be there, visible to me *and* Claire. I just have to hope that will be enough to make her behave.

So far, I haven't even seen her.

The hotel room door opens, and I look up, expecting Claire. We're supposed to start in less than ten minutes, so she should show up any second. Instead, it's the director of *Turning Tides,* Lea Cortez, who comes in. She smiles wide when she meets my gaze, and I stand, hurrying over for a hug.

"Oh, it's so good to see you!" she says, squeezing my shoulders before letting me go. Her eyes flit to where Audrey is standing just behind us, then she leans forward. "Excellent timing, Flint," she says knowingly. "You happened to get a girlfriend just in time for the premiere, huh?"

The question doesn't surprise me. Lea is fully aware of what Claire has been up to the past few months, and she knew my team was trying to figure out a way to make it stop.

"Let's call the timing fortuitous instead of suspicious," I say, reaching for Audrey's hand.

She steps forward and slips her fingers into mine.

"Lea, this is my girlfriend," I say, not even tripping over the words. Maybe because now, they feel true. "Doctor Audrey Callahan."

Audrey reaches out and shakes Lea's hand. "And this is Lea Cortez. Director of *Turning Tides* and my very good friend. She and her wife, Trista, were my neighbors when I lived in Malibu."

"You've caught yourself a good one," Lea says to Audrey, her tone warm. "Are you a doctor of medicine? What's your specialty?"

"Not medicine," Audrey says. "I have my PhD in wildlife biology."

"Oh, I love that." Lea snaps her fingers. "Actually, have you ever done any consulting? I'm reading this script right now, and *oh,* it's so gorgeous. Historical. West Virginia mountains. A little bit of coal mining, a little bit of falling in love. But there's one character who's this activist, in opposition to the mining industry for environmental reasons, and I'm feeling like the science is a little thin. Would you be willing to take a look? Give me your professional opinion?"

Audrey's eyebrows lift. "Oh. I...sure. I'd be happy to."

I give Audrey's waist a reassuring squeeze. This is the first I've heard of the script Lea's reading, but Audrey would be a perfect consultant. The woman knows *everything* about everything.

"Truly? That would be amazing," Lea says.

The door behind us opens again, and this time it really is Claire. Her gaze meets mine for the briefest second, then she looks down, a flash of trepidation crossing her features.

It isn't what I'm expecting, and I narrow my eyes.

"Okay. Looks like we're getting started. I'll see you on the other side." Lea heads across the hall to where her interviews are taking place, and I pull Audrey into my arms. She settles against me with an easy comfort that warms me from the inside out.

"I'm glad you're here," I say, smiling down at her.

"I'm glad I'm here too."

"We're ready to roll," a voice says from behind me.

"They're just waiting on you, Flint," Joni calls.

I look at Joni and nod, then lean down and kiss Audrey, lingering long enough to cause a few snickers and whispers to sound across the room. "Promise you'll stay where I can see you?" I ask when I finally pull away.

She leans up and kisses me again. "I promise."

I pass Joni on my way to the middle of the room where Claire's waiting for me, and she grabs my arm, halting my progress. "So we're kissing now?" she whispers under her breath.

"Looks like it."

"You're really selling it," she says through clenched teeth.

"Well, I'm a really good actor."

She leans back and studies me, then her gaze narrows. "You aren't acting, are you?"

I smile. "Absolutely not."

A sound guy approaches, mic in hand, and attaches it to my collar, then melts into the crowd of techie people standing behind the cameraman while a makeup artist quickly descends, powdering my face until Joni tugs her away. "That's enough," Joni says. "He looks great."

Claire offers a tentative smile when I sit down beside her. She seems fidgety, nervous, almost like she's afraid to look at me, which is incredibly out of character for her.

"Hi, Claire," I say. "How are you?"

She looks up, her expression curious, maybe even a little surprised. "Okay, I guess," she answers. "How are you?"

I don't have time to answer her because someone calls "mics on" from behind us, and then we're off.

The process is just as taxing as it always is. We answer ten different variations of the same ten questions over and over again.

What was it like working together?

Is there any animosity between us now that we're no longer together?

How was it filming on location in such a beautiful country?

What's up next for the both of us?

Do we have any plans to work together in the future?

Most of the questions steer clear of my personal life—a requirement that was made clear to all participating journalists. But that didn't stop them from asking about *Claire's* personal life. My favorite question: *Was Claire disappointed when she realized I'd moved on with someone else?*

Just before we break for lunch, a woman from LA Weekly asks me something no one else has thought to ask yet.

"Last question for you, Flint," the journalist says. "Are we supposed to assume that the new relationship in your life has something to do with your move back to North Carolina?"

Joni steps forward—this is definitely a question that crosses into personal territory—but I lift a hand and motion her away. I'm okay answering this one.

"Yes and no," I say. I look up and smile at Audrey, who's standing just off to my left. "When I moved, I knew I was looking for something. More stability, more time with my family. But there was something else I wanted, too. I didn't know what it was, really, only that I'd never found it in LA. And I didn't find it until I met Audrey. We all need people to keep us grounded, you know? Who will remind us what's really important. It's easy to lose sight of that in this business. Our relationship is still new, but if I'm lucky, I hope that's what she'll be for me."

There's a long stretch of silence after my answer, and I squirm with sudden discomfort. "What?" I quickly joke. "Was that too much? Too personal? Nobody knows how to handle Flint Hawthorne being a little vulnerable?"

It's Claire who responds. "It wasn't too much, Flint," she says softly, a hand on my arm. "It was perfect."

If this really was just an act, if my feelings for Audrey really were fake, I might regret fooling Claire because there is real and genuine warmth in her eyes. It's surprising to see, and so completely unexpected, I almost have whiplash. But then, she hasn't really seemed like the same Claire today. It could just be that the pictures of me and Audrey—and then seeing Audrey here with me—accomplished their purpose. But I'm beginning to sense there's something else to Claire's change in behavior.

I lift my eyebrows in question, and Claire shrugs. "I'm happy for you," she says, her tone low. "And I'm sorry—"

I lift a hand, cutting her off, and reach over to tug off her mic, then I do the same with mine. "Can we go ahead and cut the cameras?" I say, hoping someone in the room will listen.

Joni appears beside me and takes our mics, then ushers the LA Weekly lady and everyone else to the other side of the room.

"Thanks," Claire says softly. "I'm still so new at this."

"You're doing fine," I say gently.

She's quiet for a beat before she looks up, eyes watery and a little red. "Flint, I'm sorry about all those things I said." She takes a deep breath, hesitating the tiniest bit before she keeps going. "Simon just kept saying I needed to keep our names on everyone's minds as much as possible. It was his idea for me to hint that we were still in a relationship. He said it would create exactly the kind of buzz the movie needs."

"Wait, you're working with Simon?"

She nods, wide-eyed. "I thought you knew. He called me right after you and I broke up."

It takes me a moment to process what she's telling me.

All this time, Simon has been playing both sides of the game, telling me one thing and telling Claire something else.

I lean back in my chair.

I should have known.

Honestly, I'm surprised I didn't piece it together sooner.

"Simon can be very persuasive." I breathe out a tired sigh. "I wish you'd told me, Claire."

She nods. "I know. I should have. But Simon said I couldn't trust you on this. He said that you—" She winces and shakes her head. "Well, never mind what he said. I shouldn't have listened, and I'm sorry."

"Let me guess. He said I'm stuck on my own high horse and can't be trusted to know what my career really needs?"

"Something like that," Claire says.

"Where is Simon anyway?" I ask, suddenly realizing that he hasn't been around all morning. Normally, he would be.

Claire frowns. "He'll be here after lunch."

I nod, wondering how quickly Joni can draft up some official paperwork terminating my relationship with my publicist. It's a decision I should have made a long time ago. I haven't been on the same page with the guy in months. Knowing Joni, she already has the paperwork saved on her laptop just in case.

"Hey, can I give you some advice?" I say to Claire. The room around us is clearing out as everyone breaks for lunch, but I can't *not* say what needs to be said, no matter how difficult she's made my life the past few months.

She nods. "Of course."

"Fire Simon. He'll use you, Claire. He's a lot more concerned about his own star rising than he is yours, and I don't think you can trust him to have your best interests at heart. He didn't have mine. In fact, he went directly against what I asked of him. He played us against each other, which wasn't good for either of us."

"Yeah, I see that now." She breathes out a sigh. "Are you going to fire him?"

"The minute I see him," I say. "But not just over this. He's had it coming for a while." I stand, and offer Claire a hand, pulling her to her feet.

"Thanks, Flint. I really am sorry about everything I said. I hope I didn't cause any problems for you and your girlfriend. She seems really nice."

"I appreciate the apology." I make eye contact with Audrey and hold out my hand, hoping she'll come join me.

"Can I ask you one more thing?" Claire asks, and I nod. "At the premiere tonight, do you think we could make a show of looking like we're friends again? Simon said bringing the drama would go farther, but I don't think he's the right publicist for me anymore. All this clamoring for attention—gosh, I really don't like the way it makes me feel. I'd feel a lot better if we could all just get along."

Audrey finally reaches me and slips her hand into mine, offering Claire a warm smile.

"How about we just *be* friends again?" I say. "No show required."

Claire smiles. "Thanks, Flint. That would be great."

After I introduce Audrey, she and Claire chat for a few minutes, then we say goodbye, and Audrey and I head back to our room with Nate and Joni for lunch.

We need privacy if I'm going to fill them in on what Claire told me about Simon, and I definitely need to fill them in. If this guy has been pitting Claire and me against each other, who knows how else he's been mismanaging things.

Joni was right. I have been too trusting.

But all of that stops right now.

Chapter Twenty-Four

Flint

JONI IS LIVID, AS expected, when she hears what Simon has been doing. Fortunately, she really did have termination paperwork prepared just in case. We can even get Simon uninvited to tonight's premiere if we work quickly enough.

Audrey is quiet while I relay everything I learned, but her eyes are sharp, darting from me, to Joni, and back again as we discuss the situation. As soon as there's a pause in the conversation, she lifts a hand. "Listen. I understand your desire to *not* have Simon at the premiere. After what he's put you through, I don't really want him there either. But Flint, Simon knows a lot about you. He knows about *us*. Are you sure it's worth firing him *now*? Right in the middle of the press cycle? If he has no reason to be loyal, why would he be?"

"That's a valid point," Joni says. "I hate it because cutting ties today would be so incredibly satisfying, but Audrey might be right."

I lean forward, elbows on my knees, and run my hands through my hair. The wardrobe people will be annoyed when I go back for the rest of the interviews, but I'm too annoyed to care. I do see Audrey's point, but I *really* don't want to be around Simon anymore. Claire said he'd be here after lunch.

The idea of faking it, of playing nice—that's a hard thing to swallow.

I shake my head. "I see your point, but Simon also has a lot on the line here. He may be well-connected, but I am, too. I could ruin his reputation among other actors. He has to know that. I don't think he'll screw me over."

"You might be underestimating the size of Simon's ego," Joni says. "I'm not saying we don't fire him; I'm just saying we wait a couple of weeks until the movie press is behind us."

"That's my vote too," Audrey says. "Not that I deserve a vote. But, you know. Just in case you were curious."

I reach over and pick up her hand, threading my fingers through hers, then lifting our clasped hands to my lips. I press a kiss on her knuckles. "You definitely get a vote. And I understand what you're both saying. But now that I've discovered the kind of cancer Simon is, I can't stand the thought of working with him any longer. I just want him gone."

Joni sighs. "Okay. I'll get everything ready for you. You can talk to him after lunch."

After we eat, Audrey excuses herself to the bathroom, and Nate heads onto the balcony to make some calls about tonight's security detail. In their absence, Joni eyes me in her big-sister way. "Okay, spill it," she says, folding her arms as she leans back in her chair.

"Spill what?"

She rolls her eyes. "So Audrey likes you now, too? You're both feeling it?"

I look toward the bathroom door. "We're taking it slow."

"Slow is good. She seems like she's holding up okay."

"More than okay," I say. "She's been amazing."

"Tonight will be the true test," Joni says. "You think she's really up for this full-time?"

"Maybe not the way I've done things in the past. But I've been wanting to handle this part of my career differently anyway. If I set some stronger boundaries, say no to stuff that isn't essential. I think we can make it work. And I want to—because I really like her."

Joni's expression softens. "You know I'm up for anything that means we all get to slow down a little." Her eyes dart behind me for a moment before coming back to me. "Speaking of slowing down, what do you say you let Audrey sit out the rest of the afternoon?"

I frown. "What? Why?"

Joni motions behind me. "Because I think she needs a nap."

I turn and look through the bedroom door to see Audrey curled up on the edge of the bed.

"Besides," Joni says. "She's got a lot more getting ready to do for tonight than you do."

I nod. "It's probably better if she isn't there when everything goes down with Simon anyway. And after our conversation, I'm sure Claire is going to be fine even without Audrey nearby."

"Claire would be crazy to say anything suggestive now, even if she hadn't apologized to you. Audrey's face is all over the internet. You've sold it. You're in a relationship. No one is doubting that now."

"My face is all over the internet?" Audrey asks, appearing in the bedroom doorway.

Joni winces, like she maybe didn't want Audrey to hear her. "Don't go looking," she says as she reaches over and swipes a handful of grapes from my mostly empty plate. "But yes.

And TMZ has already figured out who you are, thanks to Flint introducing you to Lea as *Doctor Audrey Callahan.*"

"Someone heard that?" I ask.

"There was a reporter sitting ten feet behind you," Joni says. "Of course she heard you. I wouldn't stress about it though. We knew this would happen. I didn't want you to freak out about it, but it isn't a bad thing."

"What do you mean they know who I am?" Audrey asks. "I mean, they know my name, sure. But what else have they figured out?"

Joni reaches for her phone, scrolling while she talks. "Honestly, every time the story updates, it seems like they have a little more information. They found your faculty photo from Carolina Southern, and it looks like there are links to a few more articles you've published." She holds up her phone screen so Audrey and I can both see it. "This is kinda cool though. You've gotten so much attention that Amazon has sold out of your book."

"My book?"

"Reforestation and Biodiversity," Joni reads. "By Doctor Audrey Callahan."

Audrey lets out a surprised laugh. "The only people who ever buy that book are college students who have to because it's on their syllabus."

Joni shrugs. "Maybe people will learn something, then." She stands and points at Audrey. "Hey, guess what? You get the afternoon off. I suggest a real nap instead of a two-minute one on the way back from the bathroom."

Audrey's eyes dart to me. "Oh. I'm fine. I'll be fine without a nap." A yawn muffles the last few words of her sentence, and she stifles it with her fist. "Ignore that," she says. "It's just a little bit of jet lag. But I swear I'm okay."

I smile. "Stay and sleep. For real. I can manage without you for a little bit. Especially now that I've talked to Claire."

A flash of uncertainty flits across her expression, but she nods. "Okay. If you're sure."

"I'll give you two a minute to say goodbye," Joni says, moving toward the balcony to get Nate. As she crosses back through the room, she says, "You know, since this is a totally fake relationship that doesn't have anything to do with real, actual feelings."

Nate follows quickly behind, and they both disappear out the door.

"She knows?" Audrey asks as soon as the latch clicks closed behind them.

I nod. "She guessed."

Audrey nods and moves into the bedroom, dropping onto the edge of the bed. She kicks off her shoes. "Do you think we need to check in with John? If people know who I am, I worry someone might show up at the house."

"That's a good thought. I'll have Nate check in with him and tell him to be extra vigilant."

She nods, and I reach up to curve a hand around her cheek. She closes her eyes and leans into me.

"Are you okay? I know all of this is a lot."

She nods. "I'm great, actually. It *is* a lot, but I've enjoyed watching you talk about your work." She reaches over and slides her hands across my chest, toying with the buttons on the front of my shirt. "You know what I'm not excited about though?" She bites her lip in that anxious way I'm beginning to love.

"What's that?" I lean forward, needing to touch her, to kiss her before I leave.

She presses her hands into my chest, stopping me just before my lips meet hers. "I'm *not* looking forward to watching you make out with Claire."

I freeze, not grasping her meaning. I have zero plans of ever doing *that* again.

"In the movie, Flint," Audrey says softly.

Oh. *Oh.* She isn't the first person to worry about something like this. I have friends who have navigated this road before, setting boundaries, figuring out what makes them and their spouses or partners feel comfortable when it comes to on-screen intimacy. "I get that," I say gently. "But it's acting, Audrey. It isn't real."

"It was real with Claire, though, wasn't it?"

I nod, wishing I didn't have to say yes. "Not the whole time we were filming. Just for a while there at the end. By the time we started dating for real, we'd already filmed all the scenes that included us both."

I can tell Audrey's mind is working from the way her brows are creased, a tiny line appearing right between them. "How do you keep it from feeling real?" she asks. "Not just with Claire, but generally."

I run a hand across my face and consider her question. "I mean, it helps that there are normally a dozen people or more crowded around you when it's happening. Cameras in your faces, directors paying very close attention to everything from where your hands are to how long a kiss lasts to whether your eyebrows are relaxed while you're kissing. The whole thing is directed, scripted, which generally makes it about the least intimate setting ever."

"Yeah, I guess that makes sense."

"Then there's the cardinal rule of all on-screen kissing," I say, and she lifts her eyebrows.

"What's the cardinal rule?"

I grin. "No tongue."

Her eyes widen. "Ever?"

I shake my head. "Not unless it's scripted. And that's something that would have to be written into a contract. Otherwise, it's a very fast way to make other actors think you're a jerk."

She smiles and stands, shifting so she's directly in front of me, her arms wrapped around my neck.

I lift my hands to her waist, settling them on the swell of her hips. I will never get tired of standing this way, of feeling this woman under my hands.

"This actually makes me feel a lot better," she says playfully. She leans down and nudges my nose with hers.

"Yeah? Why is that?" I ask, my voice low.

"I like that there's something only *I* get to do," she whispers. She lowers herself until she's sitting across my lap, her legs straddling either side.

"Only you, huh?"

She bites her lip, a flash of trepidation crossing her face. "I mean, only if..." Her words trail off and she takes a deep breath, but then she squares her shoulders and looks at me dead on. "Actually, yes. Only me. If I thought you were doing this with other women, I'd lose my mind, Flint. If you want me, it has to be only me."

"I don't want anyone else, Audrey." I lean up and press my lips to hers. "I've never wanted anyone like I want you."

She kisses me this time, gently at first, but then her hands slide up to my jaw, and she deepens it into something that breaks every single rule of on-screen kissing.

Fire floods my veins as her tongue brushes against mine, her hair cascading forward and enveloping me in her scent. My fingers press into the fabric of her jeans as I pull her even closer. It isn't enough. *This* isn't enough.

I have to stop, go back to work, and leave her, and yet, I'm certain that if she asked me to stay, I would. I'd ignore it all. The obligations. The journalists. The premiere. I'd forget all of it just to be *right here.* And not just because I crave the feel of her skin against mine. Though, five more seconds of this, and I might be breaking all kinds of rules—especially the ones I've set for myself.

I want to stay because I want to *know* Audrey.

All of her. Everything there is.

I want to know what makes her happy and sad and angry at the world. What makes her stop and think. What challenges her. What inspires her. What makes her stand up and fight, and what makes her hole up and hide for a while.

I want to know all her favorites. Foods. Colors. Books. Countries.

Name it, and I want to know it.

I want the people who love her the most in the world to call *me* when they don't know what to buy for her birthday present. Because they know I've done the research. They know I've asked every question and cataloged every answer.

It's Audrey who breaks the kiss, and it's probably a good thing. I'm too far gone. Too consumed by her to think straight.

"You have to go," she whispers against my ear, her lips close.

"I don't want to," I say, hugging her a little tighter.

I feel her smile, even though I can't see it. "I'm not answering to Joni, Flint." She shifts backward and stands, then tugs me to my feet. "Come on. Get out of here. I'll see you in a couple of hours."

She walks me to the door, and I kiss her one last time. "Are you sure you're going to be okay?"

She grins and shoves me toward the door. "In this very fancy hotel suite, in a very comfortable bed? However will I cope?"

Joni has already gone ahead, but Nate is waiting for me outside the room, and I follow him down to the seventh floor where all the interviews are happening. Nate has a key card to get me into the interview room, but I drop a hand on his shoulder, stopping him before he can use it.

"How do you do it, man? How do you ever walk away from Joni when you feel like this?"

His eyebrows lift. "Like what?"

"Like I can't breathe. Or think about anything but her."

His eyes lift with understanding. "You and Audrey?"

"Joni didn't tell you?"

He shakes his head. "Nah, but I should have guessed."

I rub my hand against my sternum, like I can somehow soothe the ache pulsing just behind my ribs. "I don't even know what this is," I say more to myself than Nate.

He chuckles, a wide smile stretching across his face. "That's love, man." He waves the keycard in front of the lock and pushes the door open. "Better buckle up," he says as I push past him into the room. "Your heart's in control now."

Chapter Twenty-Five

Audrey

I STAND IN THE hotel bathroom and stare at my reflection in the full-length mirror.

Honestly, I think everyone on the planet could look amazing if they had this many people available to help them get ready every morning.

I have been plucked and polished and shined and glossed.

And I have never felt so beautiful.

That *could* have something to do with the billion-dollar gown I'm wearing. It's even prettier than I remember. And it's the most feminine thing I've ever worn. The tiny flowers woven into the lace overlay are so delicate, I'm afraid to even touch them.

"How are the shoes?" Joni asks as she steps into the bathroom. "Are you dying? If you are, there are four other pairs you can try."

"These are great. I feel pretty steady." I don't have a ton of experience walking in high heels, but these have a wider block heel and they aren't too high. Plus, they have some sort of memory foam insole that makes them really comfortable—something I didn't expect in a pair of heels.

"Perfect," Joni says. "Flint should be here any minute." She looks me up and down. "He's going to pass out when he sees you, Audrey. Seriously. You're stunning."

Joni had Flint's tuxedo taken to her room so he could get ready there. She claimed it was "easier," but I think she just wants us to have some ridiculous big reveal in which he sees my red-carpet look for the first time.

For all her no-nonsense displays, Joni is clearly a romantic at heart.

Not that I'm not excited about seeing Flint in a tuxedo. I totally am. But after I *see* him, we're going to the premiere, and I'm pretty sure that's going to be just like the airport. Except worse because I'm wearing heels and a dress.

Joni keeps assuring me everyone will be corralled safely behind a barricade that will keep them from getting too close. There will be cameras, people, and lots of noise, but it will all feel very civilized.

Sure. *Civilized.*

"You okay?" Joni asks. "You look a little green."

I force a deep breath. "I'm okay. Maybe I just need some air?"

"Totally. Balcony? Let's get you to the balcony."

She hovers behind me as I cross through the bedroom and into the living room, then make my way to the balcony. Fortunately, she doesn't follow me outside.

I *am* okay; I just need a minute to breathe. To process the fact that four hours ago, I told a man, whom millions of women love and lust after, that I want him to be exclusive with *me.*

Me.

It feels impossible. Ridiculous. Utterly unlike me.

And yet, when I'm with Flint, when his arms are around me, nothing feels *more right*.

I know how much he wants a normal relationship. And he deserves it. He deserves to be with someone capable of loving him despite the craziness of his life.

I press a hand to my stomach. I have no idea what this is going to look like. I just know I want to try.

Behind me, the balcony door opens, and I slowly turn.

Flint is standing in front of the door, his hands pushed into the pockets of his tuxedo.

Oh. Oh my.

I don't have adequate words to describe how good he looks. I have a sudden urge to take his picture and preserve it for scientific purposes—a representation of the perfect male species. For generations to come, researchers can look back and know that this—this man—is as good as it gets.

"Audrey, if you keep looking at me like that, we aren't going to make it out of the hotel room," Flint says through a chuckle. He walks slowly toward me.

I smile. "I could say the same thing to you."

He slips a hand around my waist, pressing it to the small of my back and tugging me against him. "I have never seen a woman so beautiful," he says, his tone low. He leans down like he's going to kiss me but freezes when Joni yells from inside the hotel room.

"No! No kissing. Her makeup is perfect, and you can't ruin it."

Flint grins. "The price to pay for red carpet perfection." He presses his lips to my forehead instead, giving me a lingering kiss that almost feels as intimate as a regular kiss. "I'll be right beside you the whole time," he says. "I promise. Just don't let go of my hand."

~ell~

Flint stays true to his word. The only time he lets go of me is when the photographers need him to pose on the red carpet by himself or with his fellow cast members.

Just as frequently, they take pictures of the two of us together. It isn't all that different from walking through the airport, except this time, people know my name.

Audrey, look this way.

Audrey, who are you wearing?

Audrey, can we see the back of your gown?

I have never been so overwhelmed. The main reason I'm making it is because Flint is my north star, taking every opportunity to look into my eyes and make sure I'm okay. But there's something else motivating me forward, too. And that's *pride.*

Flint is really good at his job. He's charming and gracious and kind to everyone he greets. When we stop for interviews along the red carpet, he's professional and generous in his efforts to praise his director and co-stars. He does not *seek* to be the star, but that only makes him shine brighter.

When people ask about me, he smiles and squeezes my hand, and says something vague about our general happiness or how we're looking forward to a future together. The only questions directed toward me are about my gown, which is fine with me. Those are easy enough to answer. Otherwise, I'm happy to let Flint soak up all the attention. This party is about him. About his amazing accomplishment. And I'm just so proud and happy to be here with him, even with all the noise and chaos.

During the movie, I sit in between Flint and Claire, who is on her own for the night. Turns out, Simon was supposed to be her date to the premiere. Earlier today, when Flint terminated his relationship with Simon, Claire did the same thing. It still makes me nervous, especially now that Simon has lost two clients instead of just one, but I trust Flint's instincts. If he believes Simon will walk away quietly, who am I to tell him any differently?

After chatting with her earlier today, I decided I actually like Claire. She seems really sweet and genuine, which makes me think it was Simon's manipulations that were turning her into the opposite.

Still, I'm nervous enough about seeing Flint on the screen.

Now I have to do it while sitting next to *Claire?*

I don't care what Flint said about on-screen intimacy. This is still going to be weird.

I brace myself for the worst, but once the movie begins and I settle into the story, it's not so bad. It's Flint on the screen, but it's not *really* Flint. He's acting. And he's so good at it, I almost want to cry.

When it's clear we're approaching a *first kiss* moment, it's Claire who reaches over, her hand resting on my forearm. She leans toward me. "So, when we were filming this scene, we'd been out in the sun for hours already. You know what I couldn't stop thinking about? How much sand I had inside my swimsuit."

I stifle a laugh, and she grins. "And the wedgie," she says with a groan. "It was the worst. I was uncomfortable and grouchy, and I'm pretty sure Flint got really irritated with how many takes I required."

I know what she's doing. And I love her for doing it.

After the movie, all I want to do is talk to Flint. Rehash all the parts I loved the most. Tell him how incredibly talented I think he is. I've had a few moments in life when I've felt as though I'm doing exactly what I was born to do. When my writing has clicked or my research has revealed something insightful and powerful and useful. Watching Flint tonight, I knew with utter certainty that this is *exactly* what he was born to do. He's an artist. A storyteller. And it's an amazing thing to watch.

But I can't tell him any of that because the minute the movie is over, we are swept up and out and we're moving through a crowd of producers and executive producers and screenwriters and studio executives, all congratulating each other and hugging and shaking hands.

I am introduced to dozens of people. I smile and nod and do my best to catalog names, but soon everyone's faces are blurring together, my feet are killing me, and I can't remember the last time I ate anything.

Maybe this is how everyone in Hollywood stays so trim. There is never any time for food.

"How are you holding up?" I ask Flint in a rare moment of silence. We're on an elevator on our way up to the penthouse of some building where there is a party happening to celebrate the movie. I'm pretty sure all the same people we were just talking to outside of the premiere will also be here, which, I'll be honest, seems a little excessive, but Claire says there will be *food* at this party, so I'm in.

Assuming I can figure out a way to eat in this dress.

Flint tugs me close, pulling my back against his broad chest, and bends his head down to nuzzle my neck. He presses a kiss just beside my ear. "I'm starving. How are you?"

"Same. Am I allowed to eat in this dress, you think?"

"Definitely yes." He's quiet for a beat before asking, "What did you think of the movie?" The vulnerability in his voice makes my heart squeeze.

I spin around to face him, pressing my hands to his chest. "Flint. I loved the movie. You were brilliant."

He smiles the slightest bit. "High praise from a woman who doesn't like movies."

I push up on my tiptoes and press my lips to his. "I just needed the right person to show me the right movies."

"Yeah? What movies are the right ones?"

I grin. "Any ones that you are in."

The elevator reaches the top floor and dings, the door sliding open, and Flint reaches for my hand and tugs me out of the elevator. Instead of walking toward the party, he heads to the right, pulling me into a small alcove just past the bank of elevators.

He leans down to kiss me, stealing my breath and sending ripples of heat through my body. He pulls back, looking at me for a long moment before pulling me into his chest and wrapping his arms around me.

It's just a hug—but this hug feels like it means something different. Something *more*.

"Things are better when you're here," he says, his lips close to my ear.

I run my hands up and down his back. "Yeah? Like what?"

"Everything," he says simply. He finally lets me go, and I look up to find his gaze fixed on my face. He smiles. "I don't want to freak you out, Audrey. But I like the man I am more when you're beside me. You make me better."

I push up on my toes and kiss him one more time. Because what else could I possibly do? Tonight, for the first time, I'm finally willing to admit that maybe I *can* handle this kind of life.

It's still so new, but as I press my palms against Flint's chest and feel the pounding of his heart, it suddenly feels magically, blissfully possible that this man will be the rest of my life.

Chapter Twenty-Six
Audrey

THE PARTY IS IMPRESSIVE. Unlike any party I've ever attended before.

Claire said there would be food, but the spread, which covers two enormous tables lining the far wall, is more elaborate than anything I've ever seen before. There is also an endless supply of champagne, which I would usually ignore without a second thought. But tonight, we're celebrating.

Flint grabs a couple of glasses from a passing tray and hands me one. "To *Turning Tides,*" I say, holding my glass.

Flint grins, then leans forward and presses a quick kiss to my lips. "You can toast the movie if you want. But I'm toasting us."

After we eat and drink and eat some more, Flint catches me yawning. All the champagne is making me sleepy.

Flint squeezes my fingers. "What do you say we find Mark Sheridan, impress him with my startling charm and your giant biology brain, then call it a night?"

I smile. "That is the sexiest thing you've ever said."

I won't take full credit if Flint ends up getting the lead in Mark's next movie. But I'm just saying, I *own* the conversation about the environmental impacts of offshore drilling. If the goal was to impress him, mission freaking accomplished. Flint keeps looking at me, his smile wide, squeezing my hand whenever I answer another one of Mark's questions.

It's not like I thought Hollywood was *only* about beautiful people talking about inconsequential things. But...okay, maybe that *is* what I thought. But after talking to Lea earlier today about consulting on her script, and after talking to Mark, it's nice to recognize there's more to it than that.

Even though our plan was to cut out early, the four of us, me, Flint, Mark, and his wife, Deidra, end up talking for hours before I finally have to excuse myself to find a bathroom.

"Hey, take Joni with you," Flint says, motioning to where Joni and Nate are sitting just behind us. "I don't want you going anywhere by yourself."

"It's just the bathroom," I say, charmed by his concern, but entirely positive I will be just fine. I press a quick kiss to his lips. "And we're at a private party. I'll be fine."

He nods, but I don't miss the concern flitting across his expression. "Okay. Just be quick."

I nod and head down the hall, a tiny bit tipsy but still steady on my feet. Honestly, I maybe should have grabbed Joni, because I'm not entirely sure how I'm going to manage my dress on my own, but I'm buzzing on intelligent conversation and champagne, so I'm just going to run with it. It's been an amazing night! Anything is possible!

I push through a door and freeze. I thought this was the bathroom, but I'm actually on some sort of outdoor rooftop terrace. *So...I'm possibly tipsier than I thought.*

I stand at the door and consider my options. The terrace is pretty, full of oversized planter boxes that are lush with vegetation. It isn't going to help with the needing-to-pee situation, but the night air feels cool against my flushed skin, and the plants are so pretty.

Betula pendula, I think, running my fingers over the shimmering leaves of a silver birch tree. That one has always been one of my favorites.

I step past the tree and grip the banister at the edge of the terrace, looking out at the glittering skyline. It isn't anything like the views in North Carolina, but there's still something magical about all the glittering lights.

"Needed a break?" a rough voice says from behind me.

I spin around and come face to face with an older, balding man wearing a smarmy expression. He's holding a camera in his thicky, meaty hands.

I close my eyes and swear under my breath.

What was I thinking coming out here like this?

"The life of a celebrity can feel pretty intense for someone like you. Someone who isn't a celebrity." He takes a step closer. "How are you feeling, Audrey?"

I take a step backward, my heart pounding in my chest, but there's nowhere for me to go. The banister is directly behind me. I grip it with both hands and force words to come out of my throat. "I'd rather not talk to anyone right now," I say.

The man licks his lips. "I watched you in the airport yesterday. Scared out of your wits, weren't you?" He tsks. "Better toughen up, sweetheart. This life isn't meant for everyone."

"I really would like to be left alone," I say, my voice stronger this time, but I might as well be speaking a different language for all the care this man is giving my words.

He lifts his camera and fires off a few shots, the flash blinding in the dim light. I lift a hand to shield my eyes.

"Step forward for me, honey. Let me get a few shots where the light is better." The man reaches forward, his free hand wrapping around my wrist before he yanks *hard*.

I stumble forward, struggling to regain my footing and pull my arm free, but the man has an iron grip. "Let me go," I say, the words sharp in my dry throat, but his grip only tightens as he pulls me closer, his breath hot on my face.

"Take your hands *off* my girlfriend," a familiar voice says, and I look up to see Flint hauling the man away from me. He holds him by the shirt collar, anger blazing in his eyes. "Don't go near her again. Do you understand me?" He shoves the man toward Nate, who is waiting just behind him, then he's in front of me, his hands gripping my shoulders, his expression intense. "Are you all right? Did he hurt you?"

I manage a stuttering breath, but I can't form words. My heart is beating too fast, the adrenaline racing through me making me hot, then cold, then hot again.

"Audrey," Flint says, giving my shoulders the tiniest squeeze.

It's enough to rattle something loose, and I lift my gaze to his. His eyes are an intense blue, fear radiating in their depths. "I'm okay," I whisper. "Can we just...I don't want to be here anymore."

He tugs me against him for a brief hug, then curls an arm around me protectively as he walks me out of the party. Nate and the photographer are nowhere to be seen. We don't talk to anyone as we make our way to the elevator.

Nate must have talked to Joni though, because she shows up downstairs right after we do, letting us know a car is already on its way to pick us up.

Flint hasn't said anything since we left the terrace, but I don't need him to say actual words for me to understand how he's feeling. His jaw is tight, tension radiating from him in palpable waves.

Somewhere in the back of my mind, I know he's only angry because he was worried, and clearly, he had reason to be because I was in way over my head when that photographer accosted me. But the longer Flint is quiet, the more defensive I feel.

How was *I* supposed to know there would be a photographer hiding out on the terrace? As far as I understood it, the party was supposed to be private—no press. I don't know how the photographer got in, but it's not *my* fault he was there.

As soon as we're in the car, Flint shifts to face me. "Audrey, what were you thinking going out there alone? I told you to take Joni with you. *I told you.*"

My indignation boils to the surface. "What was I thinking?" I shoot back. "I'm not a child who needs scolding, Flint. I just wanted some air. How was I supposed to know there would be a photographer lurking in the corner?"

He scoffs. "That man is not a photographer. At least not a credible one. His name is Ed Cooper, and he's a criminal with a mile-long list of restraining orders, a stalking charge, and the worst reputation in all of Hollywood. He has no morals, Audrey. He will cross every line there is to cross."

"Oh, great. So happy to have met him. Maybe I'll throw a party of my own and see if he'd like to be my official photographer."

Flint's expression darkens. "What are you even saying?"

"I'd like to ask you the same question. You're talking to me like it's *my fault* Ed Cooper was on that terrace. I didn't do anything wrong, and I don't appreciate you talking to me like I did."

Flint lifts his hands, some of the fire draining out of his voice. "You're right. I'm sorry. It's absolutely not your fault. He shouldn't have been there, it *was* a private party, and the fact that he found a way in doesn't have anything to do with you. *I'm sorry,*" he says again.

I fold my arms over my chest. "Thank you for apologizing."

"But Audrey, you still have to be cautious. In this city, you have to assume there is *always* a creep lurking in the corner. You can't wander off on your own. You need air? Nate goes with you. You want to go on a walk? Nate goes with you. You want food? Nate or Joni takes care of it. That's the only way this can work."

His words knock the wind right out of me. That's the only way this can work? The *only* way our relationship can work?

I want to protest, my natural instincts rearing up to claim my independence, assert that I'm perfectly capable of doing things on my own. But then I close my eyes and feel the photographer's hand closing around my wrist, and a shudder goes through me.

I understand what Flint is saying. Safety is important, and as long as I'm with him, I have to think about it differently than I did before.

I also know the thought of having people hovering near me, watching my every move, waiting on me hand and foot twenty-four hours a day makes me want to crawl out of my own skin.

I thought I could do this.

I *want* to do this. I *want* to be with Flint.

But my fight or flight response has been triggered, and all my body wants to do is flee.

"What if I don't want people waiting on me like that?" I ask, my voice small. "What if it feels too weird? Weird and presumptuous and pretentious and so many other words that make me uncomfortable."

"It's their job," Flint says, an edge to his voice.

"No, it's their job to serve *you*."

"And you, as long as you're with me," he says without hesitation. "You're the least pretentious person on the planet, Audrey. Nate and Joni aren't going to mind."

Moisture pools in my eyes, and I press them closed, letting the tears slide down my cheeks. "It isn't about Nate and Joni, Flint. It's about *me*. We both know this conversation is about *me*."

He holds my gaze for a long moment, then he drops back into his seat, his jaw resting on his hand.

Neither of us says another word until we're back in our hotel room. By then, it's close to two a.m., and talking is probably the last thing we need to do. I can't speak for Flint, but I'm exhausted all the way down to my bones. On top of that, my heart is heavy, my emotions a confusing mass of raw, jumbled feelings.

Flint shrugs off his jacket and pulls off his tie, then unbuttons the top few buttons of his shirt. He runs a hand through his hair, looking just as tired as I feel. "Should we talk about things?" he asks, but there's no oomph behind his words. He doesn't want to talk any more than I do.

I shake my head. "Let's just get some sleep. We can talk tomorrow."

He nods, his expression grateful as he steps out of his shoes.

I do the same, slipping out of my heels, then I pause. I really don't think I can get out of this dress by myself.

"Flint, can you help me with my dress?"

He moves in behind me without a word, his fingers brushing against my skin as he slowly unclasps the tiny hook and eye at the top of my dress, then slides down the zipper. I press my arms against the bodice to hold it in place, closing my eyes as sensation dances up and down my spine.

"Thank you," I say, when the zipper reaches my waist.

He lifts his hands, his fingers briefly brushing across my exposed shoulders before he steps away. "I'll give you a minute," he says, and then he disappears into the bathroom.

It only takes a few more minutes for us to both be ready for bed.

Flint turns off the light and settles onto his pillow without even saying goodnight.

I close my eyes and try to regulate my breathing, but I'm still keyed up from everything that happened, my mind jumping from the run-in with the photographer to my argument with Flint to some crazy version of a future where Nate follows me around all the time, trudging behind me through the woods, watching me do all my research, even hovering outside the bathroom when I need to pee.

I close my eyes and take a slow, intentional breath, willing myself to relax. But it's useless.

I am never going to fall asleep.

Beside me, the mattress shifts, and suddenly, Flint's warm body is right beside me. He snakes an arm around my waist and tugs me against him, curving his limbs around me, making himself the big spoon to my smaller one. His breath brushes over my ear. "Just breathe," he whispers. "I've got you."

I instantly relax, melting into the warmth of him, savoring his solid presence behind me. I didn't know this is what I would need to fall asleep, but with Flint beside me, his strong arms holding me close, I have never felt so safe.

My breathing slowly steadies, and my eyelids grow heavy.

Soon, Flint's breathing changes, and I can tell that he's asleep.

I don't want this to be complicated.

I have met a ridiculously perfect man, and I want to be with him.

More than anything.

But I can't pretend like there isn't a cost. My safety. My anonymity. My solitude. I can never take those things for granted again.

My life will never be *the same* again.

I just have to decide if it's worth it.

Chapter Twenty-Seven

Audrey

THERE IS ONLY ONE more stop before we're heading back to North Carolina, and that's the panel discussion at UCLA's film school.

Flint and I haven't talked much this morning. We only got a few hours of sleep before we had to be up, so it's possible we're both just tired. But the air seems different between us somehow. Like we're both waiting to see how the other is going to act.

A part of me wants to just throw my arms around him, apologize for the argument, and promise everything is going to be fine.

But I still feel sick whenever I think about the photographer in my face, violating my privacy, touching my skin, pulling me toward him.

I have no idea how I'm supposed to survive in Flint's world.

Trouble is, I also have no idea how I'm supposed to survive without him.

Applause and laughter echo through the auditorium, and I look up from where I'm sitting just off-stage with Nate and Joni, catching Flint's profile as he smiles. The question was a softball, something silly about staying in shape for all his shirtless scenes.

Flint lobs it right back, joking about good genetics and a team of twenty-five people all dedicated to the contours of his abdominal muscles.

Somehow, he manages to be perfectly self-deprecating while also pointing out the ridiculousness of regular people comparing themselves to celebrities who literally do *nothing* on their own.

It's the perfect answer, and clearly, the audience agrees because they're still laughing and cheering in response.

I don't envy the moderator's job, who has to somehow make the entire *Turning Tides* cast feel like they matter when clearly, the audience is mostly interested in hearing from Flint.

I drain the last of my coffee and set the cup at my feet, anxious to be done, to finally be heading home. Flint and I still have a lot to talk about, but I just keep clinging to the hope that it will be easier in Silver Creek.

Everything makes more sense there.

We make more sense there.

But a tiny voice in the back of my mind reminds me that Flint makes sense *here,* too. This is his world. And that isn't ever going to change.

The moderator sends a question over to the casting director, so I pull out my phone, using the moment to check my email. If Flint isn't the one talking, I feel much less compelled to listen.

Besides, I haven't even bothered to open my work email since Thursday afternoon. Since I'll be back in the lab tomorrow morning, it's probably smart to check in and see if I missed anything important over the weekend.

The email at the top of my inbox makes the air freeze in my lungs. The subject line alone is enough for me to know it isn't good news, and opening the message only confirms my fears.

I didn't get my grant.

Come January of next year, my funding will be gone.

I close out my email and drop my phone in my lap, not wanting to cry right here in the middle of everything that's going on. Even though I had a vague sense this was coming, it still feels like a shock. It's *real*. And it absolutely sucks.

Beside me, Joni swears and reaches for her phone as a ripple of sound moves across the auditorium. I was so distracted by my sudden job crisis, I missed whatever the question was that caused such a stir. If it was even a question at all.

"What is it? What happened?" I whisper, looking at Joni. I stand and move to the other side of Nate so I have a better view of Flint.

"I'm sorry, can you repeat your question?" Flint says, leaning toward his microphone.

I lean forward with him, straining my ears so I can hear the repeated question.

"Are you willing to comment on the story that just broke on TMZ, claiming that you faked a relationship with Audrey Callahan in order to create distance between you and your co-star?"

I gasp, my hand flying to my mouth.

What in the world?

I hold my breath while Flint clears his throat. I can't even imagine how he's feeling, what's running through his mind right now.

"You know," he finally says, his voice measured and controlled, "since you're in film school, I assume you have some aspiration to make it in this business. So I'll give you some advice. Don't pay attention to what gossip sites say about you, and don't comment on what gossip sites say about you. It's a rule I live by, and so far, it's served me well. If you've got a question about the movie or my experiences as an actor, I'd be happy to answer that one instead."

"Geez, only Flint could deflect a question like that," Joni says behind me without lifting her eyes from her phone.

"Why did someone ask it in the first place?" I say. "Who would even know to ask?" Someone beside us, Claire's manager, I think, shushes us, and Joni grabs my hand, pulling me off the stage and into a hallway behind the theater.

"Anyone who reads the news would ask the question," she says darkly. She hands me her phone, a search engine full of headlines taking up the entire screen. "Someone leaked the story, Audrey. It's everywhere."

Five minutes later, the four of us, Nate, Joni, me, and Flint, are all in a black SUV driving toward the airport. My insides are a mass of swirling, sickening emotions. First, the email from work, now this. In one thirty-minute stretch of time, my entire life has been turned upside down.

"Okay, give me the worst of it," Flint says.

Joni takes a deep breath, then begins to read. "*A-list actor Flint Hawthorne made quite the statement last month when he posted photos of a new relationship on his public Instagram account. After claiming he was moving back to his hometown of Silver Creek, North Carolina to have more privacy, it seemed an abrupt shift to suddenly be making public declarations of affection. Turns out, it* WAS *an abrupt shift, and a totally fabricated one. An anonymous source close to the actor claims Hawthorne's new relationship with wildlife biologist Audrey Callahan, a Silver Creek native, is completely fake.*

"*Our source couldn't confirm Hawthorne's specific motivations, but our best guess is it had something to do with silencing his co-star, actress, Claire McKinsey. In the past few months, McKinsey has made very public insinuations that she and her* Turning Tides *co-star are on the brink of getting back together. Which leads us to ask, what really happened between Claire and Flint? Is this a publicity stunt? A way to get back at a scorned ex? Whatever his reasons, we give two thumbs down to Flint Hawthorne and his fake girlfriend and think this actor needs to grow up. Fake relationships? This isn't middle school! The pair might have looked great on the red carpet at the* Turning Tides *premiere, but America doesn't want to be duped. Stay tuned for further updates as the story unfolds."*

Joni leans back into her seat, and a heavy silence settles over us. "I mean, it could have been worse," she finally says.

I reach over and pick up Flint's hand, entwining our fingers together. I don't know how things are between us. I'm feeling off-kilter in every way possible, so I can only imagine he's feeling it, too. But no matter what our relationship looks like in the future, I want him to know I'm here for him right now.

"'*This actor needs to grow up*'," he says, his voice hollow. He swears softly. "I should have known this would happen."

"What do you want to do, Flint?" Joni asks. "You fired Simon, but as far as everyone else knows, he's still your publicist. He's probably already gotten two dozen requests for comment."

Flint scoffs. "On the story *he* leaked."

"You really think it was him?" Joni asks.

"Of course it was him," Flint says, steel in his tone. "Simon is the only person who knows, outside of the people in this car and our immediate families." He looks at me. "You warned me. You *told* me he might do something like this, and I didn't listen." He presses his fists into the seatback in front of him and groans. "Why didn't I just listen to you? Why didn't I wait to fire him?"

I lift a hand to Flint's back, rubbing slow circles across his shoulder blades. It's such a small thing. Too small. But what else can I do?

"We just have to move forward from here," Joni says. "What's done is done. There's no use beating yourself up over it now." She pulls out her iPad and opens up her notepad app. "Okay. Bare minimum, we need to get Simon's information off your website and issue a statement saying he no longer represents you. I can see if Kenji has someone who can handle that for us. But then you'll need to decide if you want to hire a *new* publicist, or if you want to just go dark and hope this all blows over."

"Can you get Kenji on the phone?" Flint asks. "I want to know what he thinks."

As soon as Kenji is on the line, Joni gives him a quick update, all the way back to Simon's involvement with Claire and her decision to also fire Simon.

"Wow," Kenji says when Joni finishes. "You sure know how to piss a guy off."

"What do I do, man?" Flint asks. "Can I just go home? Hope all of this goes away on its own?"

"You *can,*" Kenji says. "And it might. But I'm not sure that's a gamble I'd take."

My heart sinks at Kenji's words. I don't *want* to stay in LA. I *can't* stay. Not when my professional life is falling to pieces back in Silver Creek.

Flint sighs and presses his forehead into his palm. I move my hand from his back, down to his knee, giving it a quick squeeze. He doesn't respond to my touch at all, and I pull my hand back into my lap, hating how far away he feels. Hating even more that I'm part of the reason why.

"Listen," Kenji says. "Most of what Simon is saying is inconsequential. It's annoying and it makes you look a little stupid, but if it doesn't get worse than what we're seeing right now, it isn't going to have much impact. You're a professional. You work like a professional. That holds more weight than what entertainment news has to say. My bigger worry is that Simon isn't finished."

"You think he'll try to sabotage my career?" Flint says.

"Nah," Kenji says easily. "You're too big for him to sabotage anything. But I can see him spreading rumors. Saying you're not so easy to work with. Maybe hinting that your personal drama sometimes gets in the way."

"But couldn't Flint do the same thing to Simon?" I say. I look at Flint. "That's why you felt comfortable firing him, right? Because you thought he'd be too nervous about what you could do to *his* reputation."

"It's a valid question. But Simon isn't an idiot. I'm sure it occurred to him that you could go public with what he's done and impact his credibility. The fact that he leaked the story *anyway* makes me think he's got some greater strategy in all this. I don't have any idea what that strategy might look like, but honestly, I'm more concerned about what Simon might say in the future than I am about what he said today."

"Or he just acted impulsively," I say. "He has no strategy. He was just angry and vindictive."

"Either way," Kenji says, "we need to stay a few steps ahead of him."

I don't need Kenji to say the words to sense where this conversation is going.

Flint needs to stay in LA.

"Why don't you come by the office this afternoon?" Kenji says, confirming my fear. "We'll come up with a plan and talk about a new publicist. I know a woman. She's young and not as well-connected as Simon, but she's sharp. Thinks faster than anyone else I know. I'll get her in here and see if we can draft a response to any inquiries that come in that will minimize damage, deny the story, and keep you looking like the professional you are. Then we'll talk about how to handle Simon."

"Can we do it over the phone?" Flint asks. "We're flying out in a couple of hours."

"Dude, listen. I know you hate being in LA, but this will be so much easier if you just come in. If you're hiring this publicist, you need to meet her. Get some face time. Make sure you feel good about this."

Flint breathes out a weary sigh. "Okay. I'll make it work."

"If possible, Audrey should stay too. The more the two of you are seen in public, together and obviously into each other, the easier it will be to discredit Simon's story. Either way, I'll see you this afternoon."

Kenji hangs up and Flint's gaze shifts to me, his eyebrows raised in question.

I bite my lip. I want to stay. I do. But I *can't*. I need to call the university. Talk to my summer grad students. Regroup. Figure out if there's any money out there that can keep us funded. We need to be writing grant applications. Networking. Deciding what's next.

Flint must read my hesitation because his expression shifts, his hope turning into resignation. He masks it quickly, but I don't miss the hurt in his eyes, despite the effort he's making to keep it hidden from me. "Flint, it's not you. I want to be here with you. I do. But—I just found out I didn't get my grant."

"What? Why not?"

I shrug. "The organization that's been funding me the past three years has decided to shift their efforts to research on the coast—something about the impact of global warming on oceanic temperatures. Which is timely and important, so I guess I can't really fault them."

"But your research is important, too," Flint says. "Audrey, I'm so sorry."

"That's why I need to get home. I have to find money, somehow. Revise my grant application. I don't know. This late in the year, it's going to be tough. But I have to try."

"*Of course* you do. You have to go." He drops back into his seat. "I'm really sorry this is happening. It's like everything fell apart for both of us all at once."

I have to wonder if everything has fallen apart for *us,* too. As a couple.

"We're going to get through it though, right?" I say, willing myself to cling to whatever optimism I can muster. "It's going to be okay. You'll stay here and get through your stuff, I'll go home and get through my stuff, and everything will work out?"

He frowns. "Audrey, my stuff is *your stuff,* too. We haven't really talked about this part yet, and it really, really sucks, but the next few days are not going to be easy for you. You're probably going to be bombarded with emails, voice mails, text messages. Gossip columnists will do everything they can to try to get a comment out of you."

Joni nods. "He's right, Audrey. There would have been *some* mild interest when everyone thought your relationship was real. But now that people think it was all staged, they're going to want your side of the story. They may even reach out to your sisters or parents. All of you should probably block calls from unknown numbers, at least for the next couple of weeks."

"And you shouldn't go anywhere alone until you're sure there isn't anyone in Silver Creek who doesn't belong there," Flint says. He looks at Nate. "I want you to travel home with Audrey, Nate."

"Nate isn't staying with you?" I ask.

"No," Flint says, his expression stern. "I want him with you."

His words settle over me like an itchy wool blanket. Somehow, I'd forgotten to consider the fact that the other half of Flint's fake relationship is *me*. Enduring all the attention when I have Flint around to help me through it is one thing.

I don't know how I feel about enduring it on my own.

"What about your security?" Nate asks. "I'm happy to go, but I don't like the idea of you out here by yourself."

"Honestly, I can fly home by myself," I say, but Flint is shaking his head no before I've even finished my sentence.

"You aren't traveling alone. That's not up for debate. If I can't be with you while all this nonsense blows over, then Nate has to be." He looks at Joni. "Call the security agency we used to use and have them send someone out to cover me until I fly home."

"I assume I'm staying with you?" she asks, and Flint nods.

I sink back into my seat, my brain split between worrying about my lack of funding and stressing over the unknown attention and drama I'm facing because of stupid Simon. This isn't how my trip with Flint was supposed to end. This isn't how *anything* was supposed to end.

And now we have to say goodbye with all this tension between us, all the conversations we haven't had still lingering in the air.

How do we even move on from our last conversation? We both know it didn't end well, but how else could it have ended? I *can't* be with Flint without considering my safety—my privacy—in new ways. It doesn't matter whether I like it or not. Reality is reality. End of story.

But what am I supposed to do if that reality makes me uncomfortable? It was simple to think I could handle Flint's celebrity life when everything was easy and perfect, but the second it got hard, I freaked out. That can't be a good sign.

We pull up in front of LAX, and Nate and Joni both jump out, probably to say their own goodbyes in private. Our driver gets out to retrieve our bags, leaving Flint and me alone.

Flint must feel some sense of hesitation—or maybe he's just picking up on mine—because he makes no move to touch me. "Call me when you make it home?" he says. "I don't care how late it is. I just want to know you're safe."

I nod. "I'm really sorry I can't stay."

"I'm sorry I *have* to stay." He lifts a hand like he wants to touch me, but then it falls back into his lap. "And I'm sorry you lost your grant. I wish there was something I could do."

Joni opens the passenger door behind me. "Time to go, Audrey."

"Just one more second," I say, and she nods and closes the door.

I sniff and wipe at the tears streaming down my cheeks. I hold Flint's gaze for a long moment, and then suddenly, whatever tension keeping us apart snaps, and I throw myself into his arms.

His hands lift to cradle my face and he kisses me, his thumbs wiping away my tears. When he finally breaks the kiss, I melt against him, my head falling on his chest while his hands run up and down my back.

"Why does leaving you feel so hard?" I whisper.

He presses a kiss to my temple. "We'll talk soon, all right? We'll figure things out."

Joni knocks on the window, giving us another heads-up that we're out of time.

I reluctantly pull away and gather my things, then slide across the bench toward the door of the SUV. I look back one last time. Right now, Flint doesn't look like a movie star. He looks tired and worn down and as frustrated as I feel.

I follow Nate into the airport, through security, and toward our gate, keeping my head down to avoid eye contact just like Flint taught me.

I don't know what I'm supposed to do.

I only know it feels like my body is on its way home to Silver Creek, but I'm leaving my heart in LA.

Chapter Twenty-Eight
Audrey

ALL THINGS CONSIDERED, LIFE in Silver Creek post-celebrity-relationship (fake celebrity relationship?) could be worse.

Flint and Joni weren't wrong about inquiries from gossip sites and other reporters. Fortunately, my lack of a social media presence has made me slightly more difficult to reach. Mostly, I've just gotten emails. A few people have shown up at the house or stopped by the lab, but since Nate has insisted on shadowing me everywhere I go, it's been easy to simply let him turn them away.

I pull off my glasses and drop them onto my desk, then close my eyes, pressing my fingers into my eye sockets.

"I'm not gonna lie, Audrey. You look like you need a good night's sleep," Nate says, setting a mug of coffee down on my desk. "Drink this, at least."

I manage a small smile and reach for the cup. "I don't think I've *had* a good night's sleep since I got home." *Since I left Flint.* I think of how easily I slept with his arms around me, even just after a horrible run-in with the skeevy photographer at the premiere party, and a wave of longing rushes through me.

"Hey, whatever happened to the guy at the party? Ed Cooper?"

Nate drops into an empty chair across from my desk, causing a loud creak.

Malorie, one of the forest rangers who staffs the research lab, shoots us some side-eye, and Nate squirms.

"Can you get in trouble for me being here?"

I wave a dismissive hand. "I don't work for them. My university has an agreement with the state allowing me to use the space, but I'm my own boss around here. You're fine."

"Will that be in jeopardy too?" Nate asks. "If you don't find new funding?"

I nod. "Sadly, yes. Malorie is grumpy—she's the one who just gave us angry eyes—but everyone else is really great. I'll be sad to go."

"Maybe you won't go," Nate says. "Don't give up yet."

I take a long drink of coffee. "Oh, geez," I say, putting down the mug. "I forgot how bad the coffee is here."

"Sorry," Nate says. "You looked desperate."

I press my face into my hands, rubbing them up and down like I'm trying to wake myself up, then breathe out a long sigh. "I miss him, Nate."

"I'm sure he misses you, too."

"So, Ed Cooper?"

"Right. We called the cops on him that night, but he'd somehow managed to snag an official invitation to the party, so they had to let him go. He wasn't breaking any laws by being there."

An uncomfortable shiver runs down my spine. "I just feel like there ought to be a way to stop him somehow."

"Unfortunately, there will always be guys like Ed Cooper out there. It sucks, but it's the price people like Flint have to pay."

"And people close to Flint," I say, my voice tired.

Nate leans forward, holding me with his very serious stare. It's funny to remember how intimidated I was by this man when we first met. He really is just a giant softy. "Listen," he says. "I know my opinion doesn't matter. But I worked for a security agency before Flint hired me full-time, and I shadowed a lot of famous people. Flint is one of the good ones."

Warmth spreads through my chest. Nate doesn't have to convince me. I *know* Flint is good. "Thanks, Nate. Your opinion absolutely matters."

Nate glances at his watch. "Are you working late tonight?"

It's only my second day back at the lab, and I can for sure find something to do, but if I stay late, Nate will stay late, and I don't want him to do that. He hired a second security officer to cover my house when I'm home and in for the night, but as long as I'm out and about, Nate won't stop working.

"We can go now," I say, pushing back from my desk. "I can work on grant proposals from home, and that's mainly what I need to be focusing on anyway."

Nate follows me out to the parking lot, his eyes moving from side to side like there's *actually* a possibility of danger in this sleepy corner of Silver Creek. "So, when I start teaching classes next week, will someone have to come to school with me? I bet my students would love—"

Nate grips my elbow, silencing my rambling, and tugs me behind him.

And that's when I see him. *Ed Cooper.*

"I like you in your natural habitat," he says as he lifts his camera.

My stomach rolls, a wave of nausea nearly doubling me over.

"Keep walking, Audrey," Nate says, his voice low. "Don't respond to him."

Suddenly, the distance between us and Nate's SUV seems enormous. It can't be more than twenty yards, but my shoes are full of lead, and my limbs are trembly and weak. The car could be miles away for how long it's going to take me.

"This whole look," Ed says, following behind us, the shutter on his camera clicking over and over. "It really suits you, Audrey. You look like a real biologist."

I swallow against the lump in my throat, but it's Nate who answers him. "She *is* a real biologist. And you're on private property. You need to leave."

"Touchy," he says, as he takes a step closer. "Sorry if I'm a little confused about what's real and what isn't. After all the news lately, who knows?"

Nate pulls out his keys and clicks the fob to unlock the doors. He keeps his hand on my elbow, half-leading, half-dragging my stupid functionless limbs toward the passenger side.

"What can you tell me about your relationship, Audrey? Was it all fake? Are you going to see Flint again?" *Click. Click, click.* "I saw Flint the other night. He was out with Claire McKinsey. Did you know he's still seeing her? Was all this faking just a ploy to make her jealous?"

I ignore his words. I *have to* ignore his words.

I trust Flint.

Ten times more than I trust Ed Cooper.

Nate pulls open the passenger door and helps me in, shutting it firmly behind me. Seconds later, Nate is in the driver's seat, and we're leaving Ed Cooper and his stupid camera behind.

"Are you all right?" Nate asks.

I manage a weak nod, but my mind is spinning. I can't stop thinking about what might have happened had Nate not been there.

What if I'd been alone?

Nate checks his rearview mirror at least a dozen times on the way home. I don't see anyone following behind us, but that's little comfort. If Ed Cooper figured out where I work, I'm sure he knows where I live.

"Do you think he'll come to the house?" I manage to ask, shocked by how shaken I sound.

"If he does, I'll be there," Nate says. "I won't let him close to you, Audrey."

Ten minutes later, I'm on the couch in my living room with a bowl of Lucy's chicken noodle soup in my hands, flanked by a sister on either side. Nate called the cops first—he suspects Ed Cooper broke parole when he left California—then he calls Flint. I can only hear his side of the conversation, but it's enough to tell me how worried Flint is.

I appreciate his worry. And Nate's worry. And the way my sisters are hovering like I might break apart if they aren't here to hold me up. But I also feel like I'm wearing too-small shoes.

The attention. The security measures. All this *concern* for my welfare. Two months ago, the only thing threatening my peace and safety was the occasional run-in with a black bear. And then, I knew exactly what to do to keep *myself* safe. I was capable. Confident. Strong enough to handle whatever situation I found myself in.

But I'm in over my head with this. I *did* get away from the photographer today. But what if it happens again?

After eating and reassuring my sisters that I'm okay, I escape into my room and collapse onto my bed. I stare at my ceiling fan for a long time, watching the blades spin slowly around.

Right after Flint asked me to go to LA with him, Lucy talked me down from a full-on freak-out by treating my circumstances like a science project. We examined the facts. Formed reasonable hypotheses and logical conclusions. And it worked.

Taking a deep breath, I try to do the same thing, but my thoughts are so jumbled, I just keep thinking myself in circles.

When my phone rings an hour later, the screen lighting up with Flint's face, I have no more clarity than I did before, but I can't not answer—not when I know how worried he must be.

I grab my phone, pressing a pillow against my chest as I answer the call. "Hi, Flint."

"Hey. How are you?" he asks, concern filling his voice. "How are you feeling?"

"Still a little shaken up, but I'll be okay."

"Audrey, listen," he says. "I want you to move into my house for a few days. At least until they find Cooper and arrest him. Take your sisters with you. You'll be closer to Nate, and you'll have a security system to keep you safe when Nate can't be close by."

I close my eyes. I suspected this was what Flint would want. Logically, it makes sense. If I'm in danger, his house is a lot safer than mine. But my physical safety isn't the only thing on the line here. Nate already assured me there would be eyes on my house around the clock. I'll be safe here at home. And right now, I *need* to be.

A sense of calm settles into my heart. This is the right call. Even if it's a painful one.

"I don't want to move into your house, Flint."

He's quiet for a beat. "I don't mean permanently. Just until we can make sure—"

"I know what you mean," I say, cutting him off as gently as I can. "And I appreciate the offer. But Flint..." I hesitate, hating the tremble in my voice. "I just need to be in my own space for a while. I think I'm feeling..." I pause, fresh tears streaming down my cheeks. "Swallowed, I guess? Like my life is somehow getting sucked up into yours. And that's not your fault, and I'm not saying I don't want us to be together. I just need to breathe a minute, and that's going to be a lot easier in my own house."

"I'm not sure I understand," he says.

"Flint, your house is a fairy tale. It's magical and beautiful and full of white squirrels, and I love every single thing about it. *All of it* is a fairy tale. You. The private jet and the beautiful clothes and the people ready to wait on me hand and foot. It's amazing. *Of course* it's amazing. But it also makes it easy to get swept up. I'm Cinderella at the ball, only, I was never the girl who sat around and dreamed about ball gowns. I would have totally ruined that story because I would have taken one look at the royal invitation and been like, 'You know what? I'm good. Y'all have fun at the party. I'm gonna hang back and chill with the mice.'"

He chuckles. "That's one of the things I love most about you. I don't want you to change, Audrey. I just want you to be safe."

"I know. *I know* you do, and I appreciate that. But this is about more than my safety. It's the conversation we *didn't* have when we argued after the premiere. Every time I'm faced with a new reality of *your* world, I have to stop and ask myself how it's going to impact *mine*. How will being together influence my work? Will I travel with you whenever you're filming? Will I stay in Silver Creek? Will I require a security detail even when we aren't together? Every answer impacts the level of autonomy and control I have over my own life. I realize that's the case with every relationship. But we can't pretend like there aren't special circumstances here."

Flint is quiet for a long time. *Too long.* If not for the slight sound of his breathing, I might wonder if he was still on the call.

"So you're saying you aren't sure if you want us to be together," he finally says.

"No," I say, my voice breaking under the strain of my emotions. "I'm not saying that at all. I'm just saying I'm scared and uncertain, and I want to make sure I know my own mind. Your life is so big, Flint. And it's amazing and glamorous and I love being a part of it. But my life is important, too. I just don't want to get so swept up in your world that I lose my own."

"Which is why you want to stay at your house."

"I mean, yes. But it's more than that too."

He sighs. "I understand. I don't like it. But I *do* understand it." He sniffs and clears his throat. When he speaks again, he almost sounds like a different person. "Listen, I want you to take as much time as you need, all right? Stay at your place, for sure. Nate will still be keeping an eye on things, but I'll tell him to keep his distance so your life will feel as normal as possible."

"Flint, stop," I say.

"Stop what?"

"I don't know what just happened, but your voice changed." I think back to the way he spoke to my sisters when he first met them. That's exactly what he sounds like now. "You just turned into actor Flint—like you're only saying what I want to hear. But I don't want you to pretend with me."

He's quiet for a long moment. "You can't have it both ways, Audrey," he finally says. "You can't ask me for space and also ask me to be real, because what I want *for real* is the opposite of giving you space."

Pain slices into my heart. What am I doing? Am I really pushing him away?

"I'm sorry," I say, my voice soft. "You're right. That wasn't fair of me to say."

He sighs. "Audrey, you told me from the beginning you weren't interested in a life like mine."

"But that was before I knew you, before I..." *Before I fell in love with you.* I don't finish the sentence out loud, but the realization fills my heart with perfect clarity.

I love him. *I love him.*

If that's true, everything else will have to work out, won't it?

"I think...I need to not call you for a few days, all right?" Flint says.

"Flint, wait—"

"No, this is good. I think we both need a minute to think. To figure out what we want." He's actor Flint again, protecting his heart, doing what he thinks I need in order to protect mine.

I close my eyes, tears falling freely now. "Are you still coming home?"

"I've got a few more things to do first. But soon. As soon as I can."

We end the call and I crawl under my comforter, not even caring that I haven't brushed my teeth or checked the front door lock or plugged in my phone.

I said the hard things that were sitting on my heart—the fears, the struggles, the worries—and I don't have regrets about that. A relationship with Flint will mean all kinds of conversations about how his fame impacts both of our lives.

But I still feel like my heart is broken, and I'm not sure I can fix it until Flint is here—until I see him again.

Soon better get here quick.

Chapter Twenty-Nine

Flint

FLINT: SO. PRETTY SURE I'm in love with Audrey.

Brody: WHAT? I'M SHOCKED.

Brody: We all saw this coming, dude.

Flint: For real?

Perry: You're a good actor, man. But not that good.

Lennox: Olivia made us watch the red-carpet footage from the premiere.

Brody: It made me throw up in my mouth a little. What are you wearing, Flint? Oh, you look so handsome tonight, Flint. BARF.

Flint: I was wearing Tom Ford. Thanks for asking. Brushed wool, lined in silk. I promise it felt as good as it looked. Anyone else ever wear a Tom Ford tuxedo?

Brody: Tom Ford. That's the bargain brand you rent from Men's Warehouse, right? Like, for prom and stuff?

Lennox: Hahaha. Brody's on one...

Flint: Can we please get back to the very important subject of my love life?

Perry: Yes. Right. You love Audrey.

Lennox: Does she love you back? Are we celebrating here? Or commiserating?

Flint: Not celebrating yet. Things are still...tenuous?

Perry: Explain tenuous.

Flint: She's kinda been through it. The same photographer who accosted her in LA followed her to Silver Creek and showed up at her lab. Nate was with her. She's fine. Just a little freaked out.

Lennox: Yeah. That's a lot.

Flint: And maybe not sure if it's worth it, I guess?

Flint: She said she's worried about her life getting swallowed up in mine.

Brody: I mean, your life is a lot. But it isn't ALWAYS a lot. Things will probably calm down after the initial freak-out over you being in a relationship.

Flint: Have you guys ever resented my fame?

Flint: I realize there are a million ways you could make fun of me for asking that question, but this time I need a serious answer.

Perry: I was a little annoyed when I had to hire security because your fans wouldn't stop sneaking onto the farm to take pictures with Mom's goats. But I didn't resent you.

Brody: You're family, man. And we're proud of you. If we have to deal with a little extra attention every once in a while, it just means we make fun of you harder that week.

Lennox: Blending two lives into one is never easy. You guys will figure it out.

Flint: If she loves me back.

Brody: Have you told her how you feel?

Flint: Not yet. She asked for a little bit of breathing room.

Lennox: Ohhh. That's not good.

Brody: Don't freak him out. It's probably nothing.

Flint: Probably? What does probably mean?

Brody: Actually, I think we need to survey the wives here. Hang on.

Perry: Lila says wanting breathing room COULD mean she's not interested, but it could also mean she's VERY interested but also VERY overwhelmed. She says having met Audrey, her vote is for the second one.

Brody: Yep. Kate said the same thing. She says Audrey is probably gun-shy. She needs to know you see her for HER. And not just as a celebrity girlfriend.

Flint: I do not see her as a celebrity girlfriend.

Brody: Hi! This is Kate. I know that's not how you see her, but so far, all your big gestures have been about what she's doing for YOU. Attending your premiere, walking the red carpet, posing for your Instagram photos. What have you done for HER?

Brody: Okay. Giving the phone back now. I'm done.

Flint: Oh man. That's...

Brody: THAT'S MY WIFE, Y'ALL. She's smart.

Lennox: Tatum here. Typing one-handed because I'm breastfeeding. But YES. Listen to Kate. Do something for her that lets her know you care about her life, too. And your relationship will never be JUST about your status as a celebrity.

Perry: How's the baby? Is she so big? I swear, they grow so fast at that age.

Flint: Lila, did you steal Perry's phone? WHAT IS HAPPENING TO THIS GROUP CHAT? No more breastfeeding and baby talk. Go find your own thread.

Flint: Actually, wait. Don't leave. I think you guys might be able to help me more than my idiot brothers can.

Brody: YES!! I'm back in control. Let us help. We love you. We love Audrey. We want this to work.

Perry: Why don't you start by telling us what you love about her? <3

Lennox: Ohhh yes! Good idea.

Flint: Okay. She's brilliant. It's killer sexy.

Perry: Excellent first answer!

Flint: I also love her authenticity. She is who she is, and she doesn't equivocate about it.

Lennox: This is important. Especially because you're famous. Having a partner who has a strong sense of self matters. What else?

Flint: She's gorgeous. Like, knock the breath out of me beautiful. She's the person I want to tell whenever anything good happens, but I also want to talk to her when something really sucks. I just...want her to be my person.

Brody: Sigh. <3

Perry: <3 <3 <3

Lennox: I'm literally crying right now!

Flint: Stop with the exclamation points and heart emojis or I'm making you give the phones back to your husbands.

Perry: Flint, you don't really need our help. Do you know why you're a good actor? You have high emotional intelligence. You get how people feel, and you translate that into how you act.

Brody: Ohhh, that's so true, Lila.

Lennox: Which means you know her, Flint. You know what she needs.

Brody: But also, maybe hire some female security. If you're going to have security people around all the time, might be nice if she has someone who can also be her friend.

Flint: Thanks, y'all.

Perry: We really like her, Flint. Good luck. Let us know if you need us again. <3

Brody: You can do it! Win her heart! <3

Lennox: <3 <3 <3

...

...

...

Perry: Oh wow. That's a lot of heart emojis.

Chapter Thirty
Audrey

LUCY WAKES ME UP the following morning by climbing into my bed.

"What is happening?" I mumble sleepily, squinting against the Saturday morning sunshine pouring through my window.

"Look at this," she says, snuggling in beside me and holding up her phone. "Someone stopped Flint on his way out of a restaurant the other night, and he actually answered a question about the whole fake dating thing."

"Wait, he talked about it?"

"I mean, he didn't say much, but yeah. Here. Watch." She cues up the video and holds her phone in the air above us so we can both watch. It begins with a commentator providing a summary of the allegations in the original story, then cuts to a clip of Flint's response during the panel at UCLA, and then, finally, a clip of Flint on the sidewalk outside a restaurant.

"I have nothing but positive feelings for all my co-stars from *Turning Tides*. Claire and I ended our relationship amicably, and we've remained friends. As for my current relationship, I can assure you, everything I'm feeling is very real."

Lucy drops the phone and turns her head to look at me. "So smart, right? He didn't lie by refuting the story, but he also made it seem like it was all just total baloney. And he totally did it on the spot!"

I take a deep breath, still trying to wake up, and stretch my arms over my head. "Smart, yes. But it probably *wasn't* on the spot. My guess is his publicist planted that reporter on purpose and coached Flint on how to respond."

"Really? They do that?"

"Of course they do. When we flew into LAX, why do you think there were so many people there to see us arrive? Flint's publicist leaked our travel plans on purpose. We needed to be seen together, so he made sure we were seen."

"Look at you with all your insider Hollywood knowledge," Lucy says.

"Hey, pull that video back up again," I say, motioning toward her phone. "Is there an article with it? Does it say anything about who he was with that night?"

She pulls it back up. "There was an article. Hold on." She scrolls through it, angling the phone so I can also see. "He was with Claire McKinsey, it looks like," she says. "But other people too. Wait. Here's a photo of all of them leaving." She hands me the phone. "Do you know these people? That's Joni, right?"

I study the picture closely. It's blurry, but I'm sure I see Joni just behind Flint. And Claire is there too, along with Kenji, her manager, who I remember from the UCLA panel, and one other woman I don't recognize. "That *is* Joni. And this guy is his agent, Kenji. That's Rita, Claire's manager. I'm guessing this other woman is the new publicist Flint just hired."

Either way, I feel a tiny pulse of satisfaction knowing Flint wasn't out with Claire alone, no matter what stupid Ed Cooper said.

"Is that weird?" Lucy asks. She wraps an arm around me. "To get information about his whereabouts from the internet?"

"The photographer who showed up at my lab actually said something to me about it—about Flint being out with Claire. He was just taunting me, trying to get me to react, so I didn't really believe him. But yeah. It's still weird."

Lucy is quiet for a long moment. "I never thought about how much trust you have to have. There will probably always be people saying crap about him. I guess you have to get good at filtering it out."

"Flint says it gets easier over time."

"Yeah, probably. But still. It's so easy to focus on the fairy tale part. I guess there's a lot more to it."

I take a deep breath. "Yeah."

She turns her face to look at me. "You still haven't talked to him?"

I shake my head no. It's only been four days since we last talked, but it feels more like an eternity.

"How are you feeling?"

I tug my blanket up to my chin, snuggling a little deeper into my covers. "I miss him, Lu."

"Because you love him?"

I press my lips together. So far, the only person I've admitted my feelings to is *me*. But at this point, the idea of keeping secrets is much too exhausting. If I *am* in love, I don't want to pretend like I'm not.

Lucy can clearly read my emotions because her eyes widen. "Oh my gosh. You *do* love him." She sits up. "I can see it on your face."

I lift my hands and press them to my cheeks. "It's crazy. I don't even know how it happened."

"Oh, honey, I know *exactly* how it happened." She scrambles off the bed and yanks down my blankets.

"Lucy! What are you doing?" I reach for my comforter, but she tugs it completely off the bed, then grabs my hands, pulling until I'm on my feet beside her.

"That was really rude and awful," I say, my voice still sleepy.

"I don't care. You're in love, and that means we need to celebrate."

"Celebrate what? I only admitted I love *him*. I have no idea how he feels about me."

She props her hands on her hips. "Woman, did you *watch* the footage from the premiere? He looks at you like he *worships* you." She moves to the bedroom door and heads down the hallway. "Come on. I'm making you breakfast."

I pick up my comforter and quickly make my bed. I hate leaving it unmade, but also, I need a minute to process. In the video Lucy showed me, Flint said his feelings were real—but that's not a surprise. He told me the same thing. But the joy that shot through my veins when I heard him say it so plainly—I wasn't expecting that.

I drop onto the corner of my bed.

I've been so worried, so confused the past couple of days. But is there really anything confusing about it? If I love him, why would I chose not to be with him?

Lucy is mixing pancake batter when I make it to the kitchen. She nudges a container of strawberries across the counter. "Here. Want to cut these for me?"

I fish a knife out of the drawer. "Do you and Summer even keep *any* food downstairs?"

"Very little," Lucy says. She turns to face me, leaning her hip against the counter. "So what are we going to do about this? If you love him, why aren't you with him right now, hugging and kissing and making beautiful babies?"

I roll my eyes. "It's not that easy. You know it's not that easy."

"I don't, actually," Lucy says. "I've never been in love."

This gives me pause. My little sisters have both dated a lot. I lift my eyes to meet hers. "Really? Not even with...what was his name? With the glasses and the curly hair? Tim?"

Lucy frowns. "Ugh. Definitely not Tim."

"Huh."

"Focus, Auds. What's the hold-up with you and Flint?"

I slowly slice my way through a few more strawberries. "I'm just scared, I think. Which, when you make me say it out loud, it feels incredibly lame."

"It's not lame. It's how you feel. But just because it's scary doesn't mean you shouldn't do it. People do scary things all the time."

"No, *you* do scary things all the time. Summer does scary things. I don't."

Lucy scoffs. "Says the woman who has faced down a black bear? More than once?"

"You're crazy if you think bears are scarier than people."

She pulls out my griddle pan from under the counter and turns on the stove. "You're crazy if you think life *with* Flint is scarier than life without him. You have to listen to your heart, Auds. Don't let fear ruin something that could be amazing."

"But what if it isn't amazing?" I drop the knife and spin to face her. "I mean, of course it's amazing right now, but what if the magic eventually wears off and then it's just a lot of time apart, wishing we weren't on opposite sides of the country?"

She levels me with a long look. "Then you will have been on one wild ride, and you can sell your story to *People* magazine and make millions of dollars."

"Shut up. I would never do that."

She drops butter onto the pan, watching while it slowly melts and starts to sizzle. "The point still stands. It's okay for something to be good while it's good and then end without the experience being a failure. Besides, what if it *does* stay amazing forever? You'll never know if you don't try."

Tears suddenly prick my eyes, but I'm not about to start crying when it isn't even nine a.m., so I pick up the knife and dig back into the strawberries, willing the tears away.

Lucy bumps my hip with hers. "Don't cry into the strawberries, Auds. They aren't good salty."

I hiccup a laugh and give up fighting. I drop the knife and lift my hands, using my sleeves to dry my tears. "Seriously, what are you doing to me? And when did you get so wise?"

Lucy smiles and points at me with her spatula. "Pretty sure wisdom is encoded in our DNA. I'm just not as big a chicken as you are, so I'm seeing this particular situation a little more clearly."

I huff. "I'm not a chicken."

"Then let go. Let go, and just *be* with him." She pours out the first few pancakes. "Oh! Did you bring your phone out here?" she asks. "There was one more thing I wanted to show you. Mom and Dad's TikTok has totally exploded."

"What? Why? Isn't their account already huge?" I slide the last of the strawberries into a bowl then reach for my phone, navigating through TikTok until I find Mom and Dad's account.

"I mean, it was kind of huge," Lucy says. "But someone tagged them as Flint Hawthorne's future in-laws, and they've gotten something like a million new followers in the past twenty-four hours. Watch their latest video. They just posted it yesterday."

I push play, then listen to a minute or so of Mom and Dad, playing their instruments outside their RV, but I don't recognize the song. "What is it?"

"It's the theme song to Flint's *Agent Twelve* movies. Clever, right?"

"I might say a little on the nose, but let's go with clever."

"They're playing it so cool in the comments though," Lucy says. "Like, they aren't confirming anything. They just aren't denying it either."

"I bet Mom is loving all the attention."

"She totally is." Lucy flips the pancakes and smirks. "The attention isn't always bad, Audrey. Sometimes it can be fun. Now go wake up Summer. Breakfast first, then I know exactly what we need to do to celebrate."

Lucy's idea of celebrating is watching movies all day.

And by movies, I mean *Flint Hawthorne* movies.

My first impulse is to refuse. I can't watch all his movies. Watching his movies will only make me love him more. But then I think of Lucy's words.

Let go and be with him.

I take a steadying breath, then drop onto the couch. "Fine, but you have to fast-forward through any kissing."

Summer pops some popcorn even though it's only ten-thirty and we only just finished breakfast, then drops onto my other side, plopping the bowl into my lap.

I look from one to the other. "I know what you guys are doing," I say.

"What? What are we doing?" Summer asks.

"You're *here*," I say. "I can't remember the last time either of you was around on a Saturday. I know you're staying in for me." I link my arms through each of theirs. "I just want you to know I appreciate it."

Lucy nudges my knee. "You're watching a *movie* with us, Audrey. Even if I *had* plans, I'd cancel them to see this miracle happen."

I roll my eyes and grab a handful of popcorn. "Just shut up and push play already."

One movie turns into two, then three. With my limited experience, I'm probably a poor judge, but Flint deserved the Oscar for the World War II movie. After that one is over, we watch the first two *Agent Twelve* movies back-to-back, and I fall a little bit in love with Flint as a beard-wearing, gun-wielding CIA agent. Next up is the time travel movie (my sisters say it isn't nearly as bad as Flint claimed) but we're breaking for dinner first because Lucy insists we can't survive on popcorn and Red Vines alone. I feel like we're doing a pretty solid job, but I'll feel better tomorrow if I get a little protein, so I don't need much convincing when she mentions pasta Bolognese.

Just before we start the next movie, a knock sounds on the front door.

My heart stops. I'm pretty sure Nate is still out front, and he wouldn't let anyone approach unless he trusted them. Could it be Flint? The way my chest suddenly aches tells me just how much I want it to be.

Summer gets up to answer the door, but it isn't Flint.

It's his mother.

Hannah Hawthorne smiles wide as she sets a gift basket down on my coffee table. "Well, this looks like fun," she says as she surveys my very messy living room. Soda cans, red vine wrappers, an empty ice cream carton.

I jump up and start scrambling around the room, picking up trash. "We've been watching movies all day. Had I known you were coming, I would have—"

Summer shuts me up with a hard stare and pulls the trash I've collected out of my hands. "Just sit down and stop being a weirdo," she whispers.

"Don't clean up on my account, Audrey. I don't want to interrupt your movie. But I come with news." She motions toward the basket. "And a few things from the farm."

Lucy and Summer disappear into the kitchen. "Oh. That's really sweet of you."

"There's some goats' milk soap, some fresh apples—first of the season, and they're delicious—and a box of almond pillow cookies that are going to be your new favorite. Lennox makes them," she says easily. "But he doesn't give them to just anyone, so you should feel pretty special."

I pick up a bar of soap and lift it to my nose. It smells like apple blossoms and spring sunshine. "I don't know what to say. Thank you."

We settle onto the couch, her warm gaze putting me at ease despite the tension I initially felt at her arrival. "I hear you had a bit of a scare earlier this week."

I nod.

"That's actually the news I mentioned earlier. Flint wanted me to tell you Ed Cooper was arrested. He *did* violate his parole when he left California, so the cops have been looking for him. They found him early this morning at a motel up in Hendersonville."

Relief washes over me, and I close my eyes. "That's really good news."

She smiles. "I thought so too."

"But you didn't have to come all this way just to tell me. Nate could have—" *Oh.* It suddenly occurs to me why Hannah is here. Flint told me he'd have Nate keep his distance so my life could feel as normal as possible. A visit from his mom is still significant, but it's more personal—more *normal*—than an update from his security team.

"Flint asked *you* to come," I say.

Hannah nods. "I'm sure it's tough to get used to having security around all the time."

"Yeah, it's definitely different."

"Audrey, it won't always be like this. You'll get used to some things, but people will get used to you, too. If I've learned anything watching Flint make his way in Hollywood, it's that the internet has a very short attention span."

I don't know if it's the warmth of her voice or the fact that I've been watching movies all day full of Flint in all his glory, but my heart suddenly feels like it's going to burst. Instead, I start to cry. Which is just *ridiculous*. Before Flint, I would go months without shedding a single tear. And now I'm a freaking water fountain.

"Oh, honey, come here," Hannah says. She pulls me into a hug, rubbing my back while I hiccup and sniff and leak tears all over her shirt.

"Seriously. I have no idea what's wrong with me."

Hannah smiles as I pull away. "I'm pretty sure I have an idea."

I laugh as I wipe away my tears. "But it's worth it, right?"

"What, love?" she asks. "Or loving someone like Flint?"

I shrug. "Both?"

Her expression shifts into something soft and tender. "Audrey, that boy has been a ray of sunshine every day of his life. He's worth everything. And love? Well, that's just plain fun. Of course it's worth it."

Hannah makes me try an almond pillow cookie before she leaves, and she was right. It's definitely my new favorite cookie.

I walk her out to the porch, watching as she walks down the stairs and toward her car. But there's one more thing I need to ask her.

"Hannah, wait!" She turns, and I run down the stairs, stopping in the grass a few feet away. "Is he home?"

She smiles. "He's home."

He's home.

And I need to see him *right now.*

Chapter Thirty-One
Flint

NORTH CAROLINA HAS NEVER felt more like home.

Maybe because Audrey is here. Maybe because the summer heat is finally yielding to something cooler. Maybe because the last week in Los Angeles has been so long.

Turns out Audrey was right, and Simon really did just act impulsively when he leaked the story. He claimed stress and mounting financial obligations made him irrational. I'm not sure what he meant by that, and I don't really want to know. All I care about is it only took one conversation to make it clear that if he kept talking about me, I would be forced to let people know why I *really* fired him. It's generous that I don't let people know *anyway*. I can only hope he'll learn from the situation and do better with future clients.

Either way, I have never been so happy to leave Los Angeles behind. My own house, in the mountains I love, is just the balm I need.

Well, that's not entirely true. Audrey is the balm I need. But I still don't know where we stand.

It's just after eight when I get a text from Nate.

Nate: Your brothers are at the gate. You want me to let them in?

My brothers. All of them?

I send Nate a quick thumbs up.

Five minutes later, I swing my front door open to see them standing there in a cluster, Brody, Lennox, Perry, and Tyler, my brother-in-law.

"Expecting someone else?" Lennox says dryly.

"Nah, I knew it was you. Nate texted and asked if I wanted to let you in."

"Wait, you could have said no?" Brody asks. "Rude."

"Brilliant," Perry says. "I'd love to be able to screen people before they make it to my porch."

"But then you'd just say no to *everyone*," Lennox says.

Perry smiles. "Exactly."

"What are you guys doing here?" I step back from the door, making room for them to file inside.

"We thought you might be hungry," Brody says. "Lennox has food from the restaurant."

Lennox holds up a bag as he heads toward the kitchen.

"We also have beverages," Perry says, holding up a case of beer as he follows Lennox.

Brody claps me on the back. "And also Mom is worried about you."

There it is. The real reason they're here. But whatever. I'll take it. I need all the distractions I can get right now.

We eat around the kitchen island, then take the beer outside. The night air is cool, the cicadas' song rolling through the trees like the rise and fall of a wave.

"Okay," Perry says, cracking open a beer and handing it to me. "What's the update? Where do things stand with Audrey?"

I run a hand across my face, scratching at the week's worth of beard growth I still need to shave. "I'm definitely in love with her, I'm completely miserable without her, and I'm pretty much consumed with the need to find her, tell her, then tell everyone else how amazing she is."

"So...like a regular Saturday," Lennox says, and my brothers chuckle.

"Is this seriously what it's like to be in love?"

"*Yes,*" they say in unison.

"At least at first," Perry says. "The intensity eases up after a while. But the feelings don't."

I rub my chest. "It feels...like I can't breathe right if she isn't in the room, but then she comes into the room, and it only gets worse."

Brody nods. "Like she could ask you to do anything in this world, *anything,* and you'd do it without flinching."

I nod. "Exactly."

"I once drove three states over to pick up Tatum's favorite ice cream," Lennox says.

Perry takes a swig of his beer. "I spent half my savings restoring a Steinway piano because Lila has always wanted one."

"You need to tell her, man," Brody says. "It's time."

"I just don't want to overwhelm her before—"

Brody's eyes widen and he motions behind me. "Nah, man. I mean you need to tell her *now.*"

I stand up and spin around.

Audrey is standing in the doorway leading into the house.

I take in the sight of her. A week without seeing her has only made her seem more beautiful. She's dressed casually. Jeans. A simple T-shirt. She rocked a red-carpet look, but I think I prefer this dressed-down version of Audrey.

Probably because it's more *Audrey.*

"Hey," I say, taking a step forward. "You're here."

"Nate let me in," she says. "I hope that's okay."

"It's *always* okay. It's good to see you."

Behind me, my brothers are moving, picking up empty beer bottles and straightening their chairs. In a matter of seconds, they're filing past me, each of them patting me on the back and saying hello to Audrey as they pass into the house. Perry is the last one to leave. When he reaches the door, he pauses and looks at me over his shoulder, his eyes cutting to Audrey for the briefest second. "It's not always easy. But it's the best thing that ever happened to me. And it's always worth it." He taps his hand against the door jamb, then disappears into the house.

Seconds later, the front door clicks closed, and Audrey and I are alone.

I take a step toward her and push my hands into my pockets, resisting the urge to run to her, to pull her into my arms.

"I didn't mean to break up the party," she says.

"Don't worry about it. They were just hanging out. We weren't doing anything important."

She nods. "I, um..." She looks up and breathes out a trembling breath. "I had this whole speech prepared, and now I can't remember anything I wanted to say." She tucks her hair behind her ear. "Actually, that's not true. I do remember one thing."

She lifts her eyes to meet mine, hope shining in their depths, and my heart starts pounding in my chest. "Yeah? What's that?"

She smiles, her expression tender. "Just that I'm in love with you."

I close my eyes and let the words wash over me.

"I think a part of me knew, right from the start, that I eventually *would* love you," she continues. "But I was so scared, Flint.

Scared of getting hurt. Of feeling overwhelmed. Of getting lost in a world so much bigger than the one I've made for myself. All that fear made me push you away, but I didn't even last twelve hours before I realized that the thought of living without you is so much scarier." She takes a step toward me. "I want us. I want *you.* "

I have so much I want to tell her.

But I can't say anything until I'm holding her.

I hurry forward, catching her when she launches herself into my arms. I spin her around, hugging her close, then slowly lower her to the ground, her body flush against mine.

Her hands lift to my face, and she pushes up on her toes to kiss me, stopping just before her lips meet mine. "You haven't said anything yet, Flint."

"I love you," I whisper. "I love you so much."

She smiles, her nose brushing against mine. "I love you, too."

When our lips finally touch, it feels like our first kiss all over again. All the fire, all the passion and excitement, but there's something else now too.

Now, there's a promise threaded through each touch, each caress of her skin against mine. I pull back, my hands lifting to her face. "Hey, I need to tell you something."

Her eyes flutter open. "Okay."

"Come inside and sit."

Her eyebrows lift, and she bites her lip.

"It's good. I swear it's good," I say. "Just come on."

I leave her on the couch and run to my office where I grab the list I printed off for her earlier. I take it back to the living room and sit down beside her.

"This is for you."

She takes the single sheet of paper, her brow furrowing as she looks it over.

"It took a little bit of leg work. And quite a few phone calls. Mark and Deidre helped with that—they have a lot of connections. But all these organizations have grant money that's currently available, *and* they're interested in seeing your proposal."

Audrey looks up. "You did this?"

"I mean, Mark did a lot of it. And nobody guaranteed anything. But there's a lot of money in California. And a lot of environmentalists who are concerned about development and how it impacts—"

She cuts off my words with a kiss, her fingers tangling in my hair. I could keep doing this all night, but I'm not finished yet. There's something else I still need to show her. I pull away, but she holds me close, her hands moving to the sides of my face. "I can't believe you did this," she says. "Flint. This is amazing."

"Like I said, there are no guarantees."

"I know," she says quickly. "I know. But it's a place to start."

I jump off the couch, not even trying to curb my enthusiasm. I *want* Audrey to know how excited I am about this. About *us*. "Okay, I have one more thing to show you."

She laughs. "What has gotten into you?"

This time, I head to my bedroom and grab the Feed 'n Seed bag from the top of my dresser. I carry it back to the living room and set it on the back of the chair, then pull out the camouflage sweatshirt I picked up on my way home. "I got this today. And a hat, too." I pull out a baseball cap trimmed with leaves, just like the one she was wearing when I found her hidden on the trail. "I figured, this way, if you ever want to go out to observe the squirrels or birds or whatever, I can come too."

She studies me for a long moment, her eyes shining. "Flint," she finally says. "This is the nicest thing anyone has ever done for me."

I lick my lips and hurry back to the couch, reaching for her hands. "Audrey, I know my life is big and stressful and frequently stupid. But I fell in love with a biologist, and I don't ever want you to *stop* being a biologist. I see you, all right? Your life won't get swallowed by mine because I won't let it. It's too important to me. You're too important to me."

She smiles through her tears, then kisses me for a very long time.

Later, when we're stretched out on the couch, Audrey snuggled against me, she lifts her head, propping her chin on my chest. "You know, it's okay if *some* of my life gets swallowed by yours."

"Yeah? Like what?"

"I mean, if we get to the point where we're choosing houses, I definitely choose this one."

"Good to know," I say through a grin.

"I'm just saying though. If the master bathroom isn't as pretty as the guest bathroom just past your office, I'm using the guest one instead. I've had actual dreams about that shower."

"It's nice, right?" I lean up and press a kiss to her forehead, still overwhelmed by the realization that I *can* kiss her—that she wants me to. "But trust me. You're going to love the shower in the master bathroom."

She smiles. "I can't wait to see it."

I can't wait for *everything*. All of whatever this life with Audrey is going to be.

Audrey drops her head and settles against me, breathing out a contented sigh.

I've done a lot of amazing things in my life, and I've met a lot of amazing people. But there isn't a single doubt in my mind: nothing has ever compared to this.

Epilogue
Flint

AUDREY HAS NEVER LOOKED more beautiful.

In the past three years, she's looked amazing on the red carpet half a dozen different times.

She also took my breath away on our wedding day.

And she looked *stunning* when she held our son for the first time, her sweat-streaked hair clinging to her face.

But there's something about today that feels different. Or maybe it's just that every time I look at her, she's more beautiful than she was the day before.

"What do you think?" she asks, turning away from the hotel mirror to face me. "I feel like my boobs might fall out."

"They aren't falling anywhere," I say. "You look great."

She grumbles as she adjusts the front of her dress. "Seriously. They haven't been the same since the pregnancy."

I step up behind her, wrapping my arms around her waist, and press a kiss to her collarbone. "You're perfect. Your body is perfect."

"But is it the right balance? I want to look professional, but also like...I don't know. A woman."

I turn her to face me, keeping my hands on her arms. "Audrey. You're going to be the most beautiful woman in the room. You always are." I give her shoulders a tiny squeeze. "More importantly, you're going to be the most *brilliant* person in the room."

"You really think so?"

"You're the one they're giving the award to, aren't they?"

She leans up and presses a quick kiss to my lips. "I still think it's silly we're here. If anything goes wrong with our travel, we might miss—"

I kiss her again, cutting off her protests. "We aren't going to miss anything. Besides, we already know you *won* your award. If we had to choose between your thing and mine, I'd rather be at yours."

She rolls her eyes. "That's the dumbest thing you've ever said."

"It isn't dumb. It's the truth. Now come on. Your fancy luncheon awaits."

The annual luncheon for the Weston Science Foundation is happening at a luxurious lakeside hotel just outside of Asheville. They only give one outstanding achievement award each year, and this year, it's going to Audrey for her research on biodiversity in intentional green spaces to counteract the negative impacts of urbanization.

It took me three tries to memorize that sentence.

Have I mentioned how sexy my wife's brain is?

We make our way to the elevator, then ride down to the banquet hall on the first floor. Nate is hovering near the door when we arrive, and he nods as we pass into the room. "Congrats, Audrey," he whispers, and she smiles wide.

We move toward our table, and I bristle at the eyes swiveling to watch us. Audrey has grown pretty used to the way people stare whenever we're out in public. But today, I'm the one who is uncomfortable. This is Audrey's moment. Nobody should be looking at me.

"You have to stop frowning, Flint," Audrey says. "You look miserable."

"What? I'm not! I'm so happy to be here."

She chuckles as she sits down, and I scoot her chair under her. "Then smile and lean down here to kiss me."

I do as I'm told, and she hooks her hand around my tie, holding me close long enough to say, "I don't care that they're staring at you, baby. Just sit down and relax."

Fortunately, our tablemates are much more enthusiastic about Audrey's presence than mine. They pepper her with question after question about her work, and she fields them like a pro. She is gracious and charming and funny and brilliant, and I am so in love with her, I don't think we need a plane to get us to Los Angeles tonight. I'll fly us there myself.

After lunch, the foundation president shares a few remarks, then gives the stage to Audrey so she can present her latest findings and recommendations. I reach over and squeeze her hand just before she stands. "You've got this," I whisper.

There's a slight tremble in her exhale, but she squares her shoulders and smiles. "I'm going to be so boring," she says. "Don't fall asleep."

She isn't boring. Not even a little bit. By the time she finishes, the foundation president who presents her with her award looks so enamored, I think he might propose.

Across the room, Nate lifts his head, then pointedly looks at his watch.

I resist the impulse to do the same thing. We'll be fine. And I'm not about to rush Audrey out of here on my account.

Another round of applause breaks out as Audrey leaves the stage and makes a beeline straight for me. "Okay, done," she whispers, grabbing my hand. "Let's get out of here."

Nate escorts us out of the hotel to a waiting car, which whisks us to the airport where we climb onto the private jet we hired *just* for today—our only hope if we're going to make it to Los Angeles in time.

Captain Salano, the same pilot who flew Audrey to New York, greets us at the door. "Busy day?" he jokes as he shakes my hand.

I grin. "It's up to you, now."

"Hey, is Blake single?" Audrey asks as we settle into our seats.

"I don't know. You have someone in mind?"

"Summer, actually," she says as Nate and Joni file past us to sit at the back of the plane.

"She broke up with the other guy?" I ask. "The attorney guy?"

Audrey nods. "And she's totally disheartened and positive I married the last decent man on the planet." She drops her head on my shoulder, stifling a yawn. "I swear, you and your brothers are like unicorns. How are you all so good?"

"Blake's a nice guy. I'll talk to him. See what I can find out."

"That would be amazing." Audrey yawns again. "I'm sure Summer would appreciate it."

"You going to make it, sleepyhead?"

She gives me a pointed look. "*Somebody* kept me up late last night."

Depending on the day, she could be talking about Milo, who is only nine months old and still wakes us up at least once a night. But I'll take full credit for Audrey's lack of sleep last night.

I smirk. "True. And I have zero regrets."

She bumps her arm into mine. "I'll take a nap as soon as we're in the air. Find me a blanket?"

I *do* find a blanket—one big enough for us both—and I tuck it around us, our chairs almost fully reclined.

Audrey sighs as she relaxes into the seat. "I miss Milo."

I lean over and kiss her forehead. "Me too. But your sisters will take good care of him while we're gone."

She turns and nestles into my side, making me think flying private is worth it just for the chance to travel like this, with Audrey so close. "Hey, Flint?" she says, her voice sleepy.

"Hmm?"

"You're going to win an Oscar tonight."

～elle～

Audrey

I'm biased.

I *know* I'm biased.

But I've watched all the other movies and studied all the contenders for Best Actor, and Flint's performance is just *so good*. I really think he's going to win.

His entire family has flown to California to be with us for the awards. We won't have time to see them beforehand, and we're the only two who will walk the red carpet, but we'll all be together at the hotel afterwards.

Even if he doesn't win, I'm glad his entire family is here. Flint's had such a big year, and he's worked so hard. He deserves to be celebrated.

The next few hours go by in a blur. We land in LA, hurry to the hotel where we meet our fashion people who get us dressed and coifed and looking red-carpet fabulous, then we race over to the Dolby Theatre for the Academy Awards. We hit the red carpet an hour later than Flint's publicist would have preferred, but we're here. We made it.

And I'm *so proud* to be next to Flint.

I still don't love the paparazzi. I don't love the attention and the entitlement some fans feel to the innerworkings of Flint's private life. But it *has* gotten easier. The noise has gotten quieter. And we've gotten really good at holing up at the house whenever we need to recharge.

We see Lea Cortez when we're entering the theatre, and Claire McKinsey, who comes over to give me a big hug. Through it all, Flint is kind and quick to smile, but he's quieter than usual, and he just gets quieter and quieter the closer we get to his category.

He's told me a hundred times that it's an honor to be nominated, and when he says it about the *last* nomination, I believe him. But this time, I think he really wants it. Maybe because he knows his work on this movie—Mark Sheridan's movie—is the best he's ever done.

Applause fills the room as, fittingly, Matt Damon takes the stage to present the award for Best Actor. I thread my fingers through Flint's. "You have so much to be proud of," I whisper. "Win or lose."

He wins.

He wins, and he's smiling, and I'm crying, and he's kissing me and then he's on stage.

"I, um—" He chuckles, his words trailing off. "You know, I watched my wife win an award just this morning for the work she does as a biologist, and she was so poised and collected. And here I am, a complete mess." The audience laughs, and Flint looks right at me. "Audrey, I wouldn't be up here without you. I love you. Thank you for believing in me, and for giving *me* something to believe in. And for bringing Milo into this world which is truly the most amazing thing I've ever witnessed. Hopefully, we'll get him to sleep all night someday." He smiles. "Maybe. Before he's five." Flint takes another deep breath and looks toward the balcony where the rest of his family is sitting. "To my family, my parents, my siblings, thank you. You have shown me with your unending love and support that being important to the world will never matter as much as being important to *you*."

He goes on to thank Mark and the rest of the crew that brought the movie to life, then he leaves the stage.

I close my eyes and listen to the applause filling the room. Marrying Flint, watching his dedication to his craft, the seriousness with which he approaches every single role, has given me a new appreciation for actors and everyone else who works to put art out into the world.

There is so much of Hollywood that is silly and frivolous and exhausting. But this moment—this honor given to someone who has worked tirelessly to do and be the best—this isn't silly. This is everything Flint deserves.

I can't wait to tell him how much I love him.

Back at the hotel, I sit on the couch with Hannah and watch as the four Hawthorne brothers stand together by the window. They're all still in their tuxedos, though jackets have come off and ties have been loosened.

Perry's hair is starting to gray at the temples, something I've never noticed until now, but then, he's closer to forty now than he is thirty. And the rest of them aren't far behind.

I loop my arm through Hannah's and lean my head on her shoulder. "They're good men," I say, and she reaches over and pats my hand.

"They are, aren't they?"

We watch as Olivia moves across the room and joins the circle. Flint steps to the side, making room for the youngest Hawthorne sibling, and he puts his arm around her.

One of the other brothers says something that makes them all laugh—I'm too far away to hear—and Olivia rolls her eyes. Still, it's clear how much she loves her brothers no matter their teasing.

Eventually, Flint makes his way back to me, dropping onto the couch on my other side. "I still think your award is prettier than mine," he says.

It *is* pretty—opaque crystal in the shape of a tree. It honestly looks more like living room décor than an actual award.

"We'll have to keep yours in your office then," I say, my tone serious. "Wouldn't want guests to be offended when they come over to the house."

"I like this plan." He grins and pats my leg. "You ready for bed?"

"Yes, please." I shift and let him pull me off the couch. "Oh my gosh. Flint," I say, and he pauses, his eyebrows going up. "There is no baby here. We can sleep *all night long* without waking up."

He tugs me into his chest. "Dr. Callahan, that's the sexiest thing you've ever said to me."

We say goodbye to his family as they head to their respective hotel rooms, then finally make our way to bed.

"It's been a good day, Auds," Flint says as he turns off the light. He reaches for me in the dark, curving his body around mine, his chest to my back and his arm around my waist. "I love you," he whispers. "So much."

I turn so I'm facing him and press my lips to his, deepening the kiss in a way I know he'll recognize as an invitation. I'm so tired. Ridiculously tired. But I'm also ridiculously in love with him, and I'm not ready for the night to end.

He chuckles. "Do you know how many hours we've been awake?"

I kiss him one more time. "What's one more?"

His hand moves to my back, and he tugs me close. "Fine, but I'm only doing this as a favor to you," he says playfully.

I grin into the darkness. "Your noble sacrifice is noted."

Later, when we finally go to sleep, Flint drifts off first, but that's no surprise. He usually does. It always takes me longer to slow my brain down enough to sleep.

But tonight, I don't mind the thoughts coursing through my tired mind.

Thoughts of Flint, of Milo, of our tiny, happy family. Of his extended family and the way they treat all the Callahans—my parents included—like we're part of the clan.

I know well that things will not always feel this perfect.

Just next month, Flint will come back to Los Angeles for three months, and I'll have to stay in Silver Creek to finish out my semester. It won't be the first time we'll be apart, but it will be the *longest* we'll go without seeing each other.

There will be other trials too, I know. Challenges we can't foresee and won't feel prepared to handle.

But I'm choosing to trust that whatever life brings, we'll weather it well because we'll weather it together.

I'm choosing to trust that love—our love—will always be enough.

For bonus content, including a full series epilogue, visit jenny proctor.com

Acknowledgements

You guys! This is an emotional moment. I've spent the last year and a half dreaming up the Hawthornes, getting to know them, and falling in love over and over again. I've loved every minute of it, and I'm so sad to see the series end! As always, there are always so many people who are involved in the creation of a book. My cover designer, Stephanie, thank you for giving my vision balance and clarity. Lana, I don't know how you make illustrations look hot, but you totally do and I love you for it! My critique partner, Kirsten, you make my stories stronger and smarter and I'm so grateful for you—for your brilliance and our friendship. To my editor and sister, Emily, I'm so lucky. You make my words smarter. You make my life better. You support me in all the ways. Thank you for being my person. Josh, I love you. Please don't ever stop inspiring my love stories. To my Lucy, and your Summer, thanks for letting me steal your names! Finally, and most especially, readers, you make this work possible. Thank you for reading, for sending me notes of encouragement, for letting me know when you love my books. You have no idea how much those messages and emails mean! I'm an extrovert by nature, and writing is a pretty solitary game, so it means so much when I get to connect with readers. Thanks for being so awesome. Until the next one! Happy Reading!

About the Author

Jenny Proctor grew up in the mountains of North Carolina, a place she still believes is one of the loveliest on earth. She lives a few hours south of the mountains now, in the Lowcountry of South Carolina. Mild winters and of course, the beach, are lovely compromises for having had to leave the mountains.

Jenny works full-time as an author of romantic comedy. She and her husband, Josh, have six children, and almost as many pets. They love to hike as a family and take long walks through the neighborhood. But Jenny also loves curling up with a good book, watching movies, and eating food that, when she's lucky, she doesn't have to cook herself. You can learn more about Jenny and her books at www.jennyproctor.com.

Made in the USA
Middletown, DE
07 September 2023

38141384R00215